A CONSPIRACY
OF STARS

A CONSPIRACY
OF STARS

OLIVIA A. COLE

KATHERINE TEGEN BOOKS
An Imprint of HarperCollins Publishers

Katherine Tegen Books is an imprint of HarperCollins Publishers.

A Conspiracy of Stars
Copyright © 2018 by Olivia A. Cole
All rights reserved. Printed in the United States of America.
No part of this book may be used or reproduced in any manner whatsoever
without written permission except in the case of brief quotations embodied in
critical articles and reviews. For information address HarperCollins Children's
Books, a division of HarperCollins Publishers, 195 Broadway,
New York, NY 10007.
www.epicreads.com

Library of Congress Control Number: 2017938885
ISBN 978-0-06-264421-3

Typography by David Curtis
17 18 19 20 21   PC/LSCH   10 9 8 7 6 5 4 3 2 1

First Edition

For Omaun, who makes Earth worth it.

A CONSPIRACY
OF STARS

CHAPTER 1

My father and I live under different suns. In reality, it is the same: red and hungry, an intense crimson eye that sends the sweat fleeing from my skin. It's as beautiful as it is harsh, but my father sees none of the beauty. The past has dulled his wonder, and so the light of this planet shines differently on each of us. For me, it is part of home. For him, it is a beacon over a prison. Like others in N'Terra, he had his heart set on another sun. This one is a poor replacement.

"Slow down, Octavia," he says.

I tighten my hands, made thick with the white driving gloves I wear, on the steering column. My father has been allowing me to pilot the chariot since my birthday but still insists I drive too fast. I decelerate, only slightly—I love the feeling of the wind, tinged with the scent of the jungle, whipping across my face. This is one of the few times I feel relaxed.

My father says nothing else, so I squint at the intense green of the wilderness that blurs more slowly past us now, allowing the colors to blend. A smallish smudge of brown catches my eye—I've seen that mottled texture somewhere before in one of my research projects.

"Kunike," I say out loud without really meaning to. Usually I would keep my observations to myself when driving with my father, but kunike are difficult to spot—I've never seen a live one—and I'm surprised to have happened across them. There are two: small and standing impossibly still at our approach. Their fur has blended into the grasses that surround them.

My father nods, unsmiling.

"Stop," he says.

I bring the chariot to a gentle halt, tamping down the eagerness that swells in me like helium. My father lifts one hand from where it rests on the front bar and presses the signal key by the steering column. A short, sharp sound barks from our vehicle, and the two kunike become fully visible immediately. Their fur turns vividly red, and now I can see them clearly: small and fuzzy with large wide ears like sails. One rears up on its back legs, baring its surprisingly impressive fangs.

Years ago, my father would have prompted me for knowledge: "Purpose? Adaptational trajectory?" That was when I was still a kid, allowed out of the compound and into the open air of Faloiv for the first time. By now he doesn't need to ask: he signaled the kunike merely as a demonstration—a hint of his rare generosity when it comes to his only child. But I find myself answering in my head anyway: *The sentry kunike turn red to signal the rest of the pack. In the event of an attack, they would stop and fight while the others got away. The red coloring doubles as a diversion for the predator.* Before, when my father and I would actually talk, he might have told me that the kunike turn a different color if what's approaching can be considered prey. This alternate color would signal the hidden pack to attack rather than flee. But these conversations are long past. At sixteen, I'm expected to know these things already, and I do.

I've guided the chariot into motion again—the kunike fading back into camouflage behind us—and the wind picks up dust from the road, swirling it around us in rust-colored clouds. Our goggles protect our eyes, but he motions for me to fasten my face guard. Ahead, what looks like a scarlet bird hovers in the air, scanning the ground for food. I recognize it as a carnivore from its claws. But before I can even identify it, another creature—larger, a winged blue reptile—zooms in from out of nowhere and buries its talons in the red bird's body. Both plummet to the ground, struggling.

"I'll say one thing for this miserable planet," my father says. I can barely hear him over the wind: I'm driving too fast again, but he hasn't yet noticed. "It has an interesting predator-prey hierarchy. Carnivores preying only on other carnivores? Fascinating."

I say nothing. When it comes to my father's feelings about Faloiv, I tend to keep my opinions to myself. He hasn't always hated it here, but many things have been different since my grandmother died five years ago, lost in the jungle on a scavenging trip. Perhaps the knowledge that this planet can swallow us up so easily had stirred some feelings of desperation. Faloiv has been his home for over forty years, after his birth planet became hostile to human life, and I doubt he remembers much of life before Faloiv. But home isn't just memory, I've decided: it's knowledge, knowing where you belong and where you fit. My grandmother's loss ignited something restless in him, something angry and afraid. Faloiv is different for me. Greencoats—green, the color of a young branch, the sign of our inexperience but also of our commitment to growth— were born here. This is home.

"Sir," I venture. "Will we see Dr. Adibuah today?"

"Yes," my father answers, keeping his eyes trained on the dust path ahead.

"Does Dr. Adibuah ever come to the Paw to collaborate on your projects?" I ask, refusing to let his monosyllabicity irk me. "Or do you just come here because you're on the Council?"

"I've told you not to refer to the Mammalian Compound as the Paw, Octavia. It's adolescent and unspecific."

Behind my goggles I roll my eyes. The greencoats have our own set of expressions: we call the Avian Compound the Beak, and the Amphibian Compound—where my best friend Alma lives—the Newt. Not exactly clever, but it is efficient—even if it is unspecific and adolescent. And we're supposed to be clever, we students of N'Terra, children of whitecoats. It is our skills that will determine our survival. The founders of N'Terra had not meant for us to stay forever: Faloiv was the only habitable world their scouts had time to chart before evacuating the Origin Planet, and a meteor to the *Vagantur*'s hull during descent damaged the ship's power cell irreparably. What had originally been envisioned as a brief stop on the hunt for a more survival-friendly sphere had become the final destination of the *Vagantur*. The original Council tried for twenty years to fix the ship before they gave up. Now here we are.

Outside the Beak, I pull up to a woman standing by the white, smooth-walled wigwam that serves as a gatehouse. I'm surprised by the buzzgun she carries—more and more guards have them these days, and it's jarring to see it slung so casually over her shoulder. The woman had been smiling before we pulled up, but when she sees my father alongside me, she tucks the smile away. He has that effect on people.

"Names?" she says. She has a thin, almost-transparent slate in her hands. It's a formality: she knows who we are. My father is a member of the Council—the twelve-person congress that makes decisions about N'Terra. My mother is on the Council as well, which makes for some interesting debates when we eat our evening meal. Or at least it used to, before my grandmother's absence filled all our mouths with an ash of silence too thick to talk around.

I lean back as my father stretches across the steering column.

"Dr. English, Octavius. Mammalian Compound. Daughter: English, Octavia."

"Dr. English," she says after a moment, nodding in confirmation.

The guard passes the slate to my father, who applies his thumb to the screen, then passes it to me to do the same. I take the slate, center my thumb in the red square beside a picture of my face and profile, and the slate's screen goes blank. I pass it back to her.

The solid white gates ahead of us slide apart and the woman with the buzzgun nods us through. Under my hand, the chariot whispers forward toward a cluster of other vehicles, where a small group of whitecoats stands conversing. One of them wears a strange article of clothing that I've never seen: a red cloak with a tall collar that extends well above his head, which then curves forward and outward like the palm of a hand. It covers his face in shade: I can't make out his features until I've parked alongside another chariot and the red-cloaked man moves toward us.

"English," the man says, raising a hand gloved in the same red, scaled material as his cloak.

"Dr. Albatur," my father says, nodding. He's removed his traveling gloves and his hands look comfortingly human in comparison to the other man's red fingers. "A pleasure to see you."

So *this* is Dr. Albatur. I've heard his name a lot in the last year—he's the recently elected Council Head of N'Terra. Somehow I'd pictured him differently. Younger. Stronger.

"Looking forward to hearing your proposals," Dr. Albatur says. My parents have debated Albatur's policies many a time at evening meal, but they've never mentioned his garb. I study it, trying to guess its purpose. He seems to see me for the first time and forces what could be interpreted as a smile onto his narrow mouth. "Ah, your daughter."

"Hello, sir," I say, nodding respectfully, but my eyes still wander to his covering.

"I see you're curious about my hood," he says. His tone is unpleasant to my ears, the sound of someone drawing a line and daring you to cross it.

"Yes, sir," I say without hesitating.

He squints at me.

"So. Ask."

I consider his expression, wondering if he means it. I almost look at my father for confirmation, but the idea of needing permission to ask a simple question irks me.

"What animal did we learn this technology from?" I finally say.

Dr. Albatur smirks.

"So very N'Terra of you, Miss English," he says. "To assume

everything we know is from this hot little globe. No, what I wear isn't an innovation of Faloiv. This technology is of the Origin Planet: the material is from the hull of the *Vagantur*."

My forehead wrinkles involuntarily.

"I wasn't aware we dismantled the ship for personal items," I say.

Dr. Albatur's expression clouds and he fixes me with a sharp look.

"The *Vagantur* has not been dismantled," he says quickly. "Nor will it ever be. And this is not merely a personal item. My skin and the sun of Faloiv are . . . incompatible, you see. This material acts as an effective barrier in order to keep me alive. A scrap of the hull that was damaged in the landing was salvaged when my condition became apparent."

"Oh. But why will the *Vagantur* never be dismantled?" I go on. "Faloiv is our home. We're not going anywhere."

Dr. Albatur's eyelids seem to thicken and droop: suddenly they too seem to be wearing a hood like the one over his head. He stares at me hard, the corner of his mouth twitching ever so slightly.

And then he turns his eyes to my father, transferring his gaze without moving his face. He addresses him now as if I'd never said a word.

"Dr. English," he says. "How goes the progress on our other project?"

I look at my father to hear his response and note a change

in his eyes. Normally round and wide like mine, they've narrowed slightly.

"It continues. We are still attempting to locate a specimen," my father says. "I will alert you the moment we find one."

"Good," says Dr. Albatur, nodding from deep inside the hood. "Good."

He turns abruptly, the bulky redness of him moving away from us and toward the doorway to the Beak, which guards with buzzguns are now opening—Albatur's posture suggests that he's bending slightly, bowing his head away from the sun. The whitecoats that accompany him scurry at his heels, staying close. I expect my father to follow him directly, but instead he's rubbing the material of his gloves between two fingers, staring after Albatur with an expression of preoccupation.

"I guess I shouldn't have asked," I say when Albatur is out of earshot. "It just seems strange that he was so adamant about not dismantling the *Vagantur*. It just sits over there in the jungle, growing moss."

"Dr. Albatur has many ideas as the Council Head," my father says, and I'm surprised that he's not angry with me. "The *Vagantur* is just part of them."

"What else?" I ask. This is one of the longest conversations we've had in some time.

"The Solossius," he says.

"The what?"

He looks at me then, quickly, his eyes refocusing.

"Dr. Adibuah will be waiting for us."

My father has prepared me for what awaited in the main dome of the Beak—an absence of cages, with the herbivorous birds allowed to fly freely in the wide expanse of the dome. I duck immediately upon entering, two flurried pairs of wings darting just above my head in a flash of gold and crimson. From outside, the large dome appears to be solid white, but inside, sunshine pours in through slow-traveling clouds at the highest point of a transparent ceiling. The clouds are both real and not, my father has told me: made of moisture like real clouds but engineered indoors to provide the birds with a lifelike habitat. With the birds all around me, and the clouds above, it's almost like being outside, beyond the borders of N'Terra.

Dr. Adibuah is approaching, and my enjoyment of the dome fades momentarily. His usually sunny disposition seems dimmer today, the tension in his jaw turning his face somber.

"Octavius," he says. He shakes my father's hand firmly. "I didn't know Albatur was coming."

I catch a glint of something like regret flit across my father's face before he buries it again.

"Apologies. I assumed you knew."

"I didn't." Dr. Adibuah looks at me, his eyes losing some of their gloom. "And here's O, on my turf for the first time."

I like when people call me O. Sometimes Octavia is unbearably close to Octavius: my father had claimed my name like a scientific discovery, a new species; something he thinks he owns. My mother had at least insisted on me having my own middle name, Afua.

"Hello, Dr. Adibuah."

I follow my father and Dr. Adibuah through the dome, simultaneously admiring the Beak and eavesdropping on their conversation. We pause as a large flightless bird appears at the edge of the path, eyeing us almost irritably, as if commanding us to make way. I've seen this species before—the molovu— but only in the floating three-dimensional displays of the Greenhouse, where my peers and I go for our daily classes. The animal is so close now—just out of arm's reach. My head seems to buzz with the wonder of it. I squint, looking for the tentacle it hides in its orange breast plumage, an opposable, trunk-like limb that it uses to essentially vacuum seeds from the jungle floor. But the bird disappears into the bushes on the other side of the path.

"Today is the first day that we were able to manipulate the oscree pattern to appear on a skinsuit," Dr. Adibuah is saying, not bothering to conceal his excitement.

"Good," says my father, who never gets excited about any-thing. My grandmother's death had stolen the light from his eyes, and she wasn't even his mother.

Dr. Adibuah opens his mouth to add something else, but a flash of red through the trees draws his attention and mine. We're almost through the indoor jungle to the entrance of the

Zoo, and Dr. Albatur stands ahead with his cluster of white-coats like a drop of blood seeping through gauze, the red hood still shielding his face from the sun pouring in from above. The gloom returns to Dr. Adibuah's eyes. He turns to me as if to distract himself from the sight of the Council Head.

"You'll be in the Zoo with us one day," he says.

I smile at Dr. Adibuah's teasing use of "Zoo"—whitecoats don't usually call it that; it's another greencoat nickname for the laboratories in each compound, and is the place where greencoats such as myself desire to go most—a territory we won't be allowed to enter until we're twenty-one. It's where all the important animal-focused research takes place, and while I've heard rumors that Dr. Albatur wants to cut back on zool-ogy for other avenues of research, the Zoo is still the place where my grandmother said we would find the keys to our survival.

Dr. Albatur is absorbed in conversation with one of the guards, but he turns to eye me, as if I'll come charging at the doors to the Zoo with a battering ram. Dr. Adibuah must notice my scowl because he pauses to give me one more smile before he and my father join the other whitecoats.

"One day at a time, O," he says, and it seems like something he might be saying for his own benefit as well. "I hear they're considering introducing internships, so you may be in sooner than you think."

"Internships? Seriously?"

"I hope I haven't given anything away," Dr. Adibuah says, smiling. "Let's keep that between us."

"Yes, sir," I say.

"Octavia, you can occupy yourself while I'm with Dr. Adibuah? You have your research?" my father asks as we near the Zoo's doors.

He doesn't wait for me to say yes, but instead turns to the guard, who stands aside and allows my father and Dr. Adibuah to register their thumbprints on the scanner. The door slides open without a sound. Dr. Albatur doesn't bother to scan his thumb—he sweeps in through the entrance and everyone else follows.

When the door closes, I turn back to the main dome of the Beak. As much as I'd like to be in the labs, the fact that I'm unaccompanied for my first visit to this compound means I can actually explore. Everywhere there are whitecoats with slates and recording equipment, standing and observing different birds as they hover and dart and do the things that birds do. Some of the white-coated doctors are even perched in trees, motionless as they watch a bird in a nest or an egg hatching. The animals go about their business. Many of them were born in the compound; they don't know anything else. Like me.

I eye a whitecoat twenty paces away using an oxynet to snag several avian species from a passing flock. The triggering of the oxynet is silent, but the net itself makes a whistling sound as it flies through the air, trapping the birds in a sort of bubble. It's a new technology that's supposed to be gentler on the animals than an actual net. Part of the Faloii's rules when we settled, I'm told, is that we're forbidden to cut down trees or harm wildlife, and as I wander along the dirt path, letting reaching branches brush my arms, I'm glad. I look up. Beyond the arched dome ceiling, I catch a glimpse of a cluster of birds not contained in the Beak flying fast and free. I envy them as I breathe in the scent of the towering ogwe trees. The trees aren't edible—my grandmother's studies had focused on functional nutrition, and I know as much about plants as I do about animals—but the smell is almost delicious. It's hard to explain, but even their scent is striped, like their trunks: smooth but complicated, with a pattern of undertones that cross one another inside the nose when I breathe deeply.

"What are you smelling?"

My eyes snap open—I hadn't even known they'd been closed. Beside me is Jaquot, the braggart of the Beak and my classmate in the Greenhouse.

"The trees."

"Which ones?"

He's testing me, like all greencoats do to one another.

"The ogwe."

"Distinguishing quality?"

"Each ogwe leaf is perfectly identical, for one," I say.

"Why?"

"No one knows. But we will." I recite N'Terra's motto,

reluctant to give him what he wants.

"Good," Jaquot says smugly, as if he's satisfied I'm not an idiot. "Except one thing: ogwe trees don't have a scent."

"What?" I don't need him to repeat himself, but what he's said seems so stupid that I'm not entirely sure I've heard it correctly.

"No smell," he says, smiling in a way that shows too much of his gums. "Not discernible by humans, anyway."

"Wrong," I say.

"No, I'm not."

Jaquot leaves my side and walks toward the center of the dome where the trees grow thickly. The back of his head is flat, and I mentally compare it to the thick-headed marov that stump around the bushes of the jungle. I don't follow him, but when he notices he's alone, he turns back and beckons at me.

"Come on, English!"

"Do you ever get sick of the sound of your own voice?" I stay where I am.

"Oh, you don't want to defend your theory?"

I follow him so he'll keep his voice down, and we approach an ogwe tree. He reaches out a palm, laying it flat against the gray striped skin of the trunk. He closes his eyes and inhales deeply through his nose, lifting his chin for dramatic effect. I roll my eyes.

"See?" he says. "Nothing."

"You can't prove that empirically," I say. "I have no way of

15

knowing what you do or do not smell."

"You smell something?"

I inhale deeply. I don't need to close my eyes: there it is again, the powerful, crosshatched smell of the ogwe.

"Yes," I say. "It's strong."

He looks uncertain but smiles sarcastically. "You can't prove that empirically either."

I shrug, indifferent. I'll save the debate for the Greenhouse when I have evidence to back me up.

"What are you doing here anyway?" he asks, leaning against the tree. When we were kids I had a crush on him—mainly because of the color of his eyes, the same shade as the leaves. He's still handsome. But annoying outweighs attractive.

"My father takes me to the other compounds when he goes to meet with other scientists. Occasionally."

"Seriously?" he says, impressed. His lack of conceit takes me off guard. He's always talking or bragging, and I hadn't expected him to be interested in what anyone else has to say.

"Yeah." I'm hesitant to give away how excited it all makes me—I can almost hear my father calling it adolescent. But Jaquot doesn't seem to have any concern about seeming juvenile.

"That's amazing," he says, pushing off the ogwe to face me directly. "Have you been to them all?"

"All except the Fin," I say, referring to the Aquatic Compound. Jaquot moves his hand like he's sweeping the Fin away.

"Eh, you might be able to skip that anyway. I'd rather hear

Dr. Espada lecture on grubs than fish. Mind-numbing."

I laugh. I've been rolling my eyes at him since we were six, but maybe he's not *so* bad anymore. I make a mental note to send Alma a message about it when I return to the Paw. We've always thought Jaquot was all talk and no insight, but I've never considered that he may have changed. That seems fairly unscientific, now that I think about it.

"That is really cool, though," he continues, and turns to go back down the original path that leads toward the main entrance. "What does the Slither dome look like inside? Do they let the reptiles run loose?"

We walk and talk, birds flying around us like tiny, colorful comets. Some of the comets aren't so tiny: one bright orange bird lands on a branch above us, so large that the wood makes a groaning sound. No sooner does it land than it takes off again.

"Species?" I say, pointing.

"Roigo," he says after the briefest pause. "I think. It took off too fast."

"Distinguishing quality?"

"They hatch at their adult size."

"How?"

"No one knows. But we will."

We grin at each other. It's nice to talk about specimens without all the gravity that accompanies it with my parents and the whitecoats. For many of my peers, I know being a greencoat is just about memorizing facts. For me, it's more. I open my mouth to tell Jaquot this, or some less serious version of it, when there's a commotion somewhere through the trees.

"What's that?" I look around.

"I don't know," he says, craning his head to try to get a glimpse through tree trunks. "I've never heard anyone yelling in the dome."

There's more than one someone. There's a chorus of voices, rising and falling.

"It's coming from around the main entrance," says Jaquot. "Let's check it out."

We follow the worn path through another cluster of trees. The flora in the dome isn't quite thick enough to mimic walking through the real forests of Faloiv—or at least how I imagine them to be. We approach the tree line. There are just bushes and rocks after the trees thin out, a clearing before the dome wall and its door.

"Oh man, look!" Jaquot's hand whips out and grabs my wrist, unconscious of how tightly he grips me. His eyes are wide, his mouth open. I almost jerk away from him, but then I look.

Four or five whitecoats shout, their words a combination of curses and caution, their bodies a flurry of waving arms and shuffling feet. One woman's spectacles fall off, and I watch her scramble to recover them before they're crushed . . . under a foot.

The foot isn't human. It's not even a foot: it's a collection of claws and scales, attached to a leg as thick as my calf. My breath catches in my throat, as if those claws are around my neck, choking me. The red of the plumage is shockingly bright. I've heard things described as bloodred before, but it was never accurate until now. This creature is the true color of blood, and huge: my eyes travel up its body, taller than I am. Its wingspan is as wide as the wigwam outside, and the scientists from the Beak scramble to subdue the animal, to pinion its wings with thick brown straps. One of those wings buffets a whitecoat, sending him sprawling. Then the animal throws back its colossal head, opens its curved beak, and emits a sound like a roar and a screech, a deep reverberating cry that echoes into the trees. A headache blooms in my skull.

"It's a philax," Jaquot breathes. He's still gripping my wrist and I'm too shocked to shake him off.

"We're so close," I whisper, pushing aside the headache.

"Look out!" one of the whitecoats yells, and swings one of the thick straps over his head. Fastened to the end are two smooth round objects, heavy, I can tell, by the way they whirl. After a few rotations, the whitecoat lets go and sends it sailing toward the philax, where it spins around and around the animal's feet, entangling them. The philax screeches again, and it's as if the sound shakes every cell in my body. The creature totters, wavers, and then falls, crashing to the ground in a tangle of bloodred feathers and scales.

When the philax is prone on the ground—the whitecoats leaping on top of him to secure his wings with more straps—he stretches his neck out so that it's fully extended and gives one more long, cavernous screech. And in that moment, my eyes meet his.

Lightning flows through my body, a sudden jolt of an electric current. A storm of charges invades my head, my fear becoming enlarged, intensified by some titanic presence. My body goes rigid and the eyes of the philax drill into me, wild with terror. His fear vibrates in my fingernails and in my tongue: I feel it in my earlobes and in the throbbing of my head. The philax's panic builds a nest in me alongside my own fear, which is now small beside his, dull next to his intensity. I can't tear my eyes away from his.

"Octavia! Octavia!" Jaquot is shaking me by my shoulder, but I can't quite hear him. My mind is gray, busy, filled with noise . . . and behind it all, something taps.

Someone near the philax shouts as the bird manages to rise again, words I can't make out, and a lab door opens to reveal a whitecoat with a tranq gun. Behind him is Dr. Albatur, raising his hood as he steps back out into the sun of the dome. His face is hard as his mouth forms the words, "Shoot it." The whitecoat aims the tranq gun at those beautiful bloodred feathers, pauses, and then pulls the trigger. I only hear the whispered zip of the dart leaving the barrel, and then the philax is falling, I'm falling, into dark, dark space.

CHAPTER 2

I'm dreaming of my mother. She's standing in a green field, with plants that I've learned to identify on Faloiv. They are as deep green as they are in life, but richer somehow, their smells even more complicated. And among it all stands my mother: she's younger than the way I know her to be, her locs shorter, her face slimmer. But it's my mother, and in the dream she opens her arms, although I'm not sure if she's opening them to me or to everything around us. My feet are bare, which would never be allowed on Faloiv, and buried in short green plants bearing round purple buds.

"Listen," says my mother.

"Mom?"

In the dream she puts a finger to her lips.

"Listen," she repeats.

I listen. I hear wind. I hear birds: the chipper sound of the oscree and the booming caw of the muskew. Both are soft. I hear water, somewhere distant.

"Listen," my mother says a third time.

I strain my ears. Plants swaying against each other. The creak of branches in the trees that line the meadow we stand in. My breath sighing through my nostrils. And then I hear it.

My name. I hear my name, the syllables whispering through the grass under my feet, slithering up my legs, and sliding into my ears.

"Octavia . . ."

"I hear it!" I say. "I hear it!"

"Octavia . . . Octavia?"

Dr. Adibuah is gently nudging my shoulder with the back of his hand, his voice close and soft. A doctor's voice, I think as I come awake. Calm. Soothing.

"Octavia, are you all right?"

I open both eyes and stare at him for a moment before answering.

"I think so."

It's hard to sit up—a pain throbs in my neck: a deep, sharp pain—but I do. My vision swims, and my body is clammy with sweat. Our skinsuits were designed to radiate our bodies' heat out and away from us—a technology we learned and borrowed from the cellular structure of the ears of an animal called a maigno—but usually its benefits aren't needed indoors. I look down and realize I'm staring at my bare stomach, deeply brown against the white of the skinsuit. My suit has been unfastened to the waist, meaning I'm lying there in my chest wrap in front of Dr. Adibuah. I cross my arms over my chest and struggle to fully rise.

"What happened?"

"You were unconscious," Dr. Adibuah says in his doctor voice. My father sits behind him with his hands on his knees.

I was? Why was I unconscious? The memory comes back like a spark of fire. The philax . . . his eyes . . . falling . . .

This time a pain in my head flowers, lancing out and down, gripping my heart. I cry out without meaning to, falling back onto the bench where I've been laid. I'm in a small room and the sound is louder than it should be.

"Octavia, what's the matter?" Dr. Adibuah has my shoulders in his hands and leans down over me. My father remains seated, watching.

"I . . . my head."

"What happened, Octavia?" My father stands now, his hands in the pockets of his white coat.

"The—the bird . . ."

I can't tell him. It's the feeling you get pulling your hand back from the fire before you even touch the flame—instinct. I swallow my words.

"A philax managed to escape a facility room," Dr. Adibuah says. "It somehow got out into the main dome. Did it hurt you?"

Dr. Adibuah's eyes roam down my bare arms with renewed concern, looking for wounds.

"No, it didn't hurt me."

"Did it upset you?" he asks, his voice gentle.

Did it upset me? It seems such an illogical way to describe what I felt in the dome.

"Yes," I say slowly. "It . . . upset me."

The lie tastes sour in my mouth.

"Octavia is sensitive," my father says. "I'm sure it was a shock. It happened very quickly."

I say nothing, glowering.

My father studies me, his hands still in his pockets. Dr. Adibuah's eyes are softer.

"Do you want to get her home, Octavius? Her neck has a minor sprain from her fall."

My father doesn't answer right away. One hand has crept from his pocket, the fingers curling below his lip and resting there, motionless, as he takes me in.

"Yes," he says eventually. "Octavia, can you walk?"

Pulling my skinsuit back up over my upper body, I stand quickly to prove that I'm fine. I'm punished with an array of spots before my eyes, the room spinning. I ignore it and nod but don't speak.

"Before you leave," Dr. Adibuah says, his finger raised, "you should allow me to apply some of the narruf. For her neck."

My father looks at me, his face stone. But he nods.

"I'll get it," Dr. Adibuah says, and leaves us alone.

I lean back against the platform where I awakened. My head isn't spinning and the noise that had crowded my brain earlier has subsided to a whisper. But I feel strange, open. Like a room in my mind has been unlocked, the door ajar but the room empty.

Dr. Adibuah returns with a beaker containing a gelatinous substance. He'd said "narruf," which I know is a species of bird, but I half expected him to return with the animal itself, not a jar of orange goo. I want to ask what it is—these are the things I love about what we do here: the mysteries that, once deciphered, might mean our continued survival. But my father's face is granite, so I close my mouth around the question.

"This is a substance from inside the narruf egg," Dr. Adibuah says, as if he can sense my thirst for the knowledge, dipping a small, thin spatula into the goo. "It's collected at hatching. It has healing qualities for injuries sustained after leaving the egg, such as falling from the nest."

He wipes off the excess on the jar's rim and motions for me to turn my head to the side. I obey, and he reaches forward to spread the thick substance along the side of my neck, from just under my ear down to the outside of my shoulder. My throat begins to tingle.

"Does it feel warm?" he asks, the spatula hovering.

It does. The warm feeling spreads, a small, sudden fever. I nod.

"Good." He drops the spatula into a sanitation pouch hanging from the wall and returns the lid to the jar.

My father opens the door.

"Let's go."

My father and I ride in silence, this time with him steering the chariot, at his insistence. We travel the same red dirt road, but something has changed. The distance between us is always present, but now it feels like a chasm.

"Next time I go to the Avian Compound, I know to come alone," my father says.

I jerk as if his words are a spear he's lodged in my ribs.

"Wait, what?" I say, ignoring the little stab of pain left over in my neck that spikes when I raise my voice. "Sir—"

"Octavia." He cuts me off, making an effort to sound nasty. "You do realize that to do what we do—to be a scientist—you must control yourself, don't you? Are you aware of that?"

"What? *Control* myself?"

My father takes his eyes off the road for an instant to glare over at me. I'm almost as tall as he is, but suddenly I'm rendered small. Even through his driving goggles I can feel the intensity of his stare, shrinking me.

"Science requires reserve. Calm. Control."

Reserve? It's my passion that makes science so appealing to me. Doesn't that count for something? And what about Jaquot—always bragging and telling jokes? I can't remember anyone lecturing *him* about reserve.

"Do you believe that you exhibited calm and restraint at the Avian Compound today?"

I start to tell him it wasn't my fault, but he cuts me off again.

"We study life-forms, Octavia," he says sharply. "Your first time seeing a specimen up close, and you behave this way. How do you expect to be a whitecoat when you get emotional at the mere sight of an animal being tranquilized?"

"Emotional," I repeat.

"Fainting at the sight of a tranquilization is hardly the behavior of a logical human being. A *scientist*." He's raised his voice: it rings out loud over the thrumming of the chariot.

"I'm not emotional!" I say, even louder. He's not hearing me. "I felt . . . I felt . . ."

I want to say afraid, but that's not right. He doesn't under-stand what the fear felt like, shoving its way in and occupying my body. "I felt—*something*!"

"It's not about what you *feel*!" my father shouts. "It's about what you *know*!"

I have nothing to say. He's not listening anyway. The Paw appears up ahead, but jumping off the chariot and walking into the jungle currently seems more appealing. I set my jaw and stare blankly as the guards—more buzzguns—stand aside to let us enter the compound.

"Control is how we will survive," he says more quietly but still with noticeable sharpness. "Entire cities have fallen because they weren't free to command their circumstances. N'Terra will not lose control. And neither will you."

The chariot comes to a stop between two others just like it, and I don't wait for my father to switch off the power cell before I leap off the standing platform and walk quickly away toward the main dome of the Paw. He calls me but I continue on, my steps long and hard. Right now the sound of my own name sounds too much like his, and I don't want it to belong to me.

The air of the Paw flows over me and fills me with a sense of comfort that I welcome. I jog through the sparse jungle of the main dome for a minute or two. I want to get farther away from the entrance before I rest, so that my father doesn't immediately spot me when he comes in. When I've trotted a sufficient distance, I stop and lean against an ogwe, breathing deeply. I smell the smell that Jaquot says doesn't exist: the multilayered scent seems to curl into my nostrils. My mind feels clearer now, the noise that invaded it earlier fading into silence. Don't be emotional, I think, and even though the thought makes me as annoyed at myself as I am at my father, I tell myself that maybe he was right.

I hear voices and peep my head around the trunk of the ogwe to look back the way I came. My father with—of course—another whitecoat, the two of them following the other path at the fork, the one that leads to the labs. Typical, I think bitterly, he's going to the Zoo on his rest day, even when we've been at the Beak for hours. He disappears down the path, his back tall and straight, his right hand gesturing to emphasize some point he's making to the whitecoat, who's nodding vigorously. "Yes, Dr. English," he's probably saying. "You're right, Dr. English. You're so brilliant, Dr. English!" I roll my eyes.

When my father and the whitecoat are out of sight, I carry on down to the communal dome. The doors open on their own for me when I approach.

With the main dome constructed on a small hill, the attached commune is built into the shallow valley alongside it. Above is the characteristic arching roof, transparent to let the sky in, but I'm more focused on the commune below. Things change so quickly lately, and every time I come home I pause to make sure everything is as I left it. Last week I returned from the Greenhouse to find that the curving stream that divides the dome had two additional bridges constructed across it. From here I can see the stumps of the three young trees used to build them. My father says the trees were dying.

Today a team of engineers is painting the roofs of several wigwams. Our homes are low and smooth, built with the white clay abundant around N'Terra, and with the light coming through the dome roof, they light up and shine like white stones in water. The paint the engineers are adding must serve some kind of purpose, I think, watching them work: insect repellent, perhaps—we need that. Surely it can't be for the aesthetic alone—they've chosen red—as there are ordinarily so many colors in the commune already: swatches of fabric dyed with plants grown around N'Terra, draped on the sides of 'wams and hanging from poles driven into the ground. But there are fewer flags and streamers than usual. A new decree by the Council perhaps, I think, like the one that had authorized the construction of the tower.

The tower has grown since I left the dome this morning, planted there in the exact center of the compound, a spiny-looking gray tree of a structure that the Council had ordered construction of eight weeks ago. The shadow of it falls across the commune like a thorn. After so many years standing in this same spot on the hill, I find the protrusion of the tower is strange. Instead I choose to focus on my 'wam: even from here I can see the yellow cloth that hangs on our door. It was brought here all the way from a place called Englewood, where my grandmother was born. I wonder if I—if we—will ever stop missing her. As I descend the curving steps down into the commune, I brush my fingers along the flowers that grow on either side, tiny petals that curl closed at night, bright yellow in the morning and deep blue by dusk. As always, they lean away from my fingers. I smile, sympathetic. That's how I feel right now too.

At the bottom of the stairs, it's as if some blanket of silence has been pulled back, and I'm grateful for the chaos of children laughing and running. Far across the commune the first beats of a drum rhythm come to life, people relaxing after spending their day at various kinds of work. I frown, thinking of when my father used to play. It's been a long time.

I'm so focused on the sound of the drum, I run straight into someone on the path.

"Stars!" I curse, stumbling. The sudden jolt of my body reignites some of the ache from my sprain, and I grab my neck with both hands as if to clamp down on the pain before it spreads.

"Sorry," says a low voice.

I know this voice but am surprised to find it here—it belongs to Rondo, who, until now, I've only ever seen in the Greenhouse, and who I know to live in the Beak.

"What are you doing here?" I blurt, and I realize too late that I've snapped at him, still irritated from hurting my neck.

"I live here." He adjusts the burden under his arm, a medium-size black case.

"Since when?"

"This morning. My parents transferred their study."

"That explains why you look lost."

Rondo doesn't answer. He merely smiles in the quiet way that I always see him smile in the Greenhouse. Rondo is the one our classmates listen to when he speaks, myself included. Maybe it's because he talks so rarely. There's something interesting about a person who knows what he has to say is correct but chooses to keep it to himself.

"What's in there?" I ask, nodding at the case under his arm. I realize suddenly that this is how my father apologizes—by changing the subject, making his voice gentle. Never really an apology.

Rondo withdraws the case from under his arm. I don't recognize the smooth black material.

"An izinusa," he says.

"A what?"

"An izinusa. It's an instrument."

"For the lab?"

He chuckles low in his throat. The sound has a rhythm of its own, as if it too belongs in the drum circle.

"No, a musical instrument."

"Oh."

"It makes a beautiful sound."

"You can play it?" I'm impressed. My dad tried me on his drum once or twice, but it wasn't a skill that came naturally to me.

"A little."

"How did you learn?"

"A woman in my compound was teaching me before she passed. Now I'm teaching myself. This was hers."

"Can I see it?"

We catch eyes for an instant, his as deeply brown as mine but the lashes thicker, making his expression gentle. I look away, at his hands where they grip the edge of the case.

"Of course you can." Something about the way he says it—

soft—makes my face hot.

With the case being so rigid, I envisioned the izinusa itself as metal, serious. Instead the instrument is like a lovely fruit hidden inside rough peel. I sigh at the sight of it: sloping brown wood almost the same color as his skin, elegant strings, Rondo reaching in the case and lifting part of it out so I can see better.

"Wow" is all I can say.

"I know." His voice carries a smile—I can see it without having to look.

He carefully settles the izinusa back into the case. His fingers are like instruments themselves.

"You're not going to play me something?" I tease.

"Not today, O."

He talks to me as if we've been alone like this before. As if we're always alone. Now we stand in silence, looking at each other without looking at each other. It's strange that in a class as small as ours—thirty of us, together year after year—I've never spoken to him one-on-one. N'Terra encourages rivalry, and the result is much self-chosen independent study. You have maybe one good friend, and everyone else is competition. Rondo has strictly been the latter. Perhaps we'd be closer if he had lived in the Paw. And now he does, I think.

"So you're just carrying that thing around?" I ask to distract myself.

"It was just delivered from the Beak. My dads 'forgot' to

bring it when they finished transporting our stuff today."

"You play that badly, huh?" I smile. "They tried to leave it behind?"

He grins at this, and a thrill shoots through me.

"I think they'd just prefer that I focus on my studies. I'm not exactly the best pupil."

"Disagree. Dr. Espada loves you. Whenever you contribute you're rarely wrong."

"Contributing and doing assignments on time are two different things," he says. He runs his hand along the curve of the izinusa one more time before closing and latching the case.

"Well, you'd better get it together. I heard a rumor about them introducing internships."

Why did I tell him that?

"Hmm." That's all he says, and I'm disappointed. Any other greencoat would have snapped at the bait, but as his eyes wander over the commune, I become more and more sure that Rondo isn't like any other greencoat.

"What do you think the tower is for?" he says, nodding at it. "They're building one in the Beak's commune too."

I turn to follow his gaze.

"An observation deck is what I hear."

"Observing the commune?"

"No. What purpose would that serve? It's to observe the sky. The stars."

"The stars," he says, and that's all.

"Yeah. You know how it is. Always trying something new."

He nods.

"I need to get back," I say. I'm reluctant to leave. "I don't want to run into my dad out here."

"Why not?"

I hesitate.

"It's a long story."

"Maybe next time." He catches my eye and the pain in my neck momentarily subsides, or maybe I'm just distracted by the tingle he infects me with.

"Yeah, next time."

I turn away before he has a chance to catch my eye again—otherwise I might end up standing in the commune all night. Still, I can feel his gaze on my back until I turn the corner and go out of sight. Even then I feel like I can still see his eyes.

I follow my feet along the wide path to my home, the ground made smooth by the daily travels of many feet. When I reach my 'wam, I slide my hand across the illuminated panel and the front door hums open.

I assumed my mother would be home from the Zoo since it's my parents' rest day, but the 'wam is dark and quiet. While some whitecoats run shops during their days outside the lab, rest days never really mean much to my mother and father. The Zoo is the only thing that distracts them from their grief.

My grandfather died long ago: before the *Vagantur* even rose into the stars. But somehow losing my grandmother here was a different depth of tragedy for my parents. She was my mother's mother, but my father had loved her just as much. Me too. I didn't see her often: she was even more obsessed with science than my parents. But my mother says I got my logic from them and my passion from my grandmother.

"Hey, you." I jump at the sound of my mother's voice. I didn't even hear the door hum open, which she walks through carrying a slate and a box of slides for her three-dimensional projector.

"Oh, hey." I peer at the labels of her slides to see if there's anything interesting I can sneak a look at later. "You're just getting home?"

"Yes. And I ran into your father in the lab."

"Oh."

"Yes, oh," she says, placing her slides on the kitchen platform. She levels her gaze at me, and it's like looking into deep water. I can see my reflection, but there's so much swimming behind it. "Are you all right?"

"I'm fine now. I don't even know what happened." Once upon a time I might have looked to her for comfort, a refuge from my father's stoniness. But his words on the way back from the Beak have lodged themselves in my skull: emotional. Irrational. The implication of ineptitude is too much. Bending to it now—even with my mother—might make it true.

"They say you were unconscious."

"I guess."

"What do you remember from before it happened?"

I pause before answering. Sometimes I can't tell if my parents actually care or if everything is an experiment to them.

"Not much," I say. "I mean, I remember the philax."

"Yes, your father told me."

We're silent, and I wonder what it is that's hanging inside the quiet, if she's thinking what my father was thinking.

"Do you think I'm emotional?" I ask.

She crosses her arms over her chest.

"Why do you ask me that?"

"I'm just asking."

"Someone told you you're too emotional?" I can hear the edge in her voice, the rare tone that makes whitecoats falter when telling her something they were so sure of a moment before. I feel closest to my mother when she's angry: she lights up, fierce compared to the calm, cool scientist's manner that she usually carries.

"No," I lie. As much as I like to see her when she's fired up, I don't want it directed at my father. "I'm just wondering why I fainted."

My mother hmms and goes to the kitchen, where cupboards dug into the clay wall are filled with round fruits of orange and green, plus the long thick sticks of zarum, which are dried plant tubers but taste, I overheard my father say once, like something called meat. My mother takes down one of the green hava fruits and slices it with the bowed knife that hangs on the wall. The sliced fruit goes into a misshapen ceramic bowl my grandmother had made, another artifact of her life.

"Passion, *compassion*, is not a weakness," she says. "No matter what your father says."

Seeing her now, her cheekbones still visible but less defined, I suddenly remember my dream, the one I had when waking in the room at the Beak. I open my mouth to tell her, but she's moved on to talking about a project she's working on in the neurology department, studying the brain of a kalu they'd found dead outside the compound. She loves talking about brains almost as much as I love hearing her talk about them.

"Have you finished your research for tomorrow?" She's cleaning up the hava skins, feeding them into the biotube in the kitchen.

"Yes, I finished most of it before class was over."

"My girl." She smiles without looking up.

The lights flicker a little as the hava skins are fed into our energy surplus.

"Do you know anything about internships?" I ask.

"Internships." Her eyes are on me now and I shrug.

"Yeah. Dr. Adibuah said something about it at the Beak."

"Internships for whom?" Her eyebrows are almost touching

in the middle where she's scrunched them.

"Greencoats."

"Greencoats," she repeats.

"That's what he said. But he said he wasn't sure," I add.

"Did your father know about this?"

"I don't know. I couldn't tell."

"I see."

She doesn't say anything else, so I don't either. It's easy to be quiet in a house that's already silent so much of the time. She finishes disposing of the hava skins and wipes her hands on a cloth.

"All right, Afua," she says. "I have work to do."

She scoops up the slate and slides she brought in with her and moves toward the hallway, where she'll disappear into her study and hunch over her desk until well after I'm asleep. She stops at the mouth of the hall and looks back.

"I'd avoid him tonight," she says. "I think it'd be better if you two discussed things on another day when you're both less . . . stressed."

I raise and drop one shoulder. No answer necessary.

I sit alone for a while at the platform in the kitchen. My body feels heavy. I look down at my white skinsuit—which is almost like an actual second skin, as tight as it is—and realize I've been wearing it all day. My scalp is gritty at the root of the braids that my mother calls cornrows. At one point I asked what this word meant and she couldn't remember. But the word survives, stitched into my head, part of Faloiv now. The grit in my hair motivates me to take a shower and I finally drag myself up from the kitchen platform. I pad down the hall, unfastening the neck of my skinsuit. I'm halfway to our bathroom, the material peeling off, when my mother's voice, soft and low, floats to my ears from her study. I drift closer.

"I knew nothing about the internships. And, yes, they *do* give me great cause for concern."

She pauses.

"I imagine it would be the entire age group," she says. "Pulling Octavia and no one else would be unusual. I don't want to draw attention to her."

My stomach lights up with anxiety. She's talking about pulling me out of the internships? The internships that haven't even been announced yet? My grip on the skinsuit slips as my fingers begin to tremble. I press even more closely to the door, determined to learn more.

"Yes, she had an episode today. With a philax. No, I don't think she understands."

Silence for a long moment: whoever she's talking to goes on for a while. I hold my breath.

"It's not the time for that kind of talk," she says. "They wouldn't understand how she . . ."

The rest of her sentence is lost as my ears pick up a sound from the front of the 'wam: the sigh of our front door opening.

My father is home. Lungs fluttering, I scramble away from my mother's study and into the bathroom, turning on the water in the slim bathing cell. I don't step in the water yet: I wait, my hands shaking, still half-dressed, until I hear my father make his way down the hall and into my parents' room.

I finish shedding the skinsuit, unfastening my chest wrap, and finally step into the cell, careful to keep my mouth closed. I rinse my body off thoroughly, letting the water run over my scalp and through my braids. I don't have time to wash them tonight. I must finish quickly: it takes a lot of energy from our surplus to bathe, and I don't need another grievance to add to the list my father already has. I step out, drying myself with the largest size cloth from the wall holes and wrapping myself in it.

When I slide the door open, I poke my head out into the hall. There's a light in my mother's study and a light in my parents' room. Separate again, I think. I pause in the hallway one more time, and I can hear each of their voices murmuring: two rooms, two conversations. I enter my own room, where I unsheathe from the wrap like a hatching insect. I take the little bottle of jocada oil from my desk and sit on the edge of the bed to oil my scalp. Usually the feeling of the warm oil and the pads of my fingertips relaxes me, but the events of the day churn through my head in an endless parade of shadows. When I lie down, restless, it's as if the philax is lying beside me, his fear shortening my every breath.

• • •

I don't remember falling asleep, but my room is bathed in midnight when the sound of my parents' bedroom door wakes me. My father's long stride moves almost soundlessly down the hall, toward the front of the 'wam. A heartbeat later, the whisper of the front door gliding open and then shut.

Back to the Zoo, I think, but I rise and go to my small window, sliding the shade aside. It feels strange watching him like this, but in a way it's comforting: to see him and love him without the burn of his eyes staring back. I follow the shadow of him as he moves down the path, but instead of toward the labs, he veers deeper into the commune. Odd. I lean sideways in the narrow window to keep watching.

He stops at the base of the tower that rises against the moonlight like a fang. Something curls in my heart: a sinking feeling, like watching a bird about to be crushed in the talons of a predator. But there is no shadow other than my father's; he places his hand against the slick trunk of the tower and leans heavily forward, as if it's the only thing in the world keeping him up. I watch until the clouds shift over the moon and the commune is lost in black.

CHAPTER 3

The Worm pulls through the Paw's gates a little after dawn, its geothermal energy panel gleaming blue. I'd been all but sleep-walking until Rondo emerged, but at the sight of him sleep is a memory. We stand apart, surrounded by the other Paw students, everyone yawning except Rondo. Something about him wires me, but the sluggishness brought on by sleeping poorly empties my brain of interesting things to say. The kids sit and eat slices of hava that their parents have prepared for them, and I wish I had some too, to have something to do with my hands. When the Worm comes to a stop outside the main dome and the driver signals us to climb on, Rondo herds the kids aboard as if he's been living in the Paw all his life.

When I get on the Worm, he's in my seat. And although he can't possibly have known this, when I stand next to him in the aisle and stare, he gives me a quiet smile.

"I figured you'd sit up front," he says. He's already moved over to make room for me. In my seat. "First off the Worm, so first into the Greenhouse."

"Yeah, well," I say, sitting down.

The ride to the Greenhouse isn't long: the building is situated behind the Paw, on another small rise in the land. The Greenhouse is actually in the center of the main research compounds, the others spread around it like a honeycomb. Except the Council's building, where all the meetings about the happenings in N'Terra are held. It's the newest of the domes, and I haven't laid eyes on it, as neither of my parents have offered to take me when they go. Apparently it sits just beyond the arrangement of the compounds, like a satellite observing our little solar system.

Rondo is so close his arm brushes mine when he breathes deeply. He inhales and I turn to catch whatever it is he's about to say to me when I realize his words are directed at the driver.

"Nice morning, isn't it?" he says.

"I fail to see what's so nice about it," Draco replies. I should have warned Rondo not to talk to him—Draco is always irritable. He's an old man: too old, some have said, to be driving the Worm. But trying to get the steering column out of his hands would be tempting fate.

"Well, you have us, don't you?" I'm surprised to hear the humor in Rondo's voice. Only a few words exchanged with

Draco and already he seems to have pinpointed what makes the old man tick. Or what ticks him off, to be more specific.

Draco makes a growling sound as the Worm turns a corner. Somewhat roughly, I think, as if Draco imagined trying to send Rondo off the side. I swallow a laugh.

"You?" Draco says when he's done growling. "The only thing my morning wouldn't be complete without is this drive. You don't even enter the equation, young man."

"Oh, I don't know," Rondo says, straight-faced. "I think you might be lonely if you drove without us. Otherwise what would be the point?"

"The point," Draco scoffs. I can't see his face, only his hands on the steering column: wizened and deeply tanned. "The drive itself is the point. When I was a young man on a planet you know nothing about, I'd drive for miles on my own. Miles!"

"Going where?"

"Nowhere! Can't do that here." His hands tighten on the steering column, some of the color fading from them as he squeezes hard. "Can't waste the energy. Besides, our hosts wouldn't have that, would they?"

"Who?"

"Don't be dense, young man. The Faloii."

Draco pronounces it differently than what I've learned is correct—he condenses its three syllables into two, as if the third isn't worth enunciating. Rondo catches my eye, raises his eyebrow. I keep staring—something about Rondo's eyes don't let you go. Held captive by his irises, I only hear the tail end of Draco's gripes.

"Dr. Albatur will change that though," the old man complains. "People can't live as tenants forever. Faloiv is ours now too. They'd do well to get used to that."

At the mention of Dr. Albatur's name, I finally turn my eyes away from Rondo.

"What does Dr. Albatur plan to do?" I ask.

"Take back control," Draco grates. "You kids are too young to know: you don't understand anything but your sad, small world. But at one point, *we* made the rules. We wanted to build? We built. We wanted to drive?" He slaps one palm against the steering column. "We drove!"

I have more questions, but the Worm jerks to a stop—not as gently as it usually does. Draco turns to Rondo and me with a sour expression.

"Off."

We get off.

Our Worm is gone in a heartbeat—Draco enjoying his drive—but the Worms from the other compounds are pulling up now; I put the old man out of my head, squinting in the sun for the vessel from the Newt. Alma will be on it and I have things to tell her. Looking for her, I see Jaquot step off the Worm from the Beak and we briefly make eye contact. I look around for Alma, but as usual she sees me first.

"Octavia," she calls, with a gesture of her hand to come

meet her. Alma doesn't say much without a hand gesture accompanying it.

She steps off the Worm from the Newt, her hair an enormous cloud around her head. It's different almost every day: some days she braids it to her scalp like me, some days she gathers it into six or more puffs. Today nothing restrains it—an explosion of soft brown.

"Look at *you*," I say, greeting her with a shoulder bump.

She smiles her wide smile.

"My hair is getting so long. My mother says her grandparents called this an Afro."

"That's correct," says a voice I know to be Dr. Espada's. Our teacher stands in the doorway of the Greenhouse, his arms folded and his smile broad. "One of the most regal hairstyles in the galaxy. The captain of the *Vagantur* wore one. Captain Williams."

Dr. Espada doesn't wear a white coat like the other scientists: he says it gets in his way when he's teaching. Which is true. He gesticulates a lot, like Alma. She would make a great teacher as it is, so her gestures put her ahead of the curve.

"Oh?" says Alma, patting her hair gently. "I like the sound of that."

Dr. Espada gestures for us to come into the Greenhouse, where the younger kids are already trailing off to, led by Dr. Yang, who taught us when we were younger. Dr. Espada will be my last teacher—after him, the Zoo.

"What's on the agenda, Doc?" says Alma, the first through the door after him. I follow before the other greencoats start to push in for good places.

"Always so eager." Dr. Espada laughs. "Take your seats, tortoises. We have lots of new material to cover."

"What are tortoises?" Alma says quickly.

"Ahh. A reptile from the Origin Planet. Very slow."

"I see." Alma's round face is serious, her eyes squinted. I shake my head at her, laughing. The rest of us roll our eyes when Dr. Espada and the other whitecoats use words that have no place on Faloiv, but Alma mentally records each one, as if they might be worth something later.

Alma and I take our seats down front, closest to the transparent display board where most of Dr. Espada's presentation will appear. Rondo chooses a seat behind me, and my entire body stiffens. He never sits here—always in the back with Jaquot and other Beak dwellers. Jaquot even shoots his friend a quizzical look, glancing undecidedly toward the back row, before sitting down next to him. I try to act like I don't notice, straightening my back.

"What'd you do on your rest day?" Alma asks me, settling in and powering on her slate. "I sent you a message but you didn't write back."

I swallow. I don't want to talk about what happened in the Beak here in class. Too many opportunities to be overheard—specifically by Rondo.

"All right, let's get started," Dr. Espada begins, and I can't help but feel relieved that we're interrupted. A gentle hum rumbles through the walls as Dr. Espada powers on the three-dimensional projector, the sound of energy being drawn from the Greenhouse's solar store. He's just raising his hands to start gesticulating, when his eyes flick to the doorway, away, and then back again in a double take.

"Oh," he says, and his hands drop.

The heads of my classmates turn as if attached to a single curious neck. It's rare that class is disrupted: I can recall only one other time, when the Slither was flooding, that we were excused early. But the person in the doorway doesn't look urgent as if an emergency has brought her. She glides into the classroom.

"Council," Alma murmurs in my ear, just as I glimpse the gold Council pin on the breast of the woman's lab coat—a delicate likeness of the *Vagantur* surrounded by five circles representing the compounds.

"May I come in?" the woman says, though she's already in. Her voice is unexpected for someone so broad, its tenor reedy and thin like a blade of grass.

"I . . . of course," Dr. Espada says.

"Dr. Albatur has sent me to make an announcement," she says, turning to us. I note the frown that flickers across Dr. Espada's mouth.

"He couldn't have come himself?" Alma whispers. "Everybody knows he doesn't actually do any of his own research."

49

I conceal my smile. I've heard my mother say the same thing—that it was his long rambling speeches that got him elected, not his work.

"An announcement? Has something happened?" Dr. Espada says.

"You could say that." The councilwoman shoots him a flash of teeth. Her smile remains focused on him a beat longer than is called for, and I'm not surprised when he doesn't smile back. Her expression is like the painted clay decoy animals used in some field experiments. False. Hollow.

"There has been an exciting breakthrough in N'Terra," the woman says. She spreads the fingers on each hand wide like two fans. "Tomás, could you please bring up a photo of a myn?"

"Certainly."

A moment later, we all gaze up at the image of a fish presented before us, slightly blurry: it's light gray in color with a long wispy dorsal fin, eyes an opaque orange in sharp contrast to the dull color of its body.

"And now an oscree, please," the councilwoman says. She still hasn't told us her name.

Alongside the fish appears an image of the common oscree, its delicate wings folded along the length of its body.

"Two different animals," the councilwoman says. "Two different species. And yet today we have discovered that they have more in common than we could have ever predicted."

She pauses. I dart my eyes at Dr. Espada and find that his

face has lost its frown. Instead, every wrinkle seems to have been laid smooth. It's like looking at a mask.

"Would anyone like to hazard a guess?" the councilwoman goes on. She lets her eyes drift across the room, and as they wander through my row, I swear they pause on my face for just an instant too long. I wonder, my breath becoming shallow, if Dr. Albatur had told her about me, if I'm already getting a reputation in the Zoo.

"Myn and oscree? How about"—Jaquot draws out the words comically—"they instantaneously die of boredom when they come across each other in the wild?"

A subdued current of laughter courses through the room, and the councilwoman's hollow smile widens. Her eyes don't change. I glance back at Jaquot and find him reclining in his chair, grinning. Ordinarily I would be throwing ocular poison in his direction, but today I send a subtle salute, which he accepts with a kingly nod.

"I was under the impression that your students were erudite," the councilwoman says, turning her teeth on Dr. Espada again, whose neutral mask falters. Jaquot's smile fades. "Apparently not. So I'll get right to it. In these two unrelated species, we have a confirmed study that proves myn and oscree are able to communicate without any means of physical or aural input."

"Excuse me." Alma beats me in breaking the silence. "What does that mean exactly? Psychically? If they're communicating without physical or aural signals, then you mean they're communicating . . . how? Telepathically?"

"Someone is paying attention after all," the councilwoman says, beaming, but Alma doesn't smile. "Yes, that's what our studies appear to conclude. Preliminary studies began by exploring intraspecies communication and found that mammals may be communicating psychically. Then, thanks to Dr. English's research, we realized there was more to it."

"Dr. English?" Dr. Espada says quickly.

"That's correct," the councilwoman says, and this time her gaze is definitely on me, that empty smile lasering in on me with almost predatory intensity. "Samirah English, that is."

The class claps, as we always do when one of our parents is recognized for a breakthrough in N'Terran science, but I barely hear it. I sat in the kitchen with my mother last night, eating and talking, and she didn't mention this discovery at all—she just disappeared into her study and whispered about pulling me out of the not-yet-announced internships. A movement from Dr. Espada catches my eye—he reaches for his slate at his desk, typing something in a flurry of silent finger taps while the councilwoman resumes her speech.

"Quiet now," she says, her hands fanning out again. "There's one more thing. As you know, under current policy, you won't be assigned to a specialty of study until you're eighteen, after you've shown some aptitude for a particular branch. And then won't be in the labs until you're twenty-one, after extensive guided research."

Everyone is holding their breath. I feel Rondo's eyes drilling into the back of my head. Dr. Adibuah's rumor is already at the front of my mind when the councilwoman continues.

"As you can imagine, this new discovery is significant and could change the way we gather information about survival on this planet. There will be shifting priorities in N'Terra. So as of next week, students sixteen and older will have the opportunity to take part in an internship in one of our research compounds. We'll also be introducing children to hands-on procedures at age ten, and shortening their time in the Greenhouse. . . ."

It's like being in a bubble at the center of an explosion— around me, scholarly decorum is shattered with the roar of exhilaration, the room dissolving into chatter. The council-woman has more to say about children getting less formal Greenhouse instruction, but her voice is lost. Alma is stand-ing, gripping my arm and shaking it as Jaquot fake-brags about how he'd already known about internships. Somehow the excitement doesn't sink into my skin—I'm watching the councilwoman slip out of the room, Dr. Espada's eyes on her back as if observing a dangerous species in the wild. I don't hear the notification from my slate over the din of the classroom, but I see it light up and tap the mouth icon that appears. It's a message from Rondo.

Interspecies telepathy. So even if I was a bird, I could still tell you you're pretty, it says.

I stare at the black text for a moment, allowing the feeling of pleasure to overtake the gloom the councilwoman left behind—even if I'm the only one who feels its shadow. The text is like a wave of sunshine that sweeps down from my head to my chest.

That's assuming a bird would even find me attractive, I type back.

I would say your beauty is pretty much universal.

I don't know what to say to this. My fingers tingle as if they have their own message they'd like to send. Alma, sitting again now that Dr. Espada is attempting get the class under control, leans over. I minimize my messages with one swift stroke.

"I wonder if everybody gets an internship," she says under her breath. "You know good and well some of these fools aren't ready to be around specimens."

Dr. Espada has begun to lecture, and again I'm grateful for the interruption, because if I'd had to answer right then, I might have choked. Alma's words stir a fear that hunkered low in my belly and send it fleeing into the sky. What if *I* can't go into the labs?

Another message from Rondo pops up on my slate.

What's the matter?

I swallow. Is he psychic like the damn myn?

What makes you think something is?

I pay attention.

For some reason reading these three words makes my eyes prickle. So simple, the idea of being seen. Rondo might be one of the only people on this planet who actually sees me. The thought is so sharp, like a bite, that I'm responding before I can even stop myself:

Maybe you should pay attention to Espada's lecture instead.

I regret it instantly. I want to look back at him, to feel the comfort of his brown eyes like a salve on whatever wound I've exposed in my own skin. But I force myself to keep my eyes on the screen.

He sends back one word—*Okay*—and that hurts even more.

Later, when we break for our midday meal, Alma and I are the first outside. Even the heat can't crush her excitement.

"Internships. Incredible," she gushes. We had two hours of lecture after the councilwoman dropped the news of internships on us, but it's still the first thing out of everyone's mouths when we're released for break. "Can you believe it? Incredible. Absolutely incredible."

"You just said *incredible* three times," I say.

"Because it *is*! Octavia, we have to be in the same compound. We *have* to. It's going to be incredible."

"Four."

"Okay, okay. But seriously! We could discover something amazing together! Like your mom." She sighs. "Oh, stars, your mom is brilliant. Did she tell you anything about how she discovered the telepathic thing?"

I slowly chew the bite of food I've just taken, wondering how to tell her that I hadn't a clue, that my mother cares more about protecting her secrets than sharing the truth with her daughter. Alma presses on without waiting for my answer.

"I *have* to be in the Paw. I want to learn everything there is to know from her. Your dad too, of course. But you know . . . your mom. She's a legend now."

"You'd really want to be in the Paw?" I ask. She's finally settling down and eating. "Not the Newt?"

Alma nods, one of her cheeks huge from the bite she finally took.

"Of course," she says. "Mammals have always been my favorite—you know that. Besides, if I end up working in the Newt, I'm going to have to live around my parents forever. And nothing against them but, um . . . no thanks."

We both laugh. At one point I would have welcomed working alongside my mother and father. But lately . . .

"Weird that they're letting us in now," I say.

"And ten-year-olds doing hands-on work?" she says. "Did you catch that bit? The old Council Head spent so much time building the pathway to working with actual specimens. Now Albatur wants to let kids do it."

"They trust kids a lot more than I do," I say. "Can you imagine Jaquot when he was ten? I wouldn't want that terror in the labs."

"The Council likes to switch things up. Like this," she says, gesturing around us. "They never used to let us come outside. And now look: we're out here for mid-meal every day."

"Yeah, with the company of a bunch of buzzguns," I say, glancing around at the gray-suited guards that roam the Greenhouse perimeter.

"Hey, I don't mind the company, as long as I'm out here." She squints at the sky, hoping to catch sight of something, anything. "The buzzguns are weird though."

"So many since Albatur got elected. They're everywhere now."

"Surprised Dr. Espada doesn't carry one while he teaches."

I laugh at that.

"Oh shut up. I guess they have them out here in case something dangerous happens to come by. A dirixi or something."

"Don't even say that—"

"Or to protect us from the bloodthirsty Faloii!" yells Jaquot, leaping out of the long grass behind us. We jump and he laughs.

"Don't be a fearmonger. The Faloii aren't bloodthirsty," Alma says, bopping him with her water canteen.

"Can you prove that?" He laughs, doing his best whitecoat impression. I chuckle in spite of myself. He does sound like my father.

"No," says Alma, "but if they wanted to kill us, they wouldn't have let us onto Faloiv in the first place."

"Still. The Faloii think we're their prisoners. We can't do anything without their permission."

"That doesn't disprove what I just said," Alma says. "They want a say on what happens on Faloiv—so? That's not blood-thirsty. It's their planet, after all. They let us build the compounds and they leave us alone and let us study their world."

"But never them," says Rondo, emerging out of the tall grasses behind Jaquot. My smile fades and I'm very aware of the blood in my veins. I wonder if he's mad after what I said. In any case, my blood feels happy to see him, even as nervous-ness pools in my stomach. Illogical, I tell myself, annoyed by my contradictory reactions to his presence, and I find myself examining my fingers. Is attraction quantifiable? My heartbeat is empirical, but what does it actually mean?

"Go on," says Alma, sounding like Dr. Espada. I focus on looking at her instead of Rondo.

"We know so much about the animals here, but we know almost nothing about the Faloii," he says, his voice even. He stands above us with Jaquot. I wipe my hands and stand up. Alma follows suit.

"Why does it matter?" says Alma. "They let us study the life on their planet. It's not a big deal if we don't study them specifically."

"I'm not saying it against them," he says. "I'm saying it against us."

"Why *against* us?" I ask. I try not to sound combative, but I do. Here I go again. It makes talking to him easier. If I don't make my voice hard, it will inevitably be too soft. "From what I understand, we haven't seen the Faloii since the landing. They laid out the rules and then went back to wherever they live. It's not really our fault if they don't want to be studied. Can you blame them, really?"

"I'm not saying we should study them. But it would make sense to have communication with them. Right now the only discussion I ever hear about the Faloii is when someone is angry. What they won't let us do. What they're keeping us from building. It's all pretty . . . hostile."

"Exhibit A: the drivers," Jaquot throws in. "Rondo told me about Draco. The driver for the Beak is the same way—an old guy. He knows the deal. They're always complaining about the Faloii."

"Really?" I raise my eyebrow.

Jaquot nods, still laughing.

"Always. 'The Faloii think they're benevolent rulers.' Blah, blah, blah. 'If we had our way, N'Terra would be twice the size.' Blah, blah. 'When freedom is kept under lock and key, the captive will break the lock!' On and on. I don't know what lock Draco thinks he's going to break. He's like a hundred years old."

"Freedom? We have freedom," I say, confused.

He shrugs, looking uncomfortable. I imagine the topic rising up between us like a crag in the riverbed, splitting the water's flow.

"I don't know. I guess he wants more. My dad wants to expand the compound too. Lots of people do."

I look at Alma—I always look to her when I want to know if something makes sense or not. I can generally trust my own logic, but hers is infallible. Her eyes squint the way they do when she's studying research—she's considering all the variables, weighing the arguments of everyone present.

"You don't think it's weird to live on a planet and not have any communication with its people?" Rondo adds when no one says anything.

"They probably don't speak any of our languages, my friend," jokes Jaquot. I don't know how I never noticed it before, but I'm starting to see strategy in some of his comedy. Tension diffusion. He's been a clown since we were children. I'm suddenly curious about what his parents are like, if there's a chasm in his 'wam too that he's had to build a bridge across.

"Yaya's at it again," Alma says, and nods toward the Greenhouse.

We all look. Dr. Espada's standing at the doorway, the rounded figure of Yaya beside him, her slate in her hands in note-taking position.

"There *she* goes." I sigh.

"Has she still not spoken to you since you disproved her

theory on dunikai migration?" Alma says, chuckling.

"Nope." I can't help but smirk at the memory. Yaya isn't exactly a rival since she's always preferred talking to Dr. Espada more than greencoats, but the dunikai debate was one of the few head to heads we've actually had. Since then—two years ago—she's seemed even more determined to interact solely with whitecoats. Some days I think she doesn't consider herself a greencoat at all; not a student but a colleague of Dr. Espada who just happens to sit in the audience.

"Still on her quest to the top!" Alma says, shaking her head.

"Gotta love a girl with goals," Jaquot says, and I turn my eyes on him in surprise. With Alma packing her things for class and Rondo standing off to the side in his own world, I'm the only one who hears it. Jaquot shoots me a bashful smile.

Ahead, Dr. Espada is turning to go back into the Greenhouse, when he almost bumps into the councilwoman, who doesn't make way in the entrance. He steps aside for her and she strides toward her waiting chariot. I watch my teacher watching her before my gaze wanders again to the scattering of gray-suited guards, their heads turning this way and that as they scan the trees. As my group moves toward the Greenhouse, Jaquot telling jokes and Alma gesticulating, I think of my grandmother. Since she died, I've imagined filling the void she left with my own scientific discoveries; my parents' sadness soothed by the advances I would make in turning Faloiv into a place where they can be happy. But Rondo has planted a seed in my mind that sprouts into a flower I avert my eyes from. Maybe he's onto something, and it bothers me that it's not a theory I considered before. I turn to him, not quite ready to let the subject of the Faloii drop.

"Maybe they're starting internships to begin studying the Faloii," I say. "There has to be a reason they'd let us in the labs all of a sudden."

Rondo looks past me at the guards, gripping their buzzguns with both hands.

"'Shifting priorities,'" he says. "That's what she said. Maybe you're right. But I'm interested in where they're shifting."

CHAPTER 4

I don't see my father for four days.

"He's working on a new project," my mother tells me when we eat alone in the evenings. "It's taking up a lot of his time."

A lot is an understatement, I think.

It's also been four days since the councilwoman announced the internships. I haven't broached the topic with my mother, afraid of what she'll say. It floats between us now at our kitchen platform like a bubble, invisible but present.

"How is Alma?" she asks me when we've been silent for a while. She has taken her fruit and arranged it on top of the flatbread that I made in our oven of clay bricks. She takes a bite and chews with her eyes on me.

"She's good. She wants to do her internship at the Paw," I say, and pretend to focus on breaking off a piece of the bread.

My mother stops chewing, pausing and looking at me intently. When I look back into her face, she has already resumed, as if the pause never happened.

"Well," she says, "I hope she gets what she wants. From what I understand, Dr. Espada will be asking for student input, but placing students himself based on aptitude."

"Oh. Well, she's obsessed with mammals," I say. "So I bet her aptitude will get her in."

"Most likely," she says. She's swallowed her bite and doesn't take another. "Where do you want to be placed?"

"I don't know," I say. "Probably the Beak."

"The Beak," she repeats. "What about your focus on functional nutrition? I didn't know that you'd done any of your research on avian species."

She's called my bluff. She knows what all my projects have been on—I've asked her input as a mammalian expert on almost all of them.

"Well, I haven't. But, you know, birds are interesting. Reptiles too, so maybe I'll ask about the slither."

She smiles at me, a small amused smile, and I feel foolish, transparent. I stand abruptly.

"I'm going to go see some friends," I say.

She looks surprised but nods.

"All right," she says. "Have a good time. Don't worry about your food: I'll finish it."

I leave without replying.

Out in the commune, I inhale deeply. When did it become so hard to breathe at home? I wander. I was as surprised as my mother to hear me say that I was going to see friends: we both know I don't really have any in the Paw. But it's not so bad being alone: wandering in the Paw is a lot like being outside if you don't look up and see the curving ceiling of the dome. Sometimes the walls make me claustrophobic; like they're part of a cage keeping me from the rest of the world. I look at my feet, at the grass and stones and soil, and imagine that I'm outside the compound, in the jungle and on my own. I wonder if anyone else ever feels this way: the urge to escape and see Faloiv for themselves, beyond the slides that Dr. Espada shows in class, the quick snatches of the world I see on the Worm, or on my rare trips with my father. The soil is soft under my narrow white shoes. If I were a marov, I think, I could just burrow right under the dome walls. I smile at the idea and turn to start across one of the bridges that cross the stream.

"What are you smiling about?"

It's Rondo. I'm not surprised, as if I knew that by wandering long enough he'd show up.

"I was just thinking about being a marov," I blurt.

"A marov . . . ?"

He looks confused, and I seize on his puzzlement to distract from my embarrassment.

"A marov," I say, daring him to mock me. "It's a mammal.

You might want to look it up: it'll be on an exam sometime."

He looks away, his fingers tapping out a rhythm on the bridge, gazing out at the commune. I realize now I've embarrassed *him*.

"It's just a furry, fat thing." I shrug. "Ground dwelling. Eats tubers and leaves . . ."

He returns his eyes to my face, his fingers still drumming, and says, "Honestly, I don't give a damn about mammals."

This surprises me. I can't tell if he's angry with me or not. He doesn't seem angry: his face, mostly smooth aside from a little bumpy area on one cheekbone from acne, is lineless.

"No?" It's all I can think to say.

"Nope. Not at all."

"What do you give a damn about, then?" I say, and take a few steps toward the other side of the bridge. He's just come from this way, I'm guessing, but I'm not finished with my walk. I wonder if he'll come with me, and my stomach stirs, a lone winged insect trapped in its cavern.

"People," he says, and follows. Inside me, one insect becomes two. "I'm interested in people."

"Well, there's no human compound." It's a joke, but he doesn't smile.

"No, there's not."

He says it as if this is something he's already considered and found to be a problem.

"So what would you study if you had to choose? Since people aren't an option."

He pauses.

"Music."

"Music?" I scoff, trying too late to take the judgment out of my voice. I throw a sideways look at him to see if he noticed. He did, but he doesn't look offended. "I hate to break it to you, but there's no musical compound either."

"Mmm."

"You can't choose something more . . . logical?"

"There's more to the world than logic," he says.

"Not in N'Terra."

"Yes, I know." Then finally, as if giving in, he adds, "I guess I'd study birds if I had to choose. If forced."

"Do you miss the Beak that much?"

"What's to miss? Everything I need is right here."

He doesn't look at me, but his sly smile lets me know the pleasure that blooms in my chest was planted there intentionally.

"I was there last week," I say.

"I know." He nods.

"You know?"

"Yes, I heard. A whitecoat was observing a newly hatched oscree in the main dome while you were there. He mentioned to my dad that he saw you."

He "saw" me. I can hear the philax in his voice: he knows what happened. I wish I was a marov more than ever, and imagine diving into the safety of a burrow, made invisible by soil.

"He *saw* me," I repeat, refusing to look at him. We enter a cluster of shops, many of which are closing for the day. The light coming through the transparent ceiling is softer than an hour ago, sunset approaching.

"Yeah, saw you. He said you fainted. I didn't really see you as the fainting type."

I grit my teeth. I want to snap that I'm *not* the fainting type, but then I'd have to admit what actually happened. If I haven't told Alma, then I'm not telling Rondo.

"So are you just going to stay silent, Octavia?"

The sound of my name in his mouth takes on a special sound—like a rare specimen whose name requires magic to pronounce. I don't let this magic creep into my reply.

"I can. It would be my prerogative."

"Damn, O, what happened at the Beak?" he insists.

I groan and he looks briefly surprised before laughing.

"Do you really not want to talk about it?" he says. "We don't have to if you don't want to."

"Yes, I fainted, okay?" It comes out more peevishly than I intended. "I saw something happen to a philax and I just passed out." I walk a little faster, as if to put distance between me and the subject.

He doesn't say anything for a moment, letting my words fade.

"I don't believe you."

"What?"

"There's more to it than that."

"And you know this how?" I demand. I almost laugh, but what happened at the Beak is too recent to be funny yet. Especially when its consequences are still playing out.

Rondo shrugs.

"I know people. And there's more to it than that."

I don't know what to say to this, so I say nothing. We're still on the shop side of the stream, which is mostly empty. People have gone home to their families. We walk by one gray-haired man locking up his shop, keying in his security code. When he finishes, he lets a scarlet banner billow down over the door, an image of some kind stitched on the front. I've never seen this before. When the fabric settles, I find the same emblem that the councilmembers wear as a gold pin: the likeness of the *Vagantur* and the five circular compounds.

"Excuse me," I call to the retreating shopkeeper. "What is this? The banner, I mean."

He turns, a pleasant smile on his face.

"Oh, you like it? I'm one of the first to get one. We'll all have them soon. Nice, isn't it? Dr. Albatur's suggestion."

"What is the purpose?" I say, taking a corner of the banner in my fingers. It's fine work, the stitches neat and tight.

The man gives a good-natured shrug.

"Purpose? Ah, you greencoats. Not everything has to

have a *purpose*. Not in the way you think. It just makes you feel good! Something for us all to identify with: face the galaxy as *N'Terrans*, you see? To unite us against those that might divide us."

"But I thought Dr. Albatur hated N'Terra," I blurt, thinking of my encounter with him outside the Beak. The man's smile wavers.

"I don't know what would give you that idea," he says, his voice taking on a haughty quality. "He believes there's a lot that is to be desired, but who doesn't? We only have so much to work with on this planet, but he knows our history: he knows we've been better than we are. His goal is to give N'Terrans something to be proud of!"

"Like what exactly?" Rondo says.

"It's a really nice banner," I say quickly, turning my eyes back to the banner, fake-studying it. "I hope the rest of us get ours soon."

That seems to satisfy the shopkeeper: his smile returns and he bids us good night before disappearing over the nearby bridge.

"It's a really nice banner," Rondo mocks when we're alone again.

"Word travels fast lately," I say.

Maybe it's a neurological reaction to the intense red of the fabric, but anxiety rattles through me, a restlessness I can't place.

"Let's keep walking," I say.

"Albaturean or not," he says, jerking his head over his shoulder to indicate the shopkeeper. "I wish I could do that."

"What? Make vague references to unity based on obscure references to the past?" I roll my eyes.

Rondo's laugh startles me.

"What?" I frown.

"I think that might be the realest thing you've ever said." Rondo chuckles. "Usually you're trying to give the right answer. That was just . . . *your* answer."

He laughs again before continuing.

"But, no, I meant I wish I could have a shop. Instead of working in the labs." At first I think he's joking, but one glance at his face tells me he's serious. I shake my head.

"Seems like a waste. You're one of the smartest people in our class. Dr. Espada always says you're ideal for the Zoo."

"You don't ever want to do something that doesn't fit?"

"Are you talking about the izinusa you still haven't played for me?" I say.

"You look ahead at your life and all you see is whitecoats and the Zoo?" he presses.

"I look good in white."

"Be serious, O."

What do I see when I look ahead? I glance up at the ceiling, the light filtering in orange now as the sun sinks. I think briefly of what I'd been feeling before Rondo appeared on the bridge, imagining myself as a marov burrowing under the walls of the compound and emerging free in the jungle on the other side. I inwardly cup my hands around the thought. I hadn't considered it as a secret until now, but suddenly it feels like one.

"I want to be a whitecoat," I say. "I don't think it's limiting to be able to be part of learning more about this planet. There are possibilities."

He snorts and I look at him sharply, still not convinced he can't read my mind.

"There goes the real." He laughs. "Just as it showed up, gone again."

We've walked all the way through the communal 'wams and now find ourselves at the bottom of the stairs that lead up to the main dome. The flowers I like are all curling slowly shut, their color deepening from blue to violet. I should be going home but instead I find myself climbing the stairs. I get a few steps up when I realize Rondo isn't following.

"Coming?"

"I don't usually take the stairs."

"You look ahead at your life and all you see is the elevator?" I mock, smiling.

He grins, shaking his head, and follows me up the steps.

At the top, we're both slightly out of breath, he more than I.

"What happened to your grandmother?" he says without looking at me. I think about her all the time, but for years now my parents have pretended she never existed. To hear someone else mention her is almost like a burn.

"Lost in the field," I say.

"They never found her."

"No."

"Man," he says. "That's really . . ."

I wait for him to say something generic like "sad." But he never finishes the sentence, and the silence that follows is filled with hypothetical emotions. My grandmother's loss hovers over my heart, and I want to get out from under it. I turn away, toward the doors that will take us out into the main dome of the Paw. Rondo doesn't move.

"Where are you going?" he says, raising an eyebrow.

"Obvious answer," I say, and the doors slide open in front of me.

Rondo pushes off the tree he leans on but still doesn't follow.

I understand his hesitation. We all know we're not supposed to leave the commune after dark. It's not a law, but a generally accepted rule laid out by the Council that's never broken. Ordinarily I wouldn't break it, but it's like some string has attached itself to me and pulls me onward. My father's in the lab, my mother's in her study, and my mind feels noisy. If we turn back now, the night and my time with Rondo is over. It would be like catching a glimpse of a new species only to let it wander away.

The main dome is silent. Everyone is either in their homes

OLIVIA A. COLE

or, like my father, in the Zoo. The sun is gone from the sky, and the darkness of the trees is intimidating.

"So here we are," says Rondo softly. He runs his fingers through the fronds of a large bush whose delicate leaves stretch gracefully outward like my hair when it's freshly unbraided. "What are we doing?"

"Just looking." I sigh. I close my eyes as we walk along the path through the dome and breathe in the smell of it. It's not quite outdoors, but there are many more trees here than in the commune and the scent of the ogwe is comforting. With my eyes closed, I can imagine that I'm out of the compound and my brain quiets momentarily, enjoying the rich and varied smells of the plants. The claustrophobia melts away.

I open my eyes to find Rondo watching me, a faint smile on his lips.

"You're kinda strange, aren't you?" he says softly, and I think that, in his way, he's calling me something precious. I reach out my hand to him and he takes it; and like a spark erupting into blaze, I'm wondering what it would be like to kiss him. There's no logic for where it started: the thought is just here. Maybe there is science to this but it feels like . . . art. I'm about to ask him if this is what he meant when he said there was more to the world than logic when his head snaps to the left, his eyes intense.

"Someone's coming," he says.

We're already holding hands, and I yank on his to pull

him behind the striped trunk of the nearest ogwe. We're dead center in the main dome: if someone catches us here, there will be no excuses. I have no idea what the punishment would be, but I imagine it would jeopardize our internships in some way. We crouch behind the tree, barely breathing. I'm sharply aware of the feeling of Rondo's hand in my hand. I squeeze it, hard, to make myself focus on the voices we hear and not his skin.

I hear at least three people, all speaking just above a whisper. They're coming down the path from the main entrance. They will either pass us for the commune, when they will surely see us, or continue over to the lab doors, and we'll go unnoticed. I pray they're feeling studious.

The voices draw nearer, and Rondo presses his shoulder tightly against mine, trying to make us disappear. His arm feels hard through our skinsuits. I look at him in the dark and find his eyes already on my face. Focus, I tell myself as the voices loom nearer still. It's easy to hold my breath while staring at Rondo.

"Don't take all the credit," one voice says. "I've been on this assignment a lot longer."

The response is too soft to hear. The voices go away to our right, toward the labs. I'm on the side of the tree closest to them, and I force myself to break Rondo's gaze to curl my neck around the trunk. I do it slowly, inching, peeking at the group of whisperers. At first I think they're all whitecoats: a group of four walking slowly to the lab door, which is still guarded by gray-suited N'Terrans with buzzguns. But there's something strange about one member of the walking group, the one in the center. He's not wearing white, for one thing, but besides that, he's tall—too tall. Much taller than anyone I've seen in N'Terra, and more muscular, his arms long and bare. I squint my eyes in the moonlight. Spots. He has spots on what must be his skinsuit, a complex pattern expanding over his body all the way up the back of his neck. I can't see his face, and I don't want to risk sticking my head farther out from the tree to catch a glimpse. My head is buzzing, but I can't focus on the smell of ogwe to make it fade. The spotted man is nearing the doors of the lab.

"Do you see that . . . ?" I whisper to Rondo.

"What is it?" He's on the other side of the tree, the angle and my body blocking his view.

But then the lab's entrance slides open, and my father appears in the doorway, tall and broad and facing the spotted man head-on. He pauses for what seems a long moment, staring up at the man's face, before he raises his arm, leveling his hand at the man's chest. I only realize he holds a tranq gun when it fires, the zip unmistakable as the dart leaves the barrel. I clap my hand over my mouth to keep the sound that bubbles in my throat silent. Then the man with spots is lost in the shadows, his body falling sideways, caught by the white-coats that surround him.

In the dim light, something slides from the falling man's hand, dropping to the soil. The whitecoats don't seem to notice: they carry him through the door, followed by the guards with buzzguns, leaving my father standing alone outside the entrance. He scans the dome, and then disappears into the Zoo.

CHAPTER 5

There's something shining on the ground. It's on the path where the man with spots had crumpled: a small thing, lit up and sparkling.

"You see that?" I whisper, nudging Rondo. All thoughts of kissing him have vaporized.

"I don't see anything," he says. He's finally come around to my side of the tree trunk, too late to see the spotted man or my father. "It's too dark."

"He dropped something," I breathe.

"Who did? Tell me what you saw."

The door is unattended; the shining object lies there unseen.

"I'm going to get it," I say, and leap out from behind the tree.

"Octavia, hold up!"

He snatches at my arm, but I wrench away and dash toward

the lab door. I try to crouch as I run, making for an awkward pace, but if the door opens abruptly, I need to be as low to the ground as possible so I can drop if necessary.

I can see the object now that I'm closer. It's not glowing: just shining, the moonlight through the dome gleaming down and reflecting off its surface. As I get nearer, I slow down, suddenly afraid. I have no idea what it is or what it might do. Rondo hisses my name from where he hides behind the tree, and it spurs me into action.

I trot the last few steps to the lab doors and seize the shining object. I don't pause to inspect it. The door could open at any second, revealing buzzguns or my father. I hold the thing in my hand—round, an orb—and sprint back to the ogwe, Rondo's face blending with the shadows and the bark. I'm positive that the sound of my breath combined with my footsteps is so loud it will signal the guards to return, and my ears strain for the mechanical sigh of the doors. I skid to a halt by the tree and throw myself behind its trunk. Rondo starts to admonish me.

"You really are a genius," he snaps. "If the guards caught you, you'd never—"

But then we do hear the doors sigh open, my pulse freezing, and he falls silent. I press my finger to my lips, as much for him as for myself. I peek around the tree again, trying to imagine my skin melting into it, disappearing into the safety of its wood.

It's not my father. It's the two guards, back again from helping to carry the spotted man's body. They hold their buzzguns across their chests, conversing in low tones. I strain my ears to hear what they might be saying, but they're too far away. Behind the tree, my legs quiver from dwindling adrenaline and my palm sweats against the smooth, round object.

"We need to go," Rondo whispers, tugging on my arm.

I turn slowly away. Part of me wants to march back up to the door and confront the guards, demand to know who that man was and why my father tranquilized him. But the thought of my father standing there in the shadows, tranq gun raised, sends a shiver up my spine. I don't recognize the person he's becoming. I follow Rondo through the trees, creeping slowly and avoiding branches and twigs.

The two sets of doors that lead back into the commune open for us with barely a whisper. We slide through, trying to be shadows. I don't think either of us breathes until we are back in the commune on the hill, looking down at the white 'wams, some of their round windows still illuminated with soft gold lights. It's beautiful, but looking out over the familiar scene leaves me with a heavy feeling in my chest. Somehow it all looks different, barely recognizable. I wonder if my mother would believe me if I told her what I've seen. Maybe she already knows.

"What did you find?" Rondo says softly. "By the doors?"

I've been clutching it so tightly, it's as if it's grown into my palm, become part of my skin. In the faint light of the moon, I slowly open my hand and look down.

It's an egg. Or it seems to be an egg, cream-colored and smooth. I'd thought it was round, but it's not quite: the sloping surface is slightly oblong. It catches moonlight and reflects it back out into the night with a hint of iridescence. Heavy, but small, taking up only the space of my palm.

Rondo reaches out to touch the egg-shaped object. He rests his fingers on its surface for only an instant before snatching his hand back, his gasp making me jump.

"It's hot, Octavia!" he says. "How can you hold it like that?"

"No it's not," I say, surprised. I hold it in both hands, cupping it. I bring it up to my cheek and rub it against my skin. It feels warm and smooth, but not hot.

"It burned me," he says.

"Oh please. It's not that hot."

He shrugs, rubbing his fingertips to soothe them.

"You saw it fall?"

I nod.

"From where?"

"There was a person," I say, and I tell him what I saw: the tall spotted man, my father, and the tranquilizer.

"Tranquilizing a person?" he says, shaking his head. "Dr. Albatur had to have approved this. Your father's on the Council—he wouldn't do anything the Head didn't authorize."

"But who would Dr. Albatur want to tranquilize? I've never heard of anything like this happening before."

"Things are changing," he says.

I don't respond. His words suddenly seem to apply to so much more than just what I saw. Now, even in the open air of the commune, claustrophobia grips me again, as if the roof of the dome is pressing down on me. Standing here looking down on the 'wams, I picture the rounded domes of N'Terra as a giant nest of eggs. Only I don't know what species laid them or what beasts they contain. Usually not knowing something just drives me to find the answer. . . . Why does it now make me afraid?

"Hey," Rondo says. He's beside me, but his words seem to come from a long way away.

He's staring at me in a strange way. His face is always so cool and impassive. Now he looks rumpled, as if just under his skin is something reaching for the moonlight.

"What?" I whisper when he says nothing.

Rondo takes a step closer to me. If I leaned forward we would bump heads. The egg thrums warmly in my palm. Rondo studies me with that tense expression. His lips move but I don't hear anything.

"What?" I repeat.

He raises his hand, slowly. I think maybe he's going to take my hand, but instead it rises to my face. He rests a single finger softly on my forehead before letting it trail down my cheek.

"You're . . . ," he says. He pulls his hand back, as if he's changed his mind.

Am I leaning forward? Why am I leaning forward? I settle back onto my heels, but it's as if I fight a magnetic field in doing so. There's a ring around us I can't see. I might crumple if I step outside it.

I think I say "what" again.

"Nothing," he says. His eyes leave my face, sweep back over the commune below.

We part at the bottom of the stairs. I can still feel a hot line on my face where his finger skimmed my skin. He looks at me one more time as he heads down the path toward his 'wam.

"Sleep well. Remember to dream."

I can't find any words to reply, and he's gone anyway—a shadow disappearing down the path. I stand there alone in the dark for a moment, and bring my hand to my cheek. Is this what my face felt like when he touched it? I wonder what his face feels like. I look at my hands, and am almost surprised by the egg I still clutch.

I walk back to my 'wam alone. It's so dark I can barely see the yellow cloth that was my grandmother's. I wish I had asked her more questions while she was still living, before she'd wandered into the jungle of Faloiv, never to return. Our motto comes to my mind: "No one knows. But we will." I look down at the smooth white egg in my palm, glittering softly. No one knows, I think. But I will.

CHAPTER 6

You're sure you don't know who it was? Rondo types, and I glance down as surreptitiously as possible to respond. Dr. Espada is lecturing, but he's unexpectedly called on a few people and I don't want to be caught unaware.

You keep asking me that, I write. *I couldn't see him well enough.*

We talk about the spotted man, but we haven't talked about Rondo touching my face. I've started a message at least three times broaching the subject: *What were you going to say to me in the commune?* But the moonlight had been a thing that wrapped that part of the night in secrecy. Speaking of it now seems to be breaking some unspoken pact.

"English, what do you think?" Dr. Espada asks. At the sound of my name I jerk my head up from my slate.

"Sir?" I say.

He pauses by the three-dimensional projection that is floating at the front of class. He gives me a quizzical look, unused to not having an immediate answer from me. But rather than asking me again, he continues with the lecture. Embarrassment flares in my cheeks, and I close the text box from Rondo. Stars. I can't catch a break.

"Learning what we can from animals on Faloiv about how they are able to eat on this planet is extremely important for our continued survival, and not just for identifying plants for our diet. Knowing how different plants interact with different animals' digestive systems can teach us how we can in turn interact with those animals."

"*Interact,*" Jaquot says in that annoying brazen voice. Every time I think he's not that bad, I hear him speak and detest him all over again. "We don't really need to *interact* with them to use them, right? We just need to control their abilities. Not have a conversation."

Dr. Espada looks uncomfortable.

"Well, there are those on the Council who would agree, yes," he says.

"The only ones who matter," says a guy in the back. Probably Julian, Dr. Maver's son, the only other person in the Greenhouse who has a parent on the Council. I know for a fact that Maver voted for Dr. Albatur—my mother had some choice words about him behind closed doors. Dr. Espada ignores him and continues.

"By knowing where an organism fits in its ecosystem and what tools it uses to survive, we do have the option of simply . . . controlling that organism. But that should not be the ultimate goal."

"What should it be, then?" Yaya's voice rings out from the back of the Greenhouse. I almost turn to look at her—she usually saves her questions for after class so she can have a one-on-one with Dr. Espada. I can't help but wonder if she's seized on my blankness from a moment before, seeing her opportunity to advance herself. Internships haven't even begun and she's already trying to outshine me.

Dr. Espada spreads his arms wide, as if he was hoping someone asked this, and I'm annoyed that it had to be Yaya.

"Understanding," he says. "Rather than seeking to dominate, we should seek to understand."

Jaquot laughs.

"My dad says the only understanding we need is how to take control out of the hands of the Faloii," he says.

"Hear, hear," Julian calls from the back. He never used to talk in class—if it wasn't for his father being on the Council I doubt he'd have a future in the Zoo at all. Albatur's election has made him bold.

Something crosses Dr. Espada's features: anger, maybe. Or perhaps another shadow: fear. Something about the expression makes me squint. It's like looking at one of the digital renderings of an indigenous mammal, searching for clues hidden in the skin.

"Dr. Espada," I say. Part of me wants to ask a question just to redeem myself, but as soon as I begin to speak I realize it's a thing that's been waiting on my tongue. Now I'm not sure if I even want to know the answer. To retract now would make me look foolish, so I press on. "Have we seen the Faloii since our landing?"

Dr. Espada's head tilts ever so slightly, his lips parting and then closing almost imperceptibly.

"The Faloii? No." He turns to flip off the projector. "Now it's time to discuss internships," he says, and any follow-up question I might have had is lost in the buzz of the class, eagerly turning to one another to make bets and wish luck.

"Earlier this week," Dr. Espada says, raising his voice above the din, "I asked each of you to send me a message with your preference of internship compound assignment. I have considered each of your requests and weighed them against previous exam scores for aptitude, along with other factors. I will call you up one by one and we will confer briefly about your placement. No appeals."

He moves behind his desk and takes his seat, propping up his slate and looking over his spectacles at the first name.

"Yanella Axba," he says, and Yaya flows down the aisle with her head held high like he'd called her first out of preference and not alphabetical necessity. I watch the back of her head and Dr. Espada's mouth intently, trying to read his lips and her posture to learn where she's been placed. I can't tell, but when she pivots to return to her desk, a rare smile has crept across her features. She buries it quickly as she makes her way back up the aisle, her eyes unreadable. The girl can conjure an impressive mask.

"*Someone's* excited," Alma says under her breath after Yaya has passed. But her own eagerness is like the first subtle lurch of the ground before an earthquake: she's tapping her foot, jiggling her leg, her face creased in a studious frown. The same small tremors are happening all over the room as Dr. Espada moves through the alphabet: we all know that where we're placed might change the course of our lives. So when Dr. Espada eventually calls out "Octavia English," I get up slowly. The claustrophobia I've felt in the varying domes of N'Terra crawls back into my skin. I'm suddenly not sure what I want my life to be, and I'm not sure if I'm ready for an internship to tell me.

I sit down in front of Dr. Espada's desk, where he's placed a chair. He sits with his hands clasped, studying his slate propped up before him.

"Octavia," he says. He doesn't look up. Never have I found him intimidating until now. His long face is usually smiling, even in some small, subtle way. Now his expression is serious and elongates his bones, making him seem older and more somber. "You requested to be placed in the Avian Compound for your internship."

I had. I'd debated over the decision but in the end, composing the message on my slate at home on the night I'd seen the spotted man, I realized that the trail I'd been following to become my mother had blurred. I needed to be away from the Paw, away from my parents and their secrets.

"May I ask why you requested to be placed in the Avian Compound?" Dr. Espada says.

I'm not prepared for him to ask this—everyone else had been at his desk for barely a blink.

"I find birds . . . fascinating," I choke out. I've never had to finesse my answers to cover for ignorance, so I falter while searching for the words. "Learning about new species is, um, valuable for the future of N'Terra."

Dr. Espada looks at me a second longer, his expression gentle. It ruffles me, that look.

"What happened to following in your mother's footprints? Your grandmother's pursuits? How mammals use plants? In your last paper you said you wanted to learn how we, as mammals, might learn more in that area. Functional nutrition."

I can't bring myself to look him in the eye. How can I tell him that all my plans seem inane now, born of childishness that has withered more every morning? That a creeping anxiety has taken over the way I feel about N'Terra, a feeling I can't fully explain? I shake my head, not able to answer.

"I'm afraid I must deny your request." He sighs when he realizes I have no response, rearranging the layers of his fingers on top of one another. He breaks my gaze now, studies the screen of his slate, which shines in his glasses. "Your skills in studying mammals will benefit you in the Mammalian Compound. No matter what area of focus you pursue."

"Fine," I say, and rise from the chair. Anger balloons to take the place of whatever sorrow had nestled into my heart. It's almost a relief to be angry, to replace the feeling of wilting that has planted itself in my life since my grandmother's death. I turn away from him and begin to return to my desk, but suddenly I spin back. I keep my voice down—my peers, especially Yaya, are probably already curious about why I've been up here so long—but my soft voice doesn't disguise my irritation: "Is there any other reason you're keeping me in the Paw?" I'm thinking of my mother's whispered voice in her den, and it feeds the flame of my anger. I glare at him across his desk.

"Any other reason?" he says. He doesn't seem fazed by my flare of temper—he almost seems relieved somehow, like his initial instructions of "no appeals" had been a test he was hoping I'd pass.

"Yes. You mentioned 'other factors' when you were talking to the class earlier, didn't you?"

Dr. Espada holds my eyes with his. It's uncomfortable, his gaze boring into me for such a long moment. I find myself holding my breath, afraid of what he might say.

"There are always other factors." His voice is soft but heavy with words he doesn't speak out loud. Then he raises his voice, calls to the class, "Alma Entra."

He's dismissed me. The bluntness of his answer is like an abrupt splash of cold water extinguishing the flame of my anger. I return to my desk, defeat like a toxin that spreads through my blood, avoiding Alma's eyes as she makes her way up front. She's so eager to learn about her placement she doesn't even notice my expression. I sit down quickly and stare ahead, grateful that I'm in the front row so no one can look back and see my face.

"Octavia," Rondo says quietly from behind me. I ignore him. He doesn't try again, but a moment later I hear the tapping of his fingers drumming out their gentle cadence. I can't explain it, but I know he's doing it for me. I close my eyes and focus on the slow, steady sound, trying to convince my racing heart to match it.

Alma is back in her seat next to me a moment later, vibrating with excitement.

"The Paw!" she squeals, she and her hair both bobbing. "Thank the stars. I'm going to be the next head of the Mammalian Compound. I can feel it. This. Will be. Amazing."

I smile and nod, trying to control the constricting feeling in my throat.

"Octavia?" she says, cocking her head at me. "What's wrong? Aren't you excited?"

Her face suddenly becomes grave, her eyes rounding with concern as her excitement drains.

"Oh damn," she says, her hand flying to her mouth. "Did he . . . did he put you in the Fin?"

I stare at her blankly for a half second. She stares back, her eyebrows angled high on her forehead, her mouth slightly open and ready to offer consolation. And I burst out laughing. Behind me, the drumming stops.

"Wh-what's so funny?" she says.

I can't even speak: the laughter comes in gusts like a cloud bank fleeing before a storm. My life suddenly seems terribly strange and uncertain, but the fact that the worst thing Alma can imagine is my being placed in the Aquatic Compound for my internship is so absurd that I can't contain myself.

"Nothing, nothing," I wheeze, trying to get a hold of myself. Maybe I'll explain everything to her at some point. For now I can only allay her immediate worry. "No, I'm not in the Fin. I'm in the Paw, with you."

She shrieks, causing a few of our classmates to glare in our direction, and I allow myself to smile back, pushing my doubts out of my mind for a moment, along with the look on Dr. Espada's face when he said, *There are always other factors.* I think of the egg I found in the main dome with Rondo, now hidden carefully in my room. If I'm going to be in the Paw for my internship, I can at least try to learn more about the strange object and whatever secrets hide in its beautiful shell.

"*Experientia docet,*" Alma goes on, her hands flapping like two quick-bodied birds.

"Um . . . what?"

"It means 'Experience is the best teacher'!" she squeals, babbling on in her glee. "It's just an old tongue—Dr. Espada told me scientists from the Origin Planet used it to name stuff. I come across it a lot when I'm studying old comparative files. We're going to see so many incredible things, O. Can we go into the Zoo whenever we want? I'm never going to leave, I swear to stars."

She goes on. I listen and join in every now and then, hoping her excitement will infect me.

"Rondo Okadigbo," Dr. Espada calls. Rondo walks to the front of class and is only at the desk for a second or two before he returns to his seat, expressionless. He doesn't attempt to catch my eye, just sits. Alma has finally calmed down and turned her attention to the assignment Dr. Espada beamed out to our slates to keep us busy while he calls up the rest of the class one by one, distributing everyone's fate. I pull my slate close to me, but instead of opening the assignment I open my messages. I type: *So?*

Paw.

I crinkle my eyebrows. He said that if he had to pick a concentration he'd prefer it to be birds. I wonder if he's upset.

Sorry, I respond. *I know you wanted the Beak.*

I requested the Paw, he writes.

Wait, what?

I requested the Paw, he types again. I turn around to glare at him, causing Alma to look at me with a raised eyebrow before returning her eyes to her slate.

Yeah, you said that, I type. *Why? I thought you said you'd study birds if you had to choose?*

I knew he'd put you in the Paw, he types.

I read it twice and then a third time.

What do you mean?

You know.

I know what?

But he doesn't respond, and I get sick of waiting for an answer. I turn to the assignment Dr. Espada has sent out, but by the time I open it and force myself to concentrate Dr. Espada is rising from his desk. Everyone has been called.

"Well, class," Dr. Espada says, sounding tired, "that wraps us up for today. You have your assignments. You might have noticed that the text each of you has pertains to the compound to which you've been assigned."

Alma nods and a flare of shame shoots through me. I didn't notice. I haven't even started reading yet, lost in my own thoughts. I really need to get my head together.

"This will be your last day in the Greenhouse for a while," he continues, and I think his voice sounds strained. "As of now, I'm not sure if you'll be returning to formal education post-internship. Dr. Albatur is working on developing a new structure. But the assignment that you have now will be due the day after tomorrow, when you report to your internship.

I'm giving you tomorrow off to make preparations for your new course of study. If your internship is in a compound other than the one you live in, you will be relocated for the duration within the next few days. Are there any questions?"

Alma shoots me a pointed look, and that I *do* have the energy to smile about. We're going to be living in the same compound soon, at least for a while.

Everyone rises from their desks, chattering. Even those who weren't assigned to the compound they'd hoped for—myself included—are carried along in the swell of everyone else's enthusiasm.

"You know you're going to be my host, right? A week ago we didn't think we would see the inside of the Zoo for years. A week ago I didn't think I'd see the inside of another *compound* for years. You may not be as excited because your dad has taken you to other compounds, but this is a big deal for the rest of us. Not only are we going to . . ."

She goes on and on, and I respond between her pauses with one or two words, enough to give the impression that I'm as excited as she is—I don't want to ruin this for her. We gather our things, and I look around for Rondo. He's gone, already outside, the classroom empty behind me, glowing slightly green as always from the tint of the windows. Dr. Espada remains, standing idly by his desk. Alma is still talking animatedly, but behind her voice my ears start ringing. Or at least, I think it's my ears. I hear noise in my head, a buzzing. I stick a finger in my ear and wiggle it as we approach the door to leave the classroom.

Something makes me turn back before I walk through the doorway: something like an itch inside my head. I'm surprised to find Dr. Espada staring at me pointedly, his eyes almost angry in their intensity. I pause, thinking there's something else he wants to say, a lecture he's been saving for the end of class. Alma continues on, unaware. Dr. Espada says only one word.

"Listen," he says, his eyes piercing through his spectacles, and then turns away.

Confused, I go on standing in the doorway for a moment, the buzz in my head quieting, until Alma turns back, halfway down the hall, calling for me. I slowly follow her toward the outdoors, where the sun settles low into the horizon, birds flying straight across its girth, oblivious to its heat.

CHAPTER 7

I'm dreaming of my mother. She's standing beside a building with walls that slope gently upward on all sides, evening out on top to form a flat roof. She's not looking at me: instead she's bent down, picking small orange flowers from along the building's edge. I call to her, feel the words climb up my throat, but no sound is released from my open mouth. I try again, but I have no voice. The wind sifts its fingers pleasantly through my skinsuit, cooling my body.

My mother straightens her back, holding the collection of flowers loosely in her hand, her arms hanging down at her sides. She seems unaware of me, unaware of anything. She smiles a small smile and I think I hear her humming. There's something else too: a sound between a roar and a trumpet. It doesn't frighten me: it sounds some distance away, too far to be any danger. Then I hear it again much closer. My mother appears not to notice. I call to her once more, but my voice still doesn't work.

I see the source of the roar: a gwabi, across the clearing from where the strange building stands. It's full-grown, its chest broad and covered in the beautiful markings that distinguish it from other similar predators. It sees my mother, but my mother still doesn't seem to notice, even as the animal roars again and comes loping through the clearing toward her.

My panic rises like a quick red sun. The gwabi easily weighs five hundred pounds, more if it's female. I've seen its teeth in Dr. Espada's lectures, long curving blades. I try to run toward my mother to warn her but I'm rooted to the spot, watching in horror as the gwabi bounds through the grass, its ears flat, ready to attack.

It leaps. My mother turns to face it, dropping her flowers. But there is no attack. The gwabi skids to a stop before her, all four massive paws on the ground, its shoulders reaching past my mother's waist. They stare at each other, neither making a sound, and then the gwabi opens its jaws wide, very wide, in what looks like a yawn. My mother reaches both hands into its mouth.

I watch, transfixed, and with each second that passes I become more afraid that I'm about to see my mother torn apart. But when she withdraws her hands, they aren't bloody. They're shining with the gwabi's saliva, but she's holding something, lifting it out of the animal's mouth.

I can't see what it is. Not until she turns toward me—finally acknowledging me with the smile I know so well, my grandmother's dimples on either side of it—do I see that she's holding the spotted man's egg. She holds it toward me, her head tilted to one side as if to say See?

I wake to the sound of hammers.

Dragging myself from bed, I go to the window and slide the shade aside an inch. A trio of workers has resumed construction on the tower near the center of the dome. I watch them for a moment, eyeing the metallic-looking materials they create the frame of the tower with. It gives the impression of a skeleton, which adds to its hostile appearance, and I wonder if Dr. Albatur engineered its design. Its cold angles, the pointed fang of it jutting up among the smooth tops of the 'wams . . . it's almost as if Albatur himself has taken up residence in the commune, an impression that I know would please him.

Inside my 'wam is another sound—the delicate rhythm of a knife clicking against the platform. By the time I dress, the smell of baking bread has drifted down the hall to my bedroom. Usually it's my father who cooks, and it makes me hesitate before sliding open my door. I pause and listen—sure enough, I hear my father's voice, low and rough as he speaks to my mother.

"Albatur has a vision, Samirah," he says. "He understands this world as it is, not as we'd like it to be. He sees the injustice in the death of his parents, what it means to—"

"You voted for the man because you're both orphans, Octavius? You tipped this balance because you wish you could change the past?"

"A false equivalency," he scoffs.

"Oh? And using what occurred on one planet to shape the life on another is valid? You voted for a man who—"

"The Council exists for a reason," he snaps. "The vote is the vote. You're angry with me for exercising my rights? It's finished. Be serious, Samirah."

"Be serious? Here's serious, Octavius: the only studies that have been approved for the last two cycles are those of councilmembers who voted for Albatur. With nothing but a vague half-page explanation for why those that are denied have been rejected."

"You would prefer a tome?"

"Don't you mock me. Stars, don't you mock me. Not when Albatur is *this* close to violating a *tome* of—"

I try to crack my door without a sound, but it creaks traitorously in my attempt to hear the conversation better. Both my parents fall silent, the clicking of the knife the only noise.

"Good morning," my mother says, smiling as I round the corner into the kitchen. The smile pricks at my memory—she looks so much like my grandmother sometimes.

"Hey," I say, pretending to focus on the food she's cutting so I don't have to look at either of them. My father just takes the flat brown bread out of our stone oven, places it on the platform, and walks toward the back of the 'wam, saying nothing. I order myself not to look after him.

"Sleep okay?" my mother says, still chopping. It's not a real question so I don't answer. Even with the aroma of food I can smell the Zoo on her: sterile and flat.

"Did you just get home?"

She puts some of the zarum she was cutting on a plate and hands it across the platform.

"How could you tell?"

"You smell like the lab."

"Do I?" She stretches the fabric of her skinsuit up to her nose, craning her neck down to meet it, sniffing. "I don't smell anything."

I shrug, biting off a piece of zarum, not speaking. At the thought of her in the labs, the events of yesterday—my placement in the Paw—flood back into my mind. "Other factors." Why do I get the feeling that "other factors" has something to do with her? The anger that flashed through me at Dr. Espada's desk reignites in a blaze of sparks.

"Anything the matter, Afua?"

"Nope."

She stares at me across the platform, her eyes soft. I hate when she looks at me like this. If my mouth were sewn shut, that look could pull the stitches out one by one. I'm not ready to be opened up, so I look down at my food.

"I'll be serving my internship here," I say. "In case you didn't already know."

"No, I didn't," she says, but that's all.

"So is Alma. I think they'll probably host her with us. We're both female, in the same age group. We study together. It's logical."

When I hear my words out in the air they sound like a desperate attempt to convince her I'm capable of the internship. I'm as transparent as the three-dimensional animals Dr. Espada projects in the Greenhouse.

"Yes, it's logical" is all she says.

We're silent while I eat, and I keep my eyes on my plate. There is almost always tension between my father and me: a constant thrum like the coming of a perpetual storm. But it's different with my mother. This pain is new.

"Afua." Her voice is too soft. The blaze of my anger wavers.

"Yes."

"Look at me."

My jaw trembles. I'm not quite in danger of crying, but I feel . . . something. The buzzing in my head—the same sensation I felt when Dr. Espada was staring at me intently—isn't quite there. Instead it feels like an echo of the buzzing, the shadow of noise. I grip the edge of the platform and sway ever so slightly.

"What is it?" she says. I don't know if she's referring to my apparent dizziness or my attitude.

"I don't know," I say, which isn't entirely a lie. How can I tell her I feel like I've changed but that I don't know why or how?

"And what do we say about what we don't know?" she asks, picking the knife up again.

My father returns, peering at his slate.

"I'll likely stay in the Avian compound tonight," he says. "I just received word that Albatur would like to see their progress with Oscree 32."

"Why the sudden interest in avian species?" my mother says, beginning to slice the bread. "Surely the Head of Council has more important projects to oversee. It must be fascinating. A pity that only the councilmembers who voted for him are privy to these projects."

I was nibbling a piece of zarum, but it's as if the temperature in the 'wam dropped thirty degrees: her tone freezes my jaw and everything else. My father, also ice, raises his eyes from the screen of his slate to study her. He squints, his face beginning to twist with something like anger. But then it's as if a wind blows that rearranges the expression into something else, something pained. He lowers the slate.

"While we're asking questions," he says, "maybe you'd like to use this opportunity to share some of your notes with me about telepathic contacts between predator and prey? Or perhaps the Myn 44–Kunike 27 lab comparison that you decided to pursue on an independent basis without consulting me whatsoever."

"You didn't—" my mother starts.

My father's voice inches up nearer to a shout to drown her out.

"All your criticism of N'Terran competitiveness, and yet you wanted to make that discovery yourself. Do I need to tell you again what a fool I appeared to be when Dr. Albatur came to discuss it with me?"

"Albatur is—"

This time he slices the air with his hand as well as his voice, as if physically blocking her words from entering his ears.

"Dr. Albatur is the Head. He was elected. Your refusal to work with him speaks to *your* ineptitude, not his!"

He pulls in his lips, as if trying to take back what he has just said. But then he lets them out again, glaring.

"Octavius," my mother says.

"Samirah?"

The way he says her name sends an explosion of goose bumps racing down my arms. This isn't his voice. The air I breathe doesn't fill my lungs as air would—it's as if I've walked into a cloud of the disintegrating pieces of their love and inhaled its graying vapor. They stare at each other for two heartbeats, and then my father leaves without saying another word. Before the door whispers shut behind him, the clang of hammers from the commune slides into our 'wam, stirring the still air he leaves behind.

My mother exits the kitchen in a hurry and I think she's going to follow him, but her path leads her to the wall, where the photo of her parents hangs in its chipped gold frame. She stands, gazing at them, her arms crossed over her chest. I've seen her do this before, and it occurs to me that I've never asked her how well she knew her father before he died on the Origin Planet, if Nana ever really got over losing him. The two of them here on the wall are like an altar and I'm hesitant to speak, but I do.

"Mom?"

She squeezes her eyes shut, shaking her head against my voice.

"I can't, Octavia. I can't."

"You can't what?"

"Have you not been listening?" she snaps.

I jerk my head backward, her sudden anger like a slap.

"What?"

"Pay attention, Octavia! Pay attention!"

"To *what*?" I cry. "To you? To Dad? For what? So I can learn how to be miserable?"

"So you can learn how *not* to be!"

"You don't have to worry about that," I snarl. "I have no

intention of being anything like either of you."

"You don't have a choice."

"Like hell," I shout.

She laughs, so loudly and sharply it stuns me into silence.

"Hell," she says. "I don't know where you learned about it, but you don't know what it is. I do."

She blazes out of the 'wam, the sound of the hammers louder again with the door open and muted when it closes. I long for the clanging. The silence of this room might suffocate me—my breath comes in short spurts, as if the fire of my anger has eaten up all my oxygen with its smoke.

I stalk back to my room, flinging myself on the bed. I close my eyes and try to find the smell of ogwe trees, buried in my senses somewhere. I can't actually smell anything at this moment, but the memory of the scent—the impression of it— slowly brings my heartbeat back to normal.

I breathe out in a long sigh and reach under my mattress. My fingers grope around until they find the egg. I'd raised my mattress and spent an hour carving out a hole in my bed plat- form to hide it. It hadn't been easy, but it feels safe. I stroke it with my fingers, enjoying the way it heats my fingers ever so slightly. I wonder if the spotted man knows he dropped it, or if he might have dropped it on purpose.

I hear a tiny muffled noise, a sound like a small woodchip striking another piece of wood. It's my slate telling me I have a message, buried in my bag from school. I return the egg to its hiding place and reach for the bag. The message is from Rondo.

I know something about the spotted man, his message reads. I immediately sit up to respond but he's already sending a second message. *Let's talk in person. Meet me at our spot.*

CHAPTER 8

He's already waiting for me when I near the bridge. He stands with his elbows propped on the rail, gazing over the edge at the stream running underneath. As soon as I set foot on the bridge, he speaks without taking his eyes off the water. "I wonder if the fish can hear what I'm thinking."

I don't respond. I lean my elbows on the rail too and look over the edge. Below, myn sweep their tails slowly left to right like lazy fans.

"I think your brain has to be wired a certain way for that," I say.

"How do you figure?"

I shrug.

"I would guess that if animals on Faloiv can communicate

with their brains, it's the result of adaption that has occurred on this planet."

"Thank you, Dr. English," he says, raising an eyebrow.

Ordinarily I would smile, but his words only twist my mouth into a frown as the events in my kitchen with both Dr. Englishes solidify again in my mind. I push them out.

"So . . . ," I say, turning away from the myn to look at him. I study Rondo's face and notice the way the sunlight makes the line of his jaw glow. I've been in classes with him at the Greenhouse since we were small, but he always kept to himself, the shy boy who eschewed group study. How long has he had this face? He must have grown into his nose, his ears— otherwise I should have noticed long ago how much I enjoy looking at him.

"So . . . I snuck into my dads' study," Rondo says bluntly, turning to lean his back against the rail of the bridge. I'm jarred from admiring his features.

"Um . . . what?"

He shrugs, looking out at the commune. It's early and none of the shops are open; most other people are already in the labs or at their various workstations.

"They had left for the Zoo already. So I went into the study and looked through some slides."

"Why did you do that?" I can't decide whether to laugh or be scandalized.

He shrugs again. His customary gesture. His fingers drum quietly on the bridge rail, the only thing that ever gives away how busy it must be inside his head.

"We want to know more about the Faloii," he says. "And it stands to reason that the spotted man you say you saw is Faloii."

For as long as I can remember, the Faloii have been a shadow just beyond the borders of our education at the Greenhouse. Now that shadow seems to have crept in closer. When has Dr. Espada told us anything about them? Rarely. Our recent conversations—with Espada's reluctance—have been the most our hosts have ever been discussed. The sudden presence of the Faloii in my thoughts makes me uneasy. The storms that sweep over N'Terra from the jungles never come out of nowhere. They build for several days, the clouds in the distance deepening and bruising, working themselves up into the squall that will overtake the area for three sunrises. The mention of the Faloii feels much like this: the coming of a monsoon, the building up of something heavy and furious.

"You told me I don't know what I saw," I say slowly.

"Well, now I've seen something too," he says. "So forget what I told you."

"What did you see?" I say. "Show me."

"I can't," he says. "I didn't want to extract the slide in case my dads noticed. But I'm pretty sure the person you saw was Faloii. First off, who else would it be? You said he was taller

than your dad, right? Your father's one of the tallest people in
N'Terra."

I nod, already knowing where he's going with this. I'd
thought the same thing.

"So you just suddenly decided to believe me?" I say. "Your
deductive reasoning finally kicked in?"

"It's not that I didn't believe you," he says. He stops drumming the bridge rail to run a hand down over his close-cropped
hair. "I just needed more evidence. And now I think I have
some."

"Which is what?"

"I found some slides that document the *Vagantur*'s landing," he says. "No photographic material, but two pages of text
describing our first interaction with the Faloii. I couldn't figure
out an entry point to see the rest—landing agreements and
stuff—and a lot of things were redacted, so I could only read
those two pages. But they talk about the initial impressions of
the planet and give descriptions of its people."

"Wait, wait," I say, interrupting. "You 'couldn't figure out
an entry point' for the rest? Rondo, did you hack the slides?"

He looks at me sideways, his smile narrow but obvious.

"Yes."

I laugh, disbelieving. Who is this guy? I find myself moving
a little closer to him.

"You hacked the slides," I say, still laughing. "I can't believe
you hacked your own parents' files."

"Why not?"

"Because . . . I don't know, *because*! What if they find out? I can't imagine that would go over well."

"You were the one that started all this," he says sternly, but he's teasing me. "You wanted to go into the dome that night."

I sigh. He's right. But that night I was feeling strange, bold. The boldness feels far away now.

"I just don't want you to get caught," I say.

"I won't. I covered my tracks."

"So you've done this before?"

He drops his chin, gives me a long look. I can't help but laugh. Talking to him is so easy: the words just come, the questions, the answers. Why isn't it this easy at home?

"Anyway," I say. I drop my eyes from his, suddenly self-conscious about the smile plastered on my mouth. We're not in the labs, but I've heard the word *decorum* thrown at me so many times that it almost feels strange to just . . . smile. I pull in my lips to swallow it. "You said that they described the Faloii?"

"Yes," he says, nodding. "But all of it was vague. Tall with broad faces. Hands were described as being 'like an otter's' but I don't know what that means. Wide-set eyes. And something weird about their ears."

"Weird?"

"I don't know without a photograph," he says. "But they were described as unusual."

"Hmm. Maybe who I saw wasn't Faloii then. I feel like I would have noticed ears on top of his head, and I didn't."

He pauses to consider this.

"What about a tail?" he says.

"A tail?"

"Yes. The document said that one of them had a tail."

"As in, a *tail*? A *tail* tail?"

"Yeah."

"Just one of them though? Interesting," I say, but something else nags at me, something I haven't thought about in days without someone to discuss it with. "Did you happen to see anything in the files about something called Solossius?"

"Solossius?" He pauses and looks thoughtful. "No, I don't think so. That's a strange word. I think I would have noticed."

"Hmm, okay."

"What's up?"

I sigh, wishing I actually knew.

"Nothing, just something my father mentioned outside the Beak. Something that has to do with Dr. Albatur. I don't know much more than that. But all this talk about how Albatur and other people are fed up with the Faloii's rules. I wonder if this Solossius has anything to do with that."

He runs his tongue over his teeth, his eyes on the sky. I hide a smile. He always ends up looking at the sun for answers. Or maybe his eyes are unconsciously seeking the stars.

"What about his spots?" I ask, switching gears back to the

man I saw. "Did the files say anything about the spots?"

"Yes," he says, his eyes returning to my face. "Well, kind of. The Faloii were described as having markings on their body."

"Markings."

"Yes."

"That's not very specific."

"I mean, spots *are* markings."

The commune is starting to wake up. Other greencoats are coming out to roam while their parents are in the labs, enjoying their day off before internships begin. In a few days they'll be moving into their new compounds. It's strange to think that this time tomorrow, I'll be walking into the most restricted dome of the Paw.

"What are you thinking about?" says Rondo.

A man carrying a basket walks onto the bridge, headed across the stream to open his shop. I wonder if the basket carries one of Albatur's new scarlet banners. I don't answer right away, standing aside to let the man pass.

"I don't know. Tomorrow, I guess."

"Nervous?"

"Not exactly. Curious, maybe."

"A whitecoat through and through," he says, turning his eyes back to the fish in the stream.

A while ago, it would have thrilled me to hear it. Now I'm not sure. But my fondness for science and discovery is unchanged. Hardly anyone used to spend time outside their 'wams at one point: the heat drove us straight from lab to home. But then someone in the Paw made the maigno breakthrough, making our clothing more adaptable to the heat. What we don't know, we will. I wonder if my father still wants to solve these mysteries of our home, or if his sights are set on something else entirely.

"Are you going to tell me why you requested the Paw?" I ask, turning to Rondo. I'm hoping to catch him off guard before he has time to be evasive.

"Am I wrong to want to be assigned with the two smartest people in class?" he says, holding his hands up as if in surrender.

"What, you're going to try to cheat off our exams or something?"

"Would you let me?"

"Um, no."

He chuckles. He doesn't laugh enough. I've found that I like the way it sounds.

"I brought you something," he says, and leans down to touch something at his feet.

It's the smooth black case he was carrying his first day in the Paw. I didn't even notice it until this moment, so absorbed in thoughts of the Faloii.

"Your izinusa," I say, and I can't bite back the smile that bursts out of hiding.

"Yes."

He opens the case and lifts the instrument from its bed, bringing it to his shoulder. From the bottom of its curving wood base he pulls what looks like a long feathered stem from where it had been hidden in a groove. He takes it gently in four fingers of his left hand.

"No laughing," he says, but I can tell by the crease in his forehead that he has no intention of making me laugh.

I'm not prepared for the music. From the delicate look of the izinusa's neck to the graceful arch of the feather-like bow, I had expected a lighter sound than what Rondo coaxes from the strings. Instead, what flows into my ears is deep and rich with many layers of rising and falling notes. They weave with one another in ways my ears can barely comprehend, and I stare at the bow in Rondo's fingers, the music filling me up. I feel empty and full at the same time, as if all the smells and sounds of the commune have been summoned by Rondo's izinusa and swirl around me, waiting for me to make room inside my head. I look up from Rondo's fingers and find his eyes on me as he plays. I can't look away. It feels like the red sun has planted itself in my chest. Flowers grow under my skin.

When the hammers on the tower start again, Rondo stops playing, but the music has filled my ears the way the smell of ogwe fills my nose. I'm trying to think of something to say when his hand travels the short distance between us, closing around my bicep. He squeezes the softest part of my arm, a slow gentle pressure that makes my head swirl. When he lets the squeeze go, he leaves his hand there on my skinsuit, the heat traveling through the thin material. I smile.

We stand there for a while. This is a silence I can stand. Under it is only contentment, and for a few moments my head is empty: no sadness for my grandmother, no pain for my parents and the broken pieces of their love, no concern about the egg. Just Rondo: his hand, my arm, and, above us, the sun.

CHAPTER 9

"*Octavia.*"

I snap awake from a strange dream that disintegrates as soon as my eyes open. It was my mother's voice I dreamed of, and I expect to find her in my room, stirring me for my first day in the labs. But the door is closed, my room is dark, empty. I shut my eyes again, the dream washing over me but fading. I rise and go to the window, and now the dream is fully gone, fragments dispersing into specks. I slide open the window shade and am blinded by sunlight.

"Damn!"

The sun is already up. I spin away from the window to snatch my skinsuit from where it hangs on the wall. No time to eat.

I race through a deserted commune—everyone has already

left to start their day. I try not to think about what will happen if I miss my group's entrance to the labs. Will the guards even let me in? Once I get into the main dome, I tear through the trees, down the path toward the entrance to the Zoo. A stitch in my side punishes me: I've barely been awake ten minutes and now I'm sprinting, my flat white shoes pounding the packed dirt. I round the curve toward the labs, praying that I'll see Alma and Rondo lined up, ready to go in.

I wheel around the corner and slam into Jaquot, almost knocking him to the ground.

"Hey!" he yells, catching his fall against a tree.

My group is ahead of him, filing toward the guarded doors, and, like a nightmare, the three other interns and the single whitecoat turn in surprise to find me steadying myself, reaching up and smoothing my braids, clearly out of breath. The sight of Rondo, for the smallest second, makes me stop breathing altogether, the music of his izinusa flashing across my mind like a stripe of sunlight. But any comfort it offers is gone again the instant I see that the whitecoat at the head of the small group is my father, slate in hand, his face stony. His white coat is unbuttoned, his mouth like a crack in the ground when the rains are late.

"Glad that you could join us, Miss English," he says.

I don't answer. I know that voice. He's going to pretend that he's Dr. English and I'm Intern English. No relation. Might as well be true, but I don't let my embarrassment show on my face. Stone, I think, I too am made of stone.

"As I was saying," he says, turning away, "you are to arrive here in the main dome every morning, gathering at the entrance of the labs until one of the scientists comes to admit you. Who that scientist is will vary, depending on what you are studying in a given week. You will not have unlimited access to the facilities until you have completed at least one year of your internship. Understood?"

We're all outside the Zoo now, most of us probably wondering if this has all been an elaborate ruse or if we're actually going in. I was so absorbed by showing up late, I didn't even notice the fifth member of our internship group, and when I finally look, annoyance crackles through me like a strike of lightning. Of all people, Yaya. I'll have to watch my step with her in the group: she's eager to get top marks, and I wouldn't put it past her to find a way to inform the nearest whitecoat if I'm not meeting standards. Alma catches my eye from across the group, and I expect to exchange a mutual rolled eyeball over the presence of Yaya. Instead my friend's face is open, asking a question: What is it with you? I wish I had an answer.

"I'm sure most of you have heard about the oath that will be required of you. You will take it at the end of your first week in the labs," Dr. English is saying. "Not only does it signify your commitment to research in N'Terra, it holds you to secrecy about the work you will do here."

The words are out of my mouth before I can stop them.

"Secret from whom?"

All eyes are on me, including my father's. Alma stares at me, eyes wide and disbelieving, from across the group. We've always asked questions in class, but this is a different kind of question, I know. This question has roots, talons. I order myself not to look at her. Rondo, on the other hand, has the smallest of smirks on his lips.

"The who is not a question," my father says after a pause. "The oath is a Council-implemented requisite for all who wish to enter the laboratories."

I expect him to go on, but he doesn't. I also expect him to admonish me, but he doesn't. He barely looks at me, instead just turns to the guards with the buzzguns, nodding at one. She steps aside, allowing my father to press his thumb against the entry pad, and the doors whisper open, revealing a long hallway, painted stark white. No one moves. No one even breathes. I chance a glance over at Alma and her mouth is squeezed shut, her hands clasped tightly together. Even Rondo, who "doesn't give a damn about mammals," seems to be frozen by awe. My father has stepped inside already and looks back at the huddle of us, taking in our faces. This is the moment we've been dreaming of: the Zoo has opened its doors to us. I anticipate impatience from him, annoyance, but even he can't help but chuckle.

"Come on now," he says, beckoning. "We haven't got all day."

When the doors slide shut behind us, I feel the way my

grandmother must have felt when she stepped out onto Faloiv for the first time. My first step into the Zoo feels like setting foot on a new planet entirely. The ground is hard—too hard. It doesn't give under my feet at all, solid and smooth.

"What's wrong with the ground?" Jaquot asks, scuffing it with his shoe.

"It's artificial," my father says without looking back. He leads the way down the hall. "Made of synthetic material. It makes for a more sanitary environment."

Yaya stumbles, the strange floor catching at the bottom of her shoes. Jaquot is at her side like a flash of eager lightning, his hand on her elbow. She thanks him with a smile, and I roll my eyes, even as I trip slightly myself. It's strange not seeing grass or soil at my feet. Even our 'wams are grass and dirt inside, with mats laid down in the bathroom and hallway. Walking normally doesn't seem possible: having something so hard between me and Faloiv is unfamiliar. Rondo appears beside me as the interns troop down the hall. Alma is at the head of the group where I would have been, as if nothing has changed. I don't blame her: for her, nothing has.

The rooms we pass are all empty according to their windows, but still my classmates turn their heads eagerly as we pass each one. They're looking for animals: any kind. For years we've seen projected images of them in the Greenhouse with Dr. Espada, learning their unique characteristics and their adaptive trajectory, but aside from the occasional winging oscree or scurrying kunike, that's generally where greencoat first-person experience stops.

"Where is everyone?" Jaquot says. He says "everyone" as if referring to the whitecoats, of which we've seen none, but we all know he's talking about specimens. Still, for me the thrill of the proximity to animals is lessened as I also think about another organism: the spotted man. Is he still here? What had happened to him? Every time we pass one of the windows of the research rooms, I sneak a quick, nervous look. Nothing. Brought under cover of darkness and now invisible.

We're approaching the end of the hallway, a set of doors ahead, and I glance back over my shoulder at the entrance, far behind. The hallway had seemed like it might go on eternally, the whole lab one sprawling illusion. At the sight of the doors, I can sense the eagerness of the group: beyond this are the animals. We can feel it. All those empty exam and research rooms: *this* is where the specimens are. Dr. English approaches the doors—they don't require a scan—and they slither open to reveal what we've been waiting for. . . .

Eggs. All I see are eggs. Hundreds of them. In baskets and in piles. My blood initially freezes at the sight of them, thinking of the egg I have hidden under my mattress. I shoot a glance at Rondo and find his eyes already on my face. Do I have the egg of some monstrous creature of Faloiv in my bedroom? I imagine it hatching while I'm in the Zoo, growing exponentially in a matter of moments and wreaking havoc on N'Terra from the inside. I scan the room for a sign of an egg that resembles the one I have, but nowhere do I find the same pearly iridescence. The colors here are bright and in some cases almost jarring: fuchsias and deep greens. I admire the varying sizes and shapes before me, like a vast beach of multicolored stones. The sight of them fills me with a pleasant feeling that is welcome under the harsh, artificial lights.

"Your first project," Dr. English says. "These eggs are from recent collection trips. They need to be classified and sorted so they can be transported to the correct compounds. Be gentle, but don't worry too much. Their shells are very durable."

"They *have* to be on this planet," Jaquot jokes. My father, astoundingly, actually smiles. The corners of my mouth dip in a frown, remembering him raging at me about "scientist decorum." Jaquot is anything but decorous, and besides, it baffles me when Jaquot talks about Faloiv as if he wasn't born here: as if our home is a temporary habitat.

"I didn't know N'Terra asked finders to collect eggs," Yaya says. Jaquot, of course, makes a sound of agreement.

"Only if the specimens have been abandoned or have been found to be nonviable." The smile is gone from my father's face as quickly as it appeared.

"They're beautiful," Alma says, and I wonder if she's filled with the same warm feeling as I am when looking at them.

"Yes," he says. "You have six hours."

He leaves, and for a moment we're all silent. Around us, the eggs are piles of rainbows, some as small as my fist and others so large that I think carrying them might require two people.

"Well," Yaya says. We all look at her and she shrugs. "I guess we get started?"

I know better than to let my face betray the stab of irritation that sprouts between my ribs. Instead, I study her, searching for weaknesses in her faultless scientific armor. But the penetration of my stare stops at her face, finding only perfection. Her skin is deeply black, almost blue, her eyes wide and curving upward at the outer corners. I remember hearing Jaquot tell Rondo once that she was the prettiest girl on Faloiv, which now makes perfect sense given what I've observed of Jaquot's crush, and which I agreed with at the time without much jealousy. I had no need to be jealous—Yaya's beauty is a fact, and to be envious seemed irrational. Now reason seems to mean little as I take in her prominent cheekbones, the wide curve of her nose. Before I can allow myself to explore the idea of whether Rondo also thinks she's the prettiest girl on the planet, I snatch myself back from the precipice and hope that my momentary logical stutter hasn't showed in my eyes.

"And where would you suggest we start?" I ask.

She looks me square in the eye. "I would suggest that we look in our slates for the identification charts, because I don't have a damn clue."

Disarmed, I laugh—loudly—without meaning to. She gives me a half smile and shrugs in a nonchalant way, but I glimpse a

OLIVIA A. COLE

flash of shy pleasure in the way she blinks her eyes away from mine. This is the part where I'm supposed to snap back with something as clever as it is barbed, but all my words seem dull now. Jaquot appears between us, his slate illuminated with one of the charts.

"Luckily you have your resident egg expert here to lend his genius," he says, and this time I can't tell if he's doing the thing where he defuses tension, or if he's just flirting. I think the latter, the way his smile beams onto Yaya like her own private sun.

I open my mouth to say that his project on mammalian eggs hadn't even been in the top 10 percent of Greenhouse scores, but I don't want to risk irritating him in case he decides to regale everyone with tales of my fainting at the Beak. I close my mouth and turn to my own slate.

"Remember, they're not all mammalian," Yaya says. She could have been obnoxious to him about it—the way I wanted to be—but instead she shoots him a small smile. Interesting, I think. The sun might glow both ways.

"I don't care what they are," Alma says, running her hands gently over the surface of a round orange specimen. "I just want to stare at them."

Almost as if we agreed to do so, we all allow ourselves to admire the contents of the room for a few minutes.

"Nobody younger than twenty-one has ever been this close to this stuff before," Jaquot says. At first I think he's as filled with wonder as I am, but then he adds with a laugh: "I hope I don't break one! They'll kick us out."

The idea of him breaking one of these eggs makes me want to break one of his bones.

"It makes sense that this is where they would start us," Yaya says, studying the screen of her slate on which she's pulled up the classification matrices. "There are so many subtle variations between types of eggs. If we can tell these apart, we can tell animals apart easily."

Once we've gotten over our awe we get to work, picking up on those subtle differences as we sort. There are differences in color but also in shapes and textures. Reptilian eggs are mostly oblong, and mammalian eggs tend to be rounder, little hints we use to make identifying them a bit easier. We find large empty bins at the back of the room and use them to sort the eggs by class, the bins filling as time ticks by. I pause as I pick up a globular violet egg with a texture like tiny pebbles.

I stroke its surface and it leaves my skin feeling tingly. Rubbing my fingers together, I feel the sensation traveling up my arm. Alarmed, I put the egg back in the bin it came from, as quickly as I can without dropping it. I glance up, my eyes searching the room for Rondo, but he's absorbed in trying to identify a smooth blue egg, lost in his slate's matrices. I open my mouth to call him only to close it again, knowing that if I attract his attention I'll attract everyone else's too. I can't touch my arm through my skinsuit, but I continue rubbing

OLIVIA A. COLE

my fingers together, trying not to be too frantic as the tingling dulls into something difficult to describe—as if under my clothing, my arm is transforming into air.

"Are you stuck on one?" Alma says. She hasn't spoken directly to me since we arrived in the Zoo, and I can tell from her tone she's trying to break the thin layer of ice that's crept up between us.

I look away from my tingling hands and up into her eyes. It's as if the brown of her irises drives the sensation out of my mind, because my skin abruptly feels like skin again, the vibrating residue on my hands gone. I feel nothing, and when Alma comes over, scooping up the violet egg I'd just put down, I can only stare wordlessly as she places it in the mammalian bin. She doesn't rub her fingers, she doesn't pause or look troubled.

"The egg . . . ," I start, but Yaya turns her eyes on us, listening, and I realize, with a shade of nausea, that whatever I just felt might be the reason my mother sought to keep me out of the Zoo: some hidden weakness that I'm barely concealing. One word from Yaya might get me booted. "Yeah, I was stuck. But I've got it now. Thanks."

"Are there any animals that *don't* lay eggs?" Jaquot says, and I'm grateful that his interruption draws Yaya's attention. "We could build a whole new compound with these damn things."

"*I* think it's fascinating," Alma says. "I do wonder how long we've been in here though." She stands by the reptilian bin

128

with one knee bent, her hip pushed out. Her hair, braided today like mine, is covered by the gauzy headwrap the procedure file ordered us to wear. We all wear them, but she's tied hers with a high knot to give it a decorative flair.

"Three hours," says Rondo.

"I wonder if we get food," says Yaya, stifling a yawn.

As if on cue, the doors at the front of the room slide open. I expect to see my father, but it's another whitecoat. I've seen him before in the commune, always looking busy and rushed. He's no different now and doesn't even greet us.

"How many garifula eggs have you sorted so far?" he says.

My brain scrambles to find an answer. I haven't been looking at the totals, just entering numbers for each egg I sort. I've been busy admiring the specimens, letting my mind wander. I open my mouth to provide some reason why we don't have that information, but Yaya answers instead.

"One hundred and twelve," she says without hesitation.

"Good," the whitecoat says, already melting back out into the corridor. "Come with me. It's your allotted time to eat. I'll be taking you to the Atrium."

"Yes, sir," she says, and it seems she has now established herself as the leader of our little class. I make a mental note to find a way to distinguish myself later.

We troop out into the hallway where the whitecoat had gone. I don't see him anywhere. We stand there, alone, and it feels cold compared to the sorting room: the eggs seemed to lend a warmth to the air. Despite the chill, the hallways beckon to me. I'm considering taking a few steps back down the impossibly long entrance corridor, just to peek into some of the previously empty research rooms, when the squat white-coat reappears. He tells us to follow him, Yaya leading the way under the glaring artificial lights. Out here, away from the warmth of the eggs, I realize how sluggish I am. My energy feels as if it has leaked out of my veins and pooled invisibly on the stark white floor. Alma falls back from the group and walks beside me.

"It feels so weird," she says in a soft voice. We must speak quietly if we don't want our words to bounce off the walls.

"What?"

"No windows. I'm used to seeing the sky."

I look up, expecting to find the transparent ceiling of all the domes in our compounds, including the Greenhouse. But my eyes meet only glaring white lights.

"Yeah," I agree. "I hadn't even noticed until now. Maybe that's why I feel so tired."

A cluster of whitecoats makes its way toward us, and we stand to the side to give them room as they pass us in the hall. Two women and one man, all with serious looks on their faces, murmur softly to one another. I catch a thread of their conversation as they hurry by.

"They should just build it anyway," the man says. "Damn the landing agreement."

"Truly," his colleague says. "Those people are a threat to our safety."

"If you can even call them that," the second woman whispers. "Dr. Albatur's right—we need a barrier."

"Did you hear that?" I whisper to Alma.

"Hmm?"

"Ah . . . nothing."

I dart my eyes around, looking for Rondo, but he's several paces ahead. The white-clad trio disappears down the hallway. I can only assume they were talking about the Faloii. A barrier? Rondo sees me lagging and drops back to join us.

"I've never even seen some of these people before," he says as another group of whitecoats passes.

"The woman with the freckles used to live in the Newt," says Alma.

"It's easy to forget how many of us there are," I say. "With everybody in different compounds. There's gotta be hundreds of us."

"There were already five hundred people on the *Vagantur* when it landed," Rondo says. "Over two hundred of them were scientists. And that was over forty years ago."

The whitecoat is leading us to doors at the end of the corridor. As we approach them, the doors open and two whitecoats enter the hallway. With them comes a scent from what I realize must be the Atrium, its doors still wide open. Inside there are groups of whitecoats sitting and talking at various long platforms. The light is softer, and I know even before walking through the entry that the space ahead has a transparent domed ceiling: the light we see is the sun. I feel like one of the myn that's been flopping on a bank, gasping for air, finally tossed back into the compound's stream.

"What's that smell?" Alma asks.

I ignore her, taking in our surroundings. It's a dome much smaller than our commune, and smaller than the main dome too. Thirty or so whitecoats sit and stand at various platforms, some at ground level with us and some above on a small hilltop, into which stairs have been dug. Ogwe trees dot the land, most of them average in size, aside from a large one growing near the center, around which a cluster of platforms have been molded from Faloiv's abundant white clay and in front of which a short string of whitecoats has formed a line. The scientist who escorted us from the egg-sorting room gestures toward the central ogwe.

"You can get your food there. Take your time eating. Someone will come get you when it's time to return to your duties."

He removes himself without another word, marching back the way we came. Jaquot is already making a beeline for the central ogwe, leading the way with long urgent paces. I remember now that I'd skipped first meal and my stomach clenches in a gurgling fist.

"Whatever that is, it smells amazing," says Yaya.

The whitecoats ahead of us in the line pass through with

132

their platters, and I note that the platforms bearing the food are being manned by two youngish men wearing the same headwraps we wear, except theirs are green, matching their leaf-colored skinsuits. The green is nice, and I wonder if the color has a purpose or if it serves only as a demarcation of their duties. It bothers me, for some reason, the idea that wearing green as opposed to white might not have a function other than differentiation. N'Terra has always put those who study in the Zoo on a pedestal—especially since Dr. Albatur was elected—but the scowls on the faces of the men in green makes me wonder if the pedestal is higher than I thought.

"Do we serve ourselves?" Jaquot asks, and one of the green-suited men nods.

We take our platters and pile food onto them: hava slices, strips of zarum, the thick red paste of tangy waji. Jaquot makes a big show of loading his platter into a massive mound. In a basin at the end of the platform are some brown chunks I don't recognize, flecked with black.

"What's that?" Yaya asks, pointing.

"Zunile," one of the greensuits says. The frown that had been etched on either side of his mouth eases a little when he looks at her, taking in her big brown eyes, the lashes that curl so dramatically they almost touch her eyebrows, her locs that reach her shoulder blades. She notices but just nods.

The zunile doesn't look appetizing, but new food is exciting—it takes a long time to vet whether something is safe for N'Terrans to eat. I add a small mound of it to my platter and follow Jaquot, who has made a direct path to an empty platform close to one of the smaller ogwe trees. Our group sits and eats immediately, speaking only after we've taken the edge off our hunger. It's not until after I've taken a few bites that I realize Rondo has chosen the space next to me, and even though his leg is five inches from mine, I imagine I can feel the warmth of it. Alma catches me staring at him and bats her eyelashes exaggeratedly, stopping to laugh into her waji only when I mouth *I will kill you.*

"This place is brilliant," Yaya says, looking up and around as she chews.

"It is," I agree. I'm watching a row of bright red flowers. Their stamens keep extending, reaching up several feet into the air with movements so fluid they could be underwater, before slithering back down into the conical shape of their petals. "It's so different from the rest of the Zoo in here."

"Seeing the sky helps," Jaquot says. "And, you know, having good company." He directs this to Yaya, the rest of us seemingly invisible. I take a bite of food to hide my smile, remembering how in the Greenhouse he always sat in the back row. Now I know why—that's where Yaya sits.

"What's with the face?" Jaquot says, jutting his chin at me with a smile.

"Good company does help," I say. Then I turn to Yaya. "Matter of fact, Yaya, Jaquot was just telling me how much better our group is because of you."

"What?" Yaya draws her attention back from observing the Atrium, squinting like maybe she missed a punch line. Under the platform, Jaquot's feet are searching for my shin to kick. I pull my ankles in closer to my seat.

"A small intern pool could be tricky," I say, trying to sound casual. "Only five? The wrong fifth could have made us all look like idiots. I mean, we all know Jaquot isn't the sharpest scalpel in the set, so he was really happy to hear you were placed in the Mammalian Compound."

Jaquot glares at me until he sees that Yaya has turned her wide dark eyes on him; then his expression immediately goes smooth as glass.

"I think he's plenty sharp," she says, and then dips her head to her tray of food, like she possesses only a measured volume of flirtation and is rationing the rest. Still, it was enough for Jaquot and he shoots me a grin that tells me I'm absolved. I can't help it—I grin too.

"Why did they build the labs like this to begin with?" Alma says. "Why wouldn't they make everything with a transparent ceiling? It's so much better in here."

"Looks like the whitecoats like it, too," says Rondo, nodding in the direction of a platform of them, who are laughing. The serious silence that has seemed the norm in the rest of the Zoo is like a broken spell in the Atrium: hushed voices and solemnity are abandoned as whitecoats gather around the surfaces of eating platforms, stuffing food in their mouths and talking.

"Except them."

I almost don't understand Jaquot, who continues to speak with his mouth full. But he points with his eyes at a group of whitecoats sitting at a secluded platform toward the back of the Atrium. It's almost as if they have a bubble forming an invisible atmosphere around them, deflecting the relaxed energy of the rest of the dome. Their food sits nearly untouched in front of them, their faces long and grave as they converse.

"At least two of them are on the Council," Rondo says. He doesn't look at them, instead directing his gaze upward as if studying the branches of the central ogwe. Rondo has a way of seeing everything at once, missing nothing. I start to ask him how he knows they're on the Council when even I have never been to their dome, but I realize I already know. Hacking, I think. Of course. The identity of councilmembers isn't exactly a secret, but the fact that Rondo knows them by sight tells me he's been doing more snooping than he's admitted.

I observe the councilmembers more closely: two women and two men, their gold Council pins glinting from their lapels, and one person whose face I can't see until someone leans forward to whisper across the table, revealing him. His face stands out like a bone protruding from soil: pale and unpleasant looking, with sharp edges to his cheekbones that remind me of an insect's mandibles. He's leaned forward in his chair, speaking with squinted eyes to the rest of the table.

"That's Dr. Albatur," I say. "The pale one. The Council Head."

"That's him? We saw him in the Beak that day," Jaquot says. I hear the hitch in his voice as he realizes what he's broached. He pilots right around it, and I cast him a look of gratitude. "That day you and your dad came to visit."

"You didn't tell me that," Alma says.

"Oh . . . well, it was no big deal," I say. I pretend to focus on scooping waji onto bread and tell them about my encounter with Albatur outside the Beak that day with my father, the strange red hood he has to wear. I leave out everything else.

"He seems to be okay indoors," Alma says, eyeing him. "Did he happen to say what his condition is called? I wonder if it's only direct sunlight that's a problem for his skin."

"Could be there's something protective in the dome's roof," Yaya says, pointing upward. "To block the rays and keep him safe while he's inside."

"What a wretched life," Jaquot says. "To be stuck on a planet that your body hates."

I think back to the day I met Dr. Albatur, his disdain for Faloiv. It's more than his body that hates our planet, I think. He hates it too, no matter what the shopkeeper thinks.

"What did Draco say on the Worm that day?" I muse. But Rondo only shrugs, not yet following my train of thought. "Didn't he say Dr. Albatur plans to change things?"

I almost mention that it had something to do with the Faloii, but I close my lips around this part of the thought. I want to think about it a little longer myself.

"I guarantee he has whitecoats working on projects that can help cure him," Alma says. "There has to be an organism here that we can learn something from for that. I wonder if it's genetic? I'd hate to live on this planet if I were him."

"*I'd* hate to be sitting at that table. They all look miserable," Jaquot says, and Yaya laughs. They share a small smile. Yaya has always made herself a secret, but I've been hanging out with Jaquot at the Greenhouse since I was six—it still baffles me that I missed this crush of his. A key part of what we do in N'Terra is observation, but somehow I missed this. What else have I overlooked?

"They need to eat instead of just sitting there—that would cheer them up." Alma interrupts my thoughts, turning her gaze from the whitecoats to me. "Are you going to try the zunile, O?"

The brown chunks are the only thing that remain untouched on my plate. They're the source of the tantalizing smell hanging in the room.

"I mean . . ." I raise my eyebrow at the small pile. "Do I want to?"

"It's actually pretty good," Jaquot says. He puts a piece in his mouth, the massive quantities of food he heaped almost entirely consumed. "Really chewy—I can't compare it to anything. It must be a new plant the finders discovered on one of their trips. Don't be a coward, O. You're supposed to be our future nutritionist."

"Okay, okay, fine." I pick up one of the brown chunks between thumb and forefinger and eye it. It looks fibrous and squishy. The odor is interesting. I open my mouth and bring my hand up to drop the zunile in, when another hand appears in front of me and fastens its iron grip around my wrist.

CHAPTER 10

I stare blankly at the hand for a half second, but by the time I realize it's my mother's, she's already released her grip.

"Hello, everyone," she says, smiling. "Did I scare you, Octavia? I tried to sneak up on you."

"Yeah, a little bit." I force a laugh. I dropped the piece of zunile when she grabbed me and I peek at the floor to see if I can find it. When I look back up, my plate is in my mother's hand. Walking toward the biotubes to dispose of the remains of my meal, she says over her shoulder, "Come with me, interns. It's time to get you back to the sorting room. From what I've been told, you have quite a bit left to do."

After we drop our platters off at the biotubes, my mother turns to the group to make sure we're all accounted for. I study her face, looking for traces of our argument yesterday. Her eyes wander to the back of the Atrium, where they fall on the platform that the bone-faced Dr. Albatur sits at. Dr. Albatur watches my mother too, his insect jaw set into a square, his eyes shining like two beetles. They keep eye contact for only a moment before he ducks his head and continues speaking to the other councilmembers. If they're Council, why isn't my mother sitting there with them?

My mother turns away and leads us back out into the white hall. Her face betrays nothing, but I can sense her unrest as if it's a scent seeping from her pores. She actually seems relieved by the distraction of my fellow interns, who pepper her with questions. Despite her reputation for brilliance, she also has a reputation for kindness: the stiffness that the presence of my father tends to induce is washed away and everyone relaxes under her smile. Yaya tails my mother closely, interrogating her with as much delight as Yaya's studious mask allows for.

"Dr. English, how did it feel when you first discovered that animals across different genuses and species could communicate telepathically?"

My mother chuckles, a sound I know well and have inherited. Her laugh used to fill our 'wam, and the knowledge of its absence turns those memories into ghosts, floating hollow around me. I miss those days, when I felt like I actually knew her. Both of them. It stings even more when I realize that the answer she's giving Yaya is a story I've never even heard.

"It was incredible," my mother says. "At first I wasn't entirely willing to believe what I had discovered. But all the tests were conclusive, and after two or three days of checking everything twice and thrice, I allowed myself to feel excited."

"That's amazing," Yaya says, and my mother grants her a smile that brightens the whole hallway. I didn't inherit that. Or maybe I did, but I don't think I smile enough anymore to really know. Rondo falls back to walk alongside me.

"Returning to your precious eggs," he says. I wonder if he means to make his voice low and soft like that, or if it's just how it comes out. The texture of his words almost makes me forget about my sadness—I can't believe talking to him used to make me nervous.

"I don't know about precious," I say. "So. You knew that two hundred of the original N'Terrans were scientists. More hacking, I assume?"

"How else?" He shrugs. Protocol is so important in N'Terra and Rondo just . . . doesn't give a damn.

"Always hacking. I thought you were into music." I bump him with my shoulder.

"I can't be interested in more than one thing?"

"Well, N'Terra hasn't outlawed that."

He bumps me back.

"Yet," he counters. "To be honest, the only reason I started messing around with computers was because the whitecoats are so secretive about everything. I would love to just focus on music but . . ."

"But, again, we have no musical compound," I tease.

"I'd make one," he says. "But it's like no one on the Council cares about anything except expanding N'Terra."

"So you started hacking to . . . what? Make a point?"

He laughs lightly.

"Not necessarily. Just boredom, I guess. They won't let me study what I want, so I study them instead."

"Watching the watchers," I say with mock solemnity. "Very deep."

"I don't think I'm the only one who does it though," he says, his smile fading. "When I was doing some looking around last night, I saw someone else in the files too."

I steal a glance ahead at my mother to make sure she's not listening—she's fully engaged in conversation with Yaya and Alma. Jaquot has fallen some distance behind us, alone, but he's in his own world, chewing a piece of fruit he'd brought out of the Atrium. Also against protocol, I would imagine, but that's Jaquot for you.

"Who was it in the files?"

"Don't know. Their access point was encrypted."

"Which means what exactly? They were purposefully covering their tracks?"

"Yep."

"And do you encrypt your access point?"

He twists his mouth to the side and gives me a sidelong glance, a nonverbal *obviously*.

"Good," I say. "If you got caught, they'd probably kick you out of the Zoo for a decade—you'd be on sanitation duty until your hair was gray."

"And?" he fires back. "Like I said, I don't even want to be in here."

"If they let you play the izinusa on sanitation duty, I'll come listen on my breaks."

He pauses and gives me a long look, his lips twitching in a smile before he goes on.

"Why are we talking about me? We should be talking about *you*. Wandering out into the main dome at night spying on whitecoats? Pretty sure they'd kick you out for that too, and I doubt you'd be as cool about it."

I almost expect the hypothetical idea of being barred from the labs to affect me on a gut level, prepare my stomach for the flood of theoretical panic. But it doesn't come. Instead I feel something almost like . . . relief? Like sand washing away to expose something shining and hidden under its drifts.

"We didn't get caught, did we?"

"No," he says, returning the smile. It's a small brief offering of teeth, but it feels like a gift. "Not yet anyway."

My mother, Alma, and Yaya have reached the doorway of the sorting room and turn to wait for us to catch up. Alma raises her eyebrow at me in a teasing way, but I dodge making eye contact with her, afraid of what my face might betray.

"This is where I leave you," my mother says, and the door

opens to admit us. "Three more hours and you'll be free, if you have the rest of the eggs sorted by then."

Jaquot groans, making Yaya laugh—she's in love with him, I decide: only love makes people laugh at stupid things like this—and our group files through the doorway. I'm about to go back in too, my mind still on Rondo's smile and wondering if maybe I'm stupidly in love as well, when my mother reaches out and touches my arm lightly.

"Octavia, a moment, please."

She says it in her scientist voice: *One moment please, colleague.* But scientist voice or not, I still hear mother voice in its undertones. All the warm feelings that had fluttered about when walking with Rondo crumble back down into the shadows of my stomach.

"How's it going?" she says, this time in her mother voice. But now it's the scientist voice I hear in the undertones, the roles swapped but never really independent of the other. I wonder if it's because she's in the Zoo and the whitecoat voice is hard to shake in work territory, or if it's because I'm both daughter and project.

"Fine," I say. "It's a good group."

"Are they enjoying the experience?" she says.

"I think so. How long do you think our work will be limited to the sorting room?"

"Do you not like working with the eggs?"

"No, I do. I was just curious." The thought of the violet egg and the tingling it had left on my skin emerges out of the shadows of my brain, but I push it away hurriedly, as if she might see it.

"How do they make you feel?"

My gut ties itself into an elaborate knot. Is there surveillance equipment in the sorting room? Has she been watching me, observing my reactions to the specimens?

"Um . . . how do *eggs* make me feel?"

She nods, as if this is the most natural question in the world.

"Um . . . fine, I guess? Calm?"

She looks pleased, her mouth widening into the smile I know well.

"Which ones make you feel calm?"

There is definitely a trap somewhere in the short distance between us.

"You mean, which exact eggs? Uh, I don't know. I hadn't really been paying attention." I pause, contemplating what she's actually asking, striving to see the parameters of the experiment she might have laid out around me. "Do different eggs have different effects on humans or something?"

She gives me a look I can't quite decipher. She practically glows with excitement, but I can almost see her holding something back.

"Different eggs have different . . . purposes. Not all eggs produce young, you know."

"In that case, is it really an egg, then? What does it do if it doesn't hatch?"

She studies me, saying nothing, and my head starts to buzz. I hate these bright white lights. My headache is back.

"Later," she says finally, the smile wavering. I suddenly have the impression that she's wearing a mask, a second face that she dons specifically for the white hallways of the Zoo. It plants a shudder in my spine. "Soon we'll talk all about it. Soon."

Behind the smile mask I detect concern, hidden in places only I would notice: the subtle droop of her lower lip on the left side; the creases at the outer corners of her eyes, slight wrinkles that are deeper than I remember. I have decided to ask her if she's okay, when a door just down the white hall slides open and we both turn our heads to look. Two whitecoats appear, guiding a massive rolling cart out into the wide corridor. At first I think it's a bin like the ones we've been filling with eggs all morning, but then they turn the corner of the doorway and I instead see that it's a cage. Inside crouches a very large, sleek-furred animal, blue-gray in color, ears like large round leaves, snout snubbed and short, multiple tusks sprouting from either side. My headache throbs but doesn't dampen my excitement.

"A tufali," I say. I've only ever seen it displayed on a screen as a three-dimensional projection, and now here it is, vividly alive. I'm surprised to find that I can smell it, its musk wafting down the hall toward me like an invisible, sentient cloud. I'm taking a step toward it to get a better look when my mother's fingernails bury themselves in my arm and I'm hauled around to face her.

"Stars, Mom—" I snap, surprised, swiveling my head back around to look after the tufali, but the cart is disappearing down the hall. She takes my chin in her hand and roughly directs my face to look at her.

"What the—" I gasp.

"Male or female?" she asks, her voice urgent, as if she's asking me the password to a computer that might explode at any moment.

"W-what?"

"The tufali that you just saw. Was it male or female?"

"I don't—"

Her eyes drill into mine, deeply brown and shining with a look I don't recognize. "*Think*, Octavia."

After a long pause, the pressure of her fingers on my chin making my jaw ache, I grind my answer out.

"Female."

She lets go of my face, her eyebrows raised slightly with what looks like grim satisfaction. She was leaning in toward me and now withdraws, hesitantly as if she might grab me again.

"How did you know?" she asks.

I'm not sure how to answer. It hadn't felt like a guess. But I'd glimpsed the tufali for no more than a half second before my mother pulled my gaze away. I'm angry at the thought: the first animal specimen I've seen all day—something I'd never see milling around the side of the road or grazing beyond the compound gates—and she keeps me from looking. What is her problem?

"I should get back in," I say, moving toward the door to the sorting room. All my sadness about our fight has disappeared, replaced with anger. "They won't appreciate having to do my work for too long."

She nods. She seems unsettled and glances over her shoulder, back down at the Atrium as if to see if anyone is watching us.

"Go," she says. "I'll see you at home."

"Yeah maybe," I say, the sarcasm leaking into my voice like a toxin.

Inside the sorting room, Alma and the others are all talking but stop when I walk in. I look around, waiting, but no one says anything.

"What?" I say.

"We were just talking about your mother," Yaya says.

"What about her?"

"She's brilliant," Yaya says, as if that should have been obvious. "My mother studies neonatology. Which is interesting, fine. But to study mammalian neurology—the brains of the biggest animal class on Faloiv . . . well, it's just awesome."

"Was she helping you cheat?" Jaquot asks. His grin would ordinarily rub me the wrong way, but I can tell he's just trying to show how much he admires my mother. At one point it would have been flattering; now I just feel queasy. "Giving you some tips?"

"No," I say. It's true, but I can see the disappointment on their faces: they were hoping for a peek behind the curtain, some privileged piece of information that will make knowing me worthwhile. "I did see a tufali though."

Their expressions brighten, even Rondo's. Yaya's mouth falls open.

"You did?"

"Just now?"

They all say variations of this, various expressions of excitement.

"Yeah. A female."

"How do you know? The males and females look identical. Their sex only becomes apparent when they mate." Yaya says this like she's answering a question on an exam and I can't help but laugh. We're greencoats. The nearest mention of animals and we go into Greenhouse mode, like a knee's reflex bursting out under the tap of a mallet.

"My mother told me," I lie.

They ask more questions about the tufali as we get back to sorting eggs. Most of them I can't answer because my viewing of the creature was so brief. I can still smell its musk, but I don't mention that: the scent isn't quite a real scent, hanging in my nose. It's more like a memory, an impression of the smell. I try to distract myself with the eggs but am hesitant to touch them, and when I look around for the violet egg from earlier, I don't see it anywhere.

"How are you supposed to tell the marov egg apart from the roigo egg?" Jaquot stands near me studying his chart. "They look exactly the same."

They don't look the same at all, not to me, but I don't say this out loud. I cautiously pick up a pale blue globe, waiting for the tingle in my fingertips, but nothing happens.

"The marov egg has a noticeable texture," Yaya says. "It also has a faint yellow ring at one end."

"Oh, I was just joking," Jaquot says. He wasn't. Now he's pointing at another specimen. "They're actually really easy to tell apart, but what about this one? This isn't even in the chart."

He keeps breaking my concentration. I finally turn to look at the egg he's referring to if it means he'll shut up.

"I'm sure it is. Let me see."

Jaquot reaches for the pinkish egg he's indicating and goes to pick it up, but then he yelps.

"What?" I demand. "What happened?"

"It's hot!" he says, tucking his slate under his arm and cradling his hand. "White hot."

Yaya tentatively touches the egg in question with her fingertip. She snatches her hand back.

"It is," she says, as if even she is shocked that he's right.

Without thinking, I reach for the egg, ignoring Jaquot's

words of caution. Its shell feels solid and warm in my palm, but not hot. It's smooth, comforting. A sensation thrums in my fingers as it did in my encounter with the violet egg, but it's different somehow. Not tingly this time—instead, a feeling of moisture. I rub my fingers together but they're dry.

"It's not hot to you?" Yaya says, disbelief tinting her words.

"It's not in the identification chart," Jaquot says again, frowning.

"Yeah, it's definitely hot." I turn away in case the lie doesn't look convincing on my face. I ignore Rondo's pointed gaze and move toward the bins. "I'll just put it in an empty bin by itself. The whitecoats will know what to do with it."

We're silent for a while, the mountain of eggs getting smaller and smaller as we sort them into bins. My mind goes again to the spotted man, and then to my mother's words in the hallway. The heat of the two eggs can't be coincidence— do they have a different purpose than hatching offspring? But why doesn't the heat bother me? I find myself yet again wishing that my grandmother were still alive. I was eleven when she disappeared, but it hasn't been until recently that I've begun to wish I'd asked her more questions.

Alma comes to my side, where I'm collecting three or four roigo eggs.

"Why don't you tell me anything anymore?" Alma says softly.

There are so many things to hide, I'm not sure which one she might be alluding to, and it's as if the herd of secrets inside me scatters at the glow of her searchlight, shadowy legs running for cover.

"What do you mean?" I ask.

"You acted like you'd never had zunile before, or even heard of it."

"I—what?"

"Zunile," she says impatiently. "At second meal today none of us had ever seen zunile before and you acted like you hadn't either."

She's talking about food. I'd almost laugh if I weren't so confused.

"Maybe your parents told you not to tell anyone since it's new. They were probably still researching it or whatever," she says, not looking at me. "But you could have told me. Stars, O, you always used to tell me stuff."

"I'm confused," I admit.

"While you were walking with Rondo, your mom told me you're allergic to it," she whispers sharply. "How would she know you're allergic if you've never eaten it before?"

"She said that?" Why would my mother lie?

"Yes. She made me and Yaya promise to never let you eat it since she won't always be around. Why did you try eating it today if you're allergic? You know reactions to new food can be dangerous."

The lies swim in my throat like myn, growing legs to scale my tongue. The only person who has known the truth lately is Rondo, and standing here in this too-bright room, my best friend looking in my eyes with a dozen unanswered questions, I can't figure out why. My parents are secret keepers: my mother whispering behind her closed study door, my father and the deep canyon of silence that has settled heavily between us. My mouth is open, ready to continue the lie that my mother has told. But why? If she's going to tell Yaya and Alma a lie—me being allergic to a plant I've never even heard of—then why not at least clue me in, let me know, so that I can corroborate? She truly must think I'm weak, that I can't handle whatever it is that she knows.

Suddenly all the secrets feel unbearably stupid. My mother trying to keep me out of the internships. The philax. The spotted man. The eggs. The idea of keeping them hidden inside me for another minute makes me tired. So I take a deep breath and I tell Alma the truth.

CHAPTER 11

Three days later, Alma and I are sharing my bedroom, her and the other interns' things finally packed and moved. I can only imagine Draco and the other irritable drivers complaining about having to transport interns back and forth between compounds while the whitecoats settled who would stay with whom. But now she's here. Having Alma present to fill the silence of my always empty 'wam is like a stitch across an open wound.

It's morning, and an engineer is in my room building Alma's bed. We have nothing else to do—no assigned research from sorting duty—so we stand in the doorway watching. He doesn't say much as he builds, working from a huge case of white clay he wheeled in, using a handheld flat spade to shape her sleeping platform. It's above my own, built into the wall like a shelf. The clay dries almost instantly, and watching him work, I realize it must take years of practice to get the process just right. He does it deftly, scooping the clay out of the case and turning swiftly back to my wall to create thick layers that gradually begin to take the shape of my own sleeping platform. I keep expecting to get bored, but we stand there watching until he finishes.

"What about when she moves out?" I ask. "Do I just have two beds now?"

He's cleaning up, wiping his spade on his apron. He smiles.

"No, don't worry. When she goes back to her own compound we'll come back and remove the bed. Concentrated pavi extract will turn it into dust," he says. "Then we can just sweep it up."

"Really?" It seems impossible: the bed looks as immovable as a boulder, like everything else in the compound. It occurs to me how little I know about anything that's not related to zoology—I've seen the clay used to build structures dozens of times: How had I not known about its properties? Rondo would probably have a theory about this. "I didn't know pavi was so acidic."

"Oh, it's not the acidity. Just the way the two react. It's a fairly recent discovery: before, we would break structures apart like stone." The engineer thrusts the spade into a loop in his apron and motions for us to clear the doorway. "You know Dr. Yang? It was her discovery, actually. She accidentally dissolved some lab equipment! Would still be a lot easier to build up the compounds if they let us break down the *Vagantur*, but I suppose some folks still aren't satisfied."

"What do you mean? Aren't satisfied?" I ask as he trundles the case of clay toward the front door. "Why wouldn't they be?"

He pauses to wipe his hands on his apron.

"Not sure exactly—I don't remember any world other than this. Seems just fine to me. But the way I hear it, there are some on the Council who grew up bitter about our hosts. Some folks don't like not being the boss. No boss here but the sun."

I exchange a look with Alma.

"How would that change though?" I ask as he wheels the case the last few feet to the entrance.

"The Council, girl. The decision is theirs. They decide they want to start making their own rules, and that's all it takes."

The door opens and he starts through it, but I fire one more question at his back.

"But wouldn't that break the landing agreement?"

He looks over his shoulder with a frown and doesn't stop moving to answer.

"When someone gets it in their head that their way is the right way, no type of agreement will stop that."

The door slides shut behind him, leaving me standing there staring at its smooth surface, more questions on my tongue.

"You don't think you're pushing it a little?" Alma's voice

comes from over my shoulder. Something in her tone makes me turn right away.

"What do you mean?"

She leans against the entrance to my bedroom, her eyebrows furrowed.

"I mean, come on, O," she says. Her hands, usually like two birds with their gestures, are tucked around her body like she's in a cocoon. "You've told me everything, and I understand. But what is asking all these questions going to accomplish?"

"Maybe nothing," I say. We stand across the room, looking at each other. "But you don't think it's important? You think I shouldn't ask?"

"I don't know," she says. Her hands come loose from around her body and flop at her sides. "It just doesn't seem like the best way to become a whitecoat. Your parents are already worried about that, right? If you're focused on this stuff and not your research, it's only going to be worse if . . ."

"If what? If I ask questions? You've always asked questions at the Greenhouse, same as me. Why is this different?"

She purses her lips and looks at me.

"I just—I don't know. It just is. I want to be a whitecoat, O. The questions I ask further that goal."

"Maybe being a whitecoat isn't my ultimate goal, Alma," I say.

She stares hard at me. She doesn't squint, but something about her expression narrows.

"What else is there, Octavia?"

We look at each other a moment longer and I can't find an answer. I've told her everything, but some things can't be explained. Not even to myself. She turns away to disappear back into my room. I take a deep breath before following her.

When I enter, she's perched up on her new bed, staring at her slate. It's not illuminated, however. She merely gazes at her blank screen. She's been like my distant sister since we were children: going to the Greenhouse to take classes with Dr. Yang, chanting songs about the difference between reptiles and amphibians. We were immediate friends, rarely a moment of silence between us. This particular silence seems wide and deep: I'm not sure how to bridge it. As it turns out, she does it first.

"Was that engineer Aiyana's dad?" she says.

I direct my eyes up at her where she sits. Aiyana is a couple of years older than us and had opted to work in archiving rather than begin a path to the labs. I don't know her well, but just her name seems to have planted a sparkle in Alma's eyes.

"No," I answer, grateful that she's not mad. "Aiyana's dad isn't an engineer."

"Oh. They have the same smile."

"What do you know about Aiyana's smile?" I prod.

She laughs, raising her eyebrows.

"Oh, this and that," she says.

"Look, I'm sorry, okay?" I can't just move forward like

nothing happened without at least saying this. "I know you want to be a whitecoat. I promise I'll try not mess things up for you."

She waves her hands.

"I'm going to be a whitecoat either way, O."

I stare at her a moment longer: my friend, my confidant. More than that, Alma is *smart*. I try to hold it back, but I need her input.

"Did you hear what he said, though?" I burst, and she laughs, shaking her head.

"Which part? People being bitter?"

I nod. "Yeah, and about the *Vagantur* not being dismantled because they're unsatisfied. About them wanting to change things."

"Unsatisfied or not, they better get used to it. N'Terra gave up on fixing the *Vagantur* decades ago. I don't know where else they think they'd go! This is home."

"Yeah . . ." I frown. The cloud over my father's heart has been a vague shadow for so long. Now that I've met Dr. Albatur, somehow the cloud has been given a shape. It looms over me and makes me feel cold.

Alma hops down from her perch, going to fetch her mattress from where it's rolled up in the hall.

"Are your parents coming home later?" she says once she's unrolled the mattress and is up on her ledge again.

"Yeah probably," I say, looking down.

She gives me a look, a cross between comfort and reproach.

"It's *okay*, O," she says. "It's me."

I sigh. I've told her about what happened at the Beak, about my father's anger, my mother's secrets, the spotted man, the egg—but I haven't gotten used to the feeling of needing to hide. Adaptations take time to change, I think: once an animal needs a method of camouflage or a defense mechanism, it's part of them until it's phased out over time or replaced.

"They probably won't come home," I admit after a pause. "I've seen them more in the Zoo in the past few days than I have in weeks. Whatever, I honestly prefer it like this."

"You're still mad about the zunile, huh?"

"I mean, yeah!"

She laughs, shaking her head.

"Well, everybody hides something. Like you, with this egg!" She pauses, biting her lip. "Can I see it?"

"The egg? Yeah, of course."

I shift my weight on the bed platform, pulling up the edge of my mattress. I scoop the egg out of the hole, gazing at it for a moment, its shell lineless and unmarred, before standing to present it to Alma.

She sits on the edge of her bed and stares at it curiously, her face apprehensive.

"It's beautiful," she says finally.

"Here," I say, extending it out to her.

She crosses her arms quickly, shaking her head.

"Nah, I don't want to touch it," she says. "I just wanted to see it."

"It won't hurt you," I laugh, rubbing it against my cheek. I do this sometimes when I can't sleep. The warmth of it comforts me. In a strange way it reminds me of Rondo.

"It might," she says. "Remember what happened in the sorting room? I still don't understand why that egg burned Jaquot and Yaya but not you."

I rub my thumbs over the egg.

"I don't know either. But what my mother said to me about different eggs having different purposes . . . it has to be related to that somehow."

I return the egg to its hiding place under my mattress.

"Is that where you keep it?" she says, poking her head down again. "Eventually we're going to need to ask someone about it. Dr. Espada or even your mom. You could actually get some answers. *Scientia potentia est!*"

"Alma, *what?*"

"It means 'Knowledge is power!'"

I can't help but chuckle.

"Why do you know all these stupid dead words?"

"They're not stupid! They're beautiful." She shrugs. "See: *Scientia potentia est,*" she says with a flourish. We both laugh, but I still want to know.

"Seriously. The last few years you're always asking Dr. Espada about the Origin Planet. All his crusty old artifacts. Why?"

"You don't want to know where we come from?" she says, her voice elongated with yearning. "This dead language is just one, the one they decided should survive. Think about how many other languages we probably left behind! We focus so much on Faloiv and the future, we never stop to think about the past."

"So? The past is the past. Gone. We have to focus on what will help us survive now: in the future." I realize I sound a bit like my father and frown.

She casts her eyes to the ground, fidgeting with her skin-suit. It's not often that Alma seems unsure or lacks a solid argument.

"I know, and we should. But sometimes . . . I don't know. You never feel like the future would make more sense if you knew about the past?"

"Like the names of old hairstyles?" I tease, but she doesn't smile.

"Yes," she says, nodding. "All these old words, they still carry meaning. Some more than others. We just have to figure out what it is."

She holds my gaze a moment longer, and I get the feeling there's more she wants to say. But then she shakes her head, smiling.

"Anyway. So what do you think the oath is going to be like?" She pulls her legs up again. "Your dad said we'd have to take it at the end of our first week, and that's tomorrow."

I've been wondering the same thing. My father had said the oath was a vow of secrecy to protect the work we do in the labs. I've been carrying so many secrets, the oath feels like another brick added to the stack already on my shoulders.

"Hopefully it's not some big ceremony," I say. "It's going to be really awkward if all the whitecoats are there. They all hate us for getting into the Zoo at sixteen."

"Ha! Yeah, they do. Just jealous. I do hope we get to see the kind of specimens they must be working with though."

"Maybe after the oath," I say. "I mean, so far we haven't seen anything worth keeping secret. Maybe after we'll see the real stuff."

My slate makes its faint wooden sound, and I rise to retrieve it. I slide my finger across the surface to unlock it and see a message from Rondo.

I found something. Bridge.

"What's that?" Alma says, craning her neck to see. "Rondo?" She grins.

"Yes," I say, half smiling, but impatient too. For the moment this isn't about how Rondo makes me feel: it could be important. I hesitate. I'm not used to having anyone with me in the 'wam.

"Do you want to wait here, or . . . ?" I ask.

She hops down off her bed, grinning.

"And miss this epically awkward flirtation? Not a chance."

• • •

"So many people out!" Alma says as we make our way through the commune, glancing around. We stop to let two kids race by, one carrying a hand drum. I think again of Rondo's izinusa, and guiltily wish for a split second that Alma hadn't come so he and I could be alone. "It's so different."

"What do you mean? What's the Newt commune like?"

"Quieter. You know nobody really cares about amphibians. We're born bored over there."

"Ha. It's just loud in here because they're building that damn tower." The structure continues to grow, and I haven't been able to shake the association of it with Dr. Albatur, its harsh lines in such stark contrast to the rounded warmth of everything else in the commune.

"Yeah, that thing is ugly. I hope it's worth it. Dr. Espada has wanted to introduce more astronomy into the curriculum for a while now. They must have fixed the telescope from the *Vagantur*."

"I hope so."

"I bet you do. You want to get up in that tower and use the telescope to look in Rondo's window. Damn the stars."

"Oh, shut up." I laugh.

"You guys have your own bridge?" She presses on, teasing me.

"Alma."

"He just says *bridge* and you already know which one, huh?"

"Oh, stars, he's just a friend!"

"Oh right," she says. "Sure, sure. A friend that you wander around at night with, spying on whitecoats."

"Now that you're here, I'll wander around with you instead," I say, only half meaning it. I secretly hope that whatever Rondo found means another after-dark trip to the dome.

All my thoughts of being alone with Rondo disappear when I see him on the bridge ahead. He's pacing, and I know something is up. My pulse jumps. Except for his drumming fingers, Rondo is generally very still. Everything my father would say a scientist should be . . . aside from his lack of interest in science. But right now he's in constant motion. He looks up and doesn't wait for me to reach him. He walks toward me, eager to close the distance between us. It's not until he's a few steps away that he seems to realize I haven't come alone. He peers at Alma and then back at me with a squint.

"Octavia?" he says. He doesn't need to say the rest: *What's she doing here?*

"She's rooming with me now for the course of the internships."

He nods, as if remembering.

"Jaquot moved in with me too." He's making small talk until he decides about Alma.

"It's okay," I say. "I told her everything."

He hesitates a moment longer, and then it's as if the pressure is too great and he spills a stream of words in a rush.

"We're missing a hundred passengers," he says. He's raised

his hands with the declaration and then lets them fall, flopping to his sides. His eyes are wide with excitement and agitation—I've never seen him so animated.

"Wait, what? Missing how? When?"

"Remember we were talking about how five hundred passengers arrived on Faloiv when the *Vagantur* crash-landed? That's correct: five hundred people—astronauts, scientists, engineers, anthropologists—were on the ship when they set the emergency course to land here. There was a meeting of agreement with representatives of the Faloii. But when the agreement was made and we started building a camp, they took count of the settlers in a beginning census. And that number was under four hundred."

"Four hundred?"

"Yes."

Alma starts to speak. "How do you know all—"

"Sometimes he hacks N'Terra's files," I say. "Rondo, what does this mean?"

"I don't know! I have no idea! But it's important, you know? All those people! They just disappear from N'Terra's records. I tried different files and databases to hunt down some reference to them. Nothing."

It wouldn't be as significant if it changed from five hundred to four hundred and ninety-five. But one hundred people . . .

"They must have died in the landing," I insist. "Right?"

"No," he says. "The landing was rough because of the meteor, but it mainly damaged the ship. I found records of injuries and two deaths, but both of those names were accounted for."

"Maybe it's just a clerical error?" Alma suggests.

"I thought the same thing," he says, shaking his head. "But there are names missing. Specific names. I accessed the entire passenger list of the people who were aboard the *Vagantur*. I cross-referenced those names against the list of injuries and the list of settlers in the initial N'Terra settlement. None of those names was on the list. It's not a numerical error. One hundred actual people are missing."

"Disease," I counter. "Is there any record of major illness? I mean, they were new on Faloiv. Maybe part of the population didn't survive the transition."

"Nope. I checked. No record of any catastrophic loss to the *Vagantur*'s population. No disease, no violence. There were a number of minor illnesses based on bad reactions to food, but very few. These were mostly people of science and their families," he says. "They weren't going to make any stupid mistakes."

"Whoa," Alma says, but nothing more. A woman passes us, walking toward the bridge, and we all avert our eyes. When I look back up, Rondo looks uncomfortable.

"There's one more thing," he says.

"What?"

He pauses, looks at Alma, and then back at me.

"Your grandmother's last name was Lemieux, right?"

I stare at him.

"Yes."

"Was your grandfather Jamyle Lemieux?"

"Rondo, why?" I say.

"You said your grandfather died on the Origin Planet," he says.

"He did."

He shakes his head slowly.

"I don't think so."

"What?"

He bites his lip.

"Rondo, what?" I demand.

"According to the passenger list, he was onboard when the *Vagantur* crashed. But then he disappeared."

CHAPTER 12

"Octavia? Octavia?"

Rondo's mouth is moving, but his voice seems to be coming through a thick cloud. For as long as I can remember—since I was old enough to speak—my parents have told me that my grandfather died on a planet far away. That he never saw Faloiv. What Rondo is telling me contradicts everything I've known my entire life.

"I think we should sit her down," Alma whispers, like I'm not right in front of her listening. But I can't find the way to make my mouth reply.

"Octavia?" Rondo says. He gives my shoulder a gentle shake.

I look at him. The only thing I can think to say is, "So my parents have been lying about that too."

He blinks, raises an eyebrow. He wants to tell me yes, but

is afraid to actually say it. He thinks I'm breakable right now, fragile. I almost smile. I wrap my fingers around this new secret and hold it tightly.

"We're going to find out more," I say.

They're both looking at me uncertainly and a vague current of annoyance floods through me. What did they expect? That I'd cry? Break down? An echo of a whitecoat's voice whispers, *For what purpose?*

"You said you've looked in every database for mention of the missing hundred?"

Rondo nods. He's swallowing his uncertainty, the excitement gradually returning to his face.

"Right," he says. "There's nothing."

"What about personal files? Can you get access to those?"

He raises one eyebrow.

"So much for being worried about me getting caught, huh?"

"You won't get caught," I say. "Just cover your tracks or whatever it is you do."

Then I remember something else.

"Didn't you say that you saw someone else in the files last time you were poking around?"

"Yep. Their footprints are all over the databases. Still don't know who it is though."

"But that means somebody else knows about the missing hundred."

"I'm certain."

"I bet a lot of people know, actually," Alma says. Her worry has softened and she's back into problem-solving mode. I'm glad I brought her with me. "Think about it. Our people all boarded the *Vagantur* together to come here. They'd notice if a hundred of their friends and family disappeared. A lot of the old folks who are still alive probably know something from the landing. Some of the people who were older kids when we landed probably remember too."

"Like my parents," I can't resist saying. "Pretty sure my mother would remember her father disappearing when we crash-landed on a new planet."

They both look at me helplessly. I know how I must sound: emotional. Angry. But I have a right to my anger for the moment. So many secrets, some with roots that stretch back for decades. If they'd keep my grandfather's disappearance a secret from me—what else would they hide?

"We're going to find out more," I repeat. "I wish we could get into the Zoo *now*."

"And do what?" Alma says. "We've only had access to the sorting room, and we know there's nothing to see there but eggs. Even if one or two of them are . . . different."

"I don't know." I groan. "Something. Who's someone we could talk to that might get us some answers?"

"You mean a whitecoat? No one," Alma says. "We're not even actual scientists yet, O. None of them is going to give us any time until well after we've taken the oath and started working on projects of our own."

"What about Dr. Espada? We could ask him, right?"

She looks doubtful. I can't tell if she's thinking of our argument about me asking too many questions or if she's just being logical.

"If anyone would answer our questions, it would be him," I insist. "We could slip it into conversation like it's something we heard in the Zoo."

"Maybe, but I don't know when we'll see him again."

Dr. Espada is the one I need to talk to; I think back to our last day at the Greenhouse, the day he assigned us to our internships. He seemed almost sad when I sat at his desk, so intense . . .

Suddenly, I'm listening. My mind feels sharp and open: a feeling of utter clarity. I smell ogwe trees, though I'm not near enough to one for this to make sense. My ears ring and I notice a quiet buzz swirling in my head. Now that I've noticed it, it seems to grow louder. Has it been there all along, or did it just appear? Something tugs at the back of my brain, a prickling inside my skull.

And then I'm running. Alma and Rondo call my name, but I can't answer. The tugging feeling pulls me along and I'm not even sure where I'm going until I find that my feet are carrying me back home, gliding down the dirt path as if I'm flying, barely feeling my feet hit the soil. I reach our 'wam's door, hurriedly swiping my palm across the pad and darting through as soon as it opens.

I rush through the empty kitchen, down the dim hallway, and throw open my folding bedroom door. I scramble onto my bed, pawing at the mattress, fumbling to pull up the corner. I know before I even see that the hole is empty, but my eyes confirm it: the egg is gone.

CHAPTER 13

In the morning, Alma and I are preparing for the oath ceremony. We have no idea how much of a ceremony it will actually be, but we washed our skinsuits last night, just in case this ends up being something of an event.

In addition to washing my clothing, I searched my parents' bedroom and study for the egg. Alma kept watch at the front door and I went in each room and looked in every wall compartment, under the mattress, in boxes, and between slides. Nothing. No sign that my parents—or anyone—had been home during the brief length of time Alma and I had gone to meet Rondo at the bridge. Someone must have been watching the 'wam, I decided, to know when it would be empty so they could go in and get it. But how had they known I'd had the egg at all?

At first I was furious, but the anger shrank into a knot of fear. Someone had been in my room. Maybe one of my parents, but maybe someone else. Who? And does that mean they know I've seen the spotted man?

The front door slides open and I exit the 'wam, Alma on my heels. I almost jump when Rondo appears in front of us, having just come around the corner on the path, but part of me expected him to be there. I messaged him last night, telling him what had happened, and all he said was: *I'm going to dig. See you tomorrow.*

"Hey," I say. The sight of him is like a trickle of cool air against my skin in the rising heat.

"Hey."

"So?"

He shakes his head. "Nothing. Nothing about the missing hundred and nothing about the egg either. I didn't really expect to see anything about the latter, but still. Plus Jaquot kept asking me what I was working on and it was hard to focus. I left while he was washing up. Hope that wasn't rude."

"Damn," I say. "Did you start looking at personal files?"

He waits to respond until a small group of whitecoats passes us on the path. They ignore us entirely, making their way up toward the main dome.

"Yes," Rondo says when the whitecoats have gone. "But I didn't see anything unusual. Even your parents' files look normal."

"You were in my parents' files?" I say, raising my eyebrows.

"Yes. Alma's parents too."

"Hey!" she says.

He shrugs.

"I had to start somewhere," he says as we approach the stairs. "That's what I'm doing. But I can't find anything. Your grandfather's name appears in only one place, Octavia, and that's on the records from the *Vagantur*. After the ship lands, he just . . . vanishes."

"So weird," I say. I wonder if my grandfather died in the landing after all. Maybe they neglected to put his name on some forgotten list of casualties.

"But, some good news. Kind of," he says. "That thing your father mentioned? The Solossius? I found a reference to it in your dad's files."

"Really?"

"Don't get too excited," he says. "There wasn't much. But I saw it mentioned as a relatively new project he's working on with three other members of the Council. Including Dr. Albatur."

"Solossius?" Alma says, batting at a few small vines that have grown out across the path. "That sounds like one of the dead languages."

"You and your dead languages," I can't help but tease. "What does it mean?"

"I'm not entirely sure. But *sol* is sun, obviously, and *ossius* means bones, I think. Or having to do with bones. So . . . sun bone? Sun skeleton? I don't know."

"Hmm. Well, we know Dr. Albatur has issues with the sun. But he never said anything about his bones."

We don't say anything else as we finish the climb to the main dome, all lost in thought.

Inside, Jaquot and Yaya are already waiting outside the lab door, a small distance away from the guards. Jaquot is still yawning and merely nods when we approach. Yaya tips her head in greeting. I don't quite manage a smile, but for some reason her levelheadedness eases my mind. Nothing seems to ruffle her—I should try to be more like that.

"Good morning," she says. "Ready?"

"Definitely," Alma says, grinning. She's relieved to be around someone who shares her enthusiasm for the Zoo. But nothing is like it was for me. The Zoo holds animals—the beautiful, exciting creatures I've longed to study more closely my entire life—but somewhere in the winding bright hallways is the spotted man too: a hidden prisoner. Is that what our oath is designed to protect? Another question Alma would wish I didn't have.

I snap out of my thoughts when Rondo nudges me and nods at the approaching figure of my mother.

She waves, smiling her warm smile that has always made people comfortable, but all I see is the mask of it. Looking at her and knowing that she and my father both lied to me about my grandfather . . . I can't trust her face, or her.

"Hello, everyone," she says. "I'm glad you're all here early. No doubt you're expecting to take your oath today?"

She looks around at us expectantly and we all nod, even me.

"Good. You would be correct. Today you will be taking your oath and moving on to a new area of study."

"Thank the stars," Jaquot says.

My mother chuckles, moving toward the lab doors and pressing her thumb against the entry pad.

"I suppose we know what your focus of study won't be?" She smiles. "In general, sorting does belong to a team of specialists. We gave them a break while you went through training."

We step through the doors, past the guards. At one point I was shocked at the sight of the buzzguns they now carry—when did I stop noticing them?

"So . . . what are we going to do next, Dr. English?" Yaya ventures once we're in the Zoo.

My mother looks over her shoulder, pursing her lips and raising her eyebrows.

"You'll see," she says.

We all exchange looks. I was right. The only thing standing between us and real specimens is the oath. But I have more than one purpose now, I remind myself. I want to find out who the spotted man is, where the egg went, and the truth about my grandfather.

We approach the sorting room at the end of the hall, but

instead of proceeding through its doors as we have for the past four days, we turn left, toward where I saw the tufali earlier in the week. At the thought of the tusked creature, its smell comes back to mind. So vividly, in fact, that it's almost as if it's passing by in its cage again.

My mother stops at a door with no window, leading us beyond it into a medium-size room lined with washbasins, rows of hooks where white coats hang crisp and clean. She waits for us all to file in before closing the door behind us. Ahead there is another door, this one a slider like the entrance to the lab. She stands between it and us, her arms behind her back, regarding us seriously. All of her previous mischievousness is gone.

"The oath you are about to take is one that every scientist and researcher in our compounds has taken since we landed on Faloiv. Taking this oath means that you are committed to contributing to our philosophy of discovery and research. Does everyone understand?"

No one responds, and in the silence I realize how insignificant this all seems. We had expected a ceremony, witnesses— maybe even a blood drawing. But instead here we are in this small, clean scrub room, with no one but my mother. I'm both relieved and disappointed.

"You do not have to take the oath," my mother continues. "If you do choose not to take it, then you will be removed from the internship and you will find another role in N'Terra."

There's a long pause and I hold my breath, glancing at Rondo and half wondering if he will ask to be removed. I know full well his interests aren't within these walls—science doesn't move him. Just music, I think. He's played for me only once, but even if he never played for me again, I'd remember the sound forever. He must be thinking something similar because suddenly his brown eyes are on me, sparkling, and I hear nothing else my mother says as she resumes talking—just an imaginary melody from his izinusa.

"We'll start at this end," my mother says, and I'm jerked out of the world of Rondo's eyes. She moves to her right, where Yaya stands looking almost feverish. "Repeat after me."

"Yes, ma'am," Yaya says, her usually firm voice softer than usual.

"As a whitecoat on Faloiv, I swear to uphold the values of N'Terra."

"'As a whitecoat on Faloiv, I swear'"—Yaya swallows half-way through—"'to uphold the values of N'Terra.'"

"And to seek, in my work, a better future for our people."

Yaya repeats the words.

"I will not share this work with anyone beyond our community, nor will I falter in my pursuit of discoveries that will aid us. I promise to consider the good of humans above all else, so help me stars."

Yaya repeats it word for word, and when she's finished my mother smiles, murmurs "Well done," and moves on to Jaquot.

Jaquot stumbles on some of the words, but makes it through without much difficulty. Rondo repeats the lines mechanically, once or twice not even waiting for my mother to finish her sentence. By the time she gets to Alma, my best friend has almost memorized the words and they flow out of her without pause. She beams at the end, and my mother smiles and nods before finally turning to me.

"Last but not least," she says, looking me in the eye.

I want to look away, but she holds my gaze as she says the lines of the oath to me.

"As a whitecoat on Faloiv," she says, "I swear to uphold the values of N'Terra."

"'As a whitecoat on Faloiv, I swear to uphold the values of N'Terra.'"

She moves through the rest slowly. Had she been speaking this slowly for the others? Maybe time has just blurred into a sluggish version of itself. The Council pin on her lapel, the small shape of the *Vagantur*, reflects a stab of gold into my eyes. My mind feels fuzzy, but I can hear myself saying the words back to her, so I must be doing okay. She arrives at the last line.

"I promise to consider the good of humans above all else," her lips say, but through the fog in my brain I hear her add four more words: *and do no harm.*

Her lips had not moved, but the shape of the words hangs squarely in the thick of my mind: *and do no harm.* I didn't actually hear them, I realize. There's no sound to the words:

they just are. I hesitate. What do I say? Do I repeat everything, the whole line including the last part that is sitting in front of my eyes, invisible but shimmering there as if written in a spider's web? Am I going crazy?

"'I promise to consider the good of humans above all else,'" I say, and open my mouth to continue. But I stop. I swallow the words—no one else had said them. "So help me stars."

My mother nods. "Well done," she says, her eyes still locked on mine. "Well done, everyone. You are now sworn into the scientific community of N'Terra. Congratulations."

We all shuffle our feet and look bashfully at one another, me rubbing my temples to clear my head. My mother is telling us that we're about to scrub in for the containment room, but I barely hear her. The artificial lights seem painfully bright.

Alma and the others are already washing their hands in the basins that line the room. The sound of the water fills my ears.

"Octavia," my mother says, touching my shoulder gently.

"I know," I say, even if I don't really. I go to the washbasin by Yaya and use the two different solutions to cleanse my skin up to the elbow. I dry my hands and take one of the white coats from the hook, sliding it on over my skinsuit.

"Good," my mother says, nodding at us. "I'm pleased to see everyone was prepared with the protocol for scrubbing in. These animals aren't accustomed to our germs and, though they've gradually built a tolerance for them, we don't want to make it more difficult for their immune systems. You may notice that your hands feel a little strange when you rub them together."

We all rub our hands together on cue. My skin feels bizarrely smooth, and somehow more sensitive. Waxy.

"The second solution you washed with has left a bacteria-resistant film over your skin, to prevent any oils or microbes from affecting the environment in the containment room. It will last for two hours and then be absorbed safely by your skin. Does everyone understand?"

We all nod.

"Good. In we go."

She turns her back on us and slides her palm across the pad outside the door. It opens with a sigh and we follow her through. I'm the last one to enter and the door closes swiftly behind me.

The heat hits me immediately—no cooling system in this room. The heat of Faloiv is in full effect, real sunlight streaming down through the transparent ceiling. The sun and the heat surround me and I breathe in deeply, feeling my lungs expand with the thick, damp air. But I'm the only one paying attention to the air. My peers are all ahead of me, looking around in wonder, their low exclamations punctuating the stillness in the room. I look too, and I see the animals.

CHAPTER 14

The first thing I notice is how beautiful they are. Colors and patterns that defy the digital depictions we've been raised on in the Greenhouse. There's the tufali—more than one actually—and their pastel blue coats, the silver undercoat. Their tusks are iridescent, pearly. There's the gwabi, with its glistening coat of sable, the creamy markings that cover its body irregular but uniform across all three specimens. The hortov—deeply, richly green; a foliage dweller, the scattering of shimmering dots across its belly adapted to look like moisture hanging from branches. But I only glance at each of them quickly, where they all lie still in their white-clay cages, to see that they all actually exist as real creatures outside of the classroom projections. The room that contains them is long, several times as big as the sorting room or even the Greenhouse, their clay enclosures varying in size.

The second thing I notice is the noise. I keep my eyes on the ground, feeling suddenly guilty that these beautiful creatures are caged because of us, calling to get out. The din grows and grows: a buzzing of raucous sound, patterns of noise overlapping, interrupting, blending. It doesn't sound like any particular animal's call: it all flows together, almost like words. I can't isolate any single noise. My mother leads us down the middle of the room, and I almost put my hands over my ears to blunt the clamor when I notice the third thing: my father.

He's talking to another whitecoat, comparing the screens of their slates. They don't appear to be raising their voices above the noise and I wonder how they can hear each other. I don't look back at the animals, as much as I want to. Instead, I focus on my father. When he sees me, I want him to see my calm, my restraint. Scientist demeanor, I think. I've taken the oath and I'm here, unmoved.

He finally turns to look at our group, acknowledging my mother first. His face is the way it always looks: smooth, placid. There must be a sleep ward somewhere in the labs. He hasn't been sleeping at home, but he looks rested.

"Good morning," he says. "I'm glad to see you all here. If you're in this room, you have taken the oath and entered the scientific community. This is the containment room. These specimens are animals that have yet to undergo any research or experimentation. We keep them in a separate holding area from those already involved in a project in order to prevent them from influencing one another."

"Do you mean infecting each other?" Yaya asks. "The experiments are contagious?"

"No, no, nothing like that," my father says. "We have not been working with illnesses. I mean *influence*. Thanks to Dr. English"—he nods at my mother—"we now know that animals on Faloiv are able to communicate in ways we don't fully understand, and eventually we realized that communication was affecting the outcomes of experiments, so we've learned to separate them."

"So . . . they were talking to each other about the experiments?" Alma says.

"Yes," my father says without a smile.

Alma's eyebrows knit together for an instant. Her face eventually relaxes, but a small furrow remains between her eyes. She has more questions, but my father—as usual—isn't receptive. And my mother, I realize suddenly, is gone.

"Any other questions?" He stares at me even though he's addressing the group.

I give a small shrug, trying to ignore my growing headache. "When do we start?" I say.

He smirks. I can't tell if it means he's pleased or displeased.

"Not today," he says, and he enjoys the look of disappointment that appears on Alma's, Jaquot's, and Yaya's faces.

Rondo, I know, is indifferent. So am I, or at least my face is. Although the noise of this room is making me consider a career in shopkeeping in the relative quiet of the commune or the archives like Aiyana.

"You are off sorting duty," my father continues, "but you won't begin observing lab work until next week. First you must spend some time in collection."

"Collection?" Yaya says, raising one eyebrow. I, too, imagine something distasteful: cleaning droppings from the animals' cages or collecting urine for analysis. I brace myself for my father's answer. But it's Rondo's voice I hear.

"Specimen collection," he says. "With the finders. We're going into the jungle?"

My father opens his mouth to reply, but a door at the far end of the containment room slams open and a whitecoat bursts through it.

"Dr. English!" he cries. "We need you with Tufali 8 immediately!"

"What's happened?" my father says, taking a step toward the whitecoat, hesitant to leave us.

"The specimen was sedated and Dr. Sligo attempted to run a test. The specimen woke up and it's out of control. We're having . . . difficulty containing it."

From the look on the whitecoat's face, it sounds like more than "difficulty." He looks almost on the verge of tears. I wonder if my father will call *him* emotional.

"Wait here," my father says to us. They disappear through the door.

No one says anything for a moment. We all stare at one another. Alma looks embarrassed as she opens her mouth to speak. "Should we . . . ?"

"Yes," Yaya says without waiting for her to finish, and they take off running across the containment room for the door at the end. Their feet echo slightly, even with the noise of the animals. Jaquot is on their tails. Rondo stands to my left looking slightly crestfallen.

"Well, I guess we go too," he says.

"Yep."

We run after them, and I find myself running faster than I need to, eager to escape the crushing din of this room. They're afraid, the animals. I can tell. The feeling isn't strong, but it's real. Their fear is all around me; I can almost smell it, thick and pungent.

Outside, Alma and the others are already creeping down the hall by the time Rondo and I come out.

"I can hear them from all the way out here," I say softly. "I don't know how the whitecoats concentrate with all that noise."

Rondo looks at me strangely. Ahead, Alma is creeping up to a research room that appears to be open.

"You can hear who?" Rondo asks.

"The animals."

He looks confused.

"But . . ."

"Octavia!" Alma hisses.

We trot down the hallway, trying to be silent. It seems dimmer here than in the entrance hall, but I can't tell if it actually is or if the dimness is just a result of my headache. The pain throbs like a siren, but I focus on Alma, Yaya, and Jaquot, who are peeking in at the edges of the doorway. The whitecoat who came to fetch my father is standing squarely in the entrance, his back to us. I move to Alma's right to peer into the research room.

There's blood everywhere, coating the floor behind an exam platform in a thick puddle. Behind the platform is another whitecoat, her coat stained deeply red all along one side. She breathes shallowly, motionless, staring at my father, who dominates the center of the room, a tranq gun held in both hands, aimed at the woman in the bloody coat. At first I don't understand: why is he aiming a gun at her? But then I look again.

A tusk protrudes from the front of the woman's thigh, a coat of blood tinting its bluish point with red. The tufali is behind the whitecoat, unmoving as if frozen. Its tusks are easily a foot long, the one that has impaled the whitecoat's thigh the longest.

For a moment my brain can only process the color of the blood—bright and wild like the philax's feathers that day in the Beak. My legs tremble, but my muscles are confused about what direction they want to go—part of me wants to run forward to help, and the rest of me wants to flee the scene before me. Rondo's hand shoots out to steady me, but his fingers are shaking so much he almost misses. We stare at the animal, only its tusk and feet visible.

She, I think, not *it*. The blood doesn't affect me now: I'm distracted by a smell. And I gradually realize it's the same tufali I saw that day in the hall with my mother. I don't know how I know: something about her scent—the same unique combination of odors. I wonder if she recognizes me too.

"Be careful, Dr. English," the whitecoat in the doorway murmurs. With his back to us, all I can see of him is his neck, shining with sweat.

My father takes a tiny step to his left. He's looking for an angle to shoot the tranq gun, but the tufali has positioned herself directly behind the whitecoat, as if to use the woman as a shield. The woman's leg looks bad, blood seeping from the wound like lava from a volcano, even with the tusk somewhat plugging it. Every time my father moves, looking for a shot, the tufali has to move too. The shuffling, I'm sure, causes the woman excruciating pain.

The words come to my mind without bidding. I don't know why they're there, but here they are, floating from the silent oath to the front of my mind. I don't say them out loud, but hold them in front of me like an object.

Do no harm.

Things happen very quickly.

The tufali rips her tusk out of the whitecoat's leg in one smooth motion, and the woman cries out as she tumbles to the floor. With her out of the way, we in the doorway have a clear view of the tufali's face: her long, wide head, her flaring snout, the orderly rows of tusks, one of the front spines shining with human blood. But it's her eyes that I see above all: gleaming black, impossibly deep, drilling into my core.

Look away.

I hear the command, not in actual words but in some mental impression of them. I feel it, and I obey, whipping my head away and back, squeezing my eyes shut and turning back into the hall. Behind me goes the zip-zip of the tranq gun releasing two darts, the dull thuds of them finding the tufali's body. She doesn't make a sound, but I hear something anyway: a rippling cry tearing through my brain. I am dizzy. I will not pass out, I will not pass out, I command. I will not. I open my eyes, willing myself to remain upright. I focus on the shining floor. More blood, spots of it bright and red at my feet. At first I don't understand. Had it leaked into the hall from the room? I look around, perplexed. It's not until Rondo is in front of me, his face serious and almost sad, extending the corner of his white coat to my face, that I realize the blood is coming from my nose.

CHAPTER 15

We make it back to the containment room before my father, the five of us scurrying back down the hall, me holding Rondo's coat to my face. Once inside, the buzz that's been simmering in my brain heightens again. With my father out of the room, I don't feel the need to hide how much it bothers me. I put my hands over my ears, the blood from my nose already mostly dried, trying to drown out the racket. It doesn't help.

"Octavia, what happened to your face?" Jaquot says. The others hadn't noticed the blood until we returned to the containment room, and now they crowd around me, concerned.

"I don't know," I say. I can still see the tufali's eyes, like spots in my mind after staring at the sun. The sense of something nameless and whispering remains. There aren't words for these things, and I'm helpless as my friends stare at me, waiting for answers. If only it weren't so *loud* in this room! The dozens of caged animals surround and squeeze in on me: it's almost as if their fear has a distinct language.

"I just wish they'd be quiet," I say, swinging my head to look at the cages. "I don't know how you guys can stand it!"

I finally glare at the animals, the first long look since we were brought into the containment room. I'm suddenly angry at them, for their fear, their clamoring. But my anger fades almost as soon as it rises. I see their faces: another tufali, a cage of three kunike, several marov, a long striped animal I can't identify, its ears huge and pointy. They're beautiful, but they're also asleep—all of them.

"They're . . . they're . . ."

"Tranquilized," Alma says. "Your mom said they keep them asleep in the containment to keep them from being too agitated."

"But who—where is all that noise coming from?" I cry, looking back at Alma. Yaya and Jaquot look on with furrowed brows, Yaya's mouth half open as if to diagnose me.

"Octavia, I don't hear anything. What is going on?"

"How can you—" I start, but at the end of the room the door has slid open and my father has reentered the containment room, conversing with a whitecoat in low tones. Rondo takes this opportunity to reach out his hand and wipe what must have been the last of my blood from my top lip. He takes the corner of his coat and stuffs it into his other pocket, to hide the blood on it. I wonder if my father knows we followed him down the hall.

My father rejoins us, the whitecoat he was talking with exiting the way he came. My father looks unflustered, giving no indication that he had to tranquilize a tufali after it maimed a woman only three rooms away.

"Now," he says, folding his hands in front of him and eyeing us. "Where were we?"

"Collection," Rondo says quickly before anyone can say anything else.

"Of course. Yes, collection, like sorting, is one thing most whitecoats do not do on a regular basis: that is the role of finders. However, every intern who eventually becomes a whitecoat in this compound must experience that part of the research process at least once. Where we find our specimens in the wild is as important as learning about them in captivity. A firsthand experience with this planet—however limited—outside the compound is beneficial as well."

"Will we spend an entire week doing collection?" Yaya asks. She looks uncharacteristically uneasy, as do the others. They were eager to get into the labs, I think. Going out into the jungle wasn't part of that excitement. Besides, they just witnessed a woman get mauled by an animal *inside* the lab.

My father smiles, and he looks briefly the way I remember him looking years ago, before my grandmother died. Kind. Those eyes end up on my face rather than Yaya's.

"That is unlikely," he says. "I expect you will only accompany the collection group for one or two days."

He's addressing me with this and I'm not sure why. He looks down at his slate.

"Now," he says, extending his hand toward the door we entered through originally with my mother. "I have somewhere to be. I will take you to a research room where I will ask you to complete an assignment about safety and procedure for your collection duty. Each of you must complete this before tomorrow."

"We're going *tomorrow?*" Alma says.

My father chuckles.

"Yes, but think of it this way: the sooner you complete collection, the sooner you will move on to observation."

Alma raises her eyebrow and nods. I can sense her brain cranking, her potential excitement about seeing new specimens weighing against her unease about going out into the jungle.

Back in the scrub room, Jaquot extends his hand to Rondo.

"Here, give me your coat," he says. He takes the lab coat with my blood on it and stows it behind a jumble of others, shooting me a look. "Nobody will think it was one of ours back here."

"Thank you," I say, surprised. "I . . . thanks."

"No problem," he says, grinning his lopsided grin. "They see this and the next thing you know the Zoo is too dangerous for greencoats and we're out of here. I demand my fair shot at getting mauled by a tufali!"

The rest of the group laughs, but I can't bring myself to even smile. Jaquot is a good guy. Obnoxious at times but good. Behind the buzz in my head, I make a note to cut him a break. Our little group might be better with him in it after all.

My father leads us down the corridor, still deeper into the labs. Out here, the noise in my brain slowly fades away, leaving an ache like an echo in my mind. I barely notice that we've reached a research room until a hand on my shoulder stops me and I look up into my father's eyes.

"Miss English, if you have a moment," he says, gesturing with his head. I shrug and follow him, not even bothering to look over my shoulder to see my group's reaction. My father and I walk two doors down to another door, which he opens with his thumb.

Inside, the air is cool, cooler even than our 'wam, and the light is dim; the room feels small and close. When we step fully inside, a sensor picks up our presence and the room brightens. My sluggishness fades as I look around with interest.

We're in his office. The room has been made smaller with shelves, all of them filled with various objects. Models, charts, statues. My gaze falls on a three-dimensional model of what looks like several overlapping galaxies: orbs of varying colors, some of them glowing.

"Have you seen any of these?" I say, studying it. "In person, I mean."

"One of them," my father says, not adding anything else.

Something else catches my eye: a skull, large and yellow-white, with an angled head and long fangs still curving from its open mouth.

"What was that?" I say, nodding at the skull.

"I don't know," he says, settling into a seat behind his cluttered desk. "It's a fossil, collected by our ancestors. A predator, as you probably guessed from the teeth. An apex predator, based on its size."

I look over my shoulder at him, frowning.

"Apex predator. Like the dirixi?"

I know very little about the dirixi, as no whitecoat has images of it to show us. But it is the only predator on Faloiv that has no predators of its own. Everything else on this planet is either herbivorous with no predators at all, or, if carnivorous or omnivorous, has predators that prey on it as well. The dirixi, from my limited knowledge, is a perfect killing machine. It was the subject of every cautionary tale whitecoats used to discourage us from wandering away from the Greenhouse as kids, but its terror isn't something you grow out of. We know how big a maigno is—they wander past the Greenhouse in herds sometimes. Anything that can kill *that*, alone and without the help of a pack, is nothing short of a nightmare.

"Yes," my father says. "Certainly not as dangerous. The dirixi's ability to smell blood from great distances makes it, well, a very sophisticated killer."

I take this in, still looking at the skull, then gaze around his office, its shelves lined with various stones and glass-encased plants. Other cases display objects I have no name for: something that looks like a buzzgun but smaller and shinier. A model of what looks to be some kind of vehicle, squat and green with a long rigid arm extending from its front. There is a single photograph and its scope dizzies me: a jungle of shining metal, the ground and a lake tiny and distant at the feet of the structures. I want to ask my father something, but I know he doesn't respond well to these kinds of questions. But I'm here, I think, and who knows when I might be again.

"Why do you have all this stuff?" I ask, resting my fingertips on one of the glass cubes.

"As a reminder," he says.

"Of what?"

"Of my parents, for one. My father helped build the structures you see in that image. He designed them." He pauses, his eyes on the photograph, staring through a mist visible only to him. "You know, I barely remember his face. But I remember those skyscrapers. I remember that city. He dreamed those buildings, and then made them real."

"What about your mother?" I ask, returning my gaze to the photograph on his shelf. The gray of his eyes has gone silver with ghosts.

"An astrophysicist. She died on the Origin Planet as well, one of the scientists who mapped the route to Faloiv. She . . ."

He stops, and I note a pang of guilty relief in my stomach. The past has crept from the stars through the cracks around my father's door and swirls around us. I stare at the metal jungle, thinking about my mother's father and where his death lands in my father's memories. I think of Draco, the driver of the Worm, and his complaints about Faloiv, his longing for dead memories. Dr. Albatur's desires to control this planet, bend it to his will. The concepts of freedom and control and death and life feel blurry.

"They deserved to survive," he says finally, and my skin prickles, charged with the emotion crackling from his words. "But they did not. We did. And we must continue to do so."

"We are surviving," I say. I face him again and meet his eyes, where the ghosts are shrinking as he settles his gaze on me.

"Not on our terms."

I have nothing to say to that except more questions, questions I know he won't answer.

"Well, at least you're not like Dr. Albatur," I say. "You're free to walk in the sunlight."

"Yes," he says. "That may be true. But sometimes it is our weakness that drives us, and not our strength. Dr. Albatur may have to wear his red cloak for now, but it is his captivity that will drive the rest of us to the freedom we desire."

Something unpleasant twists in my gut. Is he talking about the Solossius, whatever that is?

"Anyhow," he says, leaning forward and folding his arms on

his desk, "that's not what I wanted to discuss with you. I wanted to talk about what happened in the containment room."

I freeze. Does he know about my inexplicable nosebleed? About what I heard, what I saw? Dread creeps into my blood but also a smaller feeling of relief. He knows: good. Let's get this over with.

"I know you're afraid of going out with the collection team tomorrow," he says hesitantly, looking down at his clasped hands. "Because . . . because of what happened to your nana. And I wanted to apologize to you for not telling you about the assignment in advance. I'm sure having it sprung on you so suddenly and in front of the group was . . . unpleasant."

It takes me a moment to catch on, and I stand there gaping at him. I was anticipating an admonishment and instead I'm getting an . . . apology? I can't remember the last time my father apologized for anything.

"It's f-fine," I stammer. "I'm not worried about it. It's not like we'll be alone."

He nods, relieved.

"That's correct. You will be supervised by the finders, of course, and from what I understand, Dr. Espada will be accompanying your group as well."

"Dr. Espada?" Maybe I'll get answers after all.

"Yes," he says. "He used to go on collection trips quite frequently years ago. So did your mother."

"Mom went on collection trips?" I say, surprised. I've always pictured her as a lab type—the way Alma will be—crouched over slides of animals' brain scans, taking endless notes in her slate.

"Yes, she did," he says. "After your nana died. I imagine your mother thought she might . . ."

"Find Nana's body," I say, and swallow. We have never talked about this. The subject has been an immense black pit in our family, a canyon we don't cross.

"I should return you to your group," he says, and stands slowly, looking old. It's hard to watch him, so I don't.

We walk silently down the hallway from his office. On either side, the windows looking in on research rooms are empty, as they always are. We pass one window and I keep walking until I realize he has stopped.

"This is your room," he says, nodding at it.

I look through the window, its bare table and empty chairs.

"But it's empty. Did they leave?"

He shakes his head.

"Security feature. All the rooms appear empty until they're opened." He presses his thumb and the door sweeps open, revealing the faces of my group, all eyes turned to look. I glance again at the window before I enter: it appears empty aside from an exam platform and lab equipment. An illusion of some kind.

My father catches my arm as I go to enter the room. I can't remember the last time my father and I embraced, and the gentleness of his grip is unfamiliar. I look up at his face, expecting him to speak, but he doesn't. He just holds me with his eyes and I can't describe what I see there. Sadness. Fear. But before I can ask him what's wrong, he's released me.

My father doesn't say good-bye to the group or me. The door slides shut and he's gone, leaving the five of us staring at one another. We're silent for a moment. I'm just beginning to wonder if they're going to let me get away with simply starting the assignment without being questioned when Yaya drops her slate on the platform and leans forward in her seat.

"Is there something about the animals we should know?" she says, her pretty features even more intense than usual.

"What do you mean?" I say.

"Your nosebleed," she says, her large eyes darting down to my nose. I know there can't be any lingering blood—my father would have noticed—but I swipe at my top lip anyway. "Do the animals make you sick? Is that why your dad took you away just now?"

"Sick?" I say. I open my mouth to tell her she sounds ridiculous, but I realize she doesn't. Is this the weakness my parents see in me? *Is* there something about the animals that makes me sick? I think of my headaches, the nosebleed, fainting . . . I feel suddenly as if I could faint again, right here. But these are things Yaya need not know. "No, there's nothing you need to know. I'm fine."

I glance at Jaquot, searching for a hint that he may have told her about the Beak, but his face is purposefully blank—he's kept my secret. I wonder for how long.

"Are you sure?" she says. Her hands rest on either side of her slate, long elegant fingers, her beautiful dark skin in sharp contrast to the bright white clay of the platform. Looking at her hands, I almost decide to tell her. Almost. The idea of sharing my secrets with another person—especially a logical person like Yaya—seems almost like a good one: Alma and Rondo already know about my weird experiences with animals, the missing hundred N'Terrans, the spotted man, the egg . . . sharing the burden with them has helped, and maybe sharing it with two more people will help even more. But they can't know everything.

"It's not the animals that are bothering me," I say, choosing my words carefully. "It's . . . something else."

"Tell me," she says, leaning forward. Her suspicion is gone, replaced with curiosity. Her long fingers have curled into almost fists.

"It's the whitecoats," I say, hoping I don't regret this. "The elders aren't telling us something."

"Such as?" Yaya says.

Rondo's face is expressionless, ready to go along with whatever lie he thinks I'm about to tell. But I have no intention of lying, I realize. I may not tell her everything, but if I want to know the truth about some things, it doesn't hurt to have someone like Yaya sniffing around.

"We came across some encrypted files. There are one hundred people from the *Vagantur* missing from N'Terra," I say, watching her face go from concern to bewilderment. "And I think the whitecoats are covering it up."

"It's actually one hundred and two," Yaya says, leaning back in her chair and sighing. "And they're not missing. They're dead."

CHAPTER 16

"What did you say?" Rondo asks, before I have a chance to form words. "Dead? What are you talking about? There's no record of any mass casualty to the *Vagantur* passengers."

Yaya glances over my shoulder at the door, ensuring that it's not sliding open to reveal an eavesdropping whitecoat.

"I don't know about any records," Yaya says. "But of course they're not going to keep a record of what they don't want people to know."

"Well, exactly," I say, confused by her lack of confusion. "They're keeping it a secret. Why would they pretend that my grandfather died on the Origin Planet when he actually died on Faloiv?"

"Oh, your grandfather was one of them?" she says, looking sorry but sounding like a robot. "That's too bad. I'm sorry, but at least you know he didn't just disappear."

He *did* just disappear: he's not on a casualty list. I look at Jaquot, my mouth hanging open, to see if he's anywhere as unbothered as Yaya. But he's lost too: his eyes dart from me to Yaya, searching for a side to take. I know if it comes down to it, he'll take hers.

"What are you talking about?" Alma demands. Our slates lie forgotten on the platform.

"Well, it's obvious, isn't it?" Yaya shrugs, her eyes wide. "The Faloii killed them all."

I gawk at her, my mouth still open, trying to make sense of what she's saying.

"How—how do you know?" I manage to get out.

"Well, I didn't lose any grandparents. But my grandmother always told me about her old friend from the *Vagantur*, Dr. LaQuinta Farrow, who never made it to N'Terra. I remember hearing that name all the time growing up: Dr. LaQuinta Farrow. Dr. LaQuinta Farrow. And, well, my grandmother died last year—she was very old; don't feel bad—and in the last few months she talked a lot about things none of us really understood. And she started talking about Dr. LaQuinta Farrow again, and how it was so sad that she never got to see N'Terra, all because of the Faloii. She called them murderers."

It's an interesting theory, but I don't like it.

"How did you know about the missing one hundred? Or—whatever—the missing one hundred and two?" Rondo's fingers are tapping a soundless rhythm on his thigh.

"My grandmother. She always said 'One hundred and one, gone. Plus LaQuinta.' She'd say it all the time. My mom always shushed her, like it was confidential and she shouldn't be saying it."

"Did your mother know? About the missing?" Alma asks.

Yaya shrugs. "She said she doesn't remember a LaQuinta Farrow. She was too young to know anything about the elders on the *Vagantur*. But I believe my grandmother."

"So wait," I say. "Your only evidence is stuff your grandmother said on her deathbed?"

"Octavia," Alma says in a hushed voice, sounding like my mother.

Yaya looks indignant and jerks her neck. "No," she says. "Your encrypted files are evidence too."

"Evidence that one hundred people are missing," I say, resisting the urge to jerk my neck as well. "Not that one hundred people were murdered by the Faloii."

"It only makes sense," Yaya argues, sitting forward in her chair again. "Where else would they have gone? Boarded another starship and flew away? Impossible."

I bite my lip. This is different from the time I sought to disprove Yaya's theory on dunikai migration. When I learned the circumstances of my grandfather's death were a lie, some part of me believed that meant he might still be alive. Something inside me wilts.

"I don't want to be cruel," Yaya says, her tone gentler now, some of the mechanical pitch easing. "But the likelihood that the Faloii killed the hundred and two is high."

"There's no record of a landing war," I say.

"There's no record of the hundred and two either," Yaya says. "If anything, their deaths have been kept a secret to keep us from waging war or something. That's why the whitecoats don't tell us much about the Faloii. They threatened us."

"A blood agreement," Jaquot says, and I grit my teeth to keep from snapping at him. I don't want to hear about blood.

"Let's just work," I say. "We have to get this finished before we go into the jungle."

No one says anything. I pick up my slate and pretend to stare at the words on its screen for what feels like ages before the others follow suit. For a while I think they're not actually reading either: the air is tight with tension. But eventually it fades as they all fall into the assignment, absorbing the regulations we'll need to know for our trip outside the compound tomorrow. I don't read, however. I stare at the words, watching them blur together. I think about my father, his office filled with things he barely remembers, his parents' bones somewhere far away. My mother tells me he'd gotten close to her mother before the *Vagantur*'s landing—his own parents hadn't made it in time. My mother told me the story only once, but it's burned in my memory as if I saw it myself: my father's father bringing him to the *Vagantur*, then going back to the chaos, searching feverishly for his wife. They never made it back. It must have been terrible to lose first his birth parents and then Nana on Faloiv too, after she had become something of a mother figure for him. No wonder my parents had partnered: after so much loss, they had to come together. I think of my father in the compound that night with the spotted man—had that been why he tranquilized him? Is this why the spotted man was in our compound? Some long-stewing conflict that had begun before I was born? Eventually the idea of the assignment feels less taxing than my own thoughts, and I begin to read, trying to put the idea of my grandfather's blood out of my mind.

Alma and I agreed to go to sleep early to prepare for the collection trip the next day, and it's close to midnight when the soft wooden clink of my slate wakes me. I was studying when I fell asleep and my fingers bump the hard edge of the device down by my hip. I sleepily pull it up to my face, squinting at the brightness of the screen.

Bridge, says the message from Rondo, and I suck my teeth at the fact that his messages get more and more abbreviated. I lie there, and consider ignoring him and going back to sleep. It's the middle of the night. But the fact that it's the middle of the night is what drives me to sit up in bed, nearly smacking my head on Alma's cot above me. I duck, listening. She breathes steadily, deeply. Asleep. Like I should be.

I swing my feet to the floor, still deciding. I'm wearing my loose nightclothes, the woven pants slithering against the tops of my feet, the white shirt glowing against my skin. If I get up, I think, I'm not getting dressed. It's too much work to pull on the tight, stretchy skinsuit, let alone my chest wrap.

The wooden sound clinks again. I groan silently and look at the slate.

Door.

There's the flutter of wings in my stomach with the realization that Rondo is outside my 'wam. Wide awake now, I stand and step softly over to the door, sliding it open an inch at a time to avoid waking Alma. I pad down the hall to the front of the 'wam, praying both my parents are either deeply asleep or deep in their work in the Zoo. The kitchen is black except for the faint white light coming through the single window, moonlight guiding my path.

The 'wam door whispers open and I hold my breath, expecting to find Rondo there waiting. But there's no one. The heat of the main dome slides inside the doorway and washes over me. I've never worn my nightclothes outside before, and without a chest wrap, the flowing cloth of my shirt and pants lets the air crawl up inside the fabric and run over my skin. I cross my arms over my chest in case Rondo is watching.

Barefoot, I step out into the commune. Silence except for the distant trickle of the stream. It feels empty here, even with the trees. I wonder what the jungle outside our walls sounds like at night. Alive, I'm sure. Full of breath.

"You're awake."

I jump, even though I'd been expecting him. Rondo materializes from the shadows, moving toward me from the direction of our bridge. He's wearing his skinsuit, I notice, with a shade of disappointment. Not only would I feel less strange for wearing my nightclothes in front of him, but I'm curious what he looks like outside his skinsuit. I've never seen his collarbones, and suddenly, here in the silver light, all I can think about is his skin, those two graceful bones beneath his throat. Behind me, the door to my 'wam whooshes shut.

"Yeah, thanks to you," I whisper. "What are you doing? What happened?"

"Why do you think something happened?"

"It's the middle of the night," I hiss.

"I was awake," he says. His voice is low, but not quite a whisper. "And I was thinking about you."

I squint at him in the moonlight. As I gaze at his face, I'm reminded strangely of a lecture Dr. Espada had given about plant patterns: the mesmerizing angles and waves in tree bark. The asymmetry of Rondo's broad nose is like that: unique, strong. Elegant. The ogwe trees and their relaxing smell . . . What is Rondo's scent?

"I wish I could read your mind," he says. He's within arm's reach, my skin awakening like the flowers that grow along the stairway, changing color at his nearness.

"No you don't," I reply.

"Why not?"

"Because my mind doesn't make sense."

"Not everything has to."

"No," I say. "But I prefer it to."

He frowns, studying me. Looking at him, it's a different kind of research. I'm examining the curve of his lips and committing them to memory. My brain holds innumerable facts, but right now I'd wipe the slate clean to make more room for his face.

"Seriously, O," he says. His voice is as soft as the dark we stand in. "You're too hard on yourself. Why?"

I squeeze my arms more tightly around myself. Whenever I'm asked a question, I know the answer. If not right away, I can figure it out. But right now, every page, every text—they're all blank.

"I don't know," I say.

"But we will."

And then he's kissing me. Or maybe I'm kissing him. The smell of ogwe rises in my nostrils, making my body go loose and relaxed. His lips are softer than I thought they'd be. His hands rise from his sides and rest on my hips. My arms around his neck—had I put them there? My palms slide down to his shoulders, down his arms. My hands find his as they move up to my waist.

I'm out of breath and pull back. He squints at me in the way only he can—one eye almost winking. I swear I can hear the music of his izinusa drifting through my head like clouds moving over the moon. I smile broadly, and when he smiles back, it's as if his teeth are the source of all the light in the world.

Then his smile disappears.

"Do you hear that?"

"What?"

He grabs my arm and drags me around the side of my 'wam. Déjà vu springs up before me: we've done this before. What is it about Rondo that always makes me end up hiding in the dark?

Someone is approaching the 'wam. I chance a peek around the edge. It's my mother. She strides down the path from the direction of the Zoo, her face obscured in shadow. I recognize her from her hair—the graceful mass of her locs piled high on her head. Her gait is resolute and she stares down at her slate, its screen glowing dimly. I jerk my head back around behind the 'wam and I hold my breath as she approaches.

Silence. I don't hear the hum of her palm sliding to open the door. The door doesn't whisper. I don't hear her footsteps either. She seems to be standing at the entrance, not moving. Rondo catches my eye, his expression unreadable in the shadows. My head begins buzzing. I wiggle a finger in my ear, still holding my breath. Rondo holds a finger to his lips.

And then the moment passes. The door slides open and my mother goes inside. Rondo and I crouch alongside my 'wam for what seems like hours but what must be only a few minutes, waiting. When eternity has passed, I stand from where I've been crouching, the muscles in my thighs cramping in protest.

"Where are you going?" he whispers.

I look at him like he's a fool.

"Inside! We almost got caught!"

He is only lips and eyes in the near dark. As he starts to open his mouth to argue, I silence him with another kiss.

"Bye," I say. "I'll see you in a few hours. Outside."

He says nothing, just watches me leave. When I slip back into my 'wam, I spend a moment leaning against the wall inside, letting my heartbeat float back to normal, swaying to the music he left inside me.

CHAPTER 17

We have new skinsuits. They're bright red, made of the same maigno-inspired material but with a couple of features we don't have in our white day-to-day clothing. For one, they are infused with the smell of a rhohedron—the large flowers that grow in the jungle, only recently cataloged by N'Terra. The color imitates the flower as well. "Better for an animal to mistake you for a rhohedron than something more vulnerable," says the finder in charge of the collection group we're joining, who has asked to be called Manx.

She goes on to reiterate the majority of what we already learned from the assignment in our slates and I tune out. Instead, I watch Rondo, whose smile of greeting this morning in the commune had planted a speck of stardust in my chest, which now grows into a sun. His fingers move in their distracted rhythm—I wonder what tune he's playing on the izinusa in his head, if he's remembering our kiss and turning it into a melody.

"Yes?" Manx says, angling the question at me with a frown.

"Yes," I say quickly. I have no idea what she asked, but she looks satisfied, turning away. Manx is my height and much older than I expected any of the finders to be. Her hair is a tangle of silver spiral curls; little lines extend from the corners of her eyes. Despite her age, though, she is agile: her body leanly muscled and her gait quick and impatient.

Now we stand outside in the shade of the compound, waiting for Manx to finish doing what she calls "checks," taking stock of all the equipment and supplies that she and her group have assembled outside the compound. We're still inside the gates, but I look out beyond them and feel a thrill in my bones. The tree line of the jungle is a mere five hundred yards away. Soon we'll see more of Faloiv than any of us ever dreamed.

Manx looks up from securing a loose water canteen to a pack. She shields her eyes from the sun and directs a smile somewhere behind us.

"Ah, there you are," she says, waving at a newcomer. "I'm glad you could join us. Red suits you."

Dr. Espada wears the same red skinsuit as the rest of us. It seems strange to see him out of his ordinary clothing—the bright red makes him look younger, more daring. His gray hair doesn't appear as scholarly alongside Manx: instead they look like two silver adventurers, ready for anything.

"Hello, everyone." Dr. Espada smiles at us after exchanging words with Manx. "It's good to see some of my brightest students again. I've been happy to hear you've all been doing well in your internships so far."

"Did someone actually say that?" Alma asks him. "Or are you being generous?"

She hasn't spoken much this morning: she's still not thrilled about going out into the jungle. I tried teasing her about it this morning but that didn't go over well. She doesn't understand my enthusiasm for this part of the internship: the idea that I'm excited to be away from the safety of the compound puzzles her. On one hand, it puzzles me too—especially given my grandmother's fate. But the trees call to me. My wonder swallows my fear.

"Don't sound so dubious, Miss Entra." Dr. Espada smiles reassuringly. "You're doing well. This is just one more arrow to add in your quiver. *Experientia docet*, yes?"

She manages to smile at that and Dr. Espada picks up one of the packs Manx has finished checking, shouldering it.

"So," I say. "My father says you and my mother used to go on collection trips all the time."

He smiles a narrow smile, keeping his eyes down on the straps of the pack, which he buckles across his chest.

"Not *all* the time," he says. "But we went on a few."

"Did you or my mom ever get lost?" I've already decided I'm going to ask as many questions as he'll allow if it means getting the kind of answers I'm looking for.

He looks at me, then, his expression serious. "No," he says. "And let's hope it stays that way."

"All right," Manx calls from the front of the group. The four finders she oversees have assembled and claimed their packs—the interns don't carry packs, just canteens—and it looks like we're ready to get started. The sun has been up for an hour and it's blazing hot. "Let's get going. You know the rules now. Stay with the group, do as I do, and never stop listening."

I breathe in deeply when we start out on the road. I haven't been outside the compound in weeks, since the day I fainted in the Beak. The air is the same here as it was twenty paces behind me, but for some reason being beyond the gates feels satisfying, like a deep gulp of cool water, but not from the canteen at my hip. *Never be without water on Faloiv*—one of the first rules my father taught me. Right now I feel like I don't need anything but the jungle.

We don't say much as we walk on the red dirt road. I clasped on my face mask after two or three steps—it's windy today and specks of swirling dust have already found their way into my mouth. Rondo followed suit—but not before shooting me a look that makes me smile—and now the others do too. There's a break in the trees up ahead on our right, the entry point for the jungle, and my stomach starts to flutter, like an insect urging me onward. Manx waves an arm and one by one we allow the trees to swallow us.

When I first step into the shade of the jungle, it's as if all my blood begins to flow more freely. I unclasp my face mask. The light is multicolored, filtered in through leaves so thick that the canopy is like a vibrant, living roof. Is this what my grandmother felt, the very first time she entered this dense, green world? I close my eyes for just a moment and feel the jungle soak into my skin. Birds trilling high in the branches, the far-off warbles of canopy mammals. A buzzing has filled my head, but it's pleasant, like a purr.

"Welcome to the jungle," Manx says. "Drink."

We all sip from our canteens and replace them at our waists. Alma appears to have relaxed a little, standing by Jaquot and gaping at the gargantuan plants growing around and above us. Some of the trees are as big around as the Greenhouse, some as thick as entire domes. Ahead, Manx appears to stand in front of a wall made of wood; but it's not a wall, it's a tree trunk. Leaves the size of my sleeping platform sprout from stems as thick as my ankle. Rondo stands near me, smiling.

"What are you grinning about?" I ask, nudging him. I didn't realize until now how tense my muscles have been inside the Paw—now my body feels like it's made of water.

"You," he says, shrugging. His eyes are as warm as the sun I feel on my skin.

"What about me?"

"You're loving this."

I nod. It's true.

"Thinking of switching careers?" he says under his breath. He reaches out a hand and runs one of his fingers down my arm. "I can't picture you huddled in a white lab after seeing you out here."

"Only if I can have musical accompaniment."

Manx shushes us, issuing instructions.

"Interns, your job is to watch. Nothing more. Do not touch anything. Do not eat anything. Do not attempt to collect anything. Watch what we do and that's all. Understood?"

Though we all nod, I can't help but feel disappointed. I want to sit down on the jungle floor and run my hands over everything in arm's reach. But I know better—we all do. So instead I fall in next to Dr. Espada, Yaya on his other side, and pepper him with questions as we make our way down a worn path in the jungle.

"What's the biggest animal you've ever seen on a collection trip?" Yaya says.

"Have you seen a gwabi out in the wild?" I add, suddenly thinking of the dream I'd had of my mother.

"I saw a maigno up close once," he says, and we gasp. "It was shortly after the landing. I was fourteen or fifteen. I'd never seen anything so big in my life."

"So you were fourteen when the *Vagantur* landed?" I say.

"Around that age, yes."

Manx signals for us all to take a drink of water and we pause to do so. When we're moving again, I jump in with another strategic question.

"Did you ever get to see the Faloii? During the settlement negotiations?"

He looks at me sharply, and I stare back, undaunted.

"No," he says. "Not up close."

"But you saw them?"

"Very briefly, and from a distance."

"What were they like?"

"Tall," he says. "Quite tall. And graceful."

"What were their ears like?" I say.

Dr. Espada pauses ever so briefly in his stride, but catches himself and continues walking, unbothered.

"Their ears? I have no idea. Why are you asking about the ears of the Faloii?"

"Just curious," I say.

"Were they dangerous?" Yaya asks.

"They were . . . intimidating," Dr. Espada says, refusing to make eye contact with either of us.

We stop and drink again. It's slow going. Manx keeps us moving, but at a leisurely pace so we don't sweat too much. I wonder how deep into the jungle we'll go. It already feels as if we're in the middle of nowhere, but I look down and note that we're still on a worn path. I envy the finders for being able to do this every day.

The next time we stop I think it's time to drink again but Rondo stills my hand with his and points. One of the male finders ahead of us is crouched just off the path with a cylindrical container clutched in his hand. Manx has raised her hand to all of us, the entire group stopped motionless in our tracks, scarcely daring to breathe. What has he found? I wonder. Maigno tracks, perhaps. Scat from a wild tufali. But when the finder carefully closes the cylinder and returns to the path, it turns out to be much less exciting: a species of worm, Manx explains as we all crowd around to peer at the cylinder. It's as thick as two of my fingers and richly black, with dangerous-looking orange spines rising off its back.

"Insects are notoriously difficult to find on Faloiv," the finder says, looking pleased with himself. "That's why the entomology group is so small and shares space with the Reptilian Compound. We're hoping to change that. I stay on the lookout for little guys like this," he says, patting the tube gently. He tucks the specimen carefully into his pack. Jaquot appears next to me, a grin on his face.

"Can you believe we're out here?" he says, scanning the trees with his eyes. "If I had known there were insects like that, I might have requested the Reptilian Compound."

"That thing was disgusting." I laugh, shaking my head.

"I know. Brilliant." I smile about that. I hear my mother in his voice: the genuine adoration of study. He glances over his shoulder at the others, a few paces away, then lowers his voice.

"I never told anyone about that day in the Beak, you know."

"I didn't think you did."

"Was your nosebleed in the lab the other day the same kind of thing?"

I stare at him, searching his face for ill intent. I don't find anything; just curiosity.

"I have no idea. But it feels like it's related. I just don't know how."

He frowns, looking back out at the trees. "Yaya is going to figure it out eventually," he says. "I know you're not crazy about her, but I think she's good for stuff like this if you're willing to trust her."

"Are you?"

"Am I what?" he says. "Willing to trust her?"

"No, crazy about her," I say. His eyes twitch over to my face and he raises his hand to cover his mouth, like if I can't see his growing smile I won't notice the way the rest of his features light up.

"You don't miss a thing," he says when he drops his hand.

"Except for whatever causes me to faint and get nosebleeds."

Behind us Manx is rallying the group to start walking again.

"You're smart, O," he says. "You'll figure it out."

"Maybe." I shake my head. "I just wanted to work with animals. Now it's like I have a curse that's keeping me from doing it."

It feels good to say this to him, as if we're trading confessions. In a way, he was my first confidant about all the recent strangeness in my life. He was there when most of it began, after all. He turns and looks at me, his expression soft.

"You never know—maybe it's a gift," he says, smiling a lopsided smile. Then he's gone, walking back toward the group—toward Yaya—leaving me on the edge of the path alone.

We continue down the trail for what seems like hours. It's hard to tell how much time has passed in jungle this dense. I enjoy the feeling of time oozing into itself, punctuated by the brief water breaks. I'm so relaxed that I almost forget I'm supposed to be questioning Dr. Espada. I'm just gearing up to find an angle into broaching the topic of the egg when there's a sharp cry from the front of the group.

I think it's a signal at first, and try to remember what that particular sound means, but then I realize that Manx, her face creased with anxiety, is crouched over one of her finders who is sprawled on the path. Her hands are working quickly, rummaging in her pack and coming out with cloth.

"What happened?" Alma asks.

No one answers. Dr. Espada breaks away from where he's been walking with us and hurries toward Manx and the finders.

"It looks like something bit him," Rondo says, craning his neck. We move toward where the finder is sprawled. The bite had pierced the fabric of the skinsuit at his calf. Manx has cut off the suit from the knee down, and the bite mark bulges ugly and purple right on the muscle. It looks like it might just be swollen at first. But then, like a tiny, abrupt volcano, the swelling bursts and blood seeps from it, leaking out and down his leg before dripping to the jungle floor.

"Stars," Manx says, looking over each of her shoulders. "Start tracking *now*."

One of the other finders immediately opens her pack and yanks out her slate.

"Tracking what?" Jaquot says.

"Hurry, hurry," the wounded finder says. He's sitting up now, and I think he's looking at the wound, but instead his eyes are scanning the jungle around us.

"What is it? Is it poisonous?" I say.

"Yes, a morgantan bite contains venom. But it's not the poison we have to worry about," Manx says quickly, her hand emerging from her pack with a tube of solution, fitting it to a syringe, and injecting it into the finder's leg. The swelling lessens almost immediately but the blood continues to flow freely. "It's the smell of the blood. *Stars*. Damn, damn, damn."

"Anything on the sensors?" Dr. Espada snaps, turning to the young finder who holds a slate close to her face, her eyes searching. Her face goes ashen and she turns her eyes up to Dr. Espada.

"Yes," she says.

"God," Dr. Espada says. "One whiffed us. We need to move. Now."

Manx has just finished tying a tight knot of fabric around the injured finder's bite, hoisting him up from the ground. He stands on the leg easily, but his face is still twisted. I thought it was pain I was seeing, but now I realize that it's terror.

Alma is clinging to my arm—I'm not even sure she's aware she's doing it. Her eyes go back and forth between Dr. Espada and Manx.

"What's happening?" she says. "Tell us something."

"We are in serious danger," Dr. Espada says. He's already moved off the path to the base of an ogwe tree. He's looking up, peering into the branches. "This will do," he calls to Manx. He drops his pack and digs inside it, withdrawing what looks like a big reel with a hook on its side. He tugs on the hook and a length of cord appears, thick and black and somewhat shiny. He pulls again; more cord. When he has a few lengths, he swings the hook around his head and then releases it, launching it up into the branches. It catches somewhere up above and he gives it a tug. All his teacherly gentleness has fallen away.

Manx is already up in the tree before I fully realize that we *all* need to be in the tree.

"What are we supposed to do?" Alma barks at a finder who has gripped her by the shoulders and is hustling her toward the tree Dr. Espada has chosen. Rondo comes toward me, reaching for my wrist but is intercepted by another finder, who drags him toward the tree.

"Climb," the finder says. "Quickly."

Alma climbs, poorly, with Rondo following close behind. At one point her shoe slips on the rope and kicks him squarely in the face; he winces and keeps climbing. Yaya is hopping around at the base of the tree, waiting for them to reach the top. And then I hear it.

A sound that shakes the trees even from what must be a mile away: a roar so deep and mighty that I feel it in the soles of my feet. It's harsh, almost a scream. Above, rustling in the trees as unseen animals clamber to the safety of higher branches.

"Oh, stars," I hear Dr. Espada gasp. "It's the dirixi."

"You can't be serious," Yaya cries as a finder shoves her toward the rope. "Can't we . . . can't we use an oxynet? Incapacitate it?"

"No oxynet that big," Manx yells from the tree. "Get up here!"

Dr. Espada scrambles for another pack, emptying it in search of a second rope. He finds nothing and turns to close the gap between us with one stride. He snatches my arms, his hands rushing up to find my face, which he holds tightly. He looks in my eyes and the buzzing that has been simmering pleasantly in the back of my mind spikes. "We're going to have to run," he says.

Reality is shooting from my brain through my body in

bursts of rising adrenaline. A dirixi. My eyes dart around over Dr. Espada's shoulders, scanning the jungle frantically for the enormous reptile. My mind needlessly draws up all the lessons from the Greenhouse, recapping the features of dirixi that make them so dangerous: incredible sense of smell, drawn to blood; teeth the length of my forearm, saw-edged to tear the flesh of thick-hided animals like maigno . . .

"Octavia," Dr. Espada barks, shaking me. "Look at me! We have to run!"

"Run? Run where?" I stutter. Yaya is barely halfway up the rope and I don't see Jaquot or the other two finders anywhere. But looking at Dr. Espada, my mind fills with the image of great red flowers, a whole meadow of them. I don't know how this image got there: I've never seen it before in person. But I know the flowers: they're the same deep red as our skinsuits. Rhohedron. Even as a daydream, I can smell the sweet scent of their nectar, emanating from the blossoms in waves like a magnetic field.

"Go!" Dr. Espada shouts in my face, and we take off running in opposite directions. The jungle blurs around me. Somewhere behind me, from the branches of the tree, Rondo calls my name. His yell is broken in half by a hand clamped over his mouth, silencing him, protecting the group.

I run. The giant leaves and tree trunks speed past me, as if I'm standing still and it's the jungle that's running. In my head, the meadow of rhohedron floats in front of me like a specter.

I can still smell them, their scent beckoning to me as I hurtle through the crowded underbrush. I hear the sound of branches breaking behind me, and, far off, Dr. Espada's voice calling and calling. His words are drowned out by another screeching roar. I glance over my shoulder: I can't see the dirixi, but I know it must be nearly on my heels. Its intensity invades my consciousness, like deep space creeping in through a starship's cracked hull. I run too near a tree and my canteen strikes it, spinning off into the lush foliage. I run faster, following the phantom smell of rhohedron toward a place ahead where the light seems to change to a thinner, paler green.

I burst out of the tree line, at first thinking I must have circled far back to the red dirt road. But the red that springs up before me isn't the road: it's rhohedron, an entire field of it, some of the blossoms as large as my entire 'wam. I gape for only a moment at the stalks towering above, but the sounds in the jungle behind me spur me onward. I leap headlong into tall grass, ducking and dodging through the enormous low-hanging flowers and frantically looking for a stalk I might be able to scale.

Climbing isn't an option without the kind of gear that Dr. Espada had in his pack. I wasn't even issued a pack. I rack my brains for anything I might have learned in class that can help me in this moment, but instinct is all I have, and instinct says *hide*.

I dive into a cluster of the red rhohedron and burrow far

into them until I find myself within the petals of one of the huge hanging blossoms, my back against the thick trunk of the parent plant. I pull my knees to my chest, squeezing my eyes shut tight and pulling my lips in, trying to breathe softly. I realize that my head is buzzing: I can almost smell my own blood, the way the dirixi must smell it. I can feel its hunger, a roiling, savage sensation like lava coursing through my veins.

And then I think of rhohedron. I allow the image of the field to fill my mind; imagine that when I breathe in and out that I am inhaling and exhaling the scent of the huge red flowers. It calms me and I feel light, as if my body is made of plant fibers and the wind is blowing against me gently. Somewhere outside myself I hear the heavy, shambling steps, the dirixi snuffling at the rhohedron; can see the shadow of its hulking, scaled body through the delicate petals of the blossoms. But I am a flower, a poisonous flower.

A wave of hot breath passes through the rhohedron, blasting against the side of my body with enough force to make me wobble. The stench is like nothing I've ever smelled, a foul mixture of rotting food and something burning. I hold my breath. My mind floods with red. I tell myself the only thing that exists is the wind against my petals.

I don't know how much time has passed. Gradually I feel like a person again and slowly become aware of my fingers and toes, my back, stiff and sore against the trunk of the rhohedron. My lips are dry. Slowly I open my eyes, letting the shadows swimming in front of me slowly take the shape of the things they are. Flower petals. Stones. Stems. And a person, standing above me and looking down curiously. A person who I think is a person like any other, until I see the pattern of spots covering their skin.

CHAPTER 18

I'm too tired to be afraid. My body's senses are dull, as if the heat has enveloped me and overheated my brain. I look up at the person staring down at me, squinting against the sunlight slicing in between petals of the rhohedron. With the light behind them, it makes it difficult to see their face. I want to stand but I can't seem to find the energy. My head buzzes ceaselessly but not sharply the way it had in the containment room. It has returned to a purr almost below my consciousness.

"Hello," I say. What else can be said?

The person doesn't respond. They shift their weight from one bare leg to another; a massive brown leg as spotted as the arms and neck. The person is more difficult to see now than a moment ago. Is it the light in my eyes? I blink and refocus, but I can't make out the legs anymore, the arms.

I realize slowly that it's not a trick of the light. The person's skin has changed from the smooth brown that made them so visible a moment before to a vibrant red. In my dazed state I think that perhaps they somehow slipped on a skinsuit like mine between the slow blinks of my eyes. But it can't be. In places on the red skin I can still make out the spots, also red but a slightly different shade. My head continues to buzz.

"Your skin changed," I say.

The person's teeth are a flash of brilliant white, and then the face with the teeth comes closer, the red body kneeling down to look at me. The person is tall: I still have to tilt my head far back to see them. But this close I can make out their features. Broad face. Unusually large eyes, wide set. No nose to speak of, just a slightly raised area at the center of the face. No ears that I can see. But the face is not unfamiliar. Cheekbones, lips, defined eye sockets.

"You're Faloii," I say, not surprised, really, but at this point in my state of mind I'm only capable of making observations. Another observation floats to the surface of my mind, its origins unclear: the Faloii person is female.

"Yes," she says.

"Do you understand me?" I ask slowly, not for her benefit but for my own. My tongue feels thick and sluggish.

"*Yes* implies this, yes?"

"Yes."

We study each other. Her lips are parted a little, showing just a glimpse of her teeth. A moment later she stands again.

"Come."

She pushes through the heavy red petals of the rhohedron and disappears out into the sun. I swallow, gather my strength, and drag myself up from the ground. My legs tingle uncomfortably. I wiggle my toes inside my shoes where they're asleep, take a deep breath, and follow the Faloii woman out through the petals.

She's already almost brown again when I join her. She stands in the sweltering sun, the vibrant red disappearing from her skin like ink sinking out of sight into deep water. I stare at her. I can't help it. From her massive legs to her large feet that resemble paws, to her long muscular arms with hands also like paws, she is like no person I've ever seen. She wears what looks like a head wrap, also brown, that hangs down over the back of her head, covering the nape of her long, sloping neck. I feel tiny next to her: my head barely reaches her chest. She's studying me too. She doesn't have eyebrows like mine; rather, a pattern of darker brown, almost black, spots spread up her throat to her face, arranging around her eyes like dotted fingerprints. They fan out onto her forehead as well; and, staring at them, I realize they're moving. At first I think it's my eyes—that I stood up too quickly, came into the sunlight too fast. But no: the spots around her eyes and on her forehead shift as she inspects me. They form a pattern that gives her face an expression of curiosity, arching slightly, one side of the pattern peaked above the other.

"What's your name?" I ask. My head buzzes—with questions or exhaustion, I can't tell.

The spots shift again, spreading a little way apart, fanning out into a pleasant pattern.

"This is a question you can answer for yourself," she says in her smooth voice. Hearing it, I have an impression of wood: polished wood, deeply brown and shining. That's what her voice evokes. But I don't understand what she means. We've never met before. How can I answer for myself when I don't know her? I open my mouth to ask, but she interrupts.

"Listen," she says in the smooth, wooden voice.

Something in my mind shifts as she says the word. I almost start to speak again, but the something is tugging at me in my head, an unseen hand pulling gently at an inner ear. Inside, my mind's eye looks toward the pulling sensation, and it's as if a tunnel opens slowly before me, widening, allowing a hazy light to seep through. And there it is: a word. A word I've never known or heard or shaped in my mouth, but I find myself speaking it slowly, lilting at the end to form a question.

"Rasimbukar?"

"Yes," she says, showing her teeth again, the spots on her forehead fanning out, wide like a bird's wings. "Good."

I can't think of what to say next. My body is heavy and tired. Out in the sun, outside the protective camp of the rhohedron's petals, I'm exposed and I remember, as if from a dream, the monster.

"The dirixi," I say.

"The beast is gone," Rasimbukar says, the spots on her forehead settling low, closer to her eyes.

"Dr. Espada. My friends . . ." I take a few steps toward the jungle but pause. I can't remember where I entered the meadow. The jungle around the field of rhohedron looks uniform in its green intensity, the trees rising on all sides like mountains. I might as well be an insect, separated from the hive and easily squashed. Somewhere in the jungle my friends are hiding in a tree. Or maybe the dirixi had found them. I have no way of knowing, and no idea how to find them. I would consider crying if I weren't so thirsty: the idea of even a single drop of water leaving my body is enough to make me hold back my tears.

"Dr. Espada is safe," Rasimbukar says. Her spots cluster close to the center of her forehead. "I am not sure about the others."

"They climbed a tree."

"It is likely that they are also safe. Dirixi travel alone. This one followed you here and then continued toward the sun, not back."

I stand apart from her, trying to decide how to take these words. She might be lying. I know nothing about her or the Faloii. I take a step backward, ready to run.

"You do not need to fear me," Rasimbukar says, the spots still low but spreading into a wider, looser pattern.

"How can I be sure? How do I know you're not going to hurt me? Kill me?" My conversation with Yaya in the exam room yesterday vibrates in my mind. Rasimbukar doesn't seem dangerous but what if . . .

"You ask more questions that you could find answers to yourself."

I stay silent this time. The tunnel in my mind that had opened when I found her name has not closed: I look at it again, find the answers floating there. Not words this time but impressions. Feelings. Her gentleness emanates from the tunnel's mouth, and I can read its colors and shadows the way I would text. I feel lost, like I'm floating in the vast space of the galaxy.

"What is happening to me?" I say softly. One tear slips from my eye and I swipe at it hastily before it leads to more.

"You are listening," Rasimbukar says. The smooth woodenness of her voice is quieter now, her spots arranged along the outside of her eyes. Their position reminds me of my mother, when she's giving me "the look."

"To what?" I whisper.

"To Faloiv."

I stare at her, trying to learn something else from her wide-set eyes. They're slanting and dark, and although I can't distinguish an iris or a pupil, there are layers and shades of black so unfathomable it's like looking into deep space. She stares back, and I find myself watching the spots on her face as well, waiting for them to move, to tell me anything about what she might be thinking or feeling. But something else is moving instead, on her head. What I thought was a head wrap is shifting, rising, straightening. I hold my breath. Is this an attack? I know, somehow, that she doesn't mean me harm, but her strangeness leaves me on guard. Any bit of moisture that remains on my tongue evaporates as the material on her head rises, separates into two, and fans out to either side.

Ears. What I thought was a head wrap is actually two large, curving ears that until now have lain flat, backward over the crown of her head, hanging down loose like braids from her neck. They are brown like her, but thin and membraneous: the late-day sun shines through them, giving them a glowing quality. She was tall before, but the large ears give her another six inches and a fearsome quality as well.

"Do you . . . do you hear something?" I ask, trying to be polite. I try not to stare at the ears, but they demand attention.

The spots on her forehead seem to vibrate, rising and spreading. She shows her teeth.

"No," Rasimbukar says. "I am hot, and my bones are harvesting energy."

"Your bones," I say, tilting my head. I can't make my brain understand what she means. Instead I focus on her ears. "Your ears . . . they keep you cool? Like the maigno?"

"Yes," she says. The spots settle into the wide pattern. It's like a smile, I decide. A gentle smile. "Although their hearing abilities have lessened some through generations. We hear in other ways. The way you are beginning to," she adds.

It's as if there are pieces of a puzzle floating around in my head, just out of my grasp. Some of them have connected to form something I'm starting to see, but I can't figure out the shape of it.

"But . . . but why?" I ask.

"That is a question for your mother."

"My mother?"

"Yes. Now"—the spots settle low over her eyes in an even line—"you need to drink."

Rasimbukar turns and disappears inside another rhohedron blossom. I almost follow her but decide that if she wanted me to, she would have said so. I stand there alone in the sun. I wonder if Dr. Espada and the finders are looking for me or if they've all given up, returned to the compound, and left me to my fate in the jungle the way they did my grandmother years ago.

Rasimbukar emerges from the red petals again, her skin a mottled pattern of brown and red as the coloring from the rhohedron fades.

"Does your skin do that with other colors too?" I ask.

"Yes," she says. "Now drink."

She holds a long, thin object above me. It's red too, with a bright yellow bulb at one end, dangling near my face. A stamen from inside the blossom.

"Are you ready?" she says.

"Sure," I shrug, my eyes half-closed.

She gently pulls off the yellow bulb of the stamen and liquid immediately flows forth. It pours first onto my face: in my state of exhaustion and dehydration I haven't quite realized that the plant she's brought to me is what I'm supposed to be drinking. But when some of it gets onto my lips, soaking pleasantly into the thirsty skin, I open my mouth. The liquid is almost as thin as water but with an underlying vegetable taste, tinged with soil. It's not pleasant, but I drink it greedily. It's different from water in more ways than texture: as I drink, it courses through my body. With every swallow, my throat seems to light up. I can almost feel it flowing into my stomach and then finding its way into my bloodstream, filling me with its red energy.

The stamen is empty and Rasimbukar casts it off into the tall grasses surrounding us.

"I feel . . ." I can't finish the sentence. I'm awake now, all my limpness gone. But I don't have a word for this. My body is aglow with liquid light.

"You are not thirsty anymore," Rasimbukar says.

"No." But I know wasn't asking. She brought out a few of the stamens, a small bouquet, and breaks a bulb off another. She drinks it easily in only a few swallows. When she finishes, the spots on her forehead spread into the wide pattern.

"You are healthy," she says, turning to toss the second stamen into the grass too. When she turns back to look at me, the wide-set starry eyes find mine and hold them in a strong gaze. "And now you will do something for me."

I'm not sure what I can do for her. The jungle of Faloiv—and whatever lies beyond—is her world. What can I do for her here?

"I can try," I answer.

Looking her in the eyes, the tunnel in my mind widens quickly, almost painfully. It makes me catch my breath. For all her gentleness, now I feel her terror and, suddenly, her anger, spiking and red. Then out of the mouth of the tunnel rises a flashing succession of images: the jungle, dark, night, Rasimbukar crouching in the underbrush alone, and a group of humans—Manx's bright white curls—dragging a prone figure through the trees. Long-limbed. Brown. Spots covering his back, arms, and neck. It's the spotted man. Disappearing down the red dirt path toward the Mammalian Compound. Rasimbukar's pain echoes through my body, reverberating in my chest. She says nothing, her bottomless eyes tell me nothing, but I feel it, and fight to break away from the images before I speak.

"Your father," I say, knowing. She has told me without words. I can't quite shake off the secondhand fear—it clings to me like smoke.

"Yes," she says.

"We took him."

"Yes. He was abducted at the start of a one-moon journey, a voyage he takes regularly to survey the planet's ecosystems. When he does not return, my people will begin to look for him. I have told no one what I have seen. Only you."

"Me? B-but," I stammer. "But . . . why?"

The spots on her forehead cluster tightly together.

"To prevent war," she says. Her wooden voice sounds rougher than before, less polished. "The Faloii will go to war with the star people if they discover what I know. If you can return him to me, violence can be avoided."

"So you're protecting us?" I ask slowly.

"No." The spots remain where they are, a hard cluster. "I am protecting our planet. A war like this one would do irreconcilable harm to much of the life here. Our planet is small. Intricately connected. Violence has grave consequences for Faloiv."

I try to understand. I can feel my brain blundering through what she's saying. It's as if my thoughts lack thumbs, handling a puzzle clumsily and without context. War. *Violence has grave consequences.* The idea sends a quake through my bones. I don't know why N'Terra—my father—has taken Rasimbukar's father prisoner, but surely it's an act of war. If the consequences are grave for the Faloii, who are indigenous to this planet, then what would they be for us? There's no power cell for the *Vagantur* to flee with. End of the line for what Rasim-bukar calls the star people. The galaxy we wandered through to come here is closed.

"So if I can return your father to you without your people finding out, then it will be okay? The Faloii won't . . . kill us?"

"Your people have broken agreements in the past," she says. "The Faloii have been angry for some time. There are amends that need to be made. But we can keep the bridge from being broken if you return my father to me and if the star people break no other understandings."

From the back of my mind comes the word "control." I think of my father, of Dr. Albatur; how, under his leadership, N'Terra has swirled with the grumblings of bitter whitecoats. What have we done?

Rasimbukar looks up at the sun. It's beginning to sink, bath-ing the tops of the trees in deep golden light. The spots on her face spread a little but don't stray far from the center of her forehead.

"I must return you to your people," she says. Her voice sounds sad, though I'm not sure if what sounds sad to me actu-ally translates as sadness for her. I try to look into the tunnel, but it's closed tightly, as if she knew I'd be looking and shut herself off. "My people will soon begin to search the jungle for my father, and it is only a matter of time until they arrive at your compounds with questions. If your people lie, the Faloii will know."

"But how will I find him? How will I get him out? How will I find *you*?"

She's reaching out for me, one long brown finger extending toward my face, her eyes wide and dark and staring.

"You will find a way," she says. "He will need the kawa, so you must help him get it. When you are ready to enter the jungle, I will know."

And then her finger meets my forehead. There's an instant of stars. In the moment before the world goes dark, I think of my grandmother once more. I can almost see her stepping out into the trees, as strange and vast as the stars themselves. In a jolt, I imagine what she must have felt: her spreading wonder as the core of this new planet rose up to greet her, a precious center where all things meet. Then a sweet, warm black filled with the smell of ogwe trees surrounds me, carrying me up into their branches.

CHAPTER 19

In the dream, the stars conspire. They mutter in silver tongues, their language a pattern of chains that snare everyone in N'Terra with metal coils. Some of them sound like my father. Some of them are voices slithering from behind glass, heavy with secrets. One of them sounds like my mother for a moment, whispering my name. In the haze, I feel her running a finger up and down my jawbone.

"Octavia. Afua," she says. Her voice is warm, her face in shadows. "You can come back now. Come back."

I open my eyes. It's not a dream. The shadow that is my mother blots out some of the soft light from above, but I still blink several times as I move into full wakefulness. I'm in my parents' bed. My mother's finger pauses in its path down my jaw.

"There you are," she whispers.

I open my mouth to speak, to tell her all the things I've
learned and ask her all the questions I need answers to. My
head buzzes, my fingertips tingling: it's almost like heat, the
skin along my palms burning faintly. I struggle to lift my hands
to look at them, but they feel too heavy. I flex my abdominal
muscles to sit up, but my mother rests a gentle hand on my
chest.

"No, no," she says. "Rest. You don't have anywhere to be.
Your hands are okay. You have your father's hands now."

"My father's hands," I repeat sleepily. Am I dreaming this?
My fingers continue to tingle.

"Yes," she says, giving my arm a squeeze. "They'll get you
where you need to go."

I can't make sense of what she's saying.

"Alma . . . Rondo," I whisper. "Dr. Espada."

"Alma and Rondo are fine. So is Dr. Espada."

"Yaya? Jaquot?"

"Yaya is fine. Rest," she says, and I do. Exhaustion swallows
me whole and I drift down its throat into sleep.

When I wake again, Alma is in the chair in the corner with
her slate in her lap, studying. Her hair is loose from braids or
head wrap, free in a fluffy Afro. Watching her, my chest swells
with gratitude that she's okay, whole, alive. I can still see her
scrambling to climb the tree with Manx and the others, and all
the fear and chaos from that moment rises in me again. A tear

escapes from my eye and travels the short distance down my cheek to the pillow. I sniff.

Alma looks up and throws her slate on the floor in her haste to reach the bed.

"Octavia," she says. "Rondo, she's awake!"

I hear quick steps, then the hurried sliding open of the bedroom door. In a moment both Alma and Rondo hover above me. Rondo's eyes are red. He reaches for my hand and holds it. At the feeling of his fingers, my chest swells again.

"Hi," I say. My throat feels scratchy.

"Are you thirsty?" Alma says. "You've been getting fluids intravenously, but your mom said that if you woke up today you'd probably want actual water."

"If I woke up today?"

"They figured it would be today or tomorrow. Your vitals have been getting closer to normal."

"How long have I been sleeping?"

"Three days."

"Yes, I'm thirsty," I croak, squeezing my eyes shut.

Rondo releases my hand. When I open my eyes again, he's there holding a small bowl. He brings it to my mouth and tilts it against my lips. I drink a few sips, feel the cool liquid trickle down my throat. It tastes how I know water tastes, but I can't help but compare it to the rhohedron nectar. Plain water is pale in comparison. I sigh and look up, and see the bottom of Alma's sleeping platform.

"Was I in my parents' room before?"

"Yes, but they moved you in here with me yesterday," Alma says. "Said you'd get better quicker if you slept in the same room with someone."

"I guess they don't realize that you snore." I smile, feeling a little stronger.

They both smile back: small, strained smiles. My arm aches: I don't need to look at the needle to know where the intravenous line enters my body. Three days. It feels like it's been years. But I can still feel the footprints in my mind where Rasimbukar had been, can still feel the stretchy sensation of the tunnel opening and closing in my head.

"Are you in pain?" Alma asks.

"I don't think so," I say. Do I tell them? Do I know how? "I feel weird. Are you guys okay?"

Rondo shrugs, as is his custom. His gaze doesn't seem to want to leave my face until this moment.

"Yes," he says. "I was just . . . we were just worried about you. We didn't know where you went when Dr. Espada came back to the tree without you." He shakes his head.

"We wanted to stay and help," Alma says. "But Manx made Dr. Espada and the finder who was bitten take us back while they looked for you and Jaquot."

"Jaquot?" I say. "Where was Jaquot?"

Alma's eyes fill with tears as if I had slapped her. I turn to Rondo and he rubs his temples.

"What happened to Jaquot?" My voice gets shrill, high. "He's dead isn't he? Jaquot is dead."

Neither of them can look at me. It seems a long time until Alma says, "Yes."

I squeeze my eyes shut, trying to choke down the nausea that's rising in my throat. Jaquot. Dead. The cocky boy from the Beak, whose eyes I thought were pretty when we were children. The boy who squeezed my arm the first time we saw the philax. Alma and I used to call him a moron and I wonder if she remembers. We thought he was a moron and now he's dead. I think of Yaya, her secret smiles at Jaquot—the only person I saw make her laugh. I open my eyes to find my vision blurred with tears.

"The dirixi?" I say, trying to keep my voice from breaking.

"Yes," Rondo says, his mouth twitching as if to say more, but closing again before any other words escape.

"What? What is it?" I don't want anyone to be gentle with me right now. I'm already lying here with a needle in my arm, the lights turned low as if I'm on my deathbed. I don't want to be coddled. I want to know everything.

"We . . . we won't be able to cremate him. All Manx and her crew found was a piece of his skinsuit. And . . . and blood. They found his blood."

"Because the dirixi doesn't chew; it swallows," I say. It feels sickeningly comforting, reciting Greenhouse research as if I'm talking about a case study. Not a person. Not a guy who I'd studied next to, laughed with, rolled my eyes at. I remember his last words to me in the jungle and my chest nearly seizes.

"Yes," Rondo says. I wonder if his eyes are red from crying or sleeplessness. Both, I imagine. I wonder if he thought I was dead too. I wonder why I'm *not* dead. How had I known to find the rhohedron field, the sweet-scented flowers that had protected me but not Jaquot? The tunnel in my head . . . I try to open it now, but it stays stubbornly closed. I find myself drawing up the smell of ogwe trees, their scent of fiber and sap crosshatched in a complicated but soothing aroma.

"Do you guys know what ogwe trees smell like?" I blurt out, sitting up as much as my strength will allow.

"Ogwe trees?" Rondo asks. "No. The compound's filled with them and I've never smelled anything."

"They don't have a smell," Alma agrees.

I remember Jaquot saying the same thing and bite my lip to keep from crying.

"But they do." I sigh, closing my eyes and falling back onto my bed. "They do."

"Octavia." Alma says my name like she's talking to a child. "What happened out there? Where did you go?"

"I ran from the dirixi," I say, keeping my eyes closed. "I got lost. Just like my grandmother. Maybe the same dirixi that killed her killed Jaquot."

"Don't do that, O," Alma says. "There's no point. It's illogical and it doesn't help anything."

"Where are my parents?"

"In the Zoo," Rondo says. "Going over your charts. Making sure you don't have any toxins that will make you sick later. Your mom did a procedure on your hands too."

"My hands?" So it wasn't a dream, waking up and feeling them tingling. I look at them now: they look normal and I don't feel any burning.

"Yeah, she thinks you might have touched some jival? The poisonous vine thing," Rondo says.

"Yes, jival. She said you were fine though," Alma adds. "Just a quick laser cleansing. She hasn't been here since she brought you back from the procedure. Neither has your dad."

It occurs to me that my parents might be questioning the spotted man, Rasimbukar's father. If my father kidnapped him—for whatever reason—then he might somehow think the Faloii had kidnapped me for revenge. Who is the villain here? I try to remember the feeling of gentleness that came from Rasimbukar. She seemed to want to avoid violence, not cause it. *Violence has grave consequences. . . .*

"I met the spotted man's daughter," I say.

"You *what*?" Rondo barks. He had been sitting on the desk platform across from the bed, but now he's on his feet and standing close to me, one hand extended as if he thought to clutch my leg and then changed his mind.

"Yes." I tell them everything. "She said to find the kawa when I was ready to come to her," I finish.

"The kawa? What is *that?*" Rondo sounds almost angry.

"I have no idea. Alma?"

"I don't know that word," she says, sinking onto the chair at my desk. "How strong was her grasp of our language? Maybe she mispronounced something? *Water*, maybe? Kawa, water."

"I don't think so," I say. "She said it really clearly. And her speech was perfect: there's no way she didn't know the word *water*."

"How could it be perfect?" Rondo breathes in wonder. "They've only interacted with us a handful of times. The only thing Dr. Espada and the other whitecoats say about them is how mysterious they are. How did they learn our language?"

In spite of everything, I smile. Rondo always said he wasn't interested in studying animals. He preferred people, he said. I see it now in his fascination with the Faloii.

"I don't know," I say, shaking my head. "But Rasimbukar barely had an accent. She did have one, but nothing I can compare to anything I've heard from any whitecoat."

"Amazing." Rondo sighs. He sits on the desk next to Alma, leans his back against the wall, and breathes deeply. "Wow."

"Am I the only one freaking out?" Alma says indignantly, looking from Rondo to me and waving her hands. "Great, Octavia talked to a Faloii woman. Yes, it's cool. But what are we going to *do*? She's talking about a war here, guys! This is critical! You have to talk to your mom, O. Seriously."

"And tell her what?" I snap. Almost all the fatigue has faded from my body. "That a Faloii woman told me what happened by showing me pictures in my mind? You think my mother won't just go straight to the Council, to my father, and tell him everything?"

They're both staring at me strangely, Rondo with an expression that is open, bright, as if waiting for more.

"What did you say?" he says quickly.

"What? When? About my mother telling my father? She would, I know she—"

"No, about Rasimbukar showing you pictures in your head."

"Oh." It sounds stupid when I hear it said like this. It's more than pictures in my head: they are feelings, communicated as clearly as if spoken words. I can still call up the sensation of Rasimbukar hailing me, my mind buzzing as I felt her consciousness prick at mine.

"I thought you said you spoke to her in our language," Alma says, her frown deepening as she tries to solve this new puzzle.

"I did. Some of the time. For other parts we—we talked in a different way. Well, she did. That's how I know her name. She showed it to me."

"She showed it to you?" Alma says, her head tilted. She's not disbelieving—not quite. She's willing, but she needs more.

"Yes," I say. "I know it sounds impossible."

"No, it doesn't," Alma interrupts. "It's not impossible at all. I mean, your mother already proved it *is* possible."

"My mother?"

She nods.

"Animals on Faloiv communicate telepathically," she says. "It stands to reason that the people of Faloiv probably do too."

"But Octavia's not Faloii," Rondo says. He's working it out too. They're greencoats: this is what we do.

"No," Alma says, frowning. "She's not. I have to think about that. But maybe the Faloii can communicate with any life-form that way. We know hardly anything about our interactions with them since none of the whitecoats want to talk about it."

"But it's not just Rasimbukar," I say. The pieces are floating around in my head like petals on the surface of water. I'm crunching my brain hard, making ripples that move the petals closer to one another.

"What do you mean?" Rondo asks. They're both standing closer to my bed now.

"The containment room," I say. "The philax. The tufali. It's not just Rasimbukar who can . . . you know, reach me. I wondered before, but after meeting her, talking to her, it's starting to add up. I can hear them. The animals. And they can hear me."

There's silence in my small room; the only sound is the barely audible hum of our 'wam's power system, churning on scraps of vegetable peels. Rondo and Alma stare at me, both of their minds stirring the same way. Alma's eyes flicker. She's quicker than Rondo, she always has been. Quicker than me, if I'm being honest.

"Can you stand?" she says. She's gripping the arm without the intravenous needle and glancing down at my body.

"What?" I say, surprised.

She tugs on me gently. "Can you?"

"Yes," I say. I lean forward and swing my legs slowly over the edge of my bed.

"Rondo, hand me that," Alma says, pointing at a skinsuit hanging from the wall by my door.

"Wait, what?" Rondo demands, not moving. "She's on bed rest!"

"We have to do an experiment," she says, still pointing.

With my feet on the floor I feel strong. The bed at my back is like a trap, as if the longer I stay in it, the worse I'll feel. I reach for the bowl of water Rondo had given me before and sip from it on my own.

"Where are we going?" I ask.

"Um, nowhere!" Rondo insists. He stands closer to the door, as if to block it.

"Rondo, don't be ridiculous," Alma says with a long look. "She's fine. They only put her on bed rest because she was dehydrated and they wanted to check for toxins. Plus the procedure was on her hands, and she doesn't need her hands to walk."

"My hands feel fine," I offer.

"And what if she *does* have toxins?" Rondo says. I can't help but smile at the expression on his face. Ordinarily I would have felt awkward wearing my nightclothes in front of him, but he's already seen me in them. That just makes me smile more.

"If I have toxins, I'll have them whether I'm in this bed or out of it," I say, trying to be gentle. But he's not going to keep me in this room. "Besides, they would have been back with my test results by now if something was wrong with me."

He stares at me, saying nothing.

"Rondo," I say. "I'm fine. I'm not an eggshell. Now hand me my skinsuit."

He glares at both of us a moment longer, then removes the skinsuit from its hook and tosses it at me.

"Be careful removing your intravenous," he says, sliding open my bedroom door. Then he pauses. "Do you need help?"

"Rondo, get out!" Alma says.

He laughs and disappears.

"Honestly," she says, with a small laugh. "You'd think he was in love with you."

"Well, not exactly, but . . ."

Her fingers pause on my intravenous. "Excuse me?" she says, dropping her chin.

"I have some stuff to tell you." I grin.

"What's new?" She rolls her eyes and helps me take the needle from my arm. "Later."

On the path through the commune, I munch the hava Rondo forced into my hand, my arm linked through Alma's as they tell me about what happened in the jungle.

"Yaya hasn't talked much to us since then," Alma says. "I think what happened to Jaquot really messed her up. I didn't see him get taken, but Rondo thinks Yaya might have."

I glance at Rondo, who nods solemnly.

"It was really scary," Alma continues. "Dr. Espada came back to the tree without you and he was frantic. He had cuts all over his face from running through the jungle and he was, well, crying too. It was terrible. He said, 'Samirah will never forgive me.'"

"How did they find me?" I say.

"You found yourself," Rondo says as we turn a corner. "A search party of finders came back from looking for you in the jungle and found you curled up outside the Mammalian Compound. Somehow you got past the gate without the guards seeing you. You were right by the front door, like you just walked home."

"I think Rasimbukar brought me."

"Oh," he says, his forehead crinkled. "I guess that makes sense. You'd think the guards would have seen her for sure."

"Her skin changes, remember? Camouflage. Better than anything we've seen with the animals."

Neither of them reply. I wonder if the talk about Rasimbukar makes them afraid, or if the scientist in each of them is jealous. Maybe a little of both. The sudden quiet makes me notice the absence of hammering and I look for the tower the engineers have been working on. It stands there, unmanned. Rondo sees me looking.

"It's kind of been an unofficial rest period the last few days," he says. "With . . . what happened to Jaquot."

I nod. The desire to steer the subject away from his death is so strong it burns.

"So what's your experiment?" I say, glancing at Alma.

"Okay," she says, motioning with the hand that's not looped through my arm. "What do you feel right now? Are you thinking anything?"

"What?"

She sighs impatiently.

"Your brain, Octavia. Do you hear anything? The buzzing you've been talking about."

"Oh. Uh." I stop talking and pay attention. "No. Nothing."

"Okay." We're approaching a bridge to cross the stream and she stops us. "Rondo, think something at Octavia."

"Do what?"

"Think something at her!"

"At her?"

"Yes, at. Think something that you want her to hear."

"Um . . . okay."

He looks awkward and then settles his eyes on me and stares hard, his eyebrows raising slightly. I resist the strong urge to laugh.

"Anything?" Alma says, looking at me for confirmation.

"No. Nothing. All clear."

"Okay." She nods, and walks toward the bridge, towing me along. "Next step."

We stop in the middle of the bridge.

"Now." She pulls me to the rail and leans on it with her elbows. "Look down."

"At the water?"

"At what's in the water."

I gaze down at the flowing plants, the round red rocks that line the bottom of the streambed, the lazy ripples of the water flowing toward the other side of the dome. At first I'm not sure what Alma is asking me to look for, but a moment later I understand. The buzzing rises slowly, remaining soft, but only after a small school of myn swim into view from under the bridge. The buzz is barely noticeable, but it's there.

"I hear it," I whisper.

Alma squeezes my arm.

"Okay, okay. Now focus. What do you hear? What do you feel? Are they . . . saying anything?"

It's hard to focus on the feeling: the source of it is like a fish itself, small and slippery. But I squeeze a fist in my mind, forcing myself to focus. And among it all I find a feeling, not words, but a shapeless feeling: a need to stay near the bodies swimming around me, a wariness of the shadows looming above me, a darkness over the water before me, which I veer to avoid. The water seems to make calm second nature, but underneath it all, alert vigilance, an ever-present fear so natural it feels like breath.

But then there's a flurry of . . . something. The fish all scatter, the line I was listening on rapidly shut off: it's as if the long tunnel through which I could feel the myn's consciousness was abruptly snapped shut. In the water, the myn have disappeared, hidden away among rocks and plants. I look away and find Alma's eyes upon me, bright and eager.

"Well?" she says.

"They shut me out, I think. I could feel some of what they were feeling, but then it was like they realized I could hear them and closed the door."

"Interesting," Alma says.

"Well of course they did," says Rondo, who's been watching me intently. "Just because animals can communicate telepathically doesn't change the predator-prey relationship. Maybe they think you're a predator. This kind of mental connection between species doesn't mean animals are suddenly friends. It's just another kind of listening."

"But how am I doing it? And why now?" I feel more exasperation than awe. "Did the philax do something to my brain? Or . . . ?"

"I don't know," Alma says, shaking her head. "We need to learn more."

"Yes, we do," Rondo says, pushing off from the bridge rail abruptly. "And as soon as possible."

"He's right," Alma says.

"I'm going to go do some digging," Rondo says. He goes to walk away, but it's as if he too can hear my thoughts, how much I want him near me. He reaches for my hand and holds it, considering my palm as if all the answers we need are right there.

"And by that you mean hacking," Alma says.

He rolls his eyes, letting go of my hand finger by finger.

"Yeah. You two find out what you can from Octavia's parents. They'll have us back in the Zoo in the next day or two now that Octavia is out of bed, and we need to have a plan before we go back in."

"What should I ask my mom?" I call after him before he gets too far away.

He turns and walks backward for a few steps, spreading his arms wide with an irresistible smile.

"I'd start with figuring out what happened to that beautiful brain of yours."

CHAPTER 20

My father is home when Alma and I return to my 'wam. He must have just arrived, because he's standing in the hallway outside my room. At the sound of the front door sighing open, he turns toward us quickly, looking both relieved and annoyed.

"Octavia," he says, taking a few steps forward before stopping. His face carries an expression I haven't seen in a long time. Softness.

"Sir."

"Where did you go? I thought you were still sleeping and then I came home . . ."

"I was just getting some air. I woke up feeling much better and Alma helped me walk around. We didn't go far."

"I see," he says. He moves into the kitchen, going to the

water decontamination unit and flipping it on. "You'll need to drink a lot of water."

He glances down at my arm. "You removed your intravenous without issue, I see." He's less worried now, the softness leaking out of him. He has questions queuing on his tongue.

I nod apologetically about the intravenous. It's a strange feeling, knowing that to animals on Faloiv—and the Faloii too—my brain is an open book, but to N'Terrans, people like Alma and my father, I'm as opaque as a stone.

"You're feeling better?" he says. The light on the water decon unit has turned a soft green, indicating that it's ready to provide clean water. My father goes to it with a cup from one of the wall compartments and the clear liquid gushes out. It reminds me of the rhohedron nectar, Rasimbukar holding the plant over my wilting face. If I feel better now, it's because of her.

"Yes," I say. "But really I was fine. Just thirsty."

"Fine? I'm impressed," he says, turning to me with his eyebrows raised. He sips from the water before he goes on. I thought the cup was for me. "Out in the jungle for almost seven hours and you come back without a scratch on you. Your vitals were impressive too."

"How so?" Alma asks.

"She should have died," my father says bluntly, watching me. I stare back. "Seven hours without water on Faloiv, in the jungle no less. How she escaped the dirixi is beyond me. She didn't have her water canteen when she was found outside the compound, but she must have been drinking steadily before then, because she was remarkably hydrated for the period of time she was missing."

The fatherly concern from a moment ago has all but disappeared.

"I climbed another tree," I lie. "I never really saw the dirixi, though, just heard it."

The second part is true, at least.

"I saw it," Alma says. "Octavia had a good start on it when it went by our tree."

We all pause. If I could get a glimpse into each of their thoughts, I think I would see Jaquot. His name is a scar.

"I hid in the tree for hours," I continue. "Until the sun started to get lower. I didn't want to call for Dr. Espada and the others in case the dirixi came back. I had an idea of where the road was, so I just walked until I found it."

"I see," my father says. He's still eyeing me. If he had his way, I think, he'd probably have me in the Zoo strapped to a table, running tests on me. My father opens his mouth, ready to continue his interrogation, when my mother enters the 'wam.

Her arms are full with slides from the lab and, balancing on top, a basket of fruit. She's focused on keeping everything from toppling over and doesn't notice us all standing there right away. When she does, her eyebrows pop up and her face breaks into a smile.

"Octavia," she says. "Should you be up?"

"She's all right, Samirah," my father says. "What do you have?"

"Fruit," she says. "And work. Nothing new."

"Anything on the Hima boy?"

"Jaquot," she says. "I'm so sorry about your friend, girls."

"Thank you, Dr. English. I hope his parents are okay," Alma says.

"They're not," my mother says, squeezing my arm as she passes me for the kitchen. "But they will be. Time makes these things easier."

She slides the basket of fruit from her arms onto the kitchen platform, then places the slides next to them. She sighs, and I know she's thinking of my grandmother—that time *doesn't* make things easier. She turns back to me and Alma.

"Now that you're out of bed," she says, looking at me, "will you be ready to resume your studies? You've had a few days to recuperate, but I don't want to push you."

"I'm fine," I say. I'm eager to get back into the Zoo, for reasons that I hope are obvious only to me. "Really. I think getting back to work will help us, you know, keep our mind off things."

"My thoughts exactly," she says, still looking sad. My father reaches across the platform and rests his hand on her shoulder. I avert my eyes. My father's coldness is something I'm comfortable with; I don't understand his warmth. By the look on my mother's face, it's strange to her too.

"Is the finder okay?" I ask. "The one who was bitten."

"Oh yes," my mother says, handling the hava in her basket to find a ripe one to slice. "It was just a little morgantan bite. Finders are used to these things. But they haven't encountered something like a dirixi for nearly a year. Very"—she pauses, gazing at the fruit—"unfortunate timing."

"Your daughter says she escaped the dirixi by climbing a tree," my father says.

"Oh?" she says, glancing at me. She's retrieved the bow knife from the wall and is slicing the hava. "I didn't know you were much of a climber, Octavia."

"I guess I am," I say. I wonder what they'd say if they knew. If they knew any of it: Rasimbukar, my ability to communicate with her, with the myn. The fact that what my father has done—capturing Rasimbukar's father—could lead our world to war. I wonder if my father would release him, if I told them the truth. I don't think he would—I get the feeling that he's finished obeying the laws of the Faloii. Rasimbukar had mentioned that the star people—my people—had broken agreements in the past. I wish I had thought to ask which agreements. What have we been doing that I know nothing about?

My mother's hand floats in front of me, offering me a piece of hava. I wonder how long it's waited there while I was lost in my thoughts. I take the fruit.

"Eat some more," she says. "And then rest. You'll be back in the labs tomorrow."

• • •

Much later, after my parents have both gone to bed, Alma and I hang out in my room. We huddle on my bed so that we can whisper.

"Your dad," she says. "I don't think he believes you."

"About what?" I already know, but I want to hear it.

"About what happened in the jungle. He seemed really suspicious. Like he knows something."

"I know. I was thinking about my vitals. He said he looked at them. What if the rhohedron nectar showed up in my system?"

"You think he'd know that you met the Faloii?"

"I don't know. But if he's hiding Rasimbukar's dad, he has to know that the Faloii would eventually come looking for him. Right?"

"I wish I knew more about our agreement with the Faloii," Alma says, leaning back against the wall. "I mean, the Council has to know that holding a Faloii person hostage is breaking the rules. I don't need to know the agreement to know *that* much."

"That's the thing," I whisper. "Given everything I've been hearing about Albatur, I think he *wants* to break the agreement."

We sit in silence. When I was standing on the bridge with Alma and Rondo, I felt a strange exhilaration: a feeling of looming clarity where things finally seemed to make sense. The buzzing in my head. My reaction to the philax. Somehow I have a connection with the people and animals of Faloiv. But now that I know, I'm just as confused. Why? How? The questions are bigger than ever.

"We should send Rondo a message," I say, sitting up. "Maybe he's found something."

"Sure. *That's* why you want to message him."

"Shut up!"

"Whatever you've gotta tell yourself."

I stretch across to the desk platform and pull my slate toward me. It's like picking up an alien object—after being out in the jungle, everything that was once familiar feels foreign. I wake up the device and tap on the mouth icon. There's a pause as it loads, and then my messages appear. There are already three from Rondo, waiting to be read.

"He's already written me."

"I didn't even hear it," Alma yawns, reclining backward on the bed. "What did he say?"

I open the oldest message first. It's from yesterday.

I know you're still sleeping, it says. *I'm in your kitchen. I hope you wake up soon. I miss you.*

I smile broadly. Then I open the next message.

You there? I found something.

My smile fades. I open the last message.

Your mom knows something.

"Alma," I hiss. "He says my mom knows something."

She sits bolt upright.

"Knows what? That you met Rasimbukar?"

OLIVIA A. COLE

"I don't know."

I quickly type out a message. *Rondo, are you there? What does my mom know?*

He types back immediately. *About your brain.*

"About your brain?" Alma echoes. "You mean that you can . . . ?"

What about my brain? I type.

I don't know exactly. But remember those footprints I found in the databases? The ones with an encrypted entry point? I finally hacked a trace on it, and it's your mom's device.

I sit back against the wall. My mom has been poking around in the files, just like Rondo.

"Give it to me," Alma says, and takes the slate from my hands.

Which databases did you say you found her footprints in? she types.

Everywhere I've been looking, Rondo replies. *In the files about the* Vagantur's *landing, in the personnel files for the original N'Terrans. And today I found traces of her in your brain scans.*

What was she looking at? Alma's fingers fly across the slate's face.

She was more than looking, Rondo types. *She was making changes. I can't see what she deleted, but she deleted something and uploaded a new file.*

"What does that mean?" Alma breathes, leaning against the wall with me.

I'm sending you an image, Rondo says.

A moment later a black box appears in the message stream. When Alma taps it, the box's lid opens, releasing a file.

It's an image of a brain scan. We've studied brain research for years in the Greenhouse, and although neither of us are experts, Alma and I both know enough to know that this particular brain is unremarkable. No unusual swatches of color, no strange shapes or shadows.

So what? I take the slate back from Alma. *It looks normal to me.*

Exactly. But what did it replace? She encrypted the deletion: no one but me will probably ever notice. But the file you're looking at replaced something else.

Alma and I look at each other. Her mind is crunching, trying to come up with a theory. A ping from the slate draws our eyes back to its screen.

You have to get to her device, Rondo has typed. *If you can find the original brain scan, maybe it will tell you something about why you can communicate with the Faloii. And who knows what else you might find?*

I don't know if I can do that, I respond.

There's a long pause. I can't tell if he's typing a long response or if he's just thinking about what to say.

I don't like it either, O. But we need answers. I'm going to sleep. See you tomorrow.

"Well?" Alma says. Her face seems knotted.

"I can't," I say. I've already spied on my mother once before—listening at her door, I learned that she wanted to keep me out of the internships. It has bothered me ever since, has changed the way I look at her. That's the thing about secrets: once you uncover them, sometimes you wish you hadn't. But we need answers.

"There has to be another way," I say eventually. I put my palms over my eyes, pressing them. "I'm *not* going into her study."

Alma stares at me for a long moment, and I wonder if she's going to argue. But she doesn't. She sits up away from the wall.

"Look," she says frankly. "I told you all I care about is becoming a whitecoat, but I'm involved now. And if I'm gonna be involved, then we need to go all the way. I'm not going to tell you what to do, and we'll be in a position to learn something in the Zoo tomorrow . . . but we need to learn what we can, where we can."

"Yeah . . . ," I say, not wanting to commit to anything. Never would I have thought that it would be Alma convincing me to push harder to dig up the truth.

"I'm going to sleep," she says, and I realize how tired she must be. She's been looking after me with Rondo while I slept the days away. I nod and she extracts herself from where she's been sitting on my bed, climbing up to her own ledge, where I can hear her settling in. I stand and press my palm against the light pad, and the room goes dark.

"Alma," I whisper when I'm back in my bed.

"Mhmm."

"Thanks for . . . you know. For not telling anyone. And everything."

"Of course."

I can't sleep. My body seems to have a surplus of energy and my mind is like a cloud of insects, alive and swarming. In the dark I picture Rasimbukar. I may not know everything—about my people or hers, or even about myself—but I feel it in my bones that Rasimbukar is telling the truth. The compound has done something wrong, and I need to make it right.

I sit up in the dark. The 'wam is quiet with all the lights off—only the soft murmur of the cooling system. The pale light of the moon filters in through the cracks around my window shade. I have the urge to open the shade and look out at the sleeping commune, but I know the light would wake up Alma. Even with my eyes closed, I can picture it: the compound I was born in, the 'wams lit up like moon rocks at night, the trees sprouting up around us under the transparent dome rising into Faloiv's sky. My home. Now I picture it all burning, crumbling under the flame of a war started by my people. I remember what Rondo told me, the night we kissed in the dark: Not everything has to make sense. Maybe he was right. But some things I have to figure out.

I'm standing at my bedroom door before I've fully realized

what I'm going to do. I slowly slide it open, cautious for any creak or crack. The hallway is even darker than my bedroom. Down the hall, my parents' door is still. Before I know it, I'm passing it like a shadow, one foot in front of the other. The packed-dirt floor is forgiving of sound, not like the branches and the foliage in the jungle. But even without a dirixi hounding me, my heart pounds in my chest. It's so loud, I'm certain its rhythm will echo down the hall and into my parents' room. But I'm outside the study a moment later, my hands reaching out in the dark to find the door, sliding it slowly open, only wide enough for me to squeeze through.

Around me, the study smells like my mother: warm and rich. Technically this study is for both my parents' use, but my father prefers his den in the Zoo. I think of all the work she's done in this room, the discoveries she's made. I wonder how many of those discoveries have been against the wishes of the Faloii, violating agreements that were made before I was born.

I pick my way through the dark to the desk. I don't need to see it to know that it's cluttered with slides, a disorganized mass of research that only my mother knows the order of. I need more light, but I don't dare turn on the room's lamp. I fumble over to the window, tripping on a woven runner mat that covers the dirt floor, and inch the window shade open, just a tiny gap to let in some light.

Moonbeams flow in eagerly, illuminating the desk with their softness. I turn back and take it in, searching for her slate in the chaos of her other research.

I don't see it anywhere. I wanted to avoid moving things around—I have no way of knowing what she might notice and what she'd miss—but I don't have a choice. Gently, as if handling eggs, I move the slides around, shift the projector to free the thick transparent files trapped under its edge. I glance at them in the dim light: charts and recordings, notes on various specimens, illustrations of brains that clearly aren't human. I set them down and keep up my silent search until my fingers brush the smooth, solid edge of a slate.

I hold my breath as I ease it out from under a small tower of slides, then sink down to the floor, leaning against the desk and waking up the device.

The light from the screen blinds me at first after all my creeping around in the dark. When my eyes adjust, I see that the last screen my mother viewed before she switched off the device was her list of files. All of the file names are unremarkable. Tufali 8 Neurological Assessment. Kunike 21 Behavioral Analysis. Dozens and dozens of files, some with attached documents in the hundreds.

Then I find a folder that is unlabeled. I pause, wondering if I should open it. Anxiety gnaws at me. *Once you know something, you can't unknow it*, I tell myself. But I tap the unlabeled folder and watch as its contents fill the screen.

They're all images. Thumbnails that, when tapped, expand to their full size. All the images are of animals: even as thumbnails I recognize the wide yellow eyes of the igua, the remarkable ears of the kunike. I tap on a few, admiring them. Most of them were taken in the lab, specimens in containment, but there are a few that must have been taken by finders, the animals surrounded by the dense greenery of Faloiv. Some of the photos' subjects are blurred, capturing the motion of the specimen as it turned to flee.

One image catches my eye: a maigno. I tap the thumbnail and it expands to fill the screen. My eyes widen with surprise. The maigno isn't alone in the image. Beside it stands my grandmother.

Nana is young, her face unlined and her tight curly hair graying only at her temples—not the all-over eruption of white that I remember from my childhood. Her smile is broad and one hand is swung out to her side, gesturing toward the maigno as if to say *Do you see this beauty?* I wonder how old my mother was when the photo was taken. My age, perhaps: sulking in the half-built compounds and dreaming about the jungle, imagining what wonders her mother was out seeing. I tap the image again to make it larger and drag the focus to my grandmother's face to examine her features. So much like my mother, the angled chin and round cheekbones, the bright eyes.

But there's something about one of her eyes that isn't quite right: a pixilation of the image that distorts her pupil. I hadn't noticed when the image was regularly sized, but with it blown up and zoomed in like this, it catches my attention. I tap on

Nana's face to zoom in even further.

Her features fill the screen, slightly stretched, the wide, graceful bridge of her nose centered. I drag the image downward to find her eyes, and then I see what the distortion is.

It's a box. A black box just like the file that Rondo sent me on my slate a few hours before: small and square with a digital lid. I stare at it, the unknown yawning up at me from my grandmother's face. I sit there in the dark, the light from the slate glowing like a torch, my finger hovering over the box. I take a deep breath and tap it.

The box opens and the screen goes blank. At first I think the device has powered off, but then a window appears in the center of the screen, with the word *Password* blinking above an entry field.

I hesitate. Password? Rondo may be a hacker but I'm not.

At first I try Nana's name: Amara. The file had been hidden in a photo of her, so maybe the password is her as well. But the box turns red and blinks, the entry field flashing. What would my mother use as a password? Guessing, I type in *Vagantur*.

Red. Flashing field. No luck. Tries usually come in threes, I think, and I rack my brains for what might be my last shot. I have no ideas, so I start to type in my own name. O-*c-t-a-v-i-a*, and I pause, my finger stopped above the enter button. I delete the entry and type my middle name instead: *A-f-u-a*.

The box turns green and disappears, an instant of blankness before the box's contents assemble on the screen. Rows of files and images, some of them just repeated images of my grandmother with the maigno. Double encrypted, I think. What I see is mostly data; no species, though I'm fairly certain it's all human. I scan the files quickly—I've already been in the study longer than I wanted to be—searching for something I can use. Blood work. Heart rates. X-rays. And then I see my name.

I tap on the file, but the only thing I find when it opens is more blood work and vital data. I know there has to be something here—why else would it be in an encrypted file hidden in a photograph? I close the file and keep looking until my eye falls on two images: brain scans. My hands are shaking, the feeling of walking through the dark and knowing something is in the trees, knowing and massive.

The first file is just like the one Rondo sent me. In fact, I'm almost certain it's the same image. Normal activity, nothing unusual. I close it to look at the second image.

Most of the scan is normal: neurons firing as expected, healthy activity. Right in the center, though, knotted between the temporal and parietal lobes, is what looks like an explosion of color: bright tendrils all convening in a maze of twisting illumination, like blood spreading through water but clinging together like slime. My mind is buzzing, looking at the scan, but I barely notice.

"What *is* that?" I whisper to myself, holding the slate closer to my face.

Through the silence comes a whisper, behind me in the dark. "It's your brain."

I nearly throw the slate in my shock, too startled to gasp. It's my mother, halfway across the room, several steps from the door. She didn't make a sound, slipping into the study like an inky shadow. We stare at each other in the darkness, my mouth slightly open and hers set in a look of almost sadness. We say nothing, each waiting for what the other might say. Suddenly I notice the buzzing: the quivering feeling of an echo happening inside my head. I know that feeling. But I'm in my 'wam: no animals around. No Faloii. Looking at my mother, I slowly tilt my head sideways.

And the tunnel opens. Quickly. Enough to make me dizzy with the images that are suddenly inundating my consciousness. I'm overwhelmed, trying to understand what's happening. Images of my grandmother sitting at the very desk I lean against, smiling up at someone walking through the door. The jungle of Faloiv: Dr. Espada walking ahead and then turning back with eyebrows raised, grinning. My father, younger than he is now, in his white coat, weeping. My heart is pounding, my head swimming. I don't know if I want to cry or vomit.

And then the tunnel closes, the images retreating and growing dim as the buzzing wanes into nothing.

"I'm sorry," my mother whispers, now by my side, crouching and touching my hair. "Even after all these years, I struggle to control it. You're much better at it, I think."

The tears stinging in my eyes aren't mine—it's as if I've been injected with the sorrow from the vision and must wait for it to ebb. I struggle against the feeling of powerlessness. This doesn't make sense! My mother is not of Faloiv. Is she? Is that another lie too, my parents' lineage?

My mother takes the slate from my hands and sinks down on the floor next to me. I'm too shocked to move away. We huddle there in the dark. She holds the screen up in front of both of us.

"This is your brain, Octavia. As you can see, it's a little . . . different."

"B-but why?" I stammer. "What's wrong with me? How can you . . . ?"

She closes the file and opens another. It's an image of a brain scan. The brain she shows me now has the same extraordinarily colored tentacles, snaking out from a mass near the center. The mass is smaller, though, the colors less varied.

"And this is my brain," she says. The moonlight has shifted and falls only on our hands, up to the wrist. "And if you were to look at the brains of the Faloii people, they would look very similar. Not identical, but similar."

I stare at her. The speed at which my mind has been running seems as if it's slowed to the crawl of a worm.

"Are we . . . aliens?" I ask, barely able to get it out of my mouth.

She laughs softly and touches my cheek.

"No, Afua. No, we're not aliens. Well, to the Faloii we are. But we're human, you and me, even if you were born here."

"Then why are our brains like this?" I say, taking the slate from her hand and staring at the tendrils erupting in the image of my mother's brain. A flurry of incidents rush to the surface of my mind. "What's wrong with us? I passed out when the philax was tranquilized. My nose bled when a tufali . . ."

"Nothing. Nothing is wrong with us. Headaches, blood, fainting, your body is adjusting to a gift, Afua. It was triggered when you made eye contact with the philax. We've been given a gift."

"What kind of gift? From who?"

"The Faloii. And from Nana."

"But—"

We both freeze at a sound in the hall. It's my parents' bedroom door, sliding open.

"Samirah?" my father calls softly. "Are you sick? Are you all right?"

"Stay here," my mother whispers. "Go back to your room only when it's quiet. We'll talk soon."

She moves swiftly to the study door and out into the hall. She leaves the door open. I sit in the dark like a statue.

"I'm fine, Octavius," she says, yawning. "Just wanted to jot down a thought I had about Igua 27 before I forgot. I'm coming back to bed."

He murmurs something. A moment later the soft sliding of

their door, closing them back into their bedroom. Only then do I exhale.

I don't know how long I sit there, folded up in the shadow of my mother's desk. I hold the slate in my hands like a statue, unable to look away from the strange shapes in the center of my mother's brain, my brain. The feeling of the tunnel having been opened persists like an echo, but there is no stirring, no buzzing. The tunnel remains closed.

When I leave, I place the slate carelessly on her desk. Nothing to hide from her now.

CHAPTER 21

Yaya stands near the entrance to the Zoo, alone. Rondo, Alma, and I had been whispering about the events in my mother's study last night—Alma convinced that my father and mother are on opposing sides of a rising battle—but at the sight of Yaya, we all fall silent as if on cue. Grief encircles her like a planet's rings.

"Hi, Yaya," I say as we approach. She looks up, her face expressionless, eyes swollen.

"Hey, guys."

"Are you . . . are you doing okay?"

She shrugs, not looking at me.

"I'm . . . fine. I will be fine." She swallows. "I'm . . ."

"Did you . . . did you see . . . ?"

"Jaquot?" she says, and winces, as if just saying his name

causes her pain. "No, not exactly. I saw him run away from the group, before any of us were even up in the tree. I think he was looking for another one to climb. But he ran right into the part of the jungle the dirixi came out of a minute later, so I guess that's when . . . when it happened."

"It's so sad," I say. I don't know what other words to offer.

"Yes," she says. "We thought it got both of you. I hope we don't ever have to go back out there again."

Jaquot's absence makes us stiff. Our group stands quietly until my father appears in the door of the Zoo, beckoning us inside.

"Welcome back to work," he says. "I know you've all had a shock. But I expect you to give your duties the time and attention they require now that you're back in the labs."

None of us reply. We follow him down the long pale hall. I look side to side at the empty exam rooms. Rasimbukar's father could be in any one of them. I could be passing him as we speak.

"What are we working on today, Dr. English?" Yaya says. She's back to leading the group.

"Today you will be observing a procedure," he says. At the end of the hallway he turns left, leading us down the next corridor with its endless empty rooms on either side. The idea of observing piques my interest, of course: this is what I've always wanted, to gain insight into how we can make Faloiv a place for our future. But then I realize the procedure will probably involve a live specimen, and my stomach lurches. I know what the buzzing in my head is now, but I still have little understanding of how to control it. Like Rasimbukar, my mother had seemed able to shut the tunnel by her own volition, but I can't imagine how to begin shutting out the communication I can now expect to receive from all Faloivan life-forms.

My father leads us to a door with a sign that reads Observation Prep 4. I look around for Observation Prep 1 through 3, but I don't see them. The mazelike quality of the labs is frustrating. He opens the door and holds it for us, nodding for us to go in.

"You know the prep instructions. Dr. Depp will be in for you soon."

He steps back into the hall and closes the door, leaving us alone. Our surroundings are similar to the scrub room we prepped in before our visit to the containment room last week: washbasins and hanging white coats. Rondo pulls on a lab coat and reaches for a headwrap hanging from a hook. There are different colors and the one he grabs first is purple.

"Here," he says, handing it to me, letting his fingers brush mine. Then he lowers his voice, his next words just for me. "You look pretty in purple."

I smile but look away and busy my hands, wrapping up my braids in the purple cloth. How is it possible that with everything that's going on I still have space in my brain to think about that night outside my 'wam with him? I try to put it out of my head and focus on tying my wrap. Maybe when all this is over I can think about Rondo.

By the time Dr. Depp comes—a whitecoat I've never seen before—we're all prepped and ready for whatever happens next. Dr. Depp doesn't greet us. He just sticks his head in the door.

"Ready? Good. We're on a schedule."

We follow him down the hall, deeper into the labs. He's not unfriendly, but he's brusque in a way that reminds me of my father. Once through a thumb-locked door, he leads us to the end of a short hallway, where another door whispers open.

"In here," he says. "This is the observation deck, from which you'll be able to watch. I'll be going down into the procedure room. There is an intercom that will allow you and the other observers to hear me. I'll be available afterward if you need clarification on any of the procedures you witness."

He doesn't wait for us to reply, disappearing through another door, and we file into the observation area alone.

Inside, the room is nearly full of whitecoats, all crowded in before they have to go to procedures of their own, eager now to watch and take notes. I don't recognize any of them, and they don't look up from their murmured conversations as we shuffle into their midst. It's dimmer here than in the hallway, the front of the deck brighter with light shining through a glass wall. The procedure room on the other side is almost empty, resembling the illusion rooms that line the hallways outside, and I'm not entirely sure that this isn't an illusion too until a door in the room slides open, admitting Dr. Depp and another whitecoat, his assistant, a youngish man. Two other whitecoats enter behind them, bearing a medium-size cage.

The two whitecoats place the cage on the raised center platform, where one of them dons heavy white gloves and opens its door. Reaching in, he draws out the still, prone body of a kunike. It's very small—not yet an adult but already with the characteristic large ears. The animal appears to be sedated, the ears not standing erect but flopped loosely down from its delicate head.

"Aww . . . ," Yaya says in a hushed tone. I almost smile, to hear this kind of reaction from her of all people. It *is* cute, even if it does have razor-sharp teeth hiding in that small, fuzzy mouth.

The whitecoats place the kunike on the platform, securing it with thin white straps. They're not gentle and I frown at their careless handling of the small body.

Alma glances at me, catching my eye. She lowers her chin slightly, her eyebrows raised in a wordless question. I shake my head. No, I don't hear anything. Only a steady, buzzing lull. Maybe it's because the animal is sedated, or maybe the glass is effective at separating my mind from the kunike's.

Dr. Depp has already begun talking, describing every move that he and his assistant, Dr. Wong, make. It occurs to me that they're recording the session for future analysis, three-dimensional data that will go onto one of the innumerable slides my mother is always studying. Dr. Depp approaches the platform, grasping a long thin instrument like a wand. He brings it into contact with the kunike's small neck, and I watch as the tip of the instrument glows a pale blue.

The kunike stirs. My consciousness prickling, I feel it waking up before its body even begins to move. The tunnel in my brain widens slightly, noticing it. The kunike is afraid. His fear is mild compared to the tufali's terror, which had caused her to gore the female whitecoat, but it's also because he's groggy. Alma's eyes are on me again, as if I too am a specimen she's monitoring. This time I nod.

Dr. Depp begins the procedure, followed by the rustle of whitecoats taking notes.

"We are now removing a small sample of Kunike 13's fur. Based on the modifications we have made to its nutrition—introducing plants not normally found in its diet in the wild—we will see if its camouflage abilities have been affected by the change."

A lump of sadness hardens in my core. This sounds like something my grandmother would have studied: the effects of an animal's food on its biology. Somehow, though, I don't think she would have approved of this method of observation.

Dr. Depp is snipping a small chunk of the trembling kunike's fur from around his shoulders. I can almost hear the sound of the tiny scissors slicing in my ear. The kunike doesn't understand that only his fur is being taken: he thinks his life could end at any moment and his fur shifts to the bright red color it takes on when alarmed. I hold my breath. I wish I could soothe the kunike, and I even try sending something through the tunnel the way Rasimbukar—and my mother, I think—had. But I can't. It feels like trying to flex a phantom limb, attempting to curl fingers I can't even see or feel.

Dr. Depp painstakingly places the fur sample between two transparent films and passes them to his assistant, who binds them and moves to the other side of the procedure room. There's a projector set up that I hadn't noticed before, connected to a microscope.

"Assistant Dr. Wong is placing Kunike 13's fur sample under the microscope for examination."

The microscopic view of the kunike's fur is projected on the wall and I hear the uniform sound of the observing group's motion as we all lean to see the image. The whitecoats in the room with us murmur to one another: there must be something worth seeing.

"Kunike 13's fur sample displays minor but noticeable change after six weeks of dietary adjustment," Dr. Depp says. "This suggests that the highly advanced sets of camouflage that kunike are able to employ as their chief defense mechanism can be expanded based on the foods they consume."

Then I hear something else. At first I think it's the kunike, his fear growing larger the longer he is held captive on the platform, but it's bigger than that. The feeling pulses through the tunnel and fills my head with cavernous humming. I can't tell where it's coming from. The hall? Another procedure room? Just how far does the tunnel travel? Is the noise—this cacophony of brain activity—coming from the containment room nearby? I try to control my breathing: there are too many whitecoats in the room and I don't want to draw attention to myself. Alma, of course, notices.

"What's up?" she whispers.

In the procedure room, Dr. Wong is holding the kunike's head still while Dr. Depp swabs inside the large floppy ear. The kunike's heartbeat spikes in my mind, but the other thing—the humming—is larger, louder, more intense.

"I hear something else," I whisper. "I think it's nearby. I can't tell what . . ."

"Focus," Alma says. "Calm down and focus."

I breathe deeply through my nose, trying to widen the tunnel enough to let more through. Forcing my mind to open is like attempting to grip vapor. It twists around, following its own pattern. But I close my eyes and find myself asking it to open. Let me see, I think, but not in words. The shape of words.

At that, the tunnel opens, and the larger fear thrusts itself into my head like a fist. My breath catches. Rondo and Alma are both looking at me now, each of them glancing up at the whitecoats ahead of us to ensure that no one has noticed. Inside me, the fear is a clash of orange and yellow, and I find myself sliding along the wall to the door, which whispers open to admit me into the hallway. Rondo and Alma are on my heels, slipping through before the door has a chance to hum shut again.

"What is it?" Alma asks. "You hear something?"

"It's a vasana," I say, closing my eyes around the buzzing.

"What's that?" Rondo says. He stands very close, both of them do, bodies rigid as if to catch me if I fall.

"Herbivore," Alma says, reciting her brain's contents as if from a slate. "Large, a little bigger than a tufali. Pale green coat that's short and shiny. Long muzzle. Slopey ears."

"It's nearby," I say, opening my eyes. The feeling is like a trail laid out through empty space, glowing ahead of me. "Something is wrong."

"It's all wrong," Rondo says.

"It's worse," I say, looking around for I don't know what. "Something horrible."

It's a female. I can feel her now. Her mind is as open as mine, searching. She feels me, reaches out with the shapes of her fear. No words, just horror. She doesn't know who or what I am, but she reaches.

I race down the hall, trying to pick up on the traces of the vasana's plea. She's everywhere at once: I can't make my mind focus on finding her. I shut my eyes tightly and allow her to come galloping in. I see her as she imagines herself: her long sloping neck, her gentle ears, her round eyes. Sadness rises like a blue serpent, encircling me. She thinks she's dying.

"They're going to kill her," I gasp, and I follow her. It's as if she's leaping in front of me as I run through the white warren of the labs, streaming past doors and the false empty windows of the rooms. Behind me Rondo and Alma hiss my name, trying to run lightly.

"We are way out of bounds, O," Alma whispers urgently. "If someone sees us . . ."

I ignore her. I'm close. I don't understand how this works: I can't see her, the way I've seen the philax and the tufali in their moments of fear. Yet this feeling is more intense than anything I've felt so far. But I can't find the source: wandering through the long white halls is fruitless. We turn another blank corner and I glance from side to side. No doors, no windows, just signs in thick black print that read Restricted Access. A hallway of nothing: smooth white walls without a crack.

"Where does this go?" Alma whispers. "I don't even see any doors. What is this?"

"There has to be something," Rondo says. "It's like the illusion windows of the exam rooms O told us about. Hidden."

My brain pulses, the vasana's heart beating so fast that it's like a drumbeat of lightning in my head. I stretch out my hand to feel the smooth white wall, trail my fingertips across it. I walk very slowly, the vasana's fear reeling me in close. My fingertips tingle on the faultless white wall. And then I hear, "Enter, Dr. English."

I jump back in shock, jerking my tingling fingers away from the wall. Its blank whiteness has illuminated: not all of it, just a faintly blue square. In the middle of the blue square is a digital image of my father.

The white wall moves. Not a door like any I've seen in the compound, but a door nonetheless. It slides open to reveal a room, dimmer than the stark hallway and entirely empty.

"Octavia," Alma whispers. She and Rondo stand back away from the door as if it's a trap, their eyes wide. Rondo's neck is craned to peer into the doorway without actually going in.

"It thinks I'm my father," I say, looking at my hand. The door stands open in front of me, and the vasana's mind leaps from the emptiness. I step into the room, ignoring Alma's urgent whispers behind me.

It's an observation room, like the one we were in moments ago. Only here there are no whitecoats watching: there aren't even any benches to accommodate observers. The room is empty, the light illuminating the floor cast from the large observation window at the front of the room. I take three paces forward and then freeze. There she is: the vasana.

Two whitecoats have her on a slightly raised platform. She's bound securely in a standing position, her eyes glassy from the remaining tranquilizer in her blood. And above her, white coat pristine and glaring, is Dr. Albatur.

"Him," I whisper.

"Dr. Albatur attending Vasana 11," he says, his voice loud

and clear. "Today we will be viewing the implications of the previous session's experimental additions. In the last session, we implemented the synthetic genes, along with some alterations to the brain. The alterations, we hope, will—on command—override the specimen's first nature and revert to the programmed behavior. Dr. Jain?"

Dr. Jain, his assistant, steps forward quickly, pulling on thick padded gloves. I approach the glass, wondering if it's two-way, if Dr. Albatur will look up and see me, stop whatever he's doing that has the vasana so terrified, and curse at me. She feels me—she can't move her head, but inside she's looking right at me. I can't tell her anything. It's like being without a tongue.

With the thick gloves padding his hands, Jain reaches for the vasana's face. The animal doesn't resist, merely folds her ears backward in a submissive way as Jain grasps her muzzle and opens her mouth.

"Dr. Jain is opening Vasana 11's mouth to examine the animal's standard dental bite," Dr. Albatur says.

The vasana's teeth are white and somewhat small, the four canines at the front of its mouth—top and bottom—a little longer than the others and leading to flat molars in the back. Jain holds the animal's mouth open and looks to Dr. Albatur. I feel as if I'm floating outside my body: I've spent my entire life hoping to get into the Zoo and observe procedures with the animals of Faloiv. But the coldness of the whitecoats freezes my blood. It's not just the vasana's fear: it's the way the white-coats treat her as if she isn't alive at all, as if she's just one more piece of equipment.

"Initiating synthetic genetic command with Vasana 11," Dr. Albatur says, and takes a device from the workstation by the door. The device is like a slate but not as wide, its design thicker and more rudimentary, with actual knobs and buttons. As he manipulates the controls, a light begins to flash on the device. In my head, the vasana's heart begins to pound. She knows what's next, even if I don't. My heart pounds too. I put my hands on the glass, desperate to help. But I can't.

The vasana trembles on the table. She picks up each of her hooves one at a time, over and over, as if standing on hot coals. Then I look at her mouth, which Jain still holds pried open. The teeth—the regular, even, white teeth—are growing. They're enlarging and elongating, the canines becoming dramatically long, sharpening, narrowing; extending beyond her mouth and hanging over her lips. I know those teeth, but they don't belong in a vasana's jaws. They're the fangs of a dirixi.

"Do you see . . . ?" Alma says breathlessly, somewhere close behind me but far, far away.

Jain finally releases the animal's jaws, and the vasana attempts to close her mouth, prevented from doing so fully because of the enormous new fangs. I gape through the glass at the scene before me. The vasana is an herbivore, but terrifying fangs resembling that of the dirixi now sprout from her mouth.

OLIVIA A. COLE

I reach out to the vasana, but her terror makes her difficult to look at inside the tunnel.

"Vasana 11's teeth have responded positively to the influence of synthetic genes," Dr. Albatur says. "Now initiating sonic communication to the new brain tissue."

A hum enters the observation deck through the small speaker by the window. I've never heard the sound before, but I know immediately that it can mean nothing good. The vasana's muscles twitch as if a current is passing through her body: she begins to swing her long neck from left to right. Faintly, through the speaker, I can hear her snorting and snuffing. The buzzing in my mind quiets, almost to a whisper. *Are you there?* I try to ask, but the shape of the question stays stubbornly in my mind, where it lies flat. Her presence is receding from the tunnel, shrinking.

"Vasana 11 is displaying effects but not a positive sequence. Thirty seconds into sonic communication and no visible sequence."

I don't know what he means by *sequence*. Every word out of his mouth is like a weapon, aimed at the defenseless vasana with the intent to kill. I grope for the buzzing in my mind, but it quiets, smolders, the vasana becoming more and more agitated. Then her head snaps up from where it had been drooping and she fixes her eyes on Jain.

The tunnel in my mind roars open, so abruptly and so wide that I stagger backward away from the window. Alma gives a small scream of surprise and Rondo is by my side, grasping my arm.

"Octavia! Are you all right?"

But above his voice, above everything, I feel the vasana's rage. It's not normal, this anger: it feels false. It's red and vibrating, and in the waves of feeling that pulse through the tunnel into my head, I can feel the vasana somewhere underneath all the rage, drowning in it. It's as if a giant needle filled with magma has been thrust through the animal's flesh and injected into her blood. A foreign substance not her own, but strong enough to take over.

"No," I gasp, and in my mind I reach out for the vasana, try to fasten myself around her and pull her up for air. But she strains against the bonds that hold her to the table, eyes flaming, snarling with the huge, perilous fangs that protrude from her mouth. She growls unnaturally, scrabbling at the platform to get at Dr. Jain and Dr. Albatur. The two whitecoats look on, expressionless. My shock and horror is nowhere on their faces: this is what they expected to happen. What they wanted to happen.

"We have to get her out of here," Alma says, and she and Rondo grasp my arms, towing me toward the door. I fight them, struggling to keep my eyes on the vasana.

"No," I scream, scrambling to get back to the window. "She needs me, she needs me!"

"Do you see what I see, doctor?" Dr. Jain says, his haughty

whitecoat voice like an injection of ice into my spine.

I'm losing the vasana in the tunnel; she's slipping under the red mist of rage. Her gentle spirit is being smothered, from flame to coal, extinguished by whatever false interference the whitecoats have put inside her. Rondo and Alma drag me away, the door whispering open before us. The last thing I hear before we're closed out of the observation room is Dr. Albatur's voice, calm and smug through the intercom.

"Vasana 11 has successfully completed sequence. Will begin alteration of Vasana 12 directly."

CHAPTER 22

In the bright hallway outside the observation room, I crumple to the floor. The hidden door to the empty room slides shut, blending back into the smooth blankness of the white wall. The vibrations of the vasana's strange, unnatural rage still quiver through the tunnel.

"Octavia," Alma says. She crouches down in front of me and grabs my face in both her hands, forcing me to look at her. "You have to get it together. We can't get caught here!"

I stare into her round brown eyes, their thick black eyelashes. I focus on those eyelashes. Their blackness is comforting in this terribly bright hallway. I finally find a hold on the slippery arm in my head and wrench some central muscle, the vasana's pain and anger slowly dimming. I breathe in short gasps. The tunnel spirals shut, the red clouds disappearing inside it and my lungs expanding to take in more air.

"Better?" Alma asks, her eyebrows crunched down in the middle. I nod slowly. My mind quiets, and the only buzzing I hear is the vague hum from the lights above.

"What did we just see?" Rondo says.

"I don't know," Alma says, reaching her hands down to help me rise. "But we can't talk about it here. We need to get back to our observation room *now*."

"She's right," I say, scrambling up with Alma's help. "We need to go."

We hustle back down the direction we came. My mind prickles as we continue past stretches of blank white walls, but I grit my teeth and concentrate on keeping the tunnel shut. I need to learn how to control this better: I can't risk having it open whenever there's something on my radar. I wish I could talk to Rasimbukar; and at the thought of her, I'm stabbed with anxiety. What if she's already here? Locked up like her father probably is? Being experimented on? Seeing what we saw, feeling what I felt . . . no wonder Rasimbukar thinks her people could start a war. Members of the *Council*, the lawmakers of N'Terra. If the Faloii knew what we were doing . . .

"It's this room on the left," Alma says. "Be smooth. Maybe no one noticed we left."

Slipping inside, I expect to see two dozen pairs of eyes turning to stare at us, my father's among them. But all we see are the backs of whitecoats, right where we left them, peering into the procedure room where Dr. Depp has moved on to a young igua, which stands cowering on the table, Dr. Depp rubbing an ultrasound against its belly to view its digestive tract. I wonder if these animals will eventually be subject to painful experiments too.

I exhale softly, grateful that no one seems to notice we were gone. They're all rapt, watching the procedure and taking notes on their slates.

"Where have you three been?"

I jump at the voice so close to my ear. It's Yaya, standing even farther to the rear than we are. I hadn't noticed her leaning against the wall.

"What is wrong with you?" I demand, hissing. "Stars, you scared me. Why are you hiding at the back?"

She shrugs, her eyes wandering to the procedure.

"I came back here to ask you guys what you thought of the igua and then I realized you weren't here. Where were you?"

"Dr. English stopped by," Alma says quickly. I'm impressed with the smoothness of the lie. "She was just asking some preliminary questions about the procedure."

"Oh." Yaya looks disappointed. "She could have asked me. I hope you didn't make us look bad."

She offers a close-lipped smile to show she's kidding, but I know she's not.

"You didn't miss much," she says, turning back to the procedure room. "Besides it's kind of sad."

"Sad?" I say. I wouldn't expect her to attach any emotions to the work in the Zoo.

"Yes. They're all so scared."

"How can you tell?" I ask.

She gives me a look like maybe it's me who needs to be on an exam table.

"Look at him," she says, turning her eyes to the igua. The igua baby crouches as low as its splayed legs will allow, his body shaking. "He looks miserable."

"Yeah." I will the twisting tunnel to stay shut.

"I suppose it's just what we have to do," Yaya says.

"What do you mean?"

"How else are we supposed to learn?" she says. "We're not hurting it, even if it is scared."

I don't reply. If she could sense the igua's fear, I think she'd feel different, and after seeing what I saw of the vasana, everything seems like a horrifying precursor to a looming atrocity.

"You okay?" Rondo whispers.

"I still feel dizzy," I say.

"The vasana . . . this really is worse than we thought," he says.

"I know."

"If the Faloii found out . . ."

"I know."

The whitecoats are all standing up, their murmurs turning into ordinary voices. I crane my neck to see the procedure room and find it empty. The procedure is finished, the baby igua carted away, hopefully back to its mother.

The whitecoats file out, leaving the four of us alone—four: I can feel that we're all suddenly aware of Jaquot's absence again, a hole in our team. We try to fill the void with chatter. Yaya and Alma talk about Yaya's host family, whether she'll be going back to her home compound any time soon. I focus on not shrinking to the floor until Dr. Depp rejoins us, his skin a bit glossy from the decontamination regime.

"Thoughts?" he says to us, taking out his slate and studying something on its screen. He doesn't care about our answers; he's already on to the next procedure in his mind.

"Very interesting," Yaya says.

Dr. Depp doesn't respond, just frowns at his screen, his forehead lined with concentration. I swallow the first small ripples of panic, wondering if somehow he's receiving word that we left the observation room during the procedure.

"Good," he says finally, looking up and nodding once before turning back for the door. "I was skeptical about allowing greencoats internships, but I believe the Council was right about the value. If whitecoats are truly invested in this work, they'll be less likely to leave. Now, I'm going to hand you off to Dr. Wong. He'll get you back to the prep room so you can get a head start on your assignment."

"Sorry, leave?" Alma says in her note-taking voice, as if she just wants clarification. But I know her too well and I can hear the edge in her tone like a scalpel.

We're already following him out into the hall and he's barely acknowledging us, staring at his tablet instead.

"Yes," he says, still distracted by whatever is on his screen. Then he looks up and squints. "What? Oh, Dr. Wong, lovely. You'll take it from here?"

Dr. Wong has appeared from the procedure room with a smile, nodding at Dr. Depp, who doesn't even wait to hear Dr. Wong's reply. He's walking down the hallway, off to his next procedure. Rondo stares after him as if he has a mind to follow, but instead turns on Dr. Wong.

"Dr. Depp was just telling us about why they decided to allow interns," he says matter-of-factly.

"Why?" Dr. Wong says, a little surprised but not unfriendly. "Well, I'm not positive. But I can see a few reasons for allowing younger scientists into the labs."

He begins to move down the corridor, motioning for us to follow.

"Greencoats inducted into the labs for internships will get to spend significantly more time learning the fundamentals and getting acquainted with the methodology, for one," he says. "By the time you're old enough to be assigned a specialty, you will have lab experience on which to base it. Dr. Albatur is ambitious: he has lofty goals for N'Terra and believes that if we want to achieve them, we need to pursue them aggressively. I think the Council hopes that by training greencoats into our processes sooner, you will be better, more committed white-coats in the long run."

"If we don't start a war first . . . ," Alma mutters.

Dr. Wong doesn't hear her. "I wouldn't question it, if I were you. If I could go back and enter the labs at sixteen, I certainly would!"

Rondo turns to look over his shoulder at me and squints. These aren't the answers we were looking for. But we all heard Dr. Depp.

My head still throbs and I focus my energy inward. I ignore the white lights and the hard floor under my feet and turn my attention to the core of my brain. I don't know why I want to reach it: the pain from the vasana is still fresh, the echo of it still floating within me. But I want to know if she's alive.

Now that I know where the tunnel lives and how to summon it, it's easier to find. I pinpoint it nestled in my consciousness and nudge it, willing it to open. At first, nothing. My mind is tired. My headache intensifies as I focus on it. But then I feel the prickling, the stirring spiral of the tunnel yawning open. My brain suddenly feels wide and bright.

And then the buzzing. We pass one of the empty windows and even though my eyes tell me nothing is there, I feel a presence. A feeling like sorrow comes crawling out of the tunnel, a damp helplessness. An igua, I think. It's the mother of the baby igua Dr. Depp just examined: her worry pulses into my brain. The baby has not yet been returned.

We pass door after door; and in passing each one I sense the fear, loneliness, and anger pulsating out from the animals trapped inside. I feel them all, and even smell them: the things that come through the tunnel are various. Some impressions, some sensory details. The familiar scent of the tufali, the sharp smell of an animal I don't recognize but whose biology I can now hear and feel like a shell I've handled while blindfolded. By the time we near the end of the hallway, tears form in the corners of my eyes.

Dr. Wong leads us into the prep room to change out of our lab coats. I keep my head down as we file into the small room.

"A scientist will be in for you in a little while," he says. "I don't know if you'll be viewing any other procedures today. They'll probably just let you work on your assignments."

He smiles and then he's gone, the door sliding shut behind him. Yaya rounds on the three of us, squinting at me where I slump on a stool. I don't have the energy to conceal my exhaustion.

"Is there something you're not telling me?" she demands.

I take a long time deciding whether to answer.

"Well?" she says, sniffling against her will. "Is it something about Jaquot? Everything is strange. They couldn't find his body. Did the Faloii take him? Maybe they set the dirixi on us. Maybe the whitecoats just don't want to scare us . . . maybe that's why people are leaving the labs, like Dr. Depp said."

"He didn't say leaving the labs," Alma corrects. "He said

leaving. We don't know what he was referring to."

"What else would he mean?"

"N'Terra," Rondo says. He's not even addressing her, or any of us. He's thinking, gazing at the door but not really seeing it. His fingers tap out their silent melody, and I wish more than anything that my head was full of his music and not the buzzing.

"No one would leave N'Terra when the Faloii are out there killing people," Yaya says, and I wonder where the rational girl from the Greenhouse went. Is this what fear does to people? "The Faloii probably threatened us and people are afraid to work in the labs. Afraid of all their absurd rules."

I sit up a little straighter on the stool.

"Why would *that* be your theory?" I demand.

"You know why!" she snaps. "We don't know anything about them. I know what my grandmother told me, and Magellan said—"

"Who in the stars is Magellan?"

"*Magellan.* The finder who was bitten that day in the jungle. Weren't you paying attention? He said the Faloii won't let us expand N'Terra. And they won't let us study them to see how they survive here so easily."

"Why *should* they let us study them?" I say loudly, standing. "This is *their* planet. They don't owe us anything. And they damn sure don't owe us running experiments on them."

Rondo and Alma stand uncertainly between us, Alma's

hands half-raised as if to tell us to keep our voices down, but not wanting to say it.

"Magellan said they still act like they're the only ones that live on this planet. They won't even let us explore their part of Faloiv—"

"Why should they?" I snap again. "You're stupid enough to give that argument weight?"

"Don't call me stupid," Yaya says, taking a half step toward me. The shine of tears in her eyes is gone: she's fully angry now and it shows. But I'm angry too. Is this how humans got ourselves into this mess? By believing that we have as much right to this planet as the Faloii? Do we think we own the galaxy? I'm surprised they haven't *already* thrown us back out into the stars.

"Guys," Alma says, keeping her voice low. "We can talk about this later. This *really* isn't the place."

Yaya and I glare at each other, and I find myself wishing for the prickle in my brain. What could I hear in Yaya's mind that she's not saying out loud? Maybe I would understand her better.

"To answer your original question," I say, hearing the nastiness in my tone but unwilling to remove it, "I don't know anything about Jaquot that you don't know. But I will tell you this: if you're as smart as you think you are, it's not the Faloii you should be worried about."

The whisper of the door opening turns our attention to the

front of the room, where my father is stepping in through the doorway with his eyes on his slate.

"What's this?" he says, raising an eyebrow. "Still in white coats? You must have enjoyed the procedure."

"It was brilliant," Alma says quickly. She moves almost imperceptibly to stand between me and my father. Maybe she thinks there's still some trace of emotion left on my face. "But I do have a question about the procedure with Kunike 13," she continues. "What purpose does the data serve for human use? Altering the specimen's diet means that if it ate foods not usually in its nutritional regimen, it could eventually change its fur pattern to camouflage itself with the flora it consumes, correct? But what's the implication for humans?"

She already knows the answer, I'm sure. She's buying me time to calm down.

"The hope is that we will be able to find the proteins that give the kunike this ability and imitate them synthetically for our own use," my father replies. "Just like our skinsuits, the technology of which is a synthetic reproduction of a maigno's ears."

"Do we have their permission?" I can't stop myself from saying. My father tilts his head sideways to look past Alma, who moves out of the way so he can see me.

"Do we have the *animals'* permission?" he says. It wasn't what I meant—I had meant the Faloii—but now that he says it, it doesn't seem stupid at all, the way I know he thinks it does. "No, we haven't asked the animals' *permission*. We will, however, continue to do our duty as scientists of N'Terra and study them for our benefit. We will learn from the kunike's camouflage, for instance, as we design future skinsuits."

"For camouflage," I say. "What are we hiding from? The Faloii?"

"Not at this time," my father says. I don't think such coldness has ever existed on Faloiv. "The dirixi, for one, is high on my list of things we need to hide from."

I almost feel Yaya's heart clench at the reference to Jaquot's death. I can assume that's the part of my father's statement that got her attention, not the more sinister "not at this time." "Not at this time" doesn't mean "never."

"I have a procedure in the Avian compound very soon," he says, addressing the group without taking his eyes off me. "I'll walk you to the Atrium before I'm off. Remove your lab coats and gather your things."

We walk in silence down the long bright hallway. My father isn't even staring into his slate: he leads us down the hall with his eyes forward.

He turns to face us as we catch up to him. He ignores me, instead addressing Alma, Rondo, and Yaya.

"Get something to eat. Afterward someone will find you an empty room to work in."

He takes a step away to leave us, and Yaya surprises me by stopping him.

"Sir, may we continue our work in the Atrium?" she asks.

"The Atrium?" he says, turning slightly.

"Yes. It's . . ." She hesitates, as if realizing she shouldn't have asked. "The light. The light is better there."

"The light."

He squints at her, then glances at me, perhaps to see if this is something I put her up to. But I'm as surprised as he is.

"Yes," he says, turning back down the hall. "Stay out of the way."

"Yes, sir."

He's gone, sweeping down the hall with the tails of his lab coat waving behind him. Off to the Beak, I think—off to oversee more horrors.

"Let's go in," Alma says gently, touching my arm.

I pull away and move toward the door, which opens. Yaya catches my eye, her expression closed and flat. She's angry with me. Our friendship was really just beginning and now it's bent and broken. I was harsh with her, but I wonder which of my words had done the damage: implying that she's stupid or damaging her trust in N'Terra.

As we make our way across the Atrium, I'm grateful that it's almost empty—I have to stop myself from glaring at every whitecoat I pass. How could N'Terrans be so stupid? My temples are throbbing, as if everything I have learned is screaming inside my head. I try to relax and breathe deeply through my nose. Doing so, I catch a whiff of the smell of cooking food, the same scent from the first time we visited the Atrium. I know it's the same smell—full and smoky—but it feels different in my nose. It's as if I only smelled it on a shallow level before, and now I'm taking in the whole of it. It's pungent. Inhaling deeply, it's almost as if the scent takes the shape of something else, knotting in my nostrils and sticking there. I pause, bending slightly, nausea gripping me unexpectedly. What is wrong with you *now*? I think to myself, irritated. My friends didn't notice: they continue toward the central tree, eager to see what the men in green skinsuits offer in the way of food today.

I catch up, drawing even with Rondo. He's already taken a platter and is piling it with zarum and waji. There are the chunks of brown food that we'd seen before too, the dish I've never had a chance to try—zunile, I remember it was called. It's the source of the pungent aroma. I inhale again, trying to identify the scent. It's familiar, somehow. An echo. Rondo dips the spoon into the dish of zunile, stirring up the juices and releasing the odor more fully into the air.

I recoil. It's as if fire has sprung from the very air and burned me, and I double over, retching involuntarily.

"Octavia?" Rondo lets the spoon clatter back into the dish and he drops his platter onto the platform. He reaches out for me. "What's the matter?"

"The zunile," I gasp. It's all I can say before I clamp my mouth shut to keep from vomiting. I bite my lip so hard it bleeds, my hands trembling before I ball them into fists.

"Zunile? The food?" He glances quickly at the dish, as if expecting to see a slimy creature crawling out of the juices. "What's wrong? What's the matter?"

Now Alma and Yaya have also noticed. They swing back from the other end of the platform, their eyebrows low and faces squinted in worry. I can't wait. I turn and run, sweeping past the whitecoats, who look up with only mild interest. I race through the door, out of the warm sunlight and back into the glaring halls of the labs.

The hall is mercifully empty and I tear down the corridor, its whiteness a blur. Finally I reach the sorting room, unoccupied by both animals and humans. Far down the hall I hear Rondo and the others calling for me as loudly as they dare.

I pay them no attention, careening through the gap in the sorting room's door as soon as it opens wide enough. Inside, the piles of eggs wait there impassively. No attendants. I stumble to the corner of the room, sinking down where two walls meet. I breathe deeply, willing the vomit to stay down. Even here, far from the Atrium, I still smell the stink of the zunile. The smoky brown chunks were on the platform as if they too are food, but they're not. Zunile isn't food. The smell is of death. Zunile is a dead animal.

CHAPTER 23

I sit crouched in the corner of the sorting room for what feels like hours, my body trembling. Eventually workers will be coming in—they have to, it's been too long. If they find me here there's no doubt that my father will be summoned. I stumble to my feet, my legs shaking underneath me. I walk quickly to the door, flexing my cramped fingers. I need to get out of here, and I know where I'm going.

The door whispers open, admitting me into the hall. I look in each direction: no sign of Alma or Rondo. They've either returned to the Atrium or have been ushered off to another procedure room. I don't have time to look for them: right now I need answers, and the person who has them is my mother.

The trip from the Zoo to the commune is a blur, sounds and

colors running together. The gray-suited guards at the entrance to the labs speak to me, but even if I wanted to reply, I think the sound that escaped my throat could only be a roar. My anger is rising: it propels me at a sprint past the 'wams of my neighbors, right up to the yellow cloth hanging from the door of my own. I practically fall into the 'wam, panting.

My mother, standing in the hallway as if moving toward her study, turns at the sound of my entrance. She looks surprised to see me but pleasantly so.

"Why . . ." I pant. "Didn't. You. Tell. Me."

She raises an eyebrow, assessing me with her dark eyes.

"Tell you what, exactly?" she says.

"Everything!" I explode. I still haven't caught my breath, and I stand there with my chest heaving, glaring at her.

"I thought I could wait to tell you until everything was figured out," she says. "I didn't think you'd have any contact with actual animals until you were twenty-one, when you were in the labs. The philax was an accident and then the damned internships."

She flops her hands to her sides, the hands that look like mine.

"And the dead animals?" I demand, my anger still large and bright. "What about that? They're *eating* animals in there!"

My throat convulses at the thought of eating something dead, a body that was once alive and walking around, stripped and lifeless and cooked like zarum.

"It's wrong," my mother says, her jaw setting. "It was never supposed to happen. But it was commonplace before Faloiv—a custom passed down from the Origin Planet—and many of the elders of N'Terra resisted the Faloii's order when we landed."

"The Faloii specifically said we can't eat animals and we're doing it anyway?" I'm practically screaming. "We're barbarians! Why did our ancestors eat *animals*?"

My picture of the star people before us has changed from what I've always imagined: they look fanged and dead eyed now, crouching in the shadows like beasts.

"It was called 'meat,'" she says.

"*That's* meat? But Dad said he's eaten meat . . ." I'd managed to catch my breath but now it feels ragged again.

"Yes. I have eaten it too. You must understand: it was customary. People cling to their customs."

"*Customs?*" I demand. "Who cares about customs! You said the Faloii forbid it! Why would we do anything they *forbid* us to do?"

My mother sighs, her body leaning as if considering coming toward me for the first time. Her face is a map of sorrow, and I almost feel bad for shouting. But not quite.

"There are those in the compounds who"—she pauses, anger rippling across her face before she continues—"who don't agree that we should remove meat from our diet. Among other things. There are people in N'Terra who believe we shouldn't obey the laws of the Faloii. Who believe we should be making our own laws. This is one area I have fought against for some time now. It appears the Council is making decisions behind my back."

"And Grandfather," I say. "What about him? I know he didn't die the way you said. I saw the files. He was here. He was on Faloiv."

She looks as if she's taken completely by surprise, her eyes squinting.

"Your grandfather . . . ," she says but can't seem to finish; her eyes lose their steel and turn soft and shiny. "I miss him. But, Afua, there are things that we must do."

I shake my head, waving my hands. I don't want to hear any more. She sounds like my father: "There are things that we must do as scientists" if we want to survive. Obscure things that don't tell me anything about what happened to my grandfather. Everything I'm hearing sounds as if we're doing whatever we can to *ruin* our chances of survival.

"No!" I shout, staring at her accusingly. "You sound just like him! Things we must do to survive here? Like what? Like killing animals and eating their dead bodies? Like implanting vasana with dirixi teeth? Altering their brains so that they become killers? No wonder we're so worried about war, we—"

But she's rushing over to me from the hallway, the space

between us closed in an instant. Her fingers grip my shoulders like talons, her eyes inches from mine.

"What did you say?" she snaps, all the softness gone from her eyes.

"Wh-what?"

She shakes me and I almost hear my brain rattle.

"What did you say?" she repeats. "About the vasana? What did you say?"

I shake her off, stumbling backward, fear creeping in to share space with my fury.

"The vasana!" I shout. "I saw Dr. Albatur with Vasana 11. The dirixi fangs. I saw the procedure. I know what you're doing back there in the secret parts of the Zoo! Don't act so—"

"Dr. Albatur?" she interrupts. "You saw the Head of the Council tampering with the brain of a vasana?"

I wonder briefly if she's manipulating me: running an experiment on my strange, colorful brain; an experiment she's recording with some hidden device.

"Yes," I snarl, sizing her up for any discernible reaction. "I snuck into a restricted part of the Zoo. I saw Dr. Albatur. I saw the vasana. I saw *everything*."

At first I think she's attacking me. She springs forward and I cringe, waiting for I don't know what: for fists, for a tranq gun she hid somewhere in her lab coat. But instead she's at the front entrance to the 'wam, standing there in the open door looking back at me with her eyes slanted into piercing slits.

"Hurry up," she says, jerking her head at the commune outside.

"Wh-where are we going?" I've already taken a step toward her, but I pause, unsure. Is she taking me to the labs? To find my father and tell him what I've done? I feel the way the vasana must have felt; fear and anger erupting in my veins like a serum. If she tells me we're going to the Zoo, I think, preparing my body for my blooming plan, then I will run. I'll run and find a way out of the compound, find Rasimbukar. . . .

"To the Greenhouse," she says, turning her back on me, forcing me to follow. "We need to find Dr. Espada."

CHAPTER 24

The sun and my fear combine to wring the sweat out of my skin. The softness of my mother's face has been replaced by stone, a blank wall that fends off every one of my questions as she marches us outside to the chariots.

"Why are we going to see Dr. Espada? What's going on between you and Dr. Albatur?"

She ignores me, backing up the chariot and steering it toward the gates. Only then does she speak, the steel of her face giving way to a warm smile. I realize I was right about the second face she wears in N'Terra, and I shiver in the heat.

"Hello, Amelie."

The guard at the gates steps out of the small white 'wam, her buzzgun slung across her chest. The pleasure at being greeted by name is a ripple that stirs her solemnity. She holds out her slate, my mother's face already displayed on its screen.

"Dr. English," she says, holding out her slate. My mother presses her thumb to the corner of the screen and hands it back, and Amelie makes a few selections before passing it across to me. When I press my thumb to the square alongside the image of my face, I expect the usual nod from the guard before she opens the gates. But this time she squints at the screen.

"Is there a problem?" my mother says.

"Well," the guard says. "Sort of. Some kind of glitch. Miss English's print registers as Dr. English. Her father."

She turns the slate around so my mother can see, and there's the same image of my father that had appeared on the wall outside Dr. Albatur's hidden lab.

"That's strange," my mother says, as if it's not strange at all. "I'll mention it to Octavius. He has a meeting with Dr. Older this evening anyhow."

"Oh . . . ," the guard begins.

"Thank you, dear," my mother says. I've never heard her call anyone *dear* in my life.

"You're welcome," the guard says. She opens her mouth as if to say more, but changes her mind. She opens the gate.

My mother guides the chariot through the opening and out onto the red road. We say nothing until we are a safe distance from the compound, then I turn my head to look at her.

"Mom?"

She glances at me, her eyebrows raised.

"I told you that you had your father's hands," she says.

"What does that mean?" I say. "Why do the scanners think I'm Dad?"

"Because I reimprinted your fingers," she says.

"You *what?*"

"When I had you in my lab after you got lost in the jungle," she says. "I knew it would be . . . useful."

"What do you mean?"

She ignores me, unfolding her hood from the inside of her skinsuit and latching the mouth guard. She glances at me with a pointed look that tells me to do the same. When I do, she puts the chariot into high gear and we're buzzing down the road, red dust flying.

"Why are we going to see Dr. Espada?" I shout over the whir of the chariot and the whine of the wind.

"Listen!" she shouts back.

My mind prickles instantly, a rippling in the center of my brain. The mental muscle I use to access the tunnel feels more solid this time. I locate it without much teeth grinding, and coax the tunnel into spiraling slowly open.

I find my mother there waiting for me, images from her pushing through the tunnel almost immediately. I try to control their flow, focusing on each feeling and shape rather than letting it all rush past me in a cascade. I see my mother and father as children, becoming friends. He an orphan and she with only one parent, her father gone. I feel their loneliness, my mother's mother buried in lab work, venturing into the jungle to learn more about our new planet. My parents grow, bond, and live together, have me. I watch fragments of their lives flying through the universe of my mind like comets: my father holding me, my mother's joy for him as he revels in parenthood. They make promises to each other. My father vows to do whatever it takes to make a future that is safe. My grandmother behind him frowning.

The chariot whips past a small group of marov, which scatter into the bushes. Their clustered fear slips through the tunnel to mingle with my mother's thoughts. Above, oscree flap and cry, and a hefty roigo settles on a branch silently: I get the impression of its attention as it focuses on our chariot passing by. My brain is too loud now: too many lives and minds coming from all sides, filling my head with their worries and desires. How does my mother keep them all out? I clamp my mind around the tunnel and force it to shut, the buzz of feelings slowly fading.

"Where'd you go?" my mother calls as we round the corner to the Greenhouse.

"I can't keep everything straight! It's too much. How do you do it?"

"We're a little different," she says, but I barely hear her over the wind.

"What?"

"Just wait. We're almost there."

The Greenhouse is quiet on the outside: all the younger students will have already eaten second meal and are back in the building with Dr. Yang learning the scientific method or basic species differentiators. I'm gripped by a sudden pang of nostalgia, longing for those days when everything was simple: before abnormal brain scans and bloodthirsty dirixi, before secret labs and dead animals disguised as food. My mother brings the chariot to a stop outside the Greenhouse and hops off, walking quickly to the entrance before I'm even fully on the ground.

"Hurry," she says, disappearing through the doorway.

When we open his door, Dr. Espada is sitting at his desk, his slate shining up on a face lined deeply with concentration. A three-dimensional image of a maigno hangs suspended in the air in front of his desk, displayed there by his projector. He looks over in surprise at the sound of the door folding open, the surprise turning into a smile at the sight of us.

"The English women," he says, standing slowly. He greets my mother with a kiss on each cheek.

"Bad news, Tomás," my mother says, keeping her voice low. She motions for me to slide the door shut, then ushers Dr. Espada over to the windows, the thick green glass lending an emerald tint to both their faces. I close the door and hurry over to them.

"It's just what you were afraid of," she's saying when I join them. "Albatur has already begun weaponization."

"What?" Dr. Espada says. "How can he? The Council!"

"The Council said no before he was elected," my mother says. "Now that he's the Head, he's slowly turned more and more of them. Those spineless fools. But it's true. Octavia saw it with her own eyes. Afua, tell him what you've seen."

I tell Dr. Espada about the secret lab, about Albatur, the vasana and its terror, the horrifying teeth growing from its mouth on Albatur's command.

"Stars," Dr. Espada says, removing his glasses and rubbing the bridge of his nose.

"What did you say he called the specimen?" my mother says, looking at me.

"Eleven," I say. "Vasana 11."

"Eleven!" Dr. Espada says. "So many . . ."

"There's going to be a war, isn't there?" I say. "This is what Rasimbukar meant by us breaking the rules."

"Rasimbukar? Where did you hear that name?" my mother whispers.

"I met her in the jungle," I say. They both stare at me, their lips pressed tightly together. There are so many secrets: I forget who knows what. "She . . . she told me . . ."

"She told you what?" my mother demands.

"She told me she needed my help getting her father out."

"Has she told the rest of the Faloii that we have him?"

"Wait, what?" Now it's my turn to eye her. "You *know* her? And, wait, you knew that we have her father?"

ant I take a step away from her.

"Yes, of course," my mother says. "Not that I was supposed to know. I figured that out on my own. Now, has Rasimbukar told the rest of the Faloii that we have her father?"

"No," I say uncertainly. "They don't know that he's missing—he's not expected back from his journey yet. But they're going to find out when he doesn't come back. Or when Rasimbukar decides she's sick of waiting for me."

"I should have known she'd be out in the jungle that day," Dr. Espada says. "When I sent Octavia to the rhohedron field, I should've gone with her to explain to Rasimbukar."

"When you sent me?" I interrupt.

He puts his spectacles back on and looks at me with his usual expression of patience. "You didn't see the rhohedron field in your head?" he says. "You didn't suddenly know where you needed to run?"

I pause, remembering. The fear had been so intense, so hectic, that everything now seems blurry. I recall Dr. Espada shouting at me to run . . . and then the image of the enormous red flowers floating before my eyes.

Suddenly my brain is buzzing: something is hailing me from the tunnel. I slowly muscle the tunnel open, cautious about what I might find.

It's Dr. Espada. I gasp, feeling him there, his gentle spirit and his probing mind, nudging me with his consciousness. He's passing me an image, blurry around

326

the edges: an echo. It's us, him and me, in his classroom, the day he'd assigned the internships. I hear his voice—*Listen*—and I understand.

"You too," I say, withdrawing from the tunnel, letting it close slowly.

"Yes," he says.

"Who else?"

"Just the three of us. And your grandmother. She was the first."

"We don't have time to tell you everything right now," my mother says, and holds up a hand before I can argue. "I understand your anger. But there's too much that needs telling. I'll say this: trust Rasimbukar, and trust us. The Faloii gave us a gift to protect life on Faloiv—ours and theirs. There are those of us in the compound—N'Terrans—who are making decisions against the wishes of the Council that put us all in jeopardy. We cannot let that happen, or all is lost."

"But *why* is this happening?" I stammer. "Why did we take Rasimbukar's father to begin with?"

"It's complicated," my mother says. She shoots a look at Dr. Espada.

"What?" I growl, and when neither of them answers, I repeat it a little louder. "*What?*"

My mother looks at me frankly. "Your father is playing a dangerous game with Dr. Albatur. Albatur wants to leave Faloiv and he has convinced your father to help him."

Surely I've misheard her—the stupidity of it seems impossible to believe. Leave Faloiv?

"To go where?" I say. "Why?"

"Many reasons," Dr. Espada sighs. "They believe that the past is more valuable than what the future holds. Re-creating it is easier than imagining something new."

"Now that you've met Dr. Albatur, you can see why he would desire something else," my mother says. "His body cannot tolerate Faloiv. Tomás and I believe that he has preyed upon your father's desires to draw him into a plan. A plan that violates our agreement with the Faloii."

"I did hear them talking about a project together," I say.

She nods solemnly. "Your father wants to change the terms of N'Terra's existence on this planet. He wants N'Terrans to be in control, free to expand and alter Faloiv as we see fit. He wants the ability to power the *Vagantur*, to leave and come back at will. None of which is possible without an energy source that is precious to the Faloii. . . ."

"What energy source?" I say. I've never read about an energy source: only that when trying to repair the *Vagantur*, a power cell had always eluded N'Terra.

"We have to get Adombukar out of the labs," my mother says. "That's step one. Any attempts we make at peace will be futile if we still have one of the Faloii held prisoner. We must free him and expose Dr. Albatur—then hope the Council listens. If it turns out he's gotten to the other councilmembers before we do . . . we might be on our own."

"We might be, Samirah," Dr. Espada interjects, tugging on the short hairs of his beard. "They're serving zunile in the Atrium. The Council never voted on that, so that tells me Albatur is reaching as far as his powers as Head will allow."

My mother makes a sound of annoyance and squeezes her bottom lip.

"Albatur," she says with disgust.

"Why did you let this happen?" I demand. "You didn't know about Vasana 11, but you *did* know about the zunile and you just let it happen! People are eating that . . . that stuff! My friends are eating it! Oh, stars, if they knew."

My mother grabs one of my shoulders and jars me into silence. "This is complicated, Afua!" she snaps. "We can't trust everyone on the Council! They don't know about the gift we've been given, that we can communicate with the Faloii the way the Faloii communicate with each other. We mean to do good, but there are those in N'Terra who would see this as an act of treachery. A reversal of the Council's goals for the settlement."

"But why? You're trying to keep the peace!"

"Fear makes people stupid," Dr. Espada says. "It makes them violent."

"That's not an answer."

My mother and Dr. Espada exchange looks again and I grope in my mind for the tunnel to see if they're thinking anything I can pick up on. But my mind is silent.

OLIVIA A. COLE

"That's complicated too," Dr. Espada says. "Sometimes keeping the peace isn't peaceful. Right now, based on . . . past events, it's possible that the Council could view citizens of N'Terra who sympathize with the Faloii as traitors. Violence could ensue, and we can't allow that to happen."

"Past events? What past—"

"What matters right now is getting Adombukar out of the labs, and you're the one who needs to do it, Afua," she says.

"Why," I say, not even as a question. I have too many questions and I'm tired of asking them and not getting answers.

"Because you have a gift," she says.

"So do you," I counter.

"You're a little different."

"How?"

"Later," Dr. Espada says. "Right now we need a plan."

"No," I insist, raising my voice. "I need to know. Tell me what you're talking about. How am I . . . how is my brain different?"

My mother starts to speak, but Dr. Espada steps forward, his hands raised to placate me.

"We'll show you," he says, gesturing toward the door. "Will that satisfy you?"

I follow them back down the hall and out the Greenhouse doors that I know so well. Somewhere behind me I can hear the children in Dr. Yang's classroom singing a song that helps them memorize the scientific method. I remember myself as

330

a child, sitting cross-legged on the worn woven rug alongside Alma, my mouth open wide, chanting, "First you make an observation of the planet around, take notes to record all the things that you found." I step out into the sun and breathe a sigh of relief under its heat.

"Listen," Dr. Espada says.

It's almost easy now. I flex the invisible muscle in my mind, the unseen fist uncurling and letting the tunnel spiral open. The light comes in, my mind wide and bright. I hear little things: oscree feeding on the ground, wary of the nearby kunike. I feel the kunike, their hungry vigilance. I think of the kunike in the lab on Dr. Depp's exam table: the creature's paralyzing fear. There is fear here as well, the ever-present fear for survival, but it's natural, rhythmic—not the pounding terror and ruin in the labs.

What do you hear? Dr. Espada says.

At first I think he said it out loud, but then I realize that the shape of the words has come through the tunnel. I find him in my mind, along with my mother—their quivering concern for me, their impatience for me to see what they're showing me about myself.

"The same thing you hear," I say out loud, annoyed by their impatience. "Oscree. Kunike."

Not quite.

I notice it, then. The shape of Dr. Espada and my mother in my mind: it's missing something. Between me and the kunike and the oscree, linking each of us, is a wavering path of . . . something. Not light, not sound. But a . . . string: a feeling like a string, drawing each of us together in a web. I feel the string between me and my mother, between me and Dr. Espada, but they're connected to nothing else. They float somewhere separate from the animals: untethered, unconnected.

You can't hear the animals, I say to them, floating the words through the tunnel.

No.

"Now call to them," Dr. Espada says. "Call to the oscree."

I'm not sure what he means. Call to them? The oscree don't speak my language, and I certainly don't speak theirs.

My mother must feel my confusion because she says, *Show them your heart,* the feeling behind her words as gentle as her voice when she speaks out loud.

In my mind, I reach out to the oscree on the ground. They are six feet away, pecking at the red dust for insects, cocking their tiny blue heads toward the hidden kunike every now and then. The string between us quivers, as if I strummed it with my finger. Their consciousness prickles and leans in my direction, listening. They've noticed me all along: I'd shown up on their mental radar when I first opened the tunnel. But now they pay attention. I don't know what to tell them, what to show them, so I just think soft yellow shapes, images that, in my heart, feel safe and gentle. I close my eyes, focusing on sending the peaceful greeting down the line toward the small flock of fluttering minds.

Octavia, I hear my mother say.

I open my eyes and find the oscree in the dust at my feet. If I were only looking with my eyes, I would think they were ignoring me. They hop about, picking at things my eyes can't see, ruffling their feathers. But in my mind, they're looking at me. There are no words, only their fragile trust. *We are here*, they seem to say. *Now what do you want?*

One lands on my shoe, unafraid. I almost laugh out loud, in awe. They are so beautiful up close, free from cages and fear. They respond to my amusement: they return the yellow feelings of warmth down the tunnel, which my mind absorbs gratefully, like a stomach digesting nutrients. It feels the way the rhohedron nectar had felt as my body absorbed it in the jungle.

"There's more, baby," my mother says, reaching out to touch my cheek, her smile small. "More than you know yet. So much more."

At the sound of her voice, the oscree take flight and flap off into a nearby ogwe. They apologize as they go, tiny shapes of green coming through the tunnel whose meaning I understand perfectly, even if they lack a common language.

I allow the tunnel to close, and a moment later I'm faced with only my mother and Dr. Espada in the flesh.

"If you can't hear the animals," I say, "what can you hear?"

"Just each other," Dr. Espada says. "And the Faloii. The Faloii, of course, can hear us, each other, the animals, everything."

"Now take off your shoes," Dr. Espada says.

"What?" I don't move. The idea of taking off my shoes outside makes me nervous. I'm rarely without my shoes even in the compounds: Who knows what could be in the grass out here? I think of the morgantan and its nasty bite on the finder's leg in the jungle, the bleeding that had drawn the dirixi out of the trees.

Dr. Espada starts to repeat himself, but a noise draws my attention away. At first I think it's the wind, whipping up the dust and moving it toward us in red billows. But the whining isn't the wind: it's three chariots, speeding down the path toward the Greenhouse. One of them is a longer chariot, the Worm that used to carry me to school in the morning. I cover my nose and mouth to protect my lungs from the sweeping dirt, squinting my eyes to keep out the grit.

The chariots stop just yards away from us, their drivers leaping off the standing platforms and striding toward us and the Greenhouse. Their pace seems urgent and intent.

But they don't pass us for the Greenhouse entrance; they stop in front of us and one says, "Dr. Espada, Dr. English, we need you to come with us."

"Come with you?" Dr. Espada says. "Has something happened?"

"Come with us, doctors," the same driver says, his mouth a rigid line across his chin. I've never seen him around the compounds and I don't like his face. A square jaw with reddish hairs sprouting from it. He seems too young to be speaking with any authority, yet here he is. "You'll be briefed when you arrive at the Council."

"The Council?" my mother says, stepping forward. "I'm *on* the Council and I haven't heard anything about this. What's going on?"

"You'll need to come with us, Mrs. English," the shortest of the three says, and my mother smirks.

"Mrs. English?" she replies in a voice that very clearly says she doesn't *need* to do anything. "You will address me as Dr. English. Now tell me who has asked for Dr. Espada and myself." She says "asked for" in a peculiar way, as if she knows whoever has sent these three young men in gray uniforms had not been asking.

The one whose face I don't like moves his hand. Not any defensive movement or a gesture that says anything specific. But in its tiny motion, up toward his hip before settling again by his side, I become aware of the tranq gun in a holster there on his white belt.

"Mom . . . ," I say quietly, sending her a flare in my mind.

"Come, Tomás," my mother says, stepping forward, triggering a look of surprise on the first driver's features. "Someone at the Council wants to see us, it seems. I can't imagine what for." She drawls this last part in a voice slanted with sarcasm, and the driver tightens his jaw.

Dr. Espada follows my mother over to the Worm, where the third driver steps forward as if to put his hands on them. The square-jawed man waves his hand and the driver steps back again. My mother boards the Worm calmly, expressionless. Dr. Espada climbs on behind her, his face a picture of annoyance. The man with the square jaw turns back to me after watching them take their seats.

"Miss English, your father has asked me to inform you that he'll be waiting for you at home when you return to the compound."

For a moment I think he's going to grab me, force me onto the Worm with my mother, and I tense my body in preparation. I'm not sure if I'll run or if I'll fight if he touches me. Or maybe neither: maybe I'll just let him push and shove me over to the long chariot. But he turns his back on me.

The third driver boards the Worm and powers on its battery. The whine of it fills the air as I stand there in the red dust that has begun to swirl, watching my mother being carted off to the Council under ominous circumstances. My nails dig into my palms, balled in helpless rage. And then I sense the prickling in my mind: my mother is waiting there in the tunnel before it's even fully open.

Your empathy is your greatest asset. My mother's words come through to me as a firm shape like a stone. *Ambystoma maculatum.*

I almost yell to her, to ask her to explain, to tell her I don't understand. But I don't. The three chariots turn slowly away from the Greenhouse and leave me standing there in their churning dust, reaching out in my mind for my mother. But she's either too far away or she's closed herself off. Only when the machine bearing my mother is out of sight do I allow the tunnel to relax.

As it's spiraling shut, slowly and resolutely, something causes me to clench the muscle in my mind, gripping it tightly to hold the tunnel open a moment longer. I hear something—not hear, but feel: an abrupt pulse of energy that appears on the horizon of my mind like a sudden burst of starlight. I can't make out what it is, not quite. I'm starting to develop a sense of near and far in the tunnel: the hazy buzzing of all Faloiv, the constant pleasant thrum of the lives around me; the prickling of someone or something nearby that's prodding my conscious-ness; and then this, the hazy illumination of something close enough to register in the tunnel but just far enough to remain obscure. I wonder if this is what carnivores register as for each other, predators hunting predators, and at first it makes me afraid. But the presence is changing, right now: the pulse of it grows in clarity, and a sense of familiarity makes its way into my mind, a shape of smells and feelings and echoes that forms a name.

"Rasimbukar," I say out loud.

Nothing at first, just the increasing clarity, blurred edges of thoughts becoming close enough to read clearly.

I am here, she tells me.

Where?

In the trees.

I squint at the tree line a hundred yards away. Though I can see nothing, I feel her there, can almost imagine the dots on her forehead arranging and rearranging in a shifting frown.

They took my mother, I tell her.

Yes.

Are they going to hurt her?

I do not know. But your mother is brave. Intelligent. She will do what she needs to do.

"I didn't know we were breaking the rules," I say out loud without meaning to, and I find myself sending her my memories of the day's events: the zunile, the smell of death, my disgust.

She immediately sends me back her own revulsion, a wave of nausea, despair—and rage—that nearly doubles me over with its intensity. She isn't gentle: she pushes it through the tunnel to me and doesn't withdraw it until I'm physically gagging.

This is only one of the things your people have done, she tells me, finally withdrawing her disgust from my mind. *Now there may be war. You must return my father.*

"I'm trying," I plead, again saying the words out loud as well as thinking them.

Tonight, she tells me, and I comprehend her desperation, her anger. If Dr. Albatur could feel these things—if my father could—I wonder if they would still do the things they do.

Do your people know we have him? I ask.

No. But I will have no choice but to tell them if I do not see my father tonight. I will wait no longer.

And then she's gone.

CHAPTER 25

I reenter the Mammalian Compound's main dome amid a flurry of children. Dr. Yang had discovered me outside the Greenhouse and insisted I join the kids on their Worms back home. They scurry through the trees back to the commune, oblivious to the dark cloud that hovers over N'Terra. They know nothing of war. Neither do I. But I'm starting to see how one begins.

Something is different. A smell, a sound. I can't pinpoint it, and it nags at me as I walk slowly down the path toward the communal dome. Here and there whitecoats walk in pairs on their way to the labs or toward the entrance to leave for another compound. They whisper, which isn't unusual, but something about the *way* they whisper needles at me: their heads bend toward each other, the slightest hunch in their shoulders as they exchange words. I stand aside for two of them on the path and see their eyes dart at me, momentarily silent, before they resume conversation after they've passed. It's only when I'm on the path again, walking between the striped trunks of the ogwe, that it hits me.

I don't smell anything.

The comforting, complicated smell of the trees, their interlocking scent that always fills my nose but that no one else seems to notice, is gone. I stop abruptly on the path, and inhale deeply, desperately. I pick up the vaguest scent of something in the air: I can't decipher it. I think of what my mother had said: *There's more, baby.* Does that mean . . . ? I reach into my mind and open the tunnel, just a little.

The scent slithers into my head, a hollow empty smell that makes my stomach clench. I don't know what it is and I've never smelled it before, but it's being emitted by the ogwe trees. The comforting scent that usually fills my body when I'm around them has been yanked away. The trees no longer comfort me: they warn me. It's almost as if they're whispering to me, their whispers in the form of smells, expressing caution.

"Miss English."

A voice startles me, interrupting my thoughts, and I almost mistake it for the trees, murmuring to me. But it's a whitecoat with long curly hair tied back at the nape of his neck. I recognize him vaguely from the Zoo: angular features and dark eyes.

"Your father has been looking for you," he says.

I glance quickly up and down the whitecoat's body, looking for a tranq gun or some other thing he might use to subdue me. But this man doesn't seem to mean any harm. He holds his slate loosely under his arm, his eyes sharp in shape but soft in expression.

"He's very upset," he says.

"Upset?"

"Yes, I think something has happened with your mother. I'm not sure what." My face must betray some hint of emotion, because he extends a hand toward me, stopping short of touching me. "She's all right. But Dr. Albatur seems to be under the impression that she's . . . done something. I've never heard of the Council making an arrest—this is all very strange. But find your father. I just saw him leave the labs headed for the commune."

My thanks is barely strong enough to make it past my teeth.

My steps slow when I reach the stairs that lead into the compound—the dread of facing my father presses against my sternum like a heavy wind, almost pushing me backward. I wearily make my way down the packed-dirt stairs one at a time.

Movement below catches my eye and I pause by my favorite flowers, their stems and petals curling away from me, slowly turning the deep blue of their evening shade. Down where the 'wams begin, a cluster of people has gathered, and the rising sound of a commotion reaches my ears.

Six gray-clad guards are spread out before a crowd of people who live in the Paw. Most still wear their white coats from the labs, a few are shopkeepers and wear skinsuits of various colors. From this height, I can't make out any of their identities: just the colors of their clothing. I know not who but *what* each of them is. I can remember a time when I would have given anything to be wearing one of those white coats, to know that even a far-off eye would see me wearing it and know what I was. Now it seems stupid: Wearing it now would mean what, exactly? To Rasimbukar's eyes, it might mean that I'm an invader; an alien who came to this planet in supposed peace and then brutalized the people and creatures who were here first.

I descend a few more steps to get a better look at what's happening in the commune. The commotion has increased in volume. By the time I find myself near the bottom of the steps, the outrage in the voices is like a collection of smoldering coals. Everyone is angry, but the presence of the buzzguns covers the heat in a layer of ash.

"This is ridiculous!" one woman in a white coat squawks, gesturing with small, tight movements of her hands. I'm not close enough to see the expression on her face, but her voice teeters between anger and fear. "I've never heard of the Council coming into people's homes this way! What is the meaning of this?"

I can't hear the guards' responses, if they answer at all. Two other gray-suited guards come out of a 'wam on the edge of the commune, the inhabitant of the 'wam following them, gesturing angrily.

"Anything?" the guards outside call.

"Nothing."

The guard raises his voice to address the small crowd of people.

"We're all through now, everyone. Back to your business."

He turns to go, nodding at his cohorts, but the same woman in the white coat shouts after them.

"You barge into our homes to look for something—you won't tell us *what*—and when you don't find it, you just leave? What kind of nonsense is this? I'll be talking to Dr. English about this!"

"He already knows," a guard says.

I move closer. Why are they searching people's 'wams?

"Dr. English believes that there may be something in the compound that shouldn't be," the guard who seems to be in charge shouts. "We're checking 'wams for your own safety."

This sends a ripple of uneasy chatter through the crowd. I can almost see the vagueness of the guard's statement taking the form of many fears—I picture Dr. Albatur puffing a pipe and blowing Faloii-shaped smoke figures across the commune.

"The goal is to not cause any panic," the guard says, turning away from her again, headed toward the elevator with the others. "Go back to your meals. Everything is fine."

They disappear into the elevator and the door slides shut behind them. The small crowd of people stands grumbling, close together like a herd of nervous animals.

I continue past the crowd, the sound of their anger fading as I walk quickly down the path toward my 'wam. "Something in the compound that shouldn't be." What if it's Rasimbukar's father? I pass through the shadow of the tower, the sound of engineers' hammers clattering as if against my skull. Would Adombukar hurt anyone? Any inclination toward understanding that he had before has probably disappeared now that he's been kept prisoner in our labs for weeks. At my door, I hastily swipe my palm across the lock.

My father is sitting on one of the plain clay chairs in the small seating area outside our kitchen. There's no slate in his hands, no box of slides nearby. He merely slumps there, staring at the brushed dirt floor, and raises his eyes to my face when I stop just inside the door. I almost speak, but his face catches my tongue. His gray eyes are red, swollen; his expression slack and empty like a ghost who has only just realized he's a ghost. His lips part to whisper, "Octavia. You're home."

"What's going on?"

I almost call him "Dad," but my mouth won't let me say it. I was prepared for a fight: to face down his coldness with coldness of my own. But the man in front of me is too weak to be cold. His eyes are wet, not frozen.

"I'm glad you're here," he says. He stands up, an action that looks like it requires all but a drop of the energy in his body.

"Are you okay?" I've never seen him like this.

"All I have ever wanted is to keep you safe," he says, closing his eyes and rubbing one temple. "To build a world that you can be proud of, a world that will never disappoint you."

"Sir . . ."

He opens his eyes and stares at me. They're less wet, the look in them harder than before.

"Your mother and I know what it's like to lose our home. We didn't want you to ever know that pain—we wanted you to be free of it. We worked together with the other scientists to do what it takes to ensure our future. Your mother and I had a common goal."

I stare at him, speechless.

"I may have been wrong about that last part," he adds helplessly, tilting his head back to look at the ceiling. He blinks hard several times. When he sighs, it's the sound of an old man.

"Sir . . ."

"Did you know the Faloii can speak to the animals?" he says, his voice sharpening now. It's the sound of a stone being carved into a knife.

"Sir?" I try to imagine my voice as a stone as well. Give away nothing.

He's blinking, but it's as if he's clearing something from his eyes.

"The telepathy, they can communicate with the animals. And each other, of course—all in their minds. Your mother didn't want me to know. She pretends not to understand the significance. But she isn't stupid, Octavia. No, she isn't stupid." I get the feeling that he's talking to himself, and I don't interrupt as he continues. "There's more to it than speech. I don't understand it yet, but there's power in that connection. Do you know what we could have done if we'd known sooner? Harnessing the power of these animals, of the Faloii . . . N'Terra could have been a city by now. A kingdom. We don't know, but we will."

When he stops he has fixed his eyes on me, their pupils shifting slightly as they explore my features. I wonder if he's seeing my eyes that look like his, or the cheekbones and nose that are like my mother. I want to cover my face.

"Sir, what is going on?" I say.

He takes a step toward me.

"Why did your mother take you to the Greenhouse?" he says. His voice is like a needle pushing through my skin. "Why did you go see Dr. Espada?"

"I—she . . ." I fumble for a lie. "My hands were hurting. From touching that vine in the jungle. It was keeping me from working in the labs. She said Dr. Espada had a salve."

"Did she take anything with her?" he demands. "What did she have with her when you two left?"

"Did she *take* anything? No—what do you mean?"

"The guards were here a little while ago," he says. "Do you know what they were looking for?"

"A—a specimen escaped from the labs," I say. "That's what people are saying."

"A specimen?" He almost laughs. "No, they're not looking for a specimen. They were looking for something else."

Is he talking about Adombukar? Would he really describe him as a *thing*?

"The kawa, Octavia," he says. "Have you seen it?"

"The—the what?" I know that word. I've heard Rasimbukar speak it.

His hand jerks out and in one forceful motion, sweeps the old photo of my grandparents off the wall. The glass that encases their faces, the old gold frame, shatters against the door to our 'wam. My hands clamp over my mouth, the pulse of my palm racing against my lips.

"The kawa, Octavia!" he shouts. "The egg! Did your mother bring it into this house? Did she take it to the Greenhouse?"

I'm trembling. *The egg. The egg is the kawa?*

He closes the gap between us now and it takes everything in me not to stumble backward, away from him. He stands in front of me gazing down, all the sadness leaked from his body and replaced with an immense anger.

"An egg?" I say. My voice trembles. "Dad, I don't know about any eggs."

He turns his back on me and walks across the room, passing

the chair and reaching the kitchen. On the platform rests the lopsided bowl my grandmother had made long before I was born. He takes it in his hands, and for a moment I think perhaps the sight of it has cooled his rage. Then he lifts it high over his head and sends it crashing to the floor, a thousand pieces of Nana exploding across the 'wam.

I run. I'm out of the 'wam in a flash, ignoring the sound of my father shouting my name. I make it all the way to the tower before I stop to catch my breath. Tears won't come—my shock is a tourniquet. Here, in the center of the commune, more people have come to congregate; returning home and learning from their neighbors about what Albatur sent the guards to do. The fear on my face must blend in with the expressions of those around me: no one gives me a second look. I comb the crowd—no Rondo, no Alma. They can't still be in the Zoo: it's too late in the day. All of the interns would have been sent home by now. Or maybe they're holding them there on my father's orders, demanding to know where I am.

The thought is like the first snap of a spark that starts a fire. The blaze of fear spreads, and I weave in and out of the crowd, jogging when I break free, then sprinting toward Rondo's 'wam.

I arrive, panting. I've never been inside, only passed by, but his 'wam is the only one in its cluster that doesn't have anything hanging on its door, nothing to decorate it. It's plain in its white-clay eggness. I approach the door, too nervous to lay my palm against the lockpad. But I do, and I vaguely hear the soft, melodic tone inside the 'wam that alerts its inhabitants to a visitor.

The door slides open almost immediately and I gasp. I expected to stand there waiting for a while, if not forever. I also expected one of Rondo's parents to answer the door, but instead I find Alma in front of me.

"Alma?"

"Octavia!"

She throws her arms around me, her enormous hair covering my face.

"Alma, what are you doing here? Are Rondo's parents home?"

She releases me from the hug and pulls me inside.

"No, they're both in the Zoo. When Rondo and I left for the day, we went straight to your house to see if you were there since we couldn't find you. But it was just your dad and he was acting really weird. So we left and came here."

"I was just there." I nod. "He's freaking out. My mother . . ."

"Was taken to the Council," Alma says, biting her lip. "I know. Oh, stars! Do you know what's going to happen?"

"No." I shake my head and sit down. "I don't know what they know. But my dad is mad. Madder than I've ever seen him. He knows about the egg—"

Alma's hand shoots out and covers my mouth.

"Wait, wait," she says, jerking her head over her shoulder.

With her hand still over my lips, I lean forward and peer

down the hallway. Rondo's bedroom door is open, light spilling out into the corridor.

"Jaquot's father is here," she says, lowering her hand.

Jaquot's sleeping platform has already been dissolved, the pavi extract having done its work. Rondo sits on the remaining bed. At the desk, a man in a white coat stands with an open container, Jaquot's few belongings inside. I've never seen Jaquot's father, but I recognize the same green eyes, the same sharp cheekbones.

"I'm sorry for your loss, sir," I say from the doorway.

He doesn't turn right away, but when he does, I'm surprised by his eyes. When Nana died, my mother's eyes had turned soft with grief. Jaquot's father's are hard; their shine is wet jade.

"Another friend of my son's," he says.

"Yes, sir," I say.

"You were in the jungle that day?"

"Yes, sir."

He turns away from the desk. "And did you see the beast?" he says. "The beast they say killed my boy?"

"No, sir." I swallow. "I heard it. But I didn't see it."

"Perhaps it was a different beast," he says. "One we know less about."

His anger swells to fill the room. I exchange a look with Alma.

"Or perhaps," he continues, "the beast was sent."

"Sir," Alma says. "Surely you don't mean by the Faloii? There's no evidence—"

"Evidence," he interrupts. He opens his hands and stares at them before squeezing them into fists. "Facts are not always facts. The version of the truth we know is what is shown to us."

"Facts are facts," Alma says from behind me. "A different version of the truth is a mistruth."

He turns back to the desk and lifts the nearly empty container. Jaquot hadn't owned much—none of us do. When he reaches the front of the 'wam, he turns back and pierces us with another hard stare.

"Those things think they can control us," he says. "They will find that they are wrong."

He leaves the 'wam, the door sliding shut behind him. As soon as it's closed, Rondo rises from his bed and kisses me.

It's like sunlight spreading through my skin, and when he pulls away, the golden energy remains in my fingers and toes, thrumming. My breathlessness embarrasses me and I glance away from him, my eye falling on the izinusa, out of the restraints of its case and leaning against the wall by the bed.

He looks over his shoulder at the instrument and then his eyes return to my face, slanted with a half smile. That squint of his left eye sends music flooding through my body. It forms a bubble around me, protecting me from the storms brewing in N'Terra.

"I can show you how to play," he says.

"Oh, stars, you two." Alma rolls her eyes. "We're kind of in the middle of a crisis."

"She's right," he says, and I nod, tearing my eyes away from the izinusa. It's a similar feeling to leaving the sun of the Atrium for the cold, artificial hallways of the labs.

"From what Jaquot used to say, his dad has always been an Albatur supporter," I say. "But blaming the Faloii for Jaquot's death? That's intense."

"It's like everyone is losing their minds," Alma says. "Did you see the guards? Your dad came and asked them if they'd found your mother. He was really angry. He's the one who told them to check the commune and go to the Greenhouse."

This stops me cold, whatever music was left in me from looking at Rondo draining from my veins. I imagined the Council sending the guards for my mother, my father standing by helplessly, pleading for them to understand. But that wasn't the case at all: instead he sent them hunting for her, gave the word for her to be tracked down.

"Have you heard from Rasimbukar?" Rondo asks.

I nod. "We have to do it tonight. She's going to bring the Faloii if we don't get her father out *tonight*."

Alma rushes to the window and peers out.

"But it's almost sunset!" she cries.

"I know."

"What about your mom? Dr. Espada?"

I squeeze my eyes shut in a long, hard blink.

"I don't know. But I think she was trying to tell me something when they took her away. She told me something . . . in . . . in my head." I grasp for the words where I'd been holding them in my mind. I can still feel them in her voice. *"Ambystoma maculatum."*

"That's all she said?" Rondo says slowly. He'd been expecting something more to go on. "What does that even *mean*?"

"That's one of the old languages," says Alma.

"What?"

"Ambystoma maculatum. That's a name. It was a kind of salamander a long time ago."

Rondo and I stare at her blankly.

"Salamander?"

"It's an amphibian. Kind of like . . ." She thinks. "A morgantan? Probably smaller though."

"But . . ." My brain feels like it's crushing boulders in its effort to break down the facts in front of me. The truth is somewhere in the gravel. "Why would my mother tell me the name of an extinct salamander? That makes no sense."

No one says anything for a moment.

"The Solossius," Alma says, eyes wide. "The Solossius, remember?"

"What about it?" Rondo says.

"Remember how I said it sounded like something to do with solar power? Well, *Ambystoma maculatum,* the salamander . . . it was solar powered."

I wish I had something smart to say. Instead I can only stare at her.

"*Ambystoma maculatum*," she continues. "It had algae in cells all over its body. And that algae—a plant, you know—produced photosynthetic energy that it then provided to the salamander. So the salamander got its energy—or, you know, some of it, at least—from the sun. Like a plant, but not a plant. A salamander. A solar-powered salamander."

Rondo and I stare at her. She's grinning in her brainy way until she sees our faces.

"What? It was a brilliant animal, okay? My mom told me all about it when I was studying intergalactic species comparisons—"

"You're *so* bizarre," I interrupt. "But it doesn't explain why my mom would tell me the name of some random sun salamander."

"Unlikely that it's random," Rondo says, raising his eyebrow. "Think it's a coincidence that the Solossius and the salamander both have something to do with solar energy?"

"Whatever it is, my mother was talking about a power source precious to the Faloii. I have no idea what that connection could be, but we don't have time to figure this out right now. We have to focus on getting Adombukar out of the labs and into the jungle."

"But what about the egg?" Alma says. "The kawa? Why are they looking for it?"

"I don't know," I repeat. "But we have to set that aside right now too. We need to get into the Zoo, find Adombukar, and get him out."

"How?" says Alma. "They're not going to just let us stroll in there and take him for a walk. We don't even know where he is."

"I found the vasana," I say, as much to her as to myself. "If I'm given a little time, I can find him too. If he's still alive."

We're silent, these last words hanging in the air between us. If Adombukar is dead, then we might as well be too.

Rondo turns and lifts the izinusa from the floor, placing its case on the bed before returning the instrument to safety. He looks at it for a moment, then reaches his hand down to strum the ten delicate strings. The notes rise.

"Well," Rondo says. He closes the case. I close my eyes. "Let's do it."

CHAPTER 26

The raised voices of the crowds of compound residents have softened—fear has descended from the sky like a flock of predatory birds. We catch the whispers as we move toward the front of the commune.

"The searches were authorized by the Council," a man says. "It must be for our protection."

An old woman, supporting herself on a gnarled cane, stands near the entrance to her 'wam.

"Protection," she croaks, "is not offered in an eclipse of truth. We need to know what has happened."

"Do you really want to know?" the man snaps. "If we have nothing to hide, then we have nothing to fear."

The conversation shoots back and forth through the crowds.

"Maybe whatever it was didn't get out of the labs. Maybe it

got in from the jungle."

"When has something ever gotten in from outside? Unless it was sent by the Faloii. They already killed that boy."

The fear in their voices is like a new specimen that runs wild in N'Terra, overpopulating the compounds. Alma nudges me when we're out of earshot.

"They're talking about Jaquot."

"I know." I look over my shoulder at the group, still clustered together, muttering. I can't help but think about what Dr. Espada said: *Fear makes people stupid.* "They're idiots if they think the Faloii had anything to do with it."

"People don't know what to think," Rondo says as we begin to climb the stairs toward the main dome. "This is what the Council has done by not sharing any information about the Faloii. People are bound to think the worst when something goes wrong."

"They *are* sharing information," Alma says. "The wrong information."

The main dome is silent. We round a turn in the path and find ourselves behind the very tree Rondo and I had crouched behind the night Adombukar was brought into the compound. As usual, two guards stand on either side of the doorway to the Zoo beyond the tree line. I expect them to be on high alert with everything going on, but they seem relaxed: buzzguns in hand but held loosely, aimed at the ground.

"You'd think there would be more guards," I whisper.

"The Council may have given the impression that the threat is contained," Alma says. "With your mom and Dr. Espada in custody, they may not think they have anything else to worry about."

"Or maybe they already found the kawa," Rondo says.

"Another thing I have to find," I say.

"We'll worry about that later," Alma says. "For now, we have to figure out how to get into the lab."

I turn away from the Zoo, crouching behind the tree.

"Well, I think I have that part covered," I say, holding up my hands.

"Meaning?" Alma raises her eyebrow.

"Long story. Remember when the wall in the deep part of the Zoo thought I was my dad? Not a coincidence. My mom actually reimprinted my hands."

Rondo raises his eyebrows, impressed.

"Did she do that with hacking?" he says. "I wouldn't mind learning that."

"No," I say, rolling my eyes at him. "She actually, you know, reimprinted them."

Alma squints at me, the gears in her mind working.

"So the poison vine she says you touched . . ."

"Didn't happen."

"Oh," she says, then pauses. "Your mom is good."

"Yeah, well, the Council wouldn't agree."

"Obviously."

"Okay," Rondo says. "So you should be able to get into the labs, but those guards aren't just going to let you walk right in. They know who you are. We need a plan."

I think about this, turning to look around the dome without leaving the shelter of the tree. If this were the Beak, with its free-roaming specimens, we might have an easier time coming up with a diversion of some kind. But I don't see much to work with.

I turn back to ask if anyone has any ideas and find Rondo with his slate out, the screen illuminated and his fingers tapping away. Alma peers over his shoulder.

"What are you doing?" I whisper.

"What he's always doing," Alma says without raising her eyes.

"What are you hacking?" I ask.

"The guards' comms," he says.

"You can do that?"

His fingers stop tapping and his eyes glance up at my face, one eyebrow raised. Of course he can. I can't help but smile at him. When he makes that face . . .

"Are you going to talk to them?" Alma says.

"Yes," Rondo says.

"What are you going to say?"

His fingers pause on the screen.

"I haven't gotten that far," he says, and looks up into the branches of the ogwe for inspiration. "Something about a specimen being loose? That would get them running."

"No," Alma says. "That will probably make the ones at the front come back toward the Zoo. We need them away, toward the front of the dome."

"The egg," I whisper. "Tell them someone saw the kawa outside. That will get them away from the door."

He looks up at me. "You sure? What if they already found it?"

"I don't think so. My dad was hyperventilating about it when I was in the 'wam. I doubt they've tracked it down."

Rondo holds my gaze a second longer and then bends his head to the slate, his fingers making quick, precise selections.

"What are you doing now?" I peer over his shoulder. All I see are lines of code in two columns, one longer than the other.

"Monitoring their communication patterns," he says without looking up. "I don't want to use the wrong kind of language. They'd notice something was weird."

He straightens his neck and taps the enter key.

"Aren't you going to say anything?" Alma whispers.

"I did," he says, pointing at the lines of code as if it's obvious.

"But you didn't say anything," I say.

"I don't need to *say* it." He squints at the screen. "I took a voice pattern sequence and applied it to text. It will sound like the last person who said something on the comms. Watch."

I can't kiss him, so I reach down and squeeze his shoulder.

"They received the communication," Rondo whispers, then kisses my hand.

"But they're not moving," Alma says, chewing on her thumbnail.

They're not. The two guards listen to their comms, exchange a few words with each other—one shrugging—then go back to leaning. They show no sign of leaving their posts.

"What? What's the problem?" Rondo mutters. He turns back to his slate, peering at the lines of code. "I don't get it. My syntax is correct. I used the right sequence. Damn."

Alma leans over his shoulder, her eyes darting left to right. Her hand leaps out to point.

"You forgot to translate your compiler. All they heard was static," she says.

I have no idea what it means, but I snicker as Rondo's eyes nearly jump out of his head. He holds the slate close to his face, lips moving wordlessly as he calculates, or reads, or both.

"You're right," he says. "How did you—?"

She shrugs. "Ever since you started digging into private files and stuff, I started learning some hacking on my own. It's not that hard," she says.

"Okay, okay, try again," I whisper. He does, tapping a few lines of code, and then hitting enter once more.

We all swivel our heads around the trunk of the ogwe to look at the guards again. At first I'm afraid it didn't work, and I'm already thinking of a backup plan when the guards crane their necks again, fingers to their ears, listening. Rondo looks at the screen of his tablet.

"It's working," he whispers. "It's working!"

"Did you tell them to report to the front of the dome?" Alma says.

"Yes. Even said *immediately*."

The guards speak a few words and then jog away. I move to the other side of the tree to watch their path toward the front of the dome, terrified that they'll misunderstand the instructions and double back to where we hunker behind the ogwe.

"This is our chance," Alma says, grabbing my arm. I'm up and running before it's fully registered in my mind that we're actually doing it. I think it's my feet that are thudding on the ground as we dash toward the door, but it's my heart, clamorous in my ears. It's so loud I almost don't hear the voices coming down the path.

"They're coming back!" Alma hisses, and moves as if to sprint back to the trees. But Rondo throws an arm out, stopping her.

"Go with Octavia!" he whispers fiercely. "I've got this."

And then he's gone, running to the trees to head them off before they reach the end of the path. I place my shaking hand on the scan lock, praying that whatever my mother did to my prints hasn't worn off or changed. The square surface illuminates blue as my flesh comes in contact with its cool surface; in the long pause that follows I think my heart might explode, or my arm will be torn off by Alma's robotic grip. But the scanner turns green, my father's stern face appearing on the screen above it.

"Welcome, Dr. English," the automated voice says.

We throw ourselves through the door and against the wall inside. As the door slides closed, Rondo's voice drifts to my ears: "I was just looking for my slate. It must have fallen out of my bag when I left my internship earlier."

"So you came to look for it at night? I think we need to give Dr. Okadigbo a call. That's your father, isn't it?"

The door closes with a gentle thud and we remain pressed against the wall for a moment longer, frozen. I expect the door to open again immediately, the guards onto us. But it doesn't. The long white hallway is empty and silent aside from our breath, the seemingly endless line of empty windows continuing down into glowing oblivion.

"Ready?" Alma says, her voice sounding as pale as the walls.

No, I think.

CHAPTER 27

"Should you . . . you know, start listening?" Alma whispers. We're alone in the hallway, or so it seems, but I understand her need to whisper.

"I don't know," I tell her. "I don't want to get too tired or be overwhelmed. Sometimes there's a lot of noise, and I want to be able to hear him."

I wait until we near the end of the hallway, almost to the sorting room, and then I decide to open the tunnel. We'll waste precious time if we open every single door we pass.

I stop walking and concentrate, Alma by my side with her head swiveling and her eyes wide. All these years we wanted to have free rein in the Zoo. Well, here we are.

Just a little, I tell myself. I don't want everything to come flying into my consciousness, as it sometimes does. I'm still

OLIVIA A. COLE

figuring out how this works, but I do notice—a brief feeling of satisfaction—that my grip on the tunnel is stronger, more adroit.

My mind widens, and the buzz rises in my inner ear. There are animals here: I can feel them on either side of me. Some of them are tranquilized: their energy alive and thrumming but softened and made clumsy. They can still hear one another, I realize: the faintly glowing chain that connects my mind to them connects them to one another.

"Anything?" Alma whispers.

"Nothing," I say, taking more steps down the hall. Vasana on my left. Kunike on my right. Igua. Marov. I can feel them all, sense their uncertainty. Some of them—untranquilized— sense me and prickle on the horizon of my consciousness, trying to figure out what I am, sizing me up in their minds. Some of them close their minds to me.

"I don't think he's going to be anywhere in this hallway," I say after we've walked some distance down the corridor. Alma looks nervously over her shoulder. "I mean, they hid Vasana 11 deeper in the maze, in a secret lab. This is one of the Faloii. They're not going to have him somewhere easily found."

We pause, almost at the end of the hallway, near the sorting room where we spent our first week of the internship just ahead. Right? Left? To our right is the Atrium, with only a few doors in between, and to our left is the longer hallway that will lead to yet more hallways and the observation rooms.

"Left," she whispers. "It's the most logical."

I almost smile. Never have I heard her more displeased about something being logical.

I start to widen the tunnel to listen for Adombukar when we hear voices.

"Damn, damn, damn!" Alma whispers. Far at the other end of the hall, a group of three whitecoats has emerged from the Atrium. They look at one another, absorbed in conversation. They haven't seen us yet.

"In!" I breathe, shoving Alma toward the nearest door. I fumble to align my palm with the scanner, my eyes darting from it to the three whitecoats down the hall. The door whispers open, and Alma and I tumble through the doorway. When it closes, we're sealed inside the stillness of a small examination room. We stand frozen in the corner until the silence convinces me that the whitecoats haven't seen us.

"What are they even doing in here?" Alma says. "It's way past evening meal."

"My dad would be here all night sometimes."

Alma shakes her head. She glances back over her shoulder fearfully, as if she's still in the hallway and is checking for observers. But her eyes fasten on something; rather than moving back to the door, she turns around fully to look. Watching her, I follow suit, my mind already buzzing.

"What is it?" I say, afraid to see.

I haven't seen the animal on the table before. Pale violet in color, it has a slender snout nearly a foot long. Its whole body is slender, actually, though it's hard to tell when it's lying flat, restraints around its shoulders and its six limbs. Wait . . . six?

"Six legs?"

"A rahilla," Alma breathes, taking a step toward the table. She stops herself, even though the animal appears to be tranquilized.

"I don't remember that one," I say. Even now I want to pass some nonexistent test.

"Mammal. Insectivore. Only one of a few species whose body seems to have adapted to resemble the bodies of its prey."

"You'd think I'd remember that."

She shoots me a look and a half smile.

"You were probably messaging with Rondo." Then she turns her eyes back to the rahilla. "It looks so peaceful."

I open the tunnel just a tiny bit wider. The rahilla's consciousness materializes slowly on my mind's horizon, a smudged illumination. It's dim. It shouldn't be dim.

"I—I think he's dying," I say, the realization installing a sudden lump in my throat. The rahilla's light is fading as his life flickers out. I can't believe he's being forced to die here on this table alone, tied down and helpless. I approach the table, ignoring Alma's hiss of warning, and bury my fingers in the rahilla's long lavender fur.

The feeling is like an electric shock, traveling up my veins and into my head. I see the rahilla as it once was: his fur more vibrant, a deep, rich purple. He's lost weight as well: his legs used to be thick with muscle. I sense that he's lonely: only two of his species in the Zoo. He acknowledges my presence in his mind, but he's too weak to close himself off. If he was in the jungle, this inability to guard his mind might make him prey to a dirixi or a gwabi. My hands tingle on his body: they feel hot and almost wet. I have to pull them away to examine them, the feeling is so convincing. But my hands are just my hands, and the rahilla lies where he is, his slender body rising and falling with his slow, shallow breaths.

"Octavia, we need to go," Alma says.

I nod. But leaving him here feels wrong. I look around the room. On another platform against the wall is a variety of equipment, including the blue wand that Dr. Depp had used to wake the kunike from tranquilized slumber. I consider getting it, waking the rahilla. But that seems even crueler. There is no right thing to do here. Nothing is good enough. I carefully remove the straps that bind his body to the platform. He's not going anywhere except to death, so he might as well be comfortable. Then I walk to the other platform, take the blue wand, and put it in my pocket. I look at Alma and nod.

We peek out in the hallway to ensure no other whitecoats are making their way from the Atrium to the main dome. We don't hear any voices, but that could change, so we slip out of the room and walk as quickly as we can without jogging down the hallway. The tunnel is open slightly: rather than things entering and finding their way to my mind, I keep the crack just wide enough to register other consciousnesses on my radar. We pass room after seemingly empty room; many of them hide animals behind their illusory doors, but none of the presences are Adombukar. We pass what I know is the containment room, not because I remember its blank door but because I feel the many life-forces held prisoner there glowing in my mind. Almost all of them are tranquilized. Their energy pricks dully in my direction as I pass. I gently block them out, feeling like a coward.

"This is the hallway we took when we saw Dr. Albatur and Vasana 11," Alma says in the same hushed tone. "Do you hear anything?"

"I hear a lot," I say, frustrated. "But not Adombukar."

"What if he's . . ." She pauses, looking for a word other than *dead*. "Not listening?"

I imagine Adombukar laid out on a table like the rahilla, his light fading into nothing. Would Rasimbukar know if her father died? Would she feel it? Would she bring the Faloii thundering out of the jungle to rid Faloiv of humans? I wouldn't even blame her at this point.

The wall to our right opens—not the door, but the wall: another hidden entrance—and the whitecoat that comes out of it walks straight into us, his head bent to his slate. The edge of the slate runs straight into my face, jutting hard against the corner of my lip, enough to draw the faint metallic taste of blood.

"Oh!" I cry as much out of pain as surprise, slapping my hand to my mouth. Alma too gives a small shriek of shock, and the sound echoes down the long empty hallway. One moment it was just us, the only noise being the muted sound of our feet on the hard floor. Now a new sound joins us: Dr. Albatur.

"What are you two doing back here?" he says, more surprised than angry.

"We . . . uh . . ."

"English?" he says. His skin is pale, but up close I see the flush under the surface: a faint spiderweb of skin cells reddened by whatever condition he has that makes his body reject Faloiv. His bushy white eyebrows crush toward each other like a fat caterpillar cut suddenly in half. "Does your father know you're back here?"

"No, sir," I say before I can come up with a lie.

His hand, its thick pink fingers extended, reaches for me. It settles on my shoulder faster than my reflexes can allow me to jerk away.

"With your mother in the predicament she's in, I would think you would be more careful about toeing the line," he says.

"Meaning?" I say, pulling back.

He narrows his eyes at me and glances down the hall, as if he's angry that I'm keeping him from getting somewhere. The hand tightens on my shoulder.

"Miss English, I don't have time for this presently. If you

would like to have a discussion about your mother's situation, I'm sure we can locate your father and he will be more than obliged to explain."

I shake him off. "I don't need my dad to tell me what my mother's situation is. I know her situation. And I know yours too," I say.

His hand slowly sinks down to his side, as if every inch it falls is challenged by its desire to grab me by the throat.

"My situation?" he says. "What would you know of such things, Miss English? Anything your mother has told you is—"

"My mother hasn't told me anything," I snap. "But I know what you and my father are working on. The . . . the Solossius. I know what you're doing."

It's a shot in the dark, a wild stab into shadows. But as soon as the words are out of my mouth, I know I've hit something. The smirk leaks from his eyes, leaving the expression as hard and shiny as the metal instruments he uses in his experiments.

"You know very little," he says in a low voice. His eyes dart over my shoulder, looking to see if anyone else is around. I hear my heartbeat in my ears as those eyes settle on mine again. "Do you want to live here forever? Do you want your children to live on this hot, vicious little planet? The key to our freedom is in their bones. If your mother is too shortsighted to see that, then we can—"

"Are you threatening Octavia?" Alma pipes up, her voice shriller than I've ever heard it.

"I have no need," Dr. Albatur says. He reaches for me, but I duck away from him again. The idea of him touching me fills me with rage.

"You will come with me, English," he says, his eyes piercing blue under the white eyebrows, glinting like a broken star. "I look forward to escorting you to the Council."

"Get off me!" I yell, my voice bouncing off the walls. "I know what you're doing back here! And when they find out . . ."

The word "they" hangs between us, vibrating.

His hand drops to his side, and the eyes that had before been metallic flecks are now wholly stone. Staring at those eyes staring back at me, I almost don't notice the movement of his free hand, inching toward the waist of his lab coat. The fabric shifts, and there's a tranq gun.

"Alma, grab him!" I scream. I don't give my body any command but still somehow find myself lunging at him in the empty white hallway. In my periphery, Alma has found a hold on his other arm. The slate he'd been holding tumbles to the hard floor, its screen shattering on impact.

The three of us stand there, struggling awkwardly in the middle of the silent corridor. All I hear is our breathing and the rustling of our clothes against each other. He's a heavy man: he throws his bulk against me, trying to force me toward the wall. I plant my feet as firmly as I can, using my legs to brace against his weight. Alma, on his other side, claws at his hands, trying to keep them from closing around the tranq gun.

But he frees it from the folds of his lab coat. The weapon shines in the bright white light from the ceiling, and in the struggle its nose shifts toward Alma, whose teeth are bared in exertion.

"No!" I yell, jutting my elbow into Albatur's side, and there's a short whuff of breath as my bone connects. I grapple with the tranq gun, can feel its cold metal against my fingertips . . .

Zip!

The gun fires. I don't know who triggered it: all three of us have our hands on the tranq. Have I been hit? Has Alma? I feel numb. I must have been hit. I wait for the feeling of coldness to spread through my limbs, for my brain to slowly go fuzzy with sleep. It's not until Albatur grunts and topples heavily to the floor that I realize the tranq dart is buried in his fleshy reddish neck.

Alma and I stand, breathing heavily, staring down at his body. His chest rises and falls laboriously, a rattle rising from his open mouth. On his chest, the gold Council pin winks at us.

"Damn . . . ," Alma trails off, panting.

"He's fine," I say, reassuring myself as much as Alma. "He's fine, right? He's just . . . asleep."

"He's fine," Alma repeats, her eyes wide. She bends down to pick up the tranq gun from where it clattered to the floor next to him. What have we done?

"We need to find Adombukar," she says without taking her eyes off Dr. Albatur's body. "Before someone finds us."

There's the sound of feet striking the hard artificial floor. I've stopped breathing. The steps are slow, unhurried. Voices accompany the footsteps, from the direction in which we came. Two whitecoats, slates in hand. They stare at us for a moment, and I know they're looking from the body on the floor up to me and Alma, standing there holding a tranq gun. They say nothing. One slowly moves to a wall panel and keys in a code.

My ears fill with the alarm's wail.

CHAPTER 28

For a moment the four of us only stare at one another, the alarm shrieking in our ears, Albatur's body lying still and white on the floor. Then one of the whitecoats takes a tentative step toward us, and Alma's arm whips up to point the tranq gun in their direction. I don't even have time to admonish her before the whitecoat stumbles backward, running into his colleague. They both stand there, Alma pointing the gun unwaveringly, then together they shuffle until they're out of sight. Alma lowers the gun.

"Alma!" I turn to her, my eyes huge.

"We don't have time for this!" she yells. "And the next people to come around that corner aren't going to be so timid."

I force myself to focus on squeezing the muscle in my mind. It's more difficult with the alarm blaring all around us: sifting through the noise to find the quiet place in the center of my brain is no easy task. But I find it, struggle to get a grip on it, and then slowly open the tunnel.

The noise of the alarm seems to soften as my mind widens and what feels like light seeps in. This part of the lab is quieter in terms of activity in the tunnel: the rooms that line the walls here are actually empty, with a few exceptions. Dr. Albatur had come from a wall between two of the rooms: there are secrets in these hallways that my eyes can't see, but I find myself trusting my inner ear to uncover them.

"Anything?" Alma shouts, shifting her weight from foot to foot and looking over her shoulder where the whitecoats had disappeared.

"Not much. Come on!"

I jog down the hallway, deeper into the labs. We leave Dr. Albatur on the floor. I hope the bark of the alarm gives him terrible dreams. The horizon of my brain is dark and vacant: I reach out inside it, groping with an invisible hand, searching for anything. Alma jogs behind me, silent. We reach a fork in the hallway, one corridor continuing straight and another branching to our right: it's long and blank, no doors, no observation windows.

Pausing to look down the empty expanse, my consciousness immediately sparks. Something on the edge of my awareness, a flutter of blue. I stop jogging to focus on that smudge, and push the sound of the alarm out of my head. I reach out for the blue, try to wrap the fingers of my mind around it. It's not an animal, I know. This is different. The buzzing spikes, the attention of the thing turns toward me, sensing me too now. It's weak—tranquilized—but it feels me.

"I feel something," I shout, grabbing Alma's arm and dragging her down the hallway to the right. I rush forward with Alma in tow, my grip on the blue presence in my mind growing stronger. Any part of these white walls could be an entrance in disguise. *Help me find you*, I say. *I can't find you.*

It tries to reach out: I sense the energy spike toward me. At first I think it's too weak, but it glows brighter, pulses, and comes into the tunnel.

"It's him," I whisper.

I see him as if he's standing before me: the spotted man. Adombukar. He's nearby, and very weak, asking me to come. The glowing chain that links us feels brighter, and I walk quickly along it. I pass blank wall after blank wall, feeling their emptiness, looking for him. And then I reach one place on the featureless wall, as blank as the rest, but different somehow. Adombukar is there behind it, his presence in the tunnel flickering as he struggles to maintain the connection. I raise my palm to the wall, press my fingertips against it.

"Enter, Dr. English."

The wall slides open to reveal a small, dim room, devoid of exam table or research equipment. The only things in the room are a desk, diagrams, and a cage. Adombukar is inside it.

"Come on!" I shout, and pull Alma into the room. The door closes behind us. The alarm is quieter in here, muted by the wall.

"Do you think they know where we are?" Alma says. Her eyes are glued to Adombukar in a mixture of wonder and fear. "What we came to do?"

I don't answer, instead moving quickly to the cell and shoving my hand through the bars. It's made of the same white clay as everything else in the compound; thick bars the width of my arm contain him. Adombukar lies inside, tranquilized, his large body on its side and curled slightly. My hand hovers hesitantly over him. Would he want me to touch him? I slowly lower my palm and rest it gently on his shoulder.

He blazes through the tunnel into my mind, stronger with the physical contact. He only shows me one concept: *Hurry.*

"He's okay," I say, yanking my hand away and out from between the bars. "But we have to move fast."

I reach into the pocket of my skinsuit and draw out the blue wand that I took from the room with the dying rahilla. How had Dr. Depp used it on the kunike? I remember him placing it against the animal's neck. I examine the instrument, my hands shaking. I don't see any levers or controls, so I push my hand through the bars again, angle the wand toward the side of Adombukar's neck, and gently bring it into contact with his body.

He stirs immediately.

Adombukar, I tell him in my mind. *Are you okay?*

Behind me, Alma has backed away to the wall. She says nothing, just watching.

The cell is too small to permit him to stand, so Adombukar slowly rises into a crouch. He's much bigger than Rasimbukar, but he has the same deep brown skin, the pattern of spots covering his body like circular patterns traced in soil. This close, I see they're slightly raised. The spots on his forehead seem to wander, as if he's trying to find his bearings.

"We must go," he says out loud. His voice is deep and resonates in his chest, with the same strange wooden timbre as Rasimbukar.

"Yes," I say. "We just have to figure out how to get you out of this cell. There's no door that I can see."

"Oh, stars," Alma murmurs from behind me, and I whip my head around at the quake in her voice, expecting to see a whitecoat appearing from thin air. But she's staring at a screen on the wall above the desk: the light from it bathes her face in a white glow.

"What? What is it?" I snap.

She can only point, and I close the gap between us in two quick steps. On the left side of the screen is a diagram, being projected from a slate propped on a nearby shelf. I look quickly, scanning the projection with my eyes: a humanoid figure, its skeleton illuminated—many sketches, words, formulas. On the right side of the screen, another diagram: a tower, tall and angular, a platform at its pinnacle, bars around its perimeter. A structure like a metal tomb in the center, the size and shape of a person. The tower's spiny construction is familiar; even if the way I've seen it is incomplete, the image in my mind not quite as tall, no platform yet. . . .

To the side of the diagram a word catches my eye: "Solossius," I whisper.

"Sun. Bones," Alma says softly, covering her mouth. She peers at the sketches, finally understanding. "The tower. They . . . want to harvest energy from . . . from his bones."

"They've been building it this whole time." The truth of it crushes me, as if I've woken from a dream and found myself in the jaws of a dirixi. The diagram seems so simple and harmless. A figure on a screen. A sketch of a machine. Floating numbers and equations. But when I jerk my eyes away, forcing them to take in Adombukar, crouched in his cell, the horror of it sinks into my lungs, coating them in what feels like ash.

"Like the salamander," Alma says. "The Faloii make their own energy, and Dr. Albatur wants to harvest it with the towers."

"Right out in the open," I continue. "Right in the middle of the commune where the sun is bright. No wonder Albatur has been so focused on making everyone believe the Faloii are dangerous! He doesn't want anyone to say anything when he starts using them for energy!"

"But energy for what?" Alma cries. "We *have* energy!"

I stare hard at the diagram of the tower, the last few weeks swirling in my head, rearranging.

"The *Vagantur*," I say. "Remember? My mom said there's a power source that's precious to the Faloii—that it's what Dr. Albatur wants to use to power the ship so he can leave the planet. And my dad is helping him."

The room seems to be pulsing, but I know it can't be. It's my mind. Emotions flood my brain, tidal waves of fear. It takes me a second to realize some of the fear is coming from Adombukar, who stares at me hollowly from his prison.

"We have to get him out."

I rush back to the cage and inspect the bars, looking for a hinge, a fault line, anything. Nothing.

"Did they ever take you out?" I ask.

"Yes." He nods weakly. "But I was unconscious."

"Damn," I say. We're wasting too much time. The guards are probably mobilizing as we speak. By now the Council surely knows of intruders in the labs—sending reinforcements to protect their secrets.

"Move," Alma says, surprising me by appearing at my elbow. She looks at Adombukar. "Hello, sir."

She reaches inside her skinsuit, digging into an inside pocket. When she withdraws her hand from the material, a long blue vial is in her grip.

"What is that?" I ask.

"Pavi extract," she says, as if it's the most obvious thing in the world.

"Pavi?" I say. "Alma, where did you get that?"

She uncorks the thick vial. "I swiped it from the engineer that came to dissolve Jaquot's bed. I thought it might come in handy."

I just stare at her.

"Stand back as much as you can, sir," she says, and with quick, slightly awkward movements, she sprinkles the liquid on the bars of the cell, stretching high to reach the top of the cell, and crouching to make sure it reaches the bottom. It only takes a few drops. She stands back and I follow her lead, the pavi extract already beginning to hiss. The dust rises from the cell like fog.

Adombukar steps through the opening Alma has created before the dust has fully cleared. I stand before him as my father did that night in the main dome. I could take the tranq gun from Alma right now and put an end to all this, avoid the trouble that I know I'm in. But the screen with the Solossius diagram glares at me like a glowing white eye, the dreadfulness of that tower forcing me to turn away.

"Let's go."

I expect the hallway to be filled with guards, buzzguns aimed at the place on the wall where we appear. But it's empty aside from the sound of the alarm.

"What do we do now?" pants Alma, the vial of pavi extract

recorked but still in her hand, tranq gun in her other hand. These aren't the tools I expected us to be using in the labs.

Adombukar groans. He's barely standing, leaning against the smooth white wall for support. My mind prickles: he's trying to show me something, but I don't understand it. It's jumbled, the shapes fuzzy, lacking distinction. The spots on his forehead cluster and disperse again and again.

"Something's wrong," I say, returning to his side, the alarm grating on my ears. I take hold of his arm to help him, expecting to feel him enter the tunnel to show me what he's trying to communicate, but he's weak.

"It's probably the tranquilizer," Alma says. "Remember how disoriented the kunike was when Dr. Depp woke him up with the blue thing?"

She's right. Adombukar feels dizzy, his mind blurred and unfocused. Who knows what else they've done to him while he's been a prisoner here.

Adombukar's energy pulses: he manages to push one image through the tunnel and into my mind. The kawa. I recognize its smooth shape, can almost feel its mass, heavy in my palm. I know what he wants, even if I don't know why.

"He needs the egg," I say.

We grasp Adombukar by the arms, walking on either side of him as we half guide, half drag him down the hall. Without realizing it fully, I find that I've opened the tunnel as we walk, passing him different things through it: hope, warmth, light. I show him my last memory of Rasimbukar, even though I couldn't see her face: her presence out in the trees, demanding his return. *Hold on for her,* I tell him, wrapping the feeling of the words in comforting shapes. *Your daughter is waiting.*

We turn a corner, returning to a hallway that has actual doors and windows on either side.

"We're getting closer to the front," Alma says.

Wait, Adombukar tells me, and I freeze at the corner, Alma following suit. He's listening: his energy, though weak, pricks toward the hall ahead. Then I see them. The guards appear at the intersection of the next hallway, fifty paces ahead. There are six of them, faces covered by black mesh masks that I've never seen. Armor of some kind? Or just for intimidation? If the latter, it's effective. One of them lifts his finger to listen to his comm. Then they raise their buzzguns and start down the hall toward us.

My mind is humming. I don't have time to figure out the source of it. Instead I try to focus on Adombukar's presence in my mind. He's trying to tell me something, but with the buzzing and the blaring alarm, I can't hear him.

"In here," he finally says out loud, nodding weakly at the door to our left. "Here."

Alma's already opening the door. It's not a lab, just a scrub room. The door slides open and she shoves me and Adombukar inside. Outside, the guards' footsteps break into a jog. The door slides shut.

"What do I do! What do I do! They're coming!"

"Break it!" I yell. "I don't know! Just . . . break it!"

She still holds the tranq gun and aims it uncertainly at the door. The darts won't do anything, I think frantically.

"Smash the scanner!" I cry over the buzzing in my head. Adombukar leans on me heavily. His skin has begun to turn stark white to blend in with the scrub room's walls. I wonder if he's doing it on purpose or if it's automatic, danger compelling his body to hide. The sight of it gives me goose bumps, the deep brown leaking away.

Alma switches her grip on the gun from the handle to the muzzle. Using it as a hammer, she bashes it against the square scanner panel: once, twice, three times. On the fourth strike, sparks fly, the display screen flashing irregularly before going dark.

"Kawa," Adombukar whispers.

"That's only going to hold them off for a little while," Alma says, dropping the tranq gun, which is as smashed as the scanner now.

"Through here," I say, nodding at her to come help me with Adombukar. When we're supporting him on both sides, we stagger toward the second door of the scrub room, which opens on its own, designed to be touchless for hygienic purposes—there will be no breaking the scanner to keep them out. Behind us, on the other side of the door, I hear the muted voices of the six guards. I try to think of a plan beyond this next room, but the buzzing in my head has intensified and I can barely focus.

As we step through the doorway, I see why. We're in the containment room. I gaze around the large space, the endless rows of different-sized cages with their deathly quiet captives lying motionless in each one. I feel all of them: their fear, their loneliness, their anger, pulsing through the tunnel and widening my mind with their mass. My head feels as if it might split.

Adombukar collapses. His energy is sapped, his body too weak from his time in the cell, away from the jungle and the light of the sun. I drop to my knees, Alma joining me. We're both crying, and it doesn't occur to me to feel ashamed. Alma balls her fists.

"What do we do, O? We can't carry him!"

"I don't know!" I sob. I can't get my emotions under control. The guards are probably only minutes away from breaking through the door, and we'll be right here, a heap on the floor.

"Does he need water? Maybe he needs water! Like when we're in the jungle," Alma says.

"No!" I shout, the sleeping animals around me like a cemetery. "He doesn't need water. He needs the kawa, and I don't know where . . ."

I freeze. My gaze pauses on the gwabi, its inky body prone in its cell. I stand slowly, my legs wobbly. The buzz in my head is a roar, but I squeeze the muscle in my mind as hard as I can, identifying the source of each hum and pushing them out one by one. There's something swimming just beyond the edge of my consciousness, the image getting clearer and clearer as my mind becomes quiet. A memory, and not even a memory of something real. A dream. I'm remembering a dream I had, the pieces of it floating up through the darkness in my mind and reassembling to form a complete image: my mother, her hand in the mouth of a large, fanged beast. A gwabi. She pulls her hand from its jaws, and in it she holds . . .

"The kawa," I say.

I rush to the creature's cage, one of the largest in the room. The body of the gwabi is like a velvet boulder: enormously muscled and covered in fine sable fur. Its huge head lies just inside the bars, close enough to touch, the eyelids fluttering in sleep.

I reach out for the gwabi in my mind. She's there, waiting for me: her energy flares as we meet. I greet her—not with "hello," but with a feeling *like* hello. Open. Warm. Familiar. She feels hard at first: I can sense her perceiving me but holding back, keeping her mind just out of reach. She investigates me, the chain between us glowing brighter, and then she bends, allowing me near, letting me see her. Like all the others, she's afraid.

I reach into my skinsuit pocket and withdraw the wand I used to wake up Adombukar.

"Octavia," Alma snaps.

"Wait," I say. Behind me Adombukar is slumped on the floor, his pulse of light barely registering in my head. He's not dying, but he's drained, weak. His mind is slipping.

No time to waste. I reach my hand through the bars, work the wand through the gwabi's mane of fur, and press the tip to her neck.

She stirs, both in my mind and beneath my fingers. I withdraw my hand as slowly as I dare, just as she opens her eyes.

They are huge and green, a strange pixilated color as if painted with a thousand different overlapping shades. The eyes fix on me, and I can't help but break the gaze for a moment to glance at the huge fangs that protrude from her mouth.

I need it, I tell her, communicating not with words, but with feeling.

She knows.

"Alma, give me the pavi extract."

"Are you insane? It will kill us—"

"Give it to me!"

She slaps the vial into my palm and backs away as I uncork it. I stare into the multifaceted green eyes before me.

Not us, I tell her.

She stares back, knowing.

My nervousness grows hooves, galloping so fast in my lungs that it makes my breath ragged. I flick my wrist, splashing the thick white bars of the cage that holds her captive with a few drops of the pavi extract. A moment later, the bars are crumbling into piles of white dust, leaving an opening large enough for the gwabi to fit through. I retreat, nearly falling, and out she comes, her huge body graceful and lithe. She stops in front of me, her paws enormous, each of the six toes tipped with a fearsome claw.

The great mouth opens, each tooth as long as my finger. One snap and she'll end me.

But the mouth doesn't close. It waits there, held open. The wet heat of her breath wafts into my face, smelling of jungle and something else I can't identify. Terror makes my chest heave, but I swallow hard, move closer, and put my hand into the gwabi's mouth.

At first, nothing. Just the hot, wet sensation of her tongue on my palm; the terrifying texture of her molars brushing a fingernail. But something's grazing my fingertips: a hard, smooth object, rising from her throat and rolling into her mouth, heavy and strange. I grasp it, my hand deep in her mouth, and slowly, slowly—avoiding her curved fangs—pull it from her jaws. I don't need to look: I know it's the kawa.

I nearly drop it, slick with the gwabi's saliva. She stares at me neutrally. Her energy hums, glowing. She's pleased to be out of the cage, ignoring Alma completely. I thank the gwabi, who acknowledges and dismisses my gratitude with a coy blink of her luminous eyes, translating as a twist of pink in my mind.

"Where did that come from?" Alma breathes from the corner where she's hunched.

I rush to Adombukar's side, where he still slumps on the floor, his eyes barely open.

Adombukar. I form the shape of his name and push it through the tunnel along with the shape of the egg. He struggles to turn his head. I'm trying to figure out how to help him without dropping the kawa when Alma appears at his shoulder, glancing nervously back at the gwabi, and helps raise him into a sitting position.

"Where did it come from?" she says again.

"Here's the kawa," I whisper to Adombukar.

I put it near his face. I don't know what he needs from it, what he plans to do. Unlike the gwabi, his jaws aren't big enough to swallow it whole. Instead, though, his large paw-like hands slowly rise and take the kawa from my grasp.

"It's hot," Alma gasps, and I almost ask her how she knows— but then I feel it too. In Adombukar's hands, the kawa has begun to radiate a halo of heat, warm at first and then intensifying into a blast I have to back away from. Alma is forced to release Adombukar's shoulders to get away from it, but he doesn't need her anymore. He's growing stronger: the blue of him in my mind glowing brighter, its flame widening until the tunnel is illuminated with its blaze. He rises from the floor. It's not just in my mind that he's glowing: the kawa is illuminated, bathing him in its light. In the tunnel, I perceive something deep in his body growing stronger. His very bones seem to radiate, absorbing some unnamed energy from the core of the kawa.

Are you better? I ask him, afraid to interrupt, but we don't have time to spare.

Soon, he tells me. The spots on his forehead find a fixed pattern, evenly spaced, and stay there. The light fades from the kawa. When it flickers out, Adombukar approaches the gwabi, who obligingly opens her mouth and swallows the kawa once again.

"Now what?" Alma says, looking up at Adombukar's face. With his back straight and some of his strength regained, he's an imposing figure. "Where can we go? The only other door is the one at the back that goes deeper into the Zoo. We'd get caught for sure."

I squeeze my eyes shut tightly.

"I don't know," I say, gritting my teeth. "I don't know. Adombukar . . ."

I turn to him, but he's not listening to me. He's turned to look at the containment room, his eyes on the many cages of animals, all tranquilized. I quickly open the tunnel and find him reaching out to every creature in the room, the chains connecting him to them all like a glowing web. His connection with them is so much more powerful than mine. My communication is like rudimentary sign language. His is rich and deep and complicated. He speaks each animal's unique language. Listening in the tunnel is like standing on a cliff and staring out into space: the conversations happen like shooting stars, simultaneous and incredibly bright.

"Adombukar, we have to go."

We do.

He walks to the nearest cage, a smaller enclosure containing what appears to be a pregnant marov. I didn't notice her before and wonder how she became pregnant. Are the white-coats allowing them to mate? More likely, they have artificially impregnated her to study her process. The idea makes me burn, both with anger and shame.

I didn't know they were doing this, I tell him. He ignores me.

He opens his huge hand wide and places it against the front of the cage. It happens in an instant: the bars crumble. The dust falls to the floor in a whisper, leaving the marov free. He takes one finger and touches it gently to the animal's neck. It doesn't glow like the wand: he merely touches her. And she's awake.

He moves on to the next cage, and the next. Alma has come close to me and grabs my arm as we watch. He works quickly, far more quickly than seems possible. But what he does with his hands isn't a special trick that needs concentration: it comes as naturally to him as snapping one's fingers or clapping one's hands. Animals are out of their cages, milling about, some of them coming over to Alma and me to sniff our legs. Some of them merely stand, watching Adombukar. I'm in awe of their beauty, their bright colors, their unique movements. This is what I always thought it would be like: seeing the amazing animals of Faloiv up close, watching them live their lives. I just didn't think it would be . . . like this. When Adombukar reaches the cages of animals that are potentially dangerous—

igua and a younger gwabi—I say his name, afraid.

Adombukar. Isn't that a bad idea?

The Faloii have no predators but the dirixi. And everyone here—he glances at the animals that have awakened—*has an agreement.*

What . . . what about us? I say.

He looks at me and then at Alma and says out loud, "They will not harm you."

There's a metallic clatter and I spin around to look toward the doors, expecting to see the guards already bursting through. They're not, but it's obvious they're working on the scanner.

"Oh no," Alma moans, and then jumps involuntarily as a tufali comes to nudge her leg, inhaling her scent. I recognize the tufali: she's the same one who put one of her tusks through a whitecoat's thigh.

"The guards are going to go crazy when they see all the specimens out of their cages," I say.

"I have an idea," Alma says suddenly, grabbing my arm again. She rushes from my side across the containment room to where Adombukar is still opening cages. She pulls out the pavi extract again; using it, she begins opening cages too. "Come on! Use the wand. We need to hurry."

I rush to join her, dodging freed animals left and right. We're at the cage of a rahilla; with the bars gone, I merely reach in and wake it with the wand. Then the next cage, and the next. Between us and Adombukar, we open every cage in the containment room, then stand at the far end of the room and look at everything we've done. Piles of white-clay dust have been spread across the floor by various paws and hooves, and the owners of those paws and hooves roam freely. I watch in awe as a gwabi and an igua—natural enemies—stand near each other, completely ignoring the other's presence. They know there are bigger things at work here, I realize.

"So what's your plan?" I say, turning to Alma. I hear the metallic clattering every minute or so: either the guards are breaking down the door or they had to bring Dr. Older from the Beak to reprogram the scanner. That could be why they took so long.

"Uh, well, not much of a plan. But maybe we, uh . . . wait for the door to open and then, you know, rush them."

"Rush them?"

"They won't be expecting it, right? They're expecting us to keep running, and they probably think Adombukar's still really weak. There's no way they could know that the kawa was in the gwabi's mouth, or they wouldn't have been looking for it in the commune. They won't be expecting all three of us to be mobile. We can rush them and maybe grab their guns." She sees the shocked expression on my face and waves her hands. "No, no, we won't *use* the guns! Just so *they* can't use them. Then we make a break for it."

I look at Adombukar, who has been listening impassively. His large starry eyes seem to glow. He says nothing, shows me nothing in the tunnel. It's the only plan we've got. Ahead, the metallic clatter gets louder, the sounds closer together.

"Adombukar, can you . . . tell the animals our plan? I can show them, kind of, but you're much better."

"They know what to do," he says.

I can only nod.

We stand in the scrub room, Alma in the doorway that connects it to the containment room so it stays open. Here, the sounds of someone working on the door are easier to hear. I'm fairly sure they brought Dr. Older: the sounds I hear aren't brute smashes but mechanical noises that mean they're fixing the scanner. I look behind me at the far end of the containment room and suddenly realize there are probably guards outside that door as well: waiting. I turn back to the door ahead. They're in for a surprise. My muscles are taut, alert. When that door opens, we'll make our move. In my head, the tunnel is wide and bright, buzzing pleasantly with the energy of all the conscious creatures around me. We're all focused on one thing.

The door opens, and twenty guards crowd around the doorway, black mesh masks obscuring their faces. They never knew what hit them.

CHAPTER 29

Pandemonium.

I'm closest to the door and think I'll be the first one through, but the gwabi who had the kawa in her belly leaps over my head, landing with her full weight on the first two guards. Two igua, eager to escape the containment room, bull past me to my left, heads lowered and tusks aimed. Blood splashes. I look away. My heart feels as if it's inside every warm body around me, pulsing a hundred times too hard. Adombukar stands over the body of a guard. I can't tell if he's dead. I don't know what Adombukar did to him until I see him do it again. He dodges a blast from a buzzgun, grabs the owner of the gun with both of his strong paw-hands, then puts a gentle finger to the guard's forehead. And just like that, the guard is out.

"Come on!" Alma screams. There's a hole in the wall; the

world is filled with noise. Not just in my head but all around me: the sounds of animal rage and human terror. Even the kunike, small as they are, do what they must to make way: two of them attack a guard's ankles. He shoots one of them with a buzzgun and my whole body lurches.

"No," I moan, my limbs going weak. I can sense the kunike's death filling my mind, his energy leaked away into nothing.

Then I feel Adombukar, his presence pushing images through the tunnel and into my head: the kunike's light returning to Faloiv, his energy filtering through the ground and into the trees.

Is that true? I say.

Yes. Death has a place on every planet. But the violence must stop.

"We have to go!" I scream. I find that I am able to speak while also sending the animals an image of what we need to do. The long hallway leading to the main dome: we need to make it there.

Alma leads the way, the animals streaming after us like a river of bodies. The gwabi stays close to me, a comforting light coming from her. She means to watch over me.

More guards. The gwabi leaps on them. Her curved fangs gnash into the flesh of someone's throat, a bright arc of blood. I think of what Rasimbukar has said about war having grave consequences for Faloiv. Has the war already begun? We make it to the hallway, Adombukar catching a lone guard in his hands, shaking the gun from her grip, and then putting her gently to sleep. He lays her on the floor, then looks at me for direction.

"Down here!" I shout, motioning with my arm. We're in the long corridor that will take us to the main dome. We could make it. We're almost out. I sprint down the hall, the gwabi's breath loud and hot beside me.

One moment the hallway ahead is empty, and the next moment two struggling bodies tumble out from an open door—one of the deceptively empty exam rooms. One wears white, the other is a guard in gray; between them, the glint of a buzzgun's metal, which the two fight for. The guard throws the person in white against the wall.

"Alma, that's Rondo!"

I put on an extra burst of speed to reach them as Rondo throws himself at the guard again. The gray-suited man uses the buzzgun as a club and the dull sound of it striking Rondo's face jerks through my body. He staggers, then cocks back his arm and delivers a punch that sends the guard spinning. Adombukar overtakes me, reaches the guard as he's beginning to rise; and with one touch of Adombukar's finger, the man is sinking back to the ground, unconscious.

"What are you doing in here?" I cry, reaching Rondo and holding him by the arms. His lip is split, a trickle of red trailing down his chin.

He points over my shoulder, swiping at his blood with the back of his hand.

"Your mom!" He pants. "I found your mom."

I whirl. The window shows the room to be empty, but through the open door I see one end of an exam platform. Someone is stretched out on its surface, but all I can see are the shoes.

I shove past Adombukar, leaping over and around the animals that mill in the hallway. I shoulder past the door and enter the room to find my mother strapped to a tall platform, the arm of her skinsuit red with blood. Her eyes are closed. I rush to her side, too alarmed to cry.

"Mom!" I grab her, shaking her. "Mom!"

She doesn't move, her body deeply asleep with tranquilizer. I fumble for the blue wand as Alma appears beside me, tearing at the straps holding my mother to the platform. I reach out for my mother in my mind. *I'm coming*, I tell her, and her energy flares in response. I yank the wand out of my skinsuit and immediately press it to her neck, the tip glowing blue.

Her eyes flutter open, taking in the room in a series of blinks before they settle on my face.

"Afua," she says, a slow smile spreading across her face. "You found me. I've been calling."

I tug her into a sitting position, Alma unfastening the last of the straps around her feet.

"Where is Dr. Espada?" I cry.

She bites her lip, holding her injured arm.

"Octavia . . . he's gone, baby," she says, her eyes filling with tears. "He's gone."

Her words sink in to me too slowly. Gone? Dead? I just saw him. How could he be dead when I just saw him?

My mother pulls herself to the edge of the platform and then jerks in surprise. Adombukar fills the doorway with his body, and around him crowd the animals we freed from the containment room, all looking in on her with various shapes and colors of eyes. She can't hear them, but they're all buzzing about her, sensing that she is like me, if in a slightly different way.

"Adombukar," she says, and then looks at me. "You found the kawa I left for you."

My mind is still processing the fact that Dr. Espada is dead. It takes me a moment to hear what she says.

"You . . . ?"

She pulls herself off the platform, standing beside it and swaying just a little.

"Yes. I had to. I put it inside the gwabi while she was sleeping, I hope she doesn't mind."

The gwabi is nearby and blinks. I wonder if she understood.

"I knew your father would put things together," my mother continues. "He and I . . . we're at odds."

"Dad sent the Council for you . . ."

"Yes."

"Octavia," Alma warns. She's standing by the door now.

"We have to go, Mom," I plead.

I grasp her hand and pull her toward the door, and she follows. Outside in the hallway again, I notice that the alarm has stopped blaring.

"We have to move," Rondo calls. He's dragged the unconscious guard to the side of the hallway so he won't be trampled by animals.

"Yes," Adombukar says, and moves quickly down the hall after Rondo. I run after them, my mother in tow. The gwabi is at my side again, and together we dash in the direction of the doorway.

Something is happening in my mind: a flash of energy, a rippling in my consciousness that is as intense as it is abrupt. Adombukar feels it too: he pricks his mind toward it in the tunnel, curious. Another flare. And then another. As the intensity grows, I know something isn't right. The stirring in my mind is like the tumble of dead leaves. Ahead, Adombukar slowly comes to a stop midstride. My mind has filled with this new, wrong something. Adombukar turns to gaze down the hallway, and I look too.

At first, I think they're vasana that we left behind in the containment room, just now catching up. They mill about at the end of the hall, a herd of them. I don't recall seeing them in the cages—perhaps Adombukar had set them free? But I feel his confusion, a gray cloud of worry entering the tunnel, cautioning me, cautioning us all. The vasana move toward us slowly, their steps long and graceful, but their path puzzled and aimless.

"Should we wait for them?" my mother says, not understanding why we've stopped, Alma beside her.

"Something's wrong," I say. I grope for the vasana in the tunnel, looking for a connection. I sense their vague presence, a dim consciousness floating in the dark. But there's no chain connecting us, no glowing string. They feel stripped, hollow.

"Oh no," I whisper.

"What is this?" Adombukar says, softly at first. Then he's bellowing, "What is *this*!"

"We didn't know," I start to say, but with the realization starting to spread in my mind, I know we don't have time. "Adombukar, we have to go. *Now*."

He stands like a tree in the hallway. Like a ripple, the animals around me begin to notice that something about the herd of vasana is off. They think that the animals down the hall are sick, and some of them shuffle uncomfortably, moving toward the door where Rondo stands waiting.

"What have you done?" Adombukar turns on me and my mother, his anger and pain surging through the tunnel like a whirlwind.

I run, dragging my mother and Alma. I can't close the tunnel—I don't have enough focus to do it, and there's no time.

Adombukar, I call for him. *Please come. Your daughter needs you.*

And then there's a scream. Not a human scream, but an animal sound that tears through the air like lightning, electrifying the hairs on the back of my neck.

The herd of vasana, all twelve of them, are halfway down the hallway, their bodies trembling and writhing, stamping their feet. Even from this distance I make out the whites of their eyeballs, wide and exposed as they roll in their sockets. Their mouths are open, the screams rising from their elegant necks like a dirge. And beyond them, at the end of the hallway, stands Dr. Albatur, leaning against the wall for support. He has something in his hand, something black. It's too far to see properly, but I don't need to see it well to know that it's the control device.

"They will bring me your bones, Faloii!" he bellows, his voice echoing down the hallway.

I turn to run again just as the fangs emerge from the vasana's mouths, long shining dagger-like teeth sprouting from their jaws like nightmarish spikes. I shove Adombukar, whose heart I can feel breaking in the tunnel, shout for Alma and my mother. Rondo has disappeared, already out in the dome. In my mind, I scream for the other animals to get away, escape. Some of them run in time. Those who are farther behind I can feel being torn apart, my body on fire with their pain. Adombukar runs beside me, silent. I feel nothing from him.

A guard strides into the mouth of the door ahead, buzzgun drawn. Its muzzle is aimed squarely at Adombukar's chest, and there's nowhere to hide in the corridor, no place to dodge its blast. Inertia hurtles me forward even as my brain tries to urge retreat. I hear the zip of the gun being fired, my eyes squeezing shut involuntarily. The screech that rips from my throat could be from any one of the animals that stampede behind me.

When I open my eyes, debris is falling from the ceiling, embers and dust from disintegrated clay showering the hallway ahead. I look frantically for Adombukar, expecting to find him lying in a pool of blood beside me, but he's passed me, crouching by a tangle of two bodies lying there in the doorway.

"Rondo!"

The stampede of animals is no longer in the hallway around and behind me but in my chest. A massive egg of panic hatches deep inside, the creature bursting forth sending me sprinting to the Zoo's entrance, skidding to my knees and almost falling on top of him, pushing Adombukar away.

"Oh, stars," I scream. My voice cracks: everything inside me is cracking. "Oh, please, no, please, stars, no."

I grip the hand I can reach—his other hand holds the branch he used to strike the guard. Around me, the sound of my mother and Alma screaming my name filters in through what feels like a cloud of noise, the shrieking of the vasana echoing louder and louder.

"I see," Adombukar says. He presses his finger against Rondo's neck, as if checking his pulse, but the flare of green light in the tunnel tells me something else is happening, even if I don't know what. "Both are alive."

"Rondo, Rondo, Rondo," I repeat, as if saying his name over and over will stir him.

Another guard approaches, aiming his buzzgun. I throw my hand up at him as if the force of my rage and pain alone will stop him. Above my head is a hot blur of energy as the gwabi hurdles over me and Rondo, leaping upon the guard. She doesn't have to bite him: all five hundred pounds of her landing on him is like a meteor crushing his body.

Then pressure on my hand. My head snaps down to look at Rondo, his beautiful fingers squeezing mine ever so softly.

"Leave," he groans.

I have no choice, but I can't make my hand let go. I need his eyes to open. I can't move until I'm inside his dark eyes.

His eyelids flutter. His pupils adjust to the white hallway. He squeezes my hand, his grip weak. "Octavia, go."

I don't recognize the sound that rips from my throat as I force myself to let go. My mother drags me after Adombukar, who makes his way smoothly through the dome like the shadow of a cloud on water. His emotions are so intense it makes it difficult for me to breathe: his rage at the fate of the vasana combined with a breathless exaltation for his freedom. He looks around at the trees and then up at the sky through the transparent roof. It's night, with only the moon lighting the dome, but his relief at seeing the sky flows like grass blown by wind.

I can smell my mother's blood like I can smell the blood of the igua, the kunike, whose bodies I can't see but I feel lying behind us in the hallway, torn by the vasana. All around me, the ogwe give off their terrifying scent, transformed from a warning to its own silent alarm. It fills the animals' noses and drives them on, away from this place.

Alma makes it to the main door of the dome before the rest of us, slamming her palm against the scanner. The square turns red, refusing to let her out.

"They've locked it!" she screams. "Octavia, please do it!"

My mother releases my hand and I sprint to Alma's slide, slapping my palm on the scanner. They know I have my father's hands. They know. They've changed the prints. But the scanner turns green, the door slides open, and we stumble out into the hot night air of Faloiv.

Adombukar holds the door, silently calling for the animals. They streak off headlong toward the main gate. Behind us in the dome are the screams of the twelve vasana as they follow our scent. Whatever's been done to them has altered their brains in such a way that they can't speak to us in the tunnel, can't see us in the way that other creatures of Faloiv can. *Worse than death.*

The last of the animals we freed storm past us. Two igua throw their bodies at the gate, shoving with their tusks, digging in with their back legs. It topples underneath their immense power, the sound of the metal striking the ground echoing out into the trees. I search the tunnel for Rasimbukar, but if she's out there she's sealed herself off from me. I turn to call for Adombukar, but he's standing in the archway looking back into the dome, the spots on his forehead arranged into a low, flat line. I dash to his side, hoping to persuade him to come with me. But when I reach him, glancing into the dome to gauge the distance of the vasana, I see Dr. Albatur.

He's one hundred yards away, taking slow, almost leisurely steps toward us. He has a bit of a limp: I wonder if it's from me and Alma tranqing him, or if it's the effect of the door outside to Faloiv being open. I have no idea what else this planet does to his body—maybe even the air hates him. I hope it does. Behind him, the vasana wander loosely, dizzily—a flock following their pale shepherd. His left hand is behind his back; in his right is the black control.

"English, stop this nonsense," he calls. "You don't know what you're doing."

"*You* don't know what you're doing!" I scream. "How could you do this? The vasana? The Solossius! You're putting the whole planet in danger!"

"This planet!" he shouts, taking his left hand from behind his back and balling it into a fist. "This tiny, sweaty planet! We're only here because we have no choice. Our choice has been taken from us."

"But we're here!" I yell. "I was born here! Just because you have to wear a red hood—"

"Me? This is infinitely more vast!" he shouts. "This is about our survival: our legacy! We did not come so far to be limited to one sphere! We *will* return to our former greatness. Faloiv will be ours, and we will be free to make of it what we wish!"

"But we *are* free!" I scream. "This is our home. We're here and you're putting that all at risk by—"

"The *risk* is stagnancy," he bellows, stopping to glare at me. "This is about rebuilding the life we used to have! I came here with one purpose. I will not die here, with that purpose unfulfilled. And *his* people"—Albatur aims his finger like a buzzgun at Adombukar—"have what we need to change that! Their greed keeps us from rebuilding a civilization greater than our ancestors ever imagined. . . ."

"People like you killed our ancestors, Eric." My mother steps through the door, her arm bleeding steadily. "We came here to start over, not to make the same mistakes. Or did you forget what my parents always said? They were your peers."

"Your parents were traitors!" he roars.

Truth seems to be all around me, but every piece is wearing a mask. I want to interrupt, to demand answers once and for all, but my mother is raging on.

"If it wasn't for them, we would already be dead," my mother says.

Someone is running toward us from the labs. My father. The sight of him chokes me: love and fear like two serpents rising from the abyss between us, teeth bared as they wrap each other in their coils. I want to run to him and from him at the same time.

"Samirah," he shouts desperately at my mother as he nears us. He's on the other side of the pack of vasana and stands there hesitantly. His creation or not, he fears them. Scientist face-to-face with the monster he created. "Why are you doing this?"

"I could ask you the same thing, Octavius," my mother calls. She has none of his desperation: despite the pain from her wound, she's as calm as ever.

He shakes both his hands at her, his face a mask of storms.

"Look what you've done! The containment room is in ruins! Work lost! Death! For *them*!"

"What *I've* done? Eric did this!" My mother shouts at my father. "*You* did this!"

"The only thing I've done is pursue progress," Albatur yells, spit flying. "The Solossius will succeed and we will go on!"

"And this entire time you've been lying to me!" My father interrupts. He paces, looking for a way to get around the vasana, which stand swaying between him and us. He sounds the way he sounded when I last spoke to him in the 'wam: wild sorrow colors his voice. "Going behind my back. Sabotaging work that would get us closer to our goals! This is why I ordered that the vasana project be kept secret! I knew someone was causing trouble. And you! You tried to keep the telepathy discovery secret, when you knew something that significant could turn the tables for N'Terra. Why, Samirah?"

My mother lifts her chin.

"Because you're lost, Octavius. Because I knew you and Albatur would find a way to weaponize it all. To try to control the Faloii: make them do what you want. He has made you believe that the future is what lies behind, not ahead. . . ."

My father's voice is like thunder. The silence that has filled our family for so many years is finally broken, but the bridge across the chasm is uncrossable.

"You lied to N'Terra! You lied to me!"

"And I'd lie again," my mother shouts, "if it meant protecting this planet from people like Albatur. People like *you*."

"Albatur is a genius. He's overcoming his condition and providing us with a future—"

"I don't have a condition!" Albatur shouts. His eyes seem as empty and wild as the vasana. "This *planet* is the condition, for which I have a solution!" He pauses, his chin trembling—he looks so old. The ogwe trees pulse their warning into my nostrils. "And you will not jeopardize that."

He raises the black control, pointing at us like an arrow, and presses the button.

"Mom, run!" I scream, grabbing her shoulder and dragging her through the doorway. Adombukar runs with us, his long legs keeping him several paces ahead. I don't see Alma anywhere. But I hear her calling my name, and as I run, tripping in the dim light of the moon, I look for the source of her voice. I find her on the roof of the guards' 'wam, brandishing a buzzgun.

"Octavia! Up here!"

I don't stop to think how she got the gun or what she plans to do with it. I run toward the 'wam, gripping my mother's hand, wet with blood, thinking that if we can just get away from the vasana, maybe we can reason with Dr. Albatur. But the hope is shallow, desperate; my prayer is a shout down a well I know to be dry.

Behind me, the vasana scream so horribly it sends tears fleeing down my cheeks. I risk a glance over my shoulder: they're close, too close, their eyes dull with artificial rage, and behind them, by the door, the shape of Albatur, watching hungrily. I can't see my father.

When my mother's hand slips from my grasp, it's as if I'm in a bad dream. I grab at the air, thinking I will find her fingers again, I will hold on and not let go, and she will be running beside me as before. Empty space. The world slows. My mind is a stone, crashing through glass, the pieces shattering and piercing my heart. Held by the inescapable weight of the air, I spin around, so fast but slow, slow, slow. My mother falling, the red dust swelling around her in a cloud. Rising to one knee to stand before the herd of vasana envelops her like a wave, the moonlight on their teeth flashing like a thousand pointed stars.

My mind widens to encircle the universe. The whole world and all its pain is in my head, infinite lights extinguishing in agony. Somewhere, Rondo bleeding onto false ground. Somewhere, Alma screaming my name. My father screaming my mother's. And Adombukar's finger on my forehead, sending me sailing into blissful blackness.

CHAPTER 30

The smell of trees. Leaves brushing my face: the scent of their thick, complicated greenness filling my nose before turning into waves of color in my mind. Birds, high above, appearing in my consciousness like tiny bursts of light. I slowly open my eyes, become aware that I'm moving.

Adombukar carries me in both arms, the way one carries a child. He bears me easily, moving branches with his shoulder before passing through. He feels me waking, encourages me with small, gentle bursts of yellow like the sun. I sense him there and someone else, a familiar presence. Rasimbukar.

"You're awake," she says out loud. She's speaking rather than showing because she knows my mind is weak.

"Yes."

"Would you like to walk?"

"Yes."

Adombukar sets me down gently, keeping one hand on my shoulder as I find my balance. I'm surprised that it's day, and squint up at the sun filtering down through the trees. Beside us I find the gwabi, staring up at me with her luminous green eyes.

"She has not left us," Adombukar says, the spots on his forehead shifting into what I think is a reluctant smile. "She has been worried about you."

"We have been walking all night," Rasimbukar says. "We have nearly arrived."

"Where?"

"Home."

She continues forward on a path that is barely a path, the ground hardly visible through plant and bramble. I pick my way after her and her father, ducking under vines as thick as my arm. The pistils of flowers growing on a tree trunk trail after me like long tongues, scenting me. The jungle around us seems to pulse with heat and life. It's denser than I ever thought possible, and I know without having to be told that no finder from N'Terra has ever been this deep.

"Your home?" I ask.

"Yes. Would you like to see?" She pauses on the path ahead. I nod, moving forward to join her where she's stopped. She smiles, the spots on her forehead separating into a pleasant pattern. She reaches for the thickly vined branch ahead and sweeps it aside.

There was a time when I believed that the most beautiful place in existence was in N'Terra. When the sun flooded in through the transparent dome of the Mammalian Compound and shone on the tops of the 'wams we had built . . . I always believed there was nothing that could move me in the same way. But standing here on this hill between two people of Faloiv, looking down at their home, I know I was wrong.

They've found clay in the body of their planet that I've never even dreamed of: buildings made of pink and red, blue and yellow, some large enough to be mistaken for mountains. Some have rounded tops like ours, some are made of what looks like glass, and all of them are built directly into the terrain of Faloiv: boulders, trees, hills. A crescent-shaped lodge hugs the shore of a broad lake. Brilliant green vines and ivies spider up the sides of the domes. Around the perimeter of the city, the very trees bend outward to accommodate the buildings, growing at a curve instead of straight into the sky. And among it all are people, small from here, but people: the Faloii, living their lives, walking in and out of buildings, carrying baskets, enjoying the sun.

"My mother should have seen this," I say, and my anguish surges, hatching, my animal grief shuddering from its shell. It seems impossible. Can she actually be dead?

"Your mother was brave," Rasimbukar says, touching my cheek lightly with her paw-like hand. "She was protecting us all."

"She shouldn't have had to." I sniff, looking down at the city through blurred vision. My chest feels as if it's swelling, like my skin might tear to make room for the growing pain.

She says nothing, and I don't even want to look into the tunnel: I don't want to feel her agreeing with me.

"What do I do now?" I say. "My father . . . N'Terra . . ." I bite my lip hard. I'm alone now. What's the point? Rondo far behind, injured who knows how badly. Alma . . . they know she was in the labs with me. What will they do to her?

"Come." Rasimbukar starts down the hill, gesturing.

"What? There?" I cry, taking a step back. "I can't. They'll hate me! When they find out what we've done . . . what I've seen us do . . . When they find out . . ."

"Incorrect," she says, staring at me with her endless eyes. Beside me, the gwabi makes a snuffling sound through her nose, as if impatient. "Like your mother, you are brave, and we will need your bravery for what is coming."

I hesitate, look down at the city, its beautiful colors, the shapes of the buildings like the comforting images Adombukar passed through the tunnel to wake me. I slowly widen my mind, letting the energy of the city rise up to meet me. Everything has a color, a scent, a feeling. Gentle impressions that float, green and peaceful, into my head. It's strange, but I almost recognize pieces of it: a fuzzy echo, like glimpsing a tree that you've only seen in a dream. It smells close, familiar. It smells like . . .

Rasimbukar turns back to me on the hill, extending her hand. The spots on her forehead broaden and spread, giving the impression of a bird's wings, opening wide to welcome me.

"Come," she says, the sun behind her hot and bright. "Your grandparents are waiting."

ACKNOWLEDGMENTS

Perhaps one day I will write a book just thanking the people whose belief in me has carried me this far—there are as many of you as there are stars. Deepest thanks to my mother, father, and stepfather, whose endless love and confidence refused to allow me to give up. Cia White, who once said, "You are the real thing" and meant it. The Kentucky Governor's School for the Arts, where I first learned there is a future in art. My Soulie, Hope Lockett, who has been assuring me I was meant for more since we were working back line at KFC with Miss Dorothy. Kwame Alexander—Uncle! Rooster Man!—who has always been a model and has never closed a door behind him once he stepped through it. Jenn Jackson, who woke me up when what I perceived as consciousness was inception. Ari Harris, who puts the extra in extraterrestrial. Prathima Radhakrishnan, a whitecoat with a pure heart and a sharp eye. Tiffany Jackson and Dhonielle Clayton, whose cackles and brilliant, brilliant writing make this world more beautiful and more exciting. Daniel José Older, who has done so, so much just by being himself. Stuart Cipinko and his wife, Anne, who carries him on. Zoé Samudzi, who breathed hope into this book. My agent, Regina Brooks—to whom I never have to explain—thank you for choosing me. My editor, Ben Rosenthal, for his patience and true kindness. Chicago crew . . . you've stuck around through every rage and every happy riot. I'm always writing for you.

And finally, my deepest gratitude to Octavia Butler, who wrote: "All that you touch, You Change. All that you Change, Changes You. The only lasting truth is Change." May her memory and her work live forever.